DARKNESS

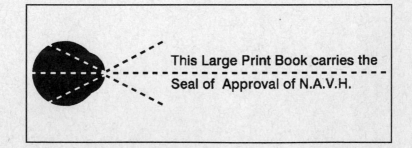

This Large Print Book carries the
Seal of Approval of N.A.V.H.

Thorndike Press® Large Print Basic.
The text of this Large Print edition is unabridged.
Other aspects of the book may vary from the original edition.
Set in 16 pt. Plantin.

LIBRARY OF CONGRESS CATALOGING-IN-PUBLICATION DATA

Names: Robards, Karen, author.
Title: Darkness / by Karen Robards.
Description: Large print edition. | Waterville, Maine : Thorndike Press Large Print, 2016. | Series: Thorndike Press large print basic
Identifiers: LCCN 2016006969 | ISBN 9781410486196 (hardback) | ISBN 1410486192 (hardcover)
Subjects: LCSH: Romantic suspense fiction. | Large type books. | BISAC: FICTION / Romance / Suspense.
Classification: LCC PS3568.O196 D43 2016b | DDC 813/.54—dc23
LC record available at http://lccn.loc.gov/2016006969

Published in 2016 by arrangement with Gallery Books, an imprint of Simon & Schuster, Inc.

Printed in the United States of America
1 2 3 4 5 6 7 20 19 18 17 16

DARKNESS

KAREN ROBARDS

THORNDIKE PRESS

A part of Gale, Cengage Learning

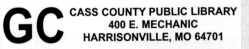
GALE
CENGAGE Learning·

Farmington Hills, Mich • San Francisco • New York • Waterville, Maine
Meriden, Conn • Mason, Ohio • Chicago

Darkness is dedicated to my three sons,
Peter, Christopher, and Jack,
and my husband, Doug,
with love

CHAPTER ONE

It was an ordinary flight, on an ordinary day, full of ordinary people.

Until it wasn't.

"Eww, gross." Nine-year-old Elijah Samuels jabbed an elbow into the ribs of his thirteen-year-old sister, Abigail, and pointed at the couple kissing in front of them. Blue-eyed, blond-haired Lije, as he was called, was sturdy and tan from three weeks spent hitting the beach with his accountant father, who'd moved to Burbank after his divorce from the children's mother the previous summer. Abby was sturdy and tan, too, with sunny streaks in her long, brown braid and a pair of gold studs in her newly pierced ears, a dad-authorized act that she was afraid her mom was going to freak out over. The siblings were near the end of what had been a long line of passengers waiting to hand over their boarding passes and walk down the ramp to take their seats on the

Airbus A320. Flight 155 was scheduled to carry them from LAX to Washington Dulles, where their mother would meet them. It was a Saturday, and a new school year would begin on Monday.

"Don't point," Abby hissed under her breath, smacking her brother on the shoulder.

"Don't hit," Lije retorted, jerking away and making a face at her.

The kissing couple, Mia and Nate Smolski, broke apart as they reached the turnstile. Nate handed over his boarding pass as Mia looked around to smile at Abby and Lije, having clearly overheard their exchange. A radiant smile lit up her thin face and made the slim brunette briefly beautiful. A long-distance runner who had attended UCLA on a scholarship, she was twenty-three years old and a newly minted nurse. Nate was twenty-six, a salesman for his uncle's car dealership. They'd gotten married the previous afternoon, and this flight was the first leg of their honeymoon. Mia followed her new husband on board, and Lije and Abby, still exchanging evil looks, followed them.

In line behind Lije and Abby were two businessmen, Don Miller and Gary Henderson. Both worked in the marketing department of a research and development company. They'd spent the week in Southern California pitching their company's services to various clients, and were glad to be going home. Both were in their forties, both married with children.

The Garcia family of Alexandria, Virginia, boarded next: grandmother Rita, mom Haylie, dad Jason, and their two-year-old twin daughters, Gracie and Helen. Grandmother and Mom were each lugging a child, and Dad was carrying two car seats and what looked like four or five backpacks. All looked tired and harassed, except the children, who were asleep on the women's respective shoulders.

Edward Thomas Jorgensen was behind the Garcias. A tall, fit man of thirty-nine, he was neatly dressed in a polo shirt and khakis and carried a briefcase. He was unmarried, childless, currently unemployed.

Nine more people boarded after Jorgensen, for a total of 243 passengers on board. The plane also carried twelve crew members.

Flight 155 took off twenty-eight minutes late at 12:58 p.m. Blue skies, perfect flying weather.

One hour and fifty minutes later, still enjoying perfect flying weather, the Airbus

A320 slammed into the side of a mountain just outside of Denver.

There were no survivors.

No cause for the crash could be determined.

NOVEMBER, ONE YEAR LATER, KAZAKHSTAN

The private jet bumped over a narrow strip of pavement as it touched down. At the end of the little-used runway in a cleared area of forest a few miles outside of Aktau, Kazakhstan, a trio of covered military-style trucks pointing their headlights toward the taxiing plane provided the only illumination. It was dark, it was snowing furiously, and those trucks held one wayward American citizen and a whole bunch of rifle-toting members of the Kazakh Armed Forces.

None of those things were designed to make James "Cal" Callahan feel all warm and fuzzy inside. The plane executed a neat one-eighty as it reached the end of the runway, turning its nose back the way they'd come so that takeoff could happen quickly.

"Keep the engines running," Cal directed the pilot, Tim Hendricks. Easing the jet to a halt, Hendricks nodded. A wiry six-two, Hendricks was, like Cal and Ezra Brown, the third member of their party, former Air

Force Special Operations Command, also known as AFSOCs or, more commonly, Air Commandos.

"Think there'll be trouble?" Ezra asked, following him to the door. Ezra was Cal's backup, his second gun, and a friend. About Cal's own height at six-four, Ezra was meatier, bald as an egg, and heavily tattooed, including a Celtic cross on his left cheek. Cal himself was more conventional looking, with neatly cut black hair, even features, and no tattoos. Despite the dark business suits that proclaimed their civilian status, they made a formidable-looking pair.

"Shouldn't be, but you never know," Cal said as the door opened and the stairs descended. "Let's make this fast."

The small leather satchel he carried as he stepped out into the biting cold held five million dollars' worth of diamonds. They weren't his diamonds, and it wasn't his money that had bought them: it belonged to the CIA, or, more properly, the US government. But the US government didn't pay ransom.

Unless it decided it wanted to. Then it employed private contractors like Cal to do the dirty work, thus keeping its official nose clean.

Ezra strode past him, taking up a position

far enough to his right that even a spray of bullets couldn't get them both at the same time. The missile launcher on his shoulder was aimed squarely at the trucks. The AK-47 slung on its strap over his shoulder was for stragglers if the missile launcher should prove less than one hundred percent effective.

Eyes narrowed against the blowing snow, Cal started walking toward the trucks.

He'd done a lot of things he didn't want to do in his thirty-four years of life. One way or another, most of them had been for money.

Getting Rudy Delgado out of Kazakhstan was about to be one of them.

Rudy was a computer hacker. One of the best. Ten years before, under the cover of his legitimate day job as an IT specialist for the CIA, he'd gone into the system, found and publicly exposed dozens of clandestine operations that at that time had been under way in the Middle East, with the justification that he opposed the United States' presence there. The public uproar had been enormous. The private backlash had cost serving officers their lives.

Having thus royally screwed the pooch, Rudy had fled the country, eventually winding up in Russia. In the years since, he'd continued working in IT, only for that country's security services. It had been a sweet deal: Rudy did what the Russian government wanted, and they protected him from the Americans and let him live.

Only Rudy being Rudy, he'd gotten ambitious. He'd hacked his way into their classified files and started poking around.

The Russians being the Russians, they hadn't liked that.

Nor had they liked what he'd found.

Rudy had fled again.

This time everybody and his mother was after him.

He'd wound up in Kazakhstan, where, via his specialty, the Internet, he dropped a bombshell on his former bosses at the CIA: he knew what had caused the crash of Flight 155 outside of Denver last year. He was prepared to trade the information, plus provide irrefutable proof of what he claimed, for a ride back to the States and a guarantee of immunity from prosecution once he got there.

His former bosses took the deal, but a complication arose. Rudy was arrested for some minor offense in Chapaev and wound up in the custody of the Kazakhstani government.

Which decided, clandestinely, to auction

him off to the highest bidder.

The CIA won, and thus here Cal and company were.

Just another day at the office.

Three men emerged from the cab of the center truck and walked toward Cal. Two were tall and straight in their military uniforms. The third, the one in the middle, was short, round, bespectacled Rudy.

It was, in Cal's opinion, a poor trade for five million dollars' worth of diamonds, but what the US government did with its money wasn't his call to make.

"Salaam." Cal greeted the soldiers in their language, bowing his head in accordance with the custom. They nodded curtly. *Not great believers in small talk, apparently,* he observed to himself, which made them his kind of guys.

The soldier on the left held out his hand for the satchel. Cal handed it over. The soldier opened it up, thrust a gloved hand inside, rooted around. Apparently satisfied, he grunted, *"Zhaksa,"* which meant "good," and closed the satchel back up again.

The soldier on the right, who'd had a hand wrapped around Rudy's arm, thrust Rudy toward Cal. As Rudy stumbled forward, the soldiers turned around and left, striding swiftly back toward the trucks.

Cal grabbed Rudy's arm in turn and started hustling him back toward the plane, which waited with steps down and engine running just ahead of them. The fuselage gleamed silver where the headlights struck it; the logo — a circle with two wavy lines under it — painted on the sides and tail gave it the look of a sleek corporate jet, which Cal supposed was the point.

The truth was he didn't really give a damn about the plane's aesthetics, especially not now — these crucial few seconds, where the Kazakhs had the diamonds and he, Ezra, and Rudy were still outside the jet, were the most likely time for an attack.

"You're American?" Rudy gasped, breathless from the pace, as he looked up at Cal. Way up, because Rudy was maybe five-five. Beneath a red knit cap with a tassel at the crown, Rudy had scared-looking hazel eyes framed by wire-rimmed glasses, a big nose, a small mouth, and a round, pale face. Besides the cap, he was wearing a black fleece jacket zipped up to the neck, jeans, and sneakers. No backpack, no gear.

"You got proof of what you say happened to that plane? Because I want to see it," was Cal's reply. Cal had been offered a nice bonus on top of his fee if he made sure Rudy brought the promised "proof" with

15

him. Of course, if Rudy couldn't produce the proof, he'd still take Rudy back with him to the States. Rudy just might not like his reception at the other end.

"Yeah, sure. See?" Digging in his jeans pocket, Rudy came up with a small object that Cal had to squint at for a second before he recognized it: a flash drive.

Cal grunted and took the flash drive from Rudy, who looked like he wanted to protest but didn't quite dare. Then they were at the plane steps. Shooing Rudy up the stairs, Cal glanced back at the trucks. They were still there at the end of the runway, still politely lighting up the pavement, waiting for their guests to leave.

"Easy enough," Ezra said, coming up behind him.

"Seems like it," Cal replied, and followed Rudy into the plane.

A few minutes later, they lifted off into what looked to be the start of a beautiful day.

Until it wasn't.

CHAPTER TWO

Freedom is a wonderful thing, Dr. Gina Sullivan thought as she watched the pair of rare white-tailed eagles disappear into the gathering storm clouds. The female of the pair had been trapped in an oil slick for nearly twenty-four hours. Cleaned up, tagged, and released, the eagle had been joined by her mate and the two were winging away toward the mountains to the north. Scudding along in a bright orange motorized rubber boat in the choppy gray waters off Attu Island's Chirikof Point, Gina, an ornithologist, had been following as best she could in hopes of discovering the approximate location of their nest for later observation. But the oncoming storm meant that she was going to have to turn back, and so she'd stopped, shifting the Zodiac into neutral as she made one last observation. Lowering her binoculars with regret, she recorded in her small notebook the time — 3:02 p.m.; the birds'

17

direction — northwest; and the birds' speed — approximately twenty knots, then shoved the notebook into the pocket of her steel-blue, fur-lined parka for safekeeping.

For a moment she sat there as the little boat rode the swells, breathing deeply of the cold sea air, taking in the majesty of the rugged island with its beautiful snow-covered mountains, the wintry sea, the turbulent sky that threatened more snow. Kittiwakes, petrels, pelicans, and gulls screeched and circled above her. She watched a trio of brown pelicans gliding high above the water suddenly tuck their wings and dive toward the surface like kamikaze pilots, fishing for a meal, and felt a warm glow of contentment.

It's good to be out in the field again.

It had been a long time — too long.

That thought she'd had about freedom? She realized that it applied to herself as much as the eagles. Only her prison was grief. And guilt. For five years now she had been mired in both as helplessly as the eagle had been mired in oil.

This trip, the first research project she had undertaken in the field since she'd lost her family, was an attempt to jump-start her life.

Baby steps.

Thunder crashed loudly in the distance, echoing off the mountains and startling the wheeling birds into silence. The clouds piling up on the horizon were noticeably darker than before.

Time to go.

Reluctantly coming about, Gina juiced the throttle and raced for camp, meaning to follow the coastline around the point until she reached Massacre Bay. The small plane burst through the heavy cloud cover approximately five minutes later.

Gina had been eyeing the amassing clouds with misgiving in the wake of another earsplitting clap of thunder. Thunder snow was never a good sign, and she'd just seen an ominous flicker of lightning behind the threatening wall of weather that was now chasing her across the sea. When the plane torpedoed out of those self-same clouds, she sat up straight in surprise on the fiberglass bench seat that ran across the bow. Muffled to the eyes by a snow mask and huddled into her waterproof parka with her hood secured tightly around a face that was all blue eyes, wide mouth, high cheekbones, and pointed chin, she gripped the wheel tighter and watched in astonishment as the plane streaked across the leaden sky toward her.

It's way too low, was her first thought, even as she registered that it wasn't a seaplane like the orange and white Reever that had delivered four of her fellow scientists to this remote atoll in the Pacific; it was, rather, a sleek silver jet. That realization was followed by an alarmed *There's something wrong* as the plane continued to descend, blasting through the snow flurries on a trajectory that would bring it down way before it reached the island's runway, which was the only one within hundreds of miles.

You're being paranoid, she scolded herself, which, given her personal history with small planes, was no surprise.

The thing was, though, the plane looked like it desperately needed to land. It was dropping fast, losing altitude if not speed.

It's going to crash. As the thought crystallized into a near certainty, Gina's heart leaped into her throat. Sucking in a lungful of the freezing, salt-laden air, she watched the plane dip low enough to disturb the flocks of birds circling the bay. Their cries, coupled with the splashing waves, the moan of the wind, and the Zodiac's own whining motor, had masked the sound of the plane until it was nearly upon her. Now the birds wheeled wildly in the face of this violent intrusion, their alarmed screeches almost drowned by the roar of the jet engines, which was close enough and powerful enough to reverberate against her eardrums. As she watched the jet shoot across the sky, she registered the logo painted on the side and tail — a circle above two wavy lines — which probably denoted some huge multinational corporation but held no meaning for her. She also had an excellent view of its smooth silver belly. There was no sign of the wheels descending, no sign of any attempt to control its descent. It was, simply, coming down.

Bone-deep fear twisted her insides. *Pull up, pull up, pull up,* she silently urged the pilot. Then, *Dear God, protect whoever's on board.*

Gina yanked her snow mask down.

"There's a runway about eight miles to the east." Her shout was drowned out by the noise of the plane, not that there was any real chance that the pilot could hear her. Still, arm waving wildly over her head in hopes that the pilot might see, she gestured in the direction of the no-longer-operational LORAN (long range navigational) Coast Guard station that was home to the only place to land on the island. It was idiotic, of course, but it was also instinctive: she couldn't just do *nothing* as

21

the plane hurtled toward the waves.

The section of cockpit windshield that was visible from her angle was black and impenetrable. It was her imagination that painted the pilot at the controls, white-faced and desperate as he fought whatever disaster that had brought the plane to this, and she knew it. She also knew that the chances that her gesture had been seen and understood were almost impossibly small.

Oomph. With her eyes on the plane rather than on where she was going, she was caught by surprise as the Zodiac hit one of the larger swells the wrong way. The impact sent her flying up off the seat and then smacked her back down onto it hard enough that her teeth snapped together. Thus reminded of where she was and the importance of keeping her mind on her business, she eased the throttle back to near-idle speed, retaining just enough forward power to keep the boat from being tossed around like flotsam by the waves. Pulse pounding, she switched her attention back to the oncoming plane.

Whether it was exhaust from the engines or actual smoke from an onboard fire she couldn't tell, but a billowing white vapor trail now marked its descending path.

Gina shuddered. The memories that trailing plume brought back made her dizzy.

Get over it, she ordered herself fiercely, shaking her head to clear it. *You're not in that plane. What happened is in the past. You're a different person now.*

Now she was twenty-eight years old, a respected ornithologist whose specialty was the environmental impact of pollution on birds, and at that moment she was out alone in the frigid Bering Sea, doing her job. This plane had nothing to do with her. Whatever happened, she was present merely as a bystander, a witness. There was no reason for her heart to pound, or her stomach to twist.

Her heart pounded and her stomach twisted anyway.

Lifting her binoculars to her eyes, she tracked the plane until it plunged into the outermost edge of the deep gray blanket of clouds that formed an ominously low ceiling above her head. The clouds swallowed it completely. Only the snarl of its engines told her that it was still racing toward her through the sky.

Her concentration was so complete that when the radio clipped to her pocket crackled, it made her jump.

"Gina. Are you there?"

The voice belonged to Arvid Kleir, a fel-

23

low scientist. The faint Swedish accent he retained even after years in the States was unmistakable. Along with the rest of the twelve-strong party culled from various top universities, he had chosen to forgo his Thanksgiving break to join the expedition. They had all arrived on Attu two days prior, eight of them, including Gina, dropped off by a chartered boat that would return for them in a week and the rest delivered by the aforementioned Reever. Their purpose was to observe and record the hazards posed by the island's unique pollution to resident and migratory bird species. Arvid came from Yale. Gina herself was an assistant professor of environmental studies at Stanford.

Yesterday afternoon, having been alerted that something was amiss by the abnormal signals emitted by the female eagle's microchip, she and Arvid had set out from camp in the Zodiac, located the bird, and rescued it from the pool of degrading oil in which it had become trapped. Attu was littered with a ton of debris from World War II, and the intermittent leakage of decades-old oil, the source of the pool, was a serious problem. Partly full oil and fuel drums, forgotten weapons, unexploded artillery, heavy equipment left to rust on hillsides and in the ocean, overturned shipping containers, and crumbling small structures abandoned by the military were everywhere. As the site of the only World War II battle on American soil, the place once had been home to more than fifteen thousand American troops as well as, on the opposite end of the island, two thousand enemy Japanese. When the war had ended, everything had been left right where it stood. Now the place was both a birder's paradise and an ecological nightmare. She and Arvid had set up a temporary camp, then spent last night and this morning painstakingly cleaning up the bedraggled eagle and making sure it was fit enough to be returned to the wild. At about one in the afternoon they'd released the bird. Arvid had then headed back to the party's main camp at the erstwhile Coast Guard station on foot while she'd followed the bird in the Zodiac.

Snatching up the radio, Gina pressed the reply button even as she craned her neck in a useless effort to locate the plane through her binoculars.

"I'm here," she said urgently into the radio. "Arvid, listen. There's a plane out here that looks like it's about to crash into the sea. You need to call the Coast Guard right now."

Gina and her eleven compatriots were the only people on the island. With cell signals nonexistent, their only means of communication with the outside world was the satellite phone they'd brought with them, which was back at the main camp.

Letting go of the button, she listened in growing dismay as Arvid responded. ". . . understand me? Gina? Are you there?"

It was clear from his tone that he hadn't heard her transmission. Interference from the oncoming storm, probably. Gina let the binoculars drop to concentrate on the radio.

"Arvid? Call the Coast Guard." Gina only realized that she was shouting into the radio when her voice echoed back at her.

Static crackled through Arvid's next words. ". . . back to camp. This storm's a doozy. You —"

Gina stared down at the radio as his voice was swallowed up by more static. Clearly, her message was not getting through. A rattling roar almost directly overhead had her thrusting the radio between her knees for safekeeping, then snatching up the binoculars and searching the churning gray ceiling for some sign of the plane.

The clouds were too thick. She couldn't see it.

Tilting her head back to the point where

her neck hurt, bracing her feet against the rocking deck for balance, she was gazing almost directly up when she saw a bright flash that looked like a horizontal lightning bolt light up the sky through the obscuring clouds. Then a deafening *boom* hit her, along with an invisible tsunami of a force field fronted by heat. A strange, high-pitched whistling sound split the air.

Oh, my God, the plane's blown up.

Her heart lurched. She was still staring up desperately as chunks of metal and other debris started pouring out of the sky like deadly rain.

Practically immobilized by shock, all she could do was lower the binoculars and watch wide-eyed as objects started splashing into the water around her with the fast rat-a-tat of machine-gun fire: *splat splat splat splat splat.*

A large chunk of metal slammed into the water inches from the starboard prow. The breeze of its passage fanned her cheeks. A shower of droplets splattered across her waterproof pants and boots. That's what it took to make her suddenly, acutely aware of the danger she was in.

Gina's throat tightened in horror as she watched the geyser-like column of water shoot skyward from where the object had hit. She was struck by an instant, appalled thought: *Looks like I just might be going to die in a plane crash after all.*

CHAPTER THREE

It was the stuff of the nightmares that still plagued her. An explosion, a flash of fire, the screams of trapped victims — the horror of being in a small plane crash stalked her, but now it only occasionally surfaced in terrifying detail while she slept. She'd lived through one as a passenger. How ironic would it be if she was killed as the result of another one when she was supposedly safe on the ground? Dropping the binoculars, heart galloping with fear, Gina ducked as closely as she could against the hard plastic console that housed the wheel as the Zodiac bucked on the resultant wave. Wrapping an arm over her head, she grabbed hold of one of the webbing straps fastened to the boat's interior sides. She cringed as more chunks of wreckage peppered the agitated gray water, sending cascades of white foam shooting skyward so that it looked like she was surrounded by a vast pod of whales surfacing to blow. Spray hit her, icy cold as it splattered across her face, pelted her coat. Waves created by the force of multiple impacts made the previously choppy surface of the bay as turbulent as the inside of a washing machine.

Gina hung on to the strap for dear life as the boat rocked and dipped precariously, praying with every breath that something wouldn't land on her directly, or that the whole boat wouldn't capsize with the force of the waves. She wore a flat orange life jacket zipped over her parka, but given the temperature of the water it was more of an empty gesture than a lifesaving device: she'd be unconscious within a few minutes of going in, and dead not long after that.

Thunk. Splash. Something large slammed into the stern on its way into the water, a glancing blow but still enough to send Gina catapulting with a cry into the air. Only her grip on the strap saved her from going overboard. She landed with a groan on her stomach across the hard, flat bench she'd been sitting on, and gasped for breath as the wind was knocked out of her. Lungs aching as she fought to fill them, listening to her pulse thundering in her ears, she stared wide-eyed at the objects now littering the water around her.

It took her a moment, but then she realized that the danger had passed. Or, at least, nothing else was falling from the sky.

Part of a wing surfed the whitecaps nearby, its jagged edge mute evidence of having been violently torn from the plane. A passenger seat, fortunately empty, was swallowed by the waves as her gaze touched it. An exterior door, easily identifiable by its handle, floated a few yards away, gleaming dull silver against the angry gray of the water. From its size and proximity, she guessed that it was what had struck the boat, fortunately not head-on.

With that one semidazed look around, she also spotted a partly submerged wheel and a seat back with a cracked tray table attached.

More objects — an iPhone, sunglasses, a coffee cup — bobbed around the boat. Sick at heart, she watched a man's large black wing-tip dress shoe tumble past on a wave. Everywhere she looked, she could see the dark blobs of more debris. Farther out, the plane's tail, still upright, was visible. There was no sign of the fuselage.

Bile rose in her throat at this irrefutable evidence of the utter destruction of the plane. Swallowing hard, she forced it back.

Grabbing her binoculars again, she focused on the triangular blade of the tail as it rose and fell with the waves, wincing at the scorch marks on it at the same time as she once again registered the insignia: a circle above two wavy lines. The logo meant nothing to her, but the fact that the tail was able to remain upright despite the turbulence did. The tail might be still attached to the fuselage, or at least some portion of the fuselage, which was acting as a kind of anchor to keep it erect.

Lowering the binoculars, Gina took a deep, meant-to-be-steadying breath. Her nostrils wrinkled with distaste. The frigid air reeked with the acrid smell of burning combined with the strong scent of airplane fuel. She could taste the metallic tang of the fuel on her tongue, feel the burn of it in her nose. It brought the reality of the crash home to her as nothing else had done.

It brought the *memory* of the crash she had barely survived home to her as nothing else had done. For a moment she thought she could once again actually feel the searing heat of flames licking at her skin, hear the screams of the others as they died.

Making a small distressed sound, she shuddered.

Stop it, she ordered herself fiercely. *That's*

gone, over with. In the past. You weren't on board this time.

The people who had been on board this time — what about them?

The thought that there might be survivors was electrifying. It was what she needed to bring her sharply back to the present. Gina got a grip and scrambled back onto the seat. From there she could see parts of the plane scattered in a wide circle around her.

The boat's sudden steep rise as it was borne aloft on a particularly tall wave gave her an excellent, if brief, view of her surroundings: parts of the plane were everywhere. The debris field was large and rapidly changing as some objects sank and others were carried away.

Could anyone have lived through something like that?

You did, she reminded herself, then pushed the unsettling memories aside in favor of using the binoculars to visually search the water. The tail was the largest visible piece of debris. If there were survivors, logic dictated that they would be near the tail.

She was looking in that direction again when her attention was caught by a small object sliding across the black rubber deck toward her foot: the radio. Dismayed by

33

how close she had come to losing the thing — the ability to communicate was all-important out here — she dropped the binoculars, snatched up the radio, and spoke urgently into it even as she slammed the throttle forward and steered toward the tail.

"Arvid? Anybody? Can you hear me?"

Nothing. Static was the only reply. Frowning as the heavy swell bounced her up and down, she watched a small black suitcase float past and winced at the thought of the probable fate of its owner.

Scrunching her face up against the bite of the wind, she desperately searched the sea for any sign of life.

Again, nothing.

The boat was small and lightweight enough, and the swells were growing big and powerful enough, that the stability of the craft was becoming a real concern: what she didn't want to do was let a wave catch her sideways. Nosing into the waves, she tried the radio once more. Still just static. Giving up for the moment, she clipped the radio to her pocket, where it would be safe and she would be able to hear any transmission sent her way.

The force of the wind made her eyes water as she scanned the area. Using the binoculars at least protected her eyes and gave her a better view of what was out there. What she saw was disheartening: debris, debris, and more debris. Blinking to refocus as she lowered the binoculars, she cast an anxious glance at the approaching storm that confirmed her worst fear: *it's coming in fast.*

When her small group of scientists had left Juneau, the week's forecast had been ideal for their purposes, calling for the weather to be moderately cold and clear with occasional light flurries, she recalled, aggrieved. The expedition members had confirmed it before boarding the ship that had carried them to Attu. Looked like things had changed.

The ominous appearance of the tumbling clouds rushing inexorably toward her made her hands clench around the wheel. The temperature was steadily dropping. The wind was cold enough now to bite at her exposed skin. Waves rose up around her in frothy, white-tipped peaks, reminding her momentarily of a bowl of fresh-whipped meringue. The boat was starting to plunge up and down like a roller-coaster car. Attu was famous for blizzards with cyclonic winds that blew up out of nowhere, and she was afraid she was staring one right in the face.

She turned her back on it. A harried search of the waves as far as she could see turned up no signs of life. Probably she was a fool to keep looking. The wheeling birds that had filled the sky earlier were gone now, although whether from the explosion or the oncoming weather she couldn't be sure. But the absence of birds was generally a bad sign.

Gina knew she needed to get to shore, but she couldn't just turn tail and run. If there were survivors, she was the only hope they had.

Firmly closing her mind to the memories that threatened to overwhelm her, she narrowed her eyes against the wind, picked up the binoculars, and set herself to searching the waves again.

The snowfall was increasing in intensity. Fat white flakes swirled around her as she guided the boat toward the tail. Scanning the water for anything that resembled a person was nearly useless: there was so much debris that it was difficult to know where to even begin to look. Plus, the water was growing so choppy that it was impossible to see more than a narrow slice of the total picture at a time.

"Can anybody hear me?" she screamed, and pushed her hood back to listen for a reply. Her hair was honey brown, midback length, straight and thick as a horse's tail. The wind caught long tendrils of it, whipping them free of her bun to send them flying around her face. It was blowing harder now, making the snowflakes feel like tiny bits of grit when they hit her skin. Keeping a wary eye on the advancing storm front, she knew that she didn't have much longer before she absolutely had to head for shore.

The thought of abandoning anyone who might be in the water made her chest tighten.

"Hell-o-o-o," she tried again at the top of her lungs. "Is anyone out here?"

The rushing sound of the wind and waves made her shout seem impossibly small. She couldn't be sure, but she didn't think it had carried very far. Certainly there was no response.

Some kind of search-and-rescue operation was needed on the scene *now*. But given the remote location, and the storm, and the time frame before it hit, she knew it wasn't going to happen. Jittery with alarm at the idea that she was the only help there might be for days, she picked up the radio again.

"There's been a plane crash," she said into it. "Arvid, can you hear me? Call the Coast Guard and get help out here. I repeat, there's been a plane crash. Can anyone hear me?" She gave her location and coordinates in hopes that Arvid or someone could hear her even if they couldn't respond. If a couple of her fellow scientists could join her with the other boat that was docked at the main camp, that would be way better than having just herself out here alone. But even as she had the thought, she realized that there wasn't time. She was probably a good half hour away by sea from the former Coast Guard station, and the storm would hit way before any of them could reach her.

Reluctantly accepting that she was on her own, Gina was grimly listening to more static in reply to her latest transmission when she spotted something floating past that was definitely human.

Her stomach dropped as she stared at it.

A man's leg, severed below the knee. Bare and white as a fish's belly except for the dark sock that still covered the foot.

Gina was watching its progress in mute horror when a movement a few hundred yards out caught her eye.

Looking up — and thankful to the core to have her attention diverted — she carefully clipped the radio to her pocket again, lifted the binoculars, and peered through the wind and blowing snow as she sought to verify what she thought she'd seen.

Yes, there it was again.

Adrenaline raced through her. Somebody was bobbing in the water. Somebody with open eyes and a gasping mouth and flailing limbs. Impossible to be certain, but from the size of him she thought it must be a man.

A survivor.

Gina's heart beat faster.

Chapter Four

He should be dead. In fact, Cal had been pretty sure that he was dead until he'd caught a glimpse of an orange boat glimmering above the icy blue world in which he'd found himself. The explosion, the hurtling into utter blackness, the sudden immersion in freezing cold water, the lack of air, the sense of being separate from his body, all made a kind of twisted sense in the context of having just lost his life.

An orange boat did not. An orange boat had no place in the Hereafter. An orange boat meant that he'd fallen into the sea instead of some icy, watery version of hell, which was where he'd always assumed he would end up when he died. Now he was freezing, and drowning, and maybe even bleeding to death, but he was not dead.

Not yet, anyway. Not ever, if he could help it.

If he was going to live, he had to have air.

Not easy when an ocean's worth of water kept slapping him in the face, smashing down on top of his head, pulling him under and spitting him back up again, toying with him like a cat with a mouse before closing in for the kill. Not easy when water gushed up his nose every time the sea bucked around him and he found himself gulping down gallons of salt water whenever he opened his mouth for air.

He was so weak it was ridiculous, so cold he was almost paralyzed with it.

What it came down to was, did he want to live or die?

If he died, would it even really matter? To whom, besides himself?

His mother was dead, killed in a car crash when he was five. His father was a tough old bastard, a now retired Air Force officer who prided himself on being a man's man. His idea of raising a son had consisted of beating the crap out of him for the smallest transgression until Cal had gotten big enough to turn what had started as a beating into a fight. After that, they'd pretty much circled each other like snarling dogs until he'd graduated high school and left home. They barely kept in touch. Would the old man grieve the death of his only offspring? Cal snorted inwardly. He'd be more

41

likely to shed a tear over getting a dent in his car.

His business partner, John Hardy, another former AFSOC, would keep the company running. Nobody who worked for them would even be out of a job.

His latest ex-girlfriend was still mad at him over the fact that he'd failed to be forthcoming with a diamond ring. She might, possibly, shed a tear over his demise. She might even give a home to Harley, his dog.

Harley would grieve. Part Irish wolfhound, part German shepherd, part God knew what else, Harley was a rescue that another previous girlfriend had left with him when it had become clear that the animal was going to grow to the size of a moose. He was six years old, clumsy as a camel on roller skates, and absolutely devoted to Cal.

Cal came to the semireluctant conclusion that he could not abandon Harley.

Besides, if he died, no one would know what had gone down on that plane. No one would know that his mission had gone catastrophically wrong, or start asking why.

He was in shock from the accident. His mind was befuddled by cold and lack of oxygen. But he knew that it was vitally important to get that information to his employer. And he was the only one who could do it.

Summoning every atom of strength that remained to him, he kicked and pushed against the angry violence of the water and forced himself up above the surface of the waves. Sucking in burning lungfuls of the briny, scorched-smelling air, he waved a leaden arm at the boat.

Hope springs eternal and all that.

The sea took instant revenge, rolling over him, carrying him under, doing its best to drown him, but not before he saw that there was only one person in the boat, a mistake if whoever it was intended to try to finish him off with a final coup de grâce. Probably, he thought as he battled back to the surface and the breath he'd been holding exploded from his body, if the boat was indeed intended as backup to the downing of his plane, they hadn't expected to find anyone alive. The boat, and the person in it, was out there as a fail-safe.

After all — and here he greedily sucked in more of the tainted air before another wave crashed down on him with what felt like all the force of Niagara Falls — how many people survived being shot out of the sky?

He probably wouldn't have survived if he hadn't been leaning against an outside wall

43

at the exact moment when what had to have been a surface-to-air missile hit them.

It had taken off the nose section. Even as he was blown into what he'd thought at the time was oblivion, he'd watched Ezra and Hendricks and Rudy, who'd all been in or near the cockpit, disintegrate into a bloom of pink mist, taken out by the concussive force of the explosion that had brought down the plane.

His mind might not be firing on all cylinders at the moment, but he retained enough of his wits to know that if his plane had just been shot out of the sky by a surface-to-air missile, then somebody on the surface had to have been close enough to have shot it. Like, say, the figure currently racing toward him in the orange boat.

CHAPTER FIVE

The survivor *was* a man. His hair, the shape of his face, the width of his shoulders — Gina was certain about his gender even though she only had a few seconds before a swell got between them again, blocking him from her view. If he was calling to her, Gina couldn't hear him over the noise of the sea. Couldn't see him now, either, as the boat plunged down the back of a wave and tall peaks of steel-gray water topped with foam and littered with pieces of wreckage rushed past her on all sides.

But she *would* find him again.

No way was she leaving this guy behind.

Dropping the binoculars, she came about and went to full throttle, sending the boat flying over the watery cliffs and valleys toward where the man had been. He was lost, temporarily, she prayed, amid the waves. As she did her best to dodge the bursts of spray breaking over the bow, the possibility that this might be the man who belonged to the leg sent a shiver of horror down her spine. If so, his life hung by the thinnest of threads, and might depend on what she did in the first moments after reaching him.

She had adequate basic first aid skills, along with a small first aid kit tucked away in her backpack, which was secured in a compartment in the stern beneath a waterproof flap, but for so severe an injury . . . her mind boggled at the thought of trying to deal with it.

That concern was forgotten as she crested a wave and saw him there in the water almost directly below her, his head bobbing, his arms barely visible as they moved back and forth in front of him in a slow, treading-water motion. His face turned up toward her even as she spotted him. It was as pale as a corpse's beneath short, soaked seal-black hair that was plastered to his skull. From that distance his eyes looked black, too, narrow slits above a triangular blade of a nose and colorless lips pressed into a thin, tight line. He saw her and gave another feeble-looking wave.

"Here," he yelled.

She barely heard the hoarse cry, and would've thought her ears were playing tricks on her if she hadn't seen his lips move. He waved again as she sent the boat toward him.

"It's okay, I've got you," she shouted to him as she throttled down and maneuvered the boat to bring it in as close to him as possible. The waves worked against them, sweeping him away before she could reach him. For a worrisome moment she lost sight of him once more. She cautiously juiced the throttle, forced to take heed because of all the objects in the water, many of which might be jagged enough to damage the boat if propelled into it with sufficient force. A moment later she was rewarded by spotting him laboring toward her with an awkward swimming stroke that made her think he might be injured. This time her eyes stayed glued to him even as she worked the wheel and throttle to close the distance between them.

Watching him struggle against the current, she realized that she might have spoken too soon when she'd assured him that she had him. Getting him on board was going to be difficult, she feared. But there was no other option: towing him to shore behind the boat while he held on wouldn't work. The water was so cold that if he stayed in it much longer he would die from hypothermia.

"Grab on to the boat," she yelled as she got close enough to see that his eyes were shadowed by dark circles and his lips were blue. His face was waxy white with cold, and so taut with effort that the strong, square bones of his cheeks and jaw were starkly visible beneath his skin.

He can't last much longer. She knew it with an utter certainty.

Another stroke of his arms and his fingers brushed the boat's starboard side. To her dismay, it instantly became clear that there was nothing for him to grab on to: the tubular sides were smooth and slick.

The increasing strength of the waves made the too-buoyant craft difficult to handle with any precision. The wheel vibrated beneath her hands as she fought to hold the boat steady long enough to give him time to climb aboard. It was useless: even as his fingers scrabbled at the rubber, the water caught him up and pulled him away.

Should she lean out and try to grab him? Gina's heart urged her to do it, but her head said no: he might latch onto her like the drowning man he was. She was five-seven and toned, but slim. From what she could see of him he looked large and solidly built. If she were to get pulled into the icy water, instead of rescuing him, she would die with him.

All she could do was get the boat as close to him as possible one more time and hope that he could get himself into it.

Taut with anxiety, pulse racing like she was the one whose life was at stake, she did battle with the rushing waves.

"Try again," she cried as the boat drew near, only to watch aghast as one of the unceasing waves broke over him without warning. He disappeared, swallowed up by the cascading torrent.

Her heart lodged in her throat. Nerves jumping, she scanned the roiling water in growing alarm. When his dark head broke the surface at last she let out a breath she hadn't realized she'd been holding. Shaking his head, throwing off water droplets like a wet dog, he started swimming toward the boat one more time.

"I'm coming!" Shrieking now, with no guarantee that he could hear her over the relentless roaring of the wind and sea, she sent the boat shooting toward him. Its blunt prow slapped up and down on the water with a sound like a hand smacking flesh. The repeated fishtailing of the stern forcibly reminded her that the craft was too flimsy and light for the increasingly harsh condi-

tions. It was meant to be used in clear weather and calm seas. Keeping her gaze firmly fixed on his dark head, she refused to acknowledge the quiver of fear that shot down her spine at the thought, or to worry about the ferocity of the storm exploding toward her. There was nothing she could do about what was coming — except get the survivor on board and then get both of them out of there as fast as she could.

Even with the sea spitting foam and the wind whistling around her ears and conditions growing worse every second, leaving him was not an option she was prepared to consider.

His head was up and he was looking at her as he dog-paddled clumsily toward her. He was shouting something, she saw, and strained to hear.

". . . *rope*".

The only word she caught of those he screamed at her was the last one, but it was also the most important: she understood instantly that he wanted her to throw him a rope.

"*No rope.*" Screaming back, she shook her head vigorously so that he would understand. There was no rope on board.

He was swimming now as she maneuvered the boat as close to him as possible, but his strokes seemed jerkier and his body rode lower in the water than before. She knew his arms and legs must be numb, and would soon be completely immobilized by cold. When that happened, he would be gone.

He could die within her view, sink beneath the waves within feet of the boat, and there wouldn't be anything she could do to save him.

Gina felt sick at the thought.

She had just reluctantly reached the conclusion that she was going to have to risk leaning out and trying to grab him when it hit her — she could use her coat. If she were to take it off and throw him one end of it — say, a sleeve, while she held on to the other sleeve — maybe she could pull him on board. But that came with its own set of problems. To begin with, her coat would inevitably get soaked, which meant that she would no longer be able to wear it, leaving her dangerously exposed to the elements. In any rescue situation, the number one rule was, don't endanger yourself.

And then suddenly her coat didn't matter, because she remembered the emergency paddles that were affixed to the interior of the stern just above the place where her backpack was stashed, covered by a rubber flap designed to keep them safe and dry and

51

out of the way.

The moment she thought of them, she throttled down into neutral. She was afraid to turn the motor all the way off in case she should have trouble getting it started again; the boat was notoriously tricky like that, and if the boat's engine went out they were both dead. Even as she swung her legs around and dropped to her knees because trying to stand up would be insane given the conditions, the boat was caught up on the shoulder of a wave. Crawling unsteadily to the stern, an exercise that was rendered way trickier than she'd expected by the pitching of the boat, she yanked the flap free of the Velcro that secured it and grabbed the uppermost paddle.

It obviously had not left the brackets that held it for a long time: she had to wrestle it free. Succeeding at last, holding it triumphantly as she sank back on her heels, she saw that it was lightweight molded plastic, about six feet long. If they were both lucky, she might be able to use it to get him into the boat. Scrambling back to her seat, she scanned the heavy swells. He was nowhere in sight. Just as fear tightened her throat, she spotted him bobbing amid the debris farther out into the bay and waved.

He did not wave back.

Was he already too weak?

Galvanized by the thought, she went after him. As the boat drew near, he rolled onto his back, his arms moving just enough to keep him afloat. Either he was resting, or, as she feared, the frigid water was taking its inexorable toll.

His head turned toward the boat as it reached him. She could feel his eyes on her, sense his desperation.

"Get ready," she yelled. Throttling down into neutral again as the prow slid past him so that he was mere inches away, she scrambled off the seat and plopped down flat on her butt on the deck. Crooking one hand around the back edge of the seat to anchor herself, she thrust the paddle toward him. The water was already catching the boat up, pulling it away. The distance between them increased at a shocking rate with every passing second.

"Grab hold," she encouraged him. The wind was louder now. She wasn't sure he'd heard her. But he definitely saw the paddle: she watched the life come back into his face, watched the muscles around his mouth and eyes tighten, watched his jaw clench as he spotted it. Grim resolve showed in every line of his face. Rolling onto his stomach, he stroked laboriously toward her. It was

obvious that he was finding it harder to move. It was also obvious that he meant to fight to the last to survive.

"Hurry," she screamed, one eye on the next line of waves rushing toward them.

He did, abandoning swimming to launch himself out of the water and latch onto the paddle in a desperate lunge. With his dead weight suddenly attached to one end, it was all she could do to retain her grip on the other. She thanked God for the nonslip material of her waterproof gloves, and for the doughnutlike design of the end of the paddle, which created a hole into which she managed to hook her fingers. Icy spray broke over them both as the waves hit, and the boat was caught up again and hurled skyward.

"Hang on," she yelled as a haze of blowing seawater obscured everything except the wave that rose like a mountain beneath them. It was the biggest one yet, a roaring monster, and with the motor in neutral they were no more than a scrap of debris caught up by it. Gina's face was so wet and cold by this time that she could feel it freezing in the wind, and her fingers started to cramp from the force of her grip on the paddle. She felt as if her arms and shoulders were being wrenched apart as she held grimly on

54

to both the paddle and the seat. Her mouth went dry with fear for him, but he managed to hang on while the boat climbed and plunged with the wave.

"Now," she screamed when the boat leveled out.

They had only a moment or two of relative calm before another series of waves hit. Letting go of the seat, she braced her feet against the side nearest him, and held on to the paddle with both hands and every bit of strength she possessed as he put what felt like a thousand pounds of force on the other end.

His head shot into view as he levered himself partway out of the water. Then the pressure lessened suddenly, and Gina exhaled with relief as he hooked a hand over the side of the boat.

"Can you climb in?" she shouted. Suddenly the top half of his drenched, haggard face came into view. He was maybe mid-thirties, she saw. His brows were thick, straight black slashes above dark eyes that were narrowed to slits. Their eyes met for an instant through the flying droplets of water that warned of yet another approaching wave, and she saw grim determination in his.

"Get out of the way," he growled. The

words were uttered in a thick, hoarse voice that she could barely hear over the roar of their surroundings. They were accompanied by a flexing of the muscles of his shoulders and arms that was a warning in and of itself. She got out of the way, scooting backward while still retaining her precautionary hold on the seat. He seemed to explode out of the water, landing across the fat sausage rolls in a mighty dive that sent the opposite side of the boat flying upward.

Squeaking with alarm, Gina threw herself back toward the rising edge. Hooking both arms outward over the rolls, she flattened her back against the inflated tubes, hoping to counteract his weight with her own. With a groan he heaved himself inside the boat. The impact of his body hitting the deck was enough to make the precariously tilting side drop back down toward the water.

Heart thudding, Gina unhooked her arms from the sides and let her head slump forward in relief.

He shifted onto his back beside her, stabilizing the boat still more, and started coughing and wheezing like he'd swallowed half the ocean. His eyes were squeezed shut, his hands rested palms down on his chest, and his legs were bent at the knee. He'd lost his shoes. His feet, in drenched black socks, were long and wide. Water poured off him in streams, adding to the puddle in the bottom of the boat. His skin was leached of all normal color. Even half-drowned and frozen as he was, though, Gina couldn't help but notice that he was way handsome in a rough-hewn, ex–prize fighter kind of way: broad cheekbones, square jaw, with a meaty, slightly crooked nose and a well-shaped mouth turned blue with cold. A shadow of stubble darkened his cheeks and chin: from the looks of it he'd shaved sometime within the last twenty-four hours. He was big enough that he took up almost the entire deck, and obviously fit, with broad shoulders and a wide chest above a flat abdomen, narrow hips, and long, powerful-looking legs. There was something dark staining his shirt on his left side around his waist, she observed with a frown, and the stain seemed to be growing as she watched.

Blood?

Gina barely had time to register the possibility before another wave snatched them up.

His eyes opened, and he grabbed on to the nearest strap as the water rose furiously under them.

"Don't move," Gina cried, because the

last thing they needed was for him to start flailing around and destabilizing the boat again. Throwing an arm over the seat, she hung on as they reached the crest of the wave amid a shower of spray, then bumped at what felt like warp speed down the rough spine into the trough.

As soon as the boat leveled out she scrambled onto the seat and reclaimed the wheel and throttle.

"We're out of here," she said to him with a palpable surge of relief. At least she once again had some degree of control. A quick glance at the approaching weather confirmed what she already knew — time was running out fast. The waves were coming in furious bunches now and seemed to be gathering size and speed by the minute. A harbinger of what was on the way, the wind blew relentlessly, driving heavy bursts of snow in angry gusts across the water. The bulk of the storm filled the horizon as far as the eye could see. Paler gray clouds mushroomed out of the billowing charcoal central mass in a way that made her pulse pound with alarm. Flickering glimmers of lightning deep inside the storm lit up various sections ominously. The whole thing seemed to be heading their way with the approximate speed of a runaway train.

Gina came about, opened up the throttle, and started heading in. Forget trying to reach camp. They needed to get to shore *now.*

A look around at her passenger made her frown. He still lay on his back. His head was near her seat; his feet touched the stern. Awash in the inch or so of icy water sloshing around in the bottom of the boat, he shivered violently. The front of her hair was damp, and water beaded on her coat and pants, but inside her clothes she was dry. Still she was cold to her marrow even in her insulated outfit. He had to be literally freezing to death.

At the moment, though, the only thing she could do for him was get him off the water.

"Are you badly hurt?" Her sharp question was prompted by the movement of his hand to press gingerly over what she was sure now was an injury to his side. Diffused by the saturation of his shirt, the stain was spreading steadily. It looked more brown than red, but still she didn't think it could be anything but blood.

He grimaced. His eyes opened a slit. "No." He took a breath. "Where are we?"

Since any except the most urgent, lifesaving treatment was going to have to wait until

59

they were ashore anyway, she moved on from his physical condition to answer his question.

"Just off the coast of Attu."

A frown creased his brow. "Attu."

"How many others were on the plane?" Her throat hurt from shouting to be heard over the wind, but she had to ask, just as she had to visually skim every piece of wreckage they passed in case there might be another survivor out there. Although she knew that there was no more time, that staying out any longer on the increasingly wild water would be little short of suicidal, she couldn't *not* search, even as she sent the boat scudding across the waves.

"Three. All dead." His voice was rough and raw. His reply ended in a violent coughing spasm that brought up a gush of seawater and had her wincing for him.

The memory of the severed leg she'd seen popped into her mind. Its owner was almost certainly dead. Even if her passenger was wrong, even if the other victims had wound up alive in the icy water, by now they would probably be beyond saving even if she could find them.

"What's your name? Where were you headed?" she asked. The sheer amount of debris was defeating her, Gina realized even as she continued to look around.

She knew there was nothing more she could do. Still, the thought that she might be leaving someone behind to die made her stomach turn inside out.

An image of the burned-out plane in which three of the people she'd loved best in the world had died flashed into her mind's eye. Her heart thudded and her breath caught even as she angrily shook her head to clear it.

Do not go there.

Her gaze again fell on her now-silent passenger, and she was immediately distracted. Not that he was doing anything. At all. In fact, he seemed to be barely breathing now, and that was just it. His eyes were closed again, and he lay motionless. The dark stain on his shirt continued to grow. She was sure now that it was blood. What alarmed her even more than the spreading blood, though, was that he had stopped shivering.

That was one of the signs of advancing hypothermia.

Was he losing consciousness? Going into shock?

Had she rescued him from the water only to have him die on her now?

"Hey," she said. His head was right behind and below her. She twisted to tap his cheek

61

with her gloved fingers. "You need to stay awake."

No response. Not even the flicker of an eyelid.

If he was unconscious, there was no way she was going to move him: he was too big. And she knew herself well enough to know that once they reached land she wasn't going to be able to just leave him behind in the boat to die.

You have to save yourself.

Gina shuddered. She could hear her father screaming those very words at her as distinctly as if she were back in that plane struggling to get him out. He'd been trapped inside when it had plunged into a Mexican jungle, and he'd died. A renowned archaeologist in the Indiana Jones mold, Gavin Sullivan had spent his life adventuring all over the world. Gina's mother had tired of his nomadic existence when Gina was ten, divorced him, and settled into an ordinary life as a history professor. She was, in Gina's father's words, *domestically inclined.* The contemptuous way in which he'd said that had made Gina, who lived with her mother most of the time, secretly terrified of having him extend that description to her. Because the truth was that she also tended to like having a home and friends and a calm, stable life. To cover up what he would consider those deplorable tendencies, when she'd been with him she'd embraced his lifestyle with outward enthusiasm, going along with his increasingly hair-raising exploits as if she lived for excitement, too.

Oh, God, after all the work she'd done to put the memories behind her, the crash of the silver jet had brought them raging back.

The next contact her hand made with her passenger's face was more of a smack. "Can you hear me?"

Still nothing.

Straightening, Gina turned her face into the wind in hopes that a blast of icy air would clear her mind, and found herself confronted by the appalling image of the tumbling clouds at the leading edge of the storm swallowing up the crashed plane's still-upright tail. This evidence of how fast the storm was closing in did what a faceful of snow-spiked wind couldn't: it cleared her mind instantly. It also terrified her.

Jerking her gaze away from the spine-chilling sight, she pushed the throttle as far forward as it would go and set the boat on a beeline for the rocky beach that was the closest practical spot to land.

Reaching down behind her, she smacked her oblivious passenger again, hard.

"You! Wake —" *up,* was how she meant to finish that, but the radio interrupted, crackling to life with a sputter of static, making her jump. God, she'd forgotten about it. It was still clipped to her pocket.

". . . blizzard conditions. Are you there? Gina? This is Ray . . ."

His voice dissolved into more static, but Gina knew who it was: Ray Wheeler. The team leader. Grabbing the radio, she depressed the speaker button and said into it, "Ray. There's been a —"

Before she could say anything more, before she could tell him about the plane crash and the survivor and where she was and that she urgently needed help to get her and her passenger safely back to camp, the radio was snatched from her hand.

Her mouth dropped open in shock as she watched it sail over the side of the boat to splash down in the churning water, where it immediately vanished.

Then her head swiveled. Her passenger had somehow managed to roll onto his knees. He was right behind her, steadying himself with a hand curled around her seat and another braced against the boat's side. Their eyes locked. There was no mistaking what was in his this time. They were hard.

Brutal. Deadly.

"No radio," he said.

CHAPTER SIX

A quiver of fear shot down Gina's spine. Her pulse kicked into overdrive. Her heart began to pound.

Looking into the hard, handsome face of the man whose life she had just risked her own to save, Gina had a terrible epiphany: the thing about rescuing a stranger was that after the rescue, he was still a stranger.

She didn't know the slightest thing about him. Except that she was now alone with him in the middle of a stormy sea, he was a hell of a lot bigger and stronger than she was, and he had just thrown her radio in the drink.

And now every internal warning system she possessed was going insane.

She tightened her grip on the wheel as it occurred to her that there wasn't a whole lot to prevent him from throwing her in after the radio. Then he'd have the boat to himself and — and what? She didn't know.

Maybe she was reading too much into what he'd just done. Maybe he was hallucinating/traumatized by the crash/unaware of what he was doing?

Yeah, no. Those narrow glinting eyes — they were the color of black coffee, she saw now that she was looking into them all up close and personal — were as aware as her own. Swallowing hard, she tore her gaze from his and forced herself to concentrate on her driving as the boat bounced like a kid on a trampoline over the tall whitecaps that raced toward shore. The truth behind the old no-good-deed-goes-unpunished saying might have just hit her over the head with a two-by-four, but she had to keep her focus: if they weren't off the water by the time the storm caught up with them, whether the guy she'd saved was up to no good probably wasn't going to matter.

Because they were both going to be dead.

"Why would you do that?" she asked angrily. Pretending that she wasn't disturbed by what he'd done was pointless: he had to know she was. Realizing that her shoulders had hunched in an automatic defensive reaction to having someone she didn't trust so close behind her, she deliberately relaxed them. "I was trying to get you some help."

"You're all the help I need." His voice was

a ragged growl. For the first time it occurred to her that his accent was American, not that it made her feel any better. She could be harmed by a fellow countryman as easily as by anyone else. He moved closer as he spoke, which put him way too close for comfort. Having the bulk of him looming up inches behind her made the skin prickle on the nape of her neck.

He could be dangerous.

Her breathing quickened. So did her pulse.

He leaned closer. She could feel the brush of his big body against her back, and her shoulders instantly tensed again in response.

He said, "Where are the people you're with?"

If he hadn't been so near, she wouldn't have been able to hear him over the escalating noise. Wind blew, surf crashed, and the motor whined with the effort of combating the increasingly massive waves. But his voice was practically in her ear, and his encroachment into her space felt — threatening. The *question* felt threatening. One thing was for sure, he wasn't asking so that he could calculate the quickest route to reaching help.

As she brushed away the pelting crystals of snow that were making her chilled face tingle, her mind went in a thousand directions at once, trying to decide the best answer to give him. Confirming that the two of them were totally alone might not be smart. On the other hand, he had the same view of their destination that she did: a shallow crescent beach rising to a rocky hillside striped with areas of brownish tundra, and, beyond that, a line of black mountains powdered with snow.

Not exactly a well-populated area.

She made the decision then not to lie to him. He had no reason to harm her. She didn't mean to give him one.

"At our camp. Most of them. Probably." Okay, that had the virtue of being the exact truth while still leaving room for reinforcements to be lurking just out of sight.

"How many?"

Wetting her lips, she told him.

"How close is your camp?"

Again, she rejected the temptation to lie. "A few miles."

"Who are you? What are you doing here?" There was a menacing undertone to that last question that sent another wary quiver snaking down her spine. Her already thudding heart thudded faster. This time she absolutely got the feeling that giving him the wrong answer might prove hazardous to her health.

Who is this guy? What have I gotten myself into?

Beating back the panicky feelings that were fluttering like butterflies in her stomach wasn't easy, but she tried, and when she spoke, her tone was measured and calm. "My name is Gina Sullivan. Dr. Gina Sullivan. I'm an environmental studies professor at Stanford, and I'm here with a group of scientists to study the effect of pollution on birds." Narrowing her eyes against the rushing wind as she marshaled her courage, she added tartly, "And I just saved your life."

"Yeah," he said, with no inflection at all. Something about that struck her as being more alarming than the menace she'd thought she'd detected in his tone before. Like her saving his life didn't matter. Like he was the kind of ruthless opportunist who would let himself be saved, and then dispose of his savior in any way he found convenient. She was reminded suddenly, irresistibly, of that old scorpion-and-frog story where the frog gave the scorpion a ride across a pond and was stung to death by the scorpion on the way. When the dying frog asked why, the scorpion replied, "Because that's my nature."

Picturing herself as the frog, Gina shivered.

Then her chin came up. She'd be damned if she was going to sit there quivering in fear of him.

"And your name is . . . ?" she prompted.

When he didn't answer, Gina's lips compressed. She flicked a wary glance back at him. Focused ahead of the boat, his eyes were obsidian slits in a face that was ashen now except for the blue tinge of his mouth, which was grim. His jaw was hard. The wind had dried his hair, which was seal black and cut so short that she wondered if he could be military. She didn't find the thought reassuring. His shirt was still so wet it clung to him. Through it, she could see exactly how heavily muscled his shoulders and chest were. Despite his clothes, which appeared to be the tattered remains of an expensive suit, the man was definitely not a desk jockey. The lower half of the left side of his shirt was now dark with blood. If he was bleeding like that despite how chilled his body had to be, then it was a serious injury. She marveled that he was still able to function. He had to be operating on pure adrenaline.

To have survived the crash, to say nothing of his immersion in the icy sea, and still be moving and functional, he had to be a fricking *machine*.

His gaze shifted. Abruptly she found herself looking into his eyes. Even with him on his knees behind her they were higher than hers, which unhappily reminded her of just how big he really was. There was not a trace of softness or compassion in them, or really anywhere in his harshly carved face.

Pulling her gaze away, Gina worked on maintaining an outward facade of calm as she looked unseeingly toward the beach.

"The storm's getting close," he said. The tickle of his breath against her cheek made her tense up. Despite his good looks, she hated having him so near. "We'll be lucky to make it in."

On that they were in full agreement. Whatever else was going on with them, they were of necessity allied against the storm. For now, it was the common enemy, chasing them across the water like a ravenous gray beast, obliterating sea and sky as it devoured everything in its path. Gina's heart pounded as she realized that it was gaining on them with alarming speed. Ahead of it, all around where the Zodiac was shooting toward the bay and beyond, the day was darkening as if dusk were falling, although it wasn't yet four p.m. and there should have been at least an hour and a half of daylight left. The waves were starting to rival skyscrapers in size, and the wind was approaching gale force. As long as they were able to stay a reasonable distance out in front of it, they were actually benefiting from the strength of the blow because it was taking them in faster. Pushed toward land, the boat skimmed the water at what felt like warp speed, touching down with a jolt and then bouncing up again, over and over and over, Gina's butt smacking the seat with each bump. If she'd been trying to do anything except go straight in, the little craft would have been impossible to control.

He asked, "Anybody going to be waiting for you up there on the beach?"

She hated admitting it. "No."

"So you're out here all alone."

Something in his tone gave her pause. She didn't answer.

"*Are* you alone?"

The menace was back in his voice. Gina barely repressed a shiver. "Yes."

By that time they'd almost reached the mouth of the bay fronting the beach that was her target. The water before them wasn't quite as rough as the waves they were riding, although tall whitecaps rolled angrily toward shore, and near the beach the surf was white with foam. As they flew past, the giant waves they were leaving behind broke over a trio of building-size rocks that served as a breakwater, booming as they showered the boat with a fine mist of icy spray.

Gina barely felt the droplets hit. She had both hands clamped around the wheel as she piloted the boat through the rocks. All her focus had to be on keeping the boat on course as she pointed it directly toward the smoothest section of beach.

Given the turbulence and what was certain to be the concurrent state of the undertow, to say nothing of the temperature of the water, she wasn't even going to try to bring the Zodiac in in the usual way, which, absent a dock, involved stopping a few yards from shore, hopping out, and pulling the boat through the surf to land.

"Hold on," she threw at him over her shoulder. "I'm going to beach it."

He didn't say anything. Instead he gripped the seat hard with both hands, one on either side of her, which she took as an acknowledgment of her words. He was so close behind her now that he was practically breathing down her neck, boxing her in with hard arms and the solid wall of his chest, but there was nothing she could do to get away from him at this point, and, anyway, she couldn't worry about *him* at the moment. Bringing the boat in had to be her only concern.

Steering as best she could given the buffeting the boat was taking from the wind and waves, she sent the boat racing toward the beach. At the last possible minute she shifted into neutral and threw the lever that lifted the motor clear of the water. Clenching her teeth, hands clamped around the wheel, she prepared herself for a hard impact as the force of the huge wave they were riding carried them the rest of the way in.

Gina let out an involuntary cry as they hit land with a grinding jolt that threw her forward, slamming her painfully into the wheel, driving the binoculars that still hung around her neck into her breastbone. The stranger crashed into her, heavy as a sack of cement, his chest colliding with her back with the approximate force of a giant sledgehammer. Gasping as the air was driven from her lungs, Gina could only lie helplessly against the wheel with him draped on top of her as the boat scraped over the beach, slewed violently sideways, and then finally shuddered to a halt maybe six feet or so beyond the reach of the surf.

For a moment after they stopped, Gina lay unmoving. The wind had been knocked out of her. Aching, slightly dazed, she gasped for air. After a moment, he levered himself off her. Free of his weight, she finally managed to suck in enough air to fill her lungs.

The world instantly came back into too-sharp and unpleasant focus.

Pushing away from the wheel, she coughed, wheezed, and coughed some more.

"Okay?" he asked. At least he sounded minimally concerned about her well-being, which she took as a good sign. He wouldn't care if she was hurt if he meant to hurt her himself, would he?

Not that she intended to wait around to find out. Now that they were safely ashore, she was going to ditch him just as fast as she could. She'd saved his life, repaid a little of her karmic debt as it were, and at this point taking care of number one became the most important item on her agenda. He didn't know it yet, but as soon as she could get off the boat they were going to go their separate ways.

"Yes." Gina was still taking careful breaths and trying not to wince from what felt like the severe bruising of her chest. If it hadn't been for the cushioning properties of the life vest and her parka, she thought the impact probably would have cracked a rib. There wasn't time to sit around assessing any possible injuries she might have suffered, however. She needed to *move.*

The storm was already barreling into the bay. The breakwater rocks were no longer visible. The waves that had carried the boat in had increased in size until they were now towering walls of water thundering to shore. In the few minutes since the boat had skidded to a stop, the air around them had darkened and taken on a greenish tinge. The surf had risen to the point where frothy fingers slithered under the far side of the boat. The wind howled rather than moaned.

Slanting lines of snow obscured her vision. What once had been flakes now felt like hundreds of icy needles hitting her skin. The temperature had dropped so that each exhalation frosted the air. She could see individual bolts of lightning as they zapped to earth inside the clouds. The pounding of the waves against the no-longer-visible breakwater boomed like cannon fire.

What was immediately, abundantly clear was that there wasn't going to be time to get anywhere that could actually be considered safe. They were lucky they'd made it off the water.

Pulse racing, Gina swung her legs around on the seat, stood up, and stepped quickly past him. In the process of laboriously getting to his feet, he made no move to stop her. She could feel his gaze on her as she ripped off the binoculars and stuck them in her pocket, then shucked the life jacket and crouched by the stern to free her backpack from its hidey-hole.

It was a big backpack, weighing in at a little over thirty pounds. A similar one had been issued to each of the scientists when they had arrived on Attu. All the expedition members were expected to take their backpacks with them whenever they left camp as a precaution against Attu's unpredictable weather (her current situation provided clear proof of the advisability of that). The Eskimos who'd once made Attu their home had called the sudden, fierce storms that blew in without warning williwaws, which in Gina's opinion was way too poetic a name for the violence of what was happening around them. At first she'd been skeptical of the need for so much stuff. Now she thanked God for the basic survival gear that the backpack was loaded with, including a small pop-up tent and a sleeping bag, in addition to food supplies and extra water. It should be enough to allow her to ride out the storm, provided she was able to find a spot relatively shielded from the wind where she could deploy the tent.

"We need to find shelter," he said as she straightened with the backpack slung over one shoulder. His voice was a harsh rasp, and he was starting to slur his words. Standing to his full height, he was, indeed, as tall and athletically built as she'd thought, and as attractive. Under other, better, conditions, she might even have been slightly bowled over by him. As she watched, he bent a little to one side, grimacing, a hand pressed to his injury. His clothes clung to him like a second skin, and she was reminded of how wet he still was, and how deathly — and *deathly* was the word — cold he had to be. The color of the stain had deepened and brightened so that it was now clearly red, clearly blood.

As she looked at him, a particularly strong gust of wind hit. It caught them both, and he took a stumbling step backward before recovering. At what she calculated was about six-four and two hundred–plus pounds, he was way too big to be blown backward by the wind, especially when the same blast hadn't moved *her.* He was also way too buff to be the kind of fat-cat businessman that his clothes seemed to indicate, or that she would have expected to find on a high-end private jet like the one he'd crashed in. Once again she wondered who and what he was, and could come up with nothing that she found even mildly reassuring. Ordinarily she didn't think any wind short of hurricane force would have been enough to budge him. But his strength was clearly waning: even through the storm-created twilight and blowing snow, she could see that his eyes seemed to have sunk into his skull and his rugged features were pinched and drawn. Every bit of him that she could see that wasn't pasty white was tinged with blue.

He was hurt and bleeding. Possibly suffering from other injuries that didn't show. Probably in the throes of hypothermia. Certainly traumatized by the plane crash and perhaps on the verge of collapsing, of going into shock.

In desperate need of help.

Her help. Because she was all the help there was.

Gina's lips tightened. The state he was in would have roused her utmost compassion if he hadn't given her reason to be wary of him. But he *had* given her reason to be wary of him, and she wasn't about to simply forget about that because right at this moment he needed her. She had many faults: stupid wasn't one of them.

So it was decided. Flinging first one leg and then the other over the side of the boat, she slid the three feet or so down the slippery rubber rolls onto the beach. The coarse sand crunched beneath her boots as she landed. Because it was (semi)dry land, she silently blessed it.

"Hey," he said. She didn't know whether he meant it as a question or a protest. She didn't care.

"You need to get off the beach in case of a storm surge." Turning to face him, she shrugged into her backpack. Because he stood in the center of the boat and she was now some six or seven feet away from it, she found herself yelling again to be heard over the wind whipping in from the bay. "There are abandoned structures all over the island. Finding one of those and taking shelter in it would be your best bet."

Turning, she started walking quickly away, head down, back to the wind, pulling her hood up and securing it in place as she went. She needed to get well away from the beach before she pitched her tent, and there wasn't much time.

"Wait," he called after her. Hunching her

shoulders defensively, she lengthened her stride. Her conscience did not smite her. She was not, not, *not* going to even so much as look back.

He let out a whoop, the sound high-pitched and startling. It was followed by a heavy thud.

She looked back and got sandblasted in the face by snow mixed with sleet for her trouble. Swiping a hand across her face to get rid of the snow and then shielding her eyes as she tried to make out what had happened, she saw that he was sprawled flat on his face in the wet, grainy sand. Clearly he'd tried to get out of the boat and fallen.

Grimacing, she looked beyond him. Black and ominous, already halfway across the bay, the bulk of the storm hurtled toward them. The wind was now strong enough to pick up small rocks and send them flying across the beach. The waves crashing against the shore and sending spray flying skyward were huge. Even as she watched, the boat was caught up by the rising tide and pulled into the surf. A receding wave whirled it away.

He lay unmoving, inches from the surging foam.

Indecision rooted her to the spot.

If she left him where he was, he would

die. If he didn't get pulled into the surf like the boat and drown, the storm surge would get him. If nothing else, he'd certainly die of exposure.

Damn it to hell.

Muttering every curse word she knew, Gina ran back toward the stranger's prone form.

CHAPTER SEVEN

Somewhere he'd read that freezing to death didn't hurt, Cal reflected groggily. Whoever had written that was wrong. He was freezing to death as he lay facedown in the grit on that bitterly cold, storm-swept beach, and the process hurt like a mother. His skin burned as the icy blast of the wind froze his sea-soaked clothes to his body. His bones and muscles ached as if a dozen thugs armed with baseball bats had just worked him over. His head pounded unmercifully. His throat was parched and dry.

He didn't think he could get up. No, he was pretty sure he couldn't get up. It didn't help that he didn't see much point in it. He'd gotten a good look at the desolate terrain before the boat had pitched up on it and there was no shelter from the elements in sight.

If he did manage to get to his feet, he could stagger a few yards, even a few hundred yards, and *then* collapse and die.

Seemed like a lot of effort for the same result.

Upon discovering that his purported savior in the boat was a young woman, his first reaction had been a feeling of immense relief. He'd let go of the suspicion that she was a cog in the plan to murder Rudy and everybody who might be party to the information he had possessed, and accepted at face value his good luck at having an innocent civilian in a boat available exactly when and where he'd needed one.

Lying there in the bottom of her boat, he'd been so exhausted, so wet and cold and nearly drowned, in so much pain and, he saw now, so close to going into shock, that it had taken him a little while to remember that his luck had never been that good.

To remember that the world was a violent and unpredictable place where trusting anybody was a good way to wind up dead.

The last harrowing minutes aboard the plane had underlined that for him. He'd been in the back with Rudy, in the small, private, windowless, lockable room that the plane had been outfitted with for the precise purpose of transporting individuals like Rudy who were untrustworthy and needed to be contained. Some people might have called it a cell, but no one who had ever been in a real cell would have done so: this one had four big leather chairs that reclined into beds, with basically all the comforts of a very luxurious home readily available. He and Rudy were alone. Rudy was chatty, proud of his exploits and eager to talk about them. One of the reasons Cal personally had been tapped for this job was because of his background in avionic military weapons systems, something he'd studied at the Air Force Academy. He'd been tasked with evaluating Rudy's claims as to what had happened to Flight 155. His opinion as to the plausibility of Rudy's story would be included in the oral briefing he would give his employer upon handing Rudy over. He'd been prepared to coax/scare/bully the details out of Rudy, but as it turned out he hadn't had to do anything but sit there and listen. Among a whole lot of nonessential information, Rudy told him exactly what he was claiming had happened to the plane.

"That Jorgensen guy was the target," Rudy said. After a hearty meal (the equivalent of a TV dinner zapped in an onboard microwave) and a nap, he kicked back in a chair munching Peanut M&M's like they guaranteed long life and happiness. Wearing a plaid flannel shirt with chinos, his dark brown hair hanging in an uneven bang across his forehead, he looked as comfortable as if he were sitting in his own living room. During the briefing he'd received before taking off for Kazakhstan, Cal had been given the NTSB report (which basically said that the plane had flown into a mountain for unknown reasons), along with a host of technical information and a dossier on the passengers and crew. On the flight to pick up Rudy, Cal had reviewed that material, and had watched a number of security videos, including one of the passengers passing through security and another of them boarding the plane. He'd done all that as part of his preparation for grilling Rudy later, because in his opinion what Rudy was suggesting had happened to that plane was all but impossible.

Of course, whether to believe Rudy wasn't his call to make. His job was to get the guy out of Kazakhstan and bring him back to American soil, and add his opinion to all the other opinions and the rest of the material that was being gathered.

"Edward Thomas Jorgensen," Cal said. He knew precisely whom Rudy was talking about. He'd read the guy's bio, seen his picture, watched on video as he'd passed through security and boarded the plane. His first impression had been: Special Forces. Then he'd checked and been struck by the paucity of information on the man — no family listed, no employment, no military or criminal record — as well as by something indefinable in the way he carried himself. A constant alertness. An air of expecting trouble.

Cal realized that he recognized it because he moved through the world like that himself: it took one to know one. For those reasons, Cal had flagged him as a person of interest before Rudy ever mentioned him. Not that he meant to share that, or anything else, with Rudy.

His and Rudy's conversation was strictly one-way.

Cal's internal radar pinged in response to Rudy's assertion that Jorgensen had been the target.

"Yeah?" Cal settled more comfortably in his chair and raised a skeptical eyebrow. He'd already learned that skepticism drove Rudy into paroxysms of revelations.

"Jorgensen's not his real name." Rudy tossed a couple more Peanut M&M's into his mouth and crunched. "Steven Carbone. Former DIA, Navy SEAL. Left the military and the US under a cloud. Something about passing secrets. Anyway, after that he did some freelance work for some bad actors. Part of the team that took out Victor Volkov — you know, that Russian billionaire who challenged Putin for the presidency a couple of years ago but got killed in a car accident before the election? Let's just say that wasn't no accident. There's a top-secret investigation going on into that and other murders of Putin opponents in DC right now, and Carbone was on his way to talk to them. Hand them the smoking gun, you might say, in return for a full pardon for anything he might have done in the past. He got whacked before he could."

"So a whole airplane full of people was taken out to get rid of one guy." Cal kept the note of skepticism going, although he was starting to get extremely interested in what Rudy was telling him. It meshed with certain rumors he'd heard. That Jorgensen/Carbone was formerly with the Defense Intelligence Agency and a SEAL tracked, too.

"If it wasn't for me, you wouldn't know that Carbone was the target," Rudy pointed out as he tossed back more M&M's. "No one would. It's easy to hide a murder in the middle of a terrible accident with two-hundred-some-odd victims."

True enough.

Cal got down to the nitty-gritty. "Who did it, and how did they do it?"

Rudy shrugged. "People loyal to Putin. What, I'm supposed to know their names? What I got is how. And I already told your bosses that."

"Tell me."

"They hacked the flight controls. Gained access through the plane's entertainment system, went through a couple of firewalls, and voilà! They got control of the plane. Probably for a few minutes only, but when you're flying over the Rocky Mountains, losing altitude for a few minutes is all it takes. *Boom-pow.*" The bag in his hand apparently empty, Rudy turned it upside down, shook it disconsolately, and asked, "Got any more M&M's?"

Cal didn't change expression, but he was thinking furiously. What Rudy described — it sounded more doable than he'd originally thought. A modern jetliner at cruising altitude is on autopilot, which means that it practically flies itself. If there was a program that could interfere with the autopilot . . . He felt his shoulders tighten with concern. "When you tell me what I want to know. And what I want to know are specifics. Everything. How the program works, who designed it, what kind of system it needs to run on. Who's using it. Who has access to it."

"It's on the market as we speak. Anybody with the money to buy it can get access to it, what do you think? Course, that's a short list, because a program like this is worth tens of millions to the right group. The FSB has it for sure, that's how I found it. Also, at a guess, some factions of the Bratva." Having clearly assumed that Cal knew that the FSB was the latter-day KGB and the Bratva was the Russian Mafia, Rudy screwed up his face in the pained expression of an expert conversing with the uninitiated as he moved on to describing the technical side. "As to how it works, it's like a virus. All it takes is for one passenger to turn on his individual entertainment unit and it's in the system. Then —" He broke off, frowning. "Look, it's all on the flash drive I gave you. Steps A through Z, so simple a kid — no, that's not right — a grandpa could follow it. It's fucking amazing, let me tell you. I only wish I'd come up with it." Cal got a glimpse of what looked like professional jealousy shining out of Rudy's eyes before the other man continued, "Give it back to me, and get me a laptop, and I'll walk you through it."

The flash drive was secured at that moment inside Cal's belt, which was of the type — offered by travel companies — that had an inside zipper in the back for the concealment of cash and small items. He'd been using it on various jobs for various purposes for years. The thing was so low-tech that it had never been compromised.

"Just talk me through it," Cal said, because until he got inside a secure facility he wasn't putting anything on a computer that he didn't want the whole world to have access to. Rudy was a great hacker, but there were more just like him. Lots of people out there were looking real hard for Rudy, and one way to look for him, or the information he'd stolen, would be to scan the Web. Cal didn't believe in taking unnecessary chances. He got the job he was hired to do done with a minimum of fuss, which was why he kept getting hired.

"You're making this difficult." Rudy frowned at him. Cal shrugged. Rudy sighed.

"Who created the program?" Cal said.

Rudy made a face. "I don't know. What, you think it was signed or something? Whoever it was sold it to the Russkies. Or maybe they just took it. Whatever. From whomever. The point is, it's out there, and there are people looking to buy it or get hold of it however they can. What happened to Flight 155 is almost foolproof." He smirked a little. "Without me, it would have been foolproof. Nobody had a clue."

Cal thought about that. His first reaction — why not just shoot the plane down, or place a bomb on board and blow it out of the sky? — was followed by a quick and terrifying answer. A missile strike would leave a heat signature; so would a bomb, not just on the plane itself but as a record on the satellites and other sensitive devices that monitored what was going on in the world. Investigators would figure out that the plane had been brought down on purpose, and would go hunting for the perpetrators. There weren't that many with that kind of capability. The culprits would be identified.

But if the plane's own systems were compromised, all investigators would be able to determine was that, for reasons unknown, the plane flew into a mountain.

Rudy was right: as a method of bringing down a plane, it was almost foolproof.

The hair rose on the back of Cal's neck.

Rudy said, "What makes what I'm selling even more valuable is that there's chatter it's getting ready to happen again."

Cal sat up straighter. "When? Where?"

"I don't know. These kinds of people don't

exactly post up schedules. The talk is coming out of Ukraine. I figure your people are smart enough to track it down."

"Tell me how it works," Cal said through his teeth.

"All right, jeez. Don't go getting mad at me. I'm the one who found the thing. I'm the good guy here."

"Right." His voice was dry. "How does it work?"

"Think of the program as a simple" — Rudy broke off, gripping the arms of his chair while the plane bucked through a pocket of turbulence; as the air smoothed out he continued — "repurposing of any basic remote control program. The program itself is not the trick. The trick is getting it on the plane. In this case, they used a private jet to get within range and then —" Without warning, the plane dropped like it was falling down an elevator shaft.

Rudy gasped out, "Holy moly!" and hung on so hard that his nails made visible indentations in the soft leather of the armrests.

As the seat seemed to drop out from under him, Cal grabbed for his armrests, too. Cruise altitude for this segment of the flight was thirty-three thousand feet. No way should there be this kind of turbulence at thirty-three thousand feet.

Even as he had the thought, the plane shimmied like a belly dancer, then dropped some more.

"Put your seat belt on and stay put," Cal ordered, and got up to go investigate. As soon as he opened the private room's door and stepped into the main cabin, the plane dropped so abruptly that he was almost thrown off his feet.

Grabbing hold of the nearest seat back, he made his way toward the cockpit. The interior was all plush beige leather and polished teak, with four additional passenger seats facing each other and a couch on the left side. Although it was the middle of the afternoon, Cal looked out the windows to see darkness encroaching on all sides. He frowned. The plane's rocking and pitching gave him his answer: what he was seeing were storm clouds. The plane was flying through a storm.

As if in confirmation, a clap of thunder reverberated through the plane. Lightning flashed. Clearly they were right in the middle of a violent weather system. From the way the plane was being buffeted, the wind had to be blowing at least a hundred knots. His ears popped suddenly, giving him incontrovertible evidence that they were descending.

What the *hell*?

The cockpit door was shut. Cal tried the handle: locked. Quickly keying in the code meant to unlock the door, Cal tried the handle again.

Still locked.

He tried once more. Same result.

Christ, had something gone wrong in the cockpit? Were they unconscious in there? Dead? Visions of a cockpit fire, a decompression accident, electrical trouble resulting in some kind of freak electrocution — the gamut of possibilities ran through his head in the space of seconds. He even spared a passing thought for the scenario Rudy had described — a remote takeover of the plane's controls — only to dismiss it. No entertainment system. No means of access. A remote takeover of the plane wouldn't have disabled Ezra and Hendricks.

Thumping the metal panel hard with his fist to let them know he was out there, he pressed the button on the intercom system that connected the cabin to the cockpit, one unit of which was set into the wall right beside the door.

"Ezra? Hendricks?" His voice was sharp. He could feel tension coiling inside him, feel the strong kick of his heart.

No answer.

He tried once more. "You guys alive in there?"

No answer.

Shit. Adrenaline spiked through his system. He pounded the door harder. *"Ezra? Hendricks?"*

"What's going on?" Rudy was behind him.

"I told you to stay put," Cal flung over his shoulder, looking around for some kind of tool he could use to break the handle off the door, which should, he hoped, at least weaken the lock. In his pocket, attached to his key ring, was a small but effective Leatherman tool. With the handle out of the way and the lock accessible, he thought he could use the tool's screwdriver to jimmy the locking mechanism. Since 9/11, cockpit doors were practically impregnable. He would have hit this one with everything he had if he'd thought it would do any good. It wouldn't. The lock was his only chance.

"There's a problem. Oh, jeez, I knew there was a problem," Rudy moaned, wringing his hands. Thunder boomed. Lightning flashed. The plane shook and dropped. Rudy staggered and caught hold of a seat back to keep from going down.

Grabbing a fire extinguisher from its mount on the wall, Cal barked at him, "Stay out of my way. Sit down."

The cabin rang with the crash of metal on metal as Cal slammed the case of the fire extinguisher into the handle multiple times in quick succession. By the time the handle popped off, Rudy, collapsed in a seat right behind him, was jabbering what sounded like a prayer, the plane was bouncing and yawing like a boat in high seas, and Cal was drenched in sweat.

His worst fear was that they were going to run out of time. The plane was heading down, and the clock stopped ticking when it ran into something other than air.

Steadying himself against the plane's gyrations with a shoulder propped against the wall, he probed the lock with his small screwdriver.

It slid into the opening, found what he hoped and prayed was the latch —

"Damn it, Cal, stand down!" Ezra's voice boomed at him through the intercom.

Cal's shoulders sagged with relief. Whatever the hell had gone down, it was over. Straightening, he braced a hand against the wall for balance and depressed the speaker button.

"What the hell, man?" he said. He was breathing hard. His heart was hitting about three times its normal rate.

"Stand down," Ezra repeated. "Leave the lock alone."

Cal frowned. The plane was still bucking, still descending through what felt like the mother of all storms.

"You want to tell me what's going on?" he said into the intercom. He had a bad feeling. A gut-tightening, breath-stealing bad feeling.

"We're landing. Sit down, buckle up."

"We're in the middle of the fucking ocean!"

"We got a better offer for Delgado. Thirty million. You'll get your cut."

It took Cal a moment to process. His finger still on the button, he leaned right up close to the intercom to say, "No. Hell no. Motherfucking hell no." With each variation of "no" his voice increased in volume until at the end he was shouting at the top of his lungs.

"It's a done deal," Ezra replied. "We got people waiting for him on the ground."

Cal heard a click. He knew what that meant: the cockpit side of the intercom had been turned off.

Curses exploding from his mouth, Cal kicked the door, hammered on it, yelled through it, "You fucking idiots, we're on a job. What do you think is going to happen if we turn up without Delgado? What are you going to say, you lost him? You think there won't be hell to pay?"

Behind him, Rudy whimpered with fear. He babbled, "You can't do this, you can't let them do this, jeez, I trusted you. Oh, man, oh, man —"

"Shut the fuck up," Cal snapped over his shoulder at him, and turned his attention back to the door.

Feet planted wide apart to try to counter-act the plane's jolting, Cal inserted the tiny screwdriver back inside the broken handle. Bracing a shoulder against the door in an effort to keep himself reasonably steady, he probed the lock.

"Damn it, Cal, leave it the hell alone," Ezra boomed at him. *Not* over the intercom. From the sound of his voice, Cal could tell that he was standing just on the other side of the door.

"If you think there won't be blowback for this, you're a goddamned moron," Cal roared, manipulating the screwdriver. The blade connected with what he was almost sure was the latch —

"Get away from the fucking door," Ezra roared back.

Cal turned his wrist, jiggled the screw-driver, heard a click, knew he had it.

Bang!

Something hit him in the gut with the force of a lightning bolt. Pain blasted through his system, blowtorching his insides, obliterating everything except mushrooming agony. Clapping both hands to its source, which was low on his left side, Cal staggered backward, past Rudy, who was rising to his feet, shrieking as he watched. Flickering lightning cast weird shadows over everything. The plane bounced over the rough air currents like a rock on a pond. Gasping, Cal fell heavily against the wall. As he started sliding down it, as he felt the warm stickiness of his blood bubbling up between his fingers, Ezra yanked the door open and stepped through it. Behind him, Cal could see into the cockpit, see Hendricks at the controls.

"I told you to stand down." Ezra's voice was tight. He held a gun in his hand.

That was when Cal understood that he'd been shot. Ezra had shot him.

Their eyes met.

"You fucking —" Cal broke off to launch himself at Ezra with murderous force. Taken by surprise, Ezra dropped the gun and stumbled back as Cal cannoned into him, knocking him into Hendricks, who was thrown from his chair. Hendricks scrambled around on the steeply tilting floor after the gun, Cal grappled with Ezra, and Ezra got his legs bunched against his chest and mule-kicked Cal, sending him flying backward into the cabin to slam against the wall.

Ezra was charging him, barreling through the cockpit door with a roar, when the front of the plane blew up. The cockpit, the first small section of cabin, the first two leather seats, Hendricks, Ezra, Rudy — disintegrated before his eyes.

Boom! Gone.

A split second later there was nothing around him but air. He would have screamed, but it was as if he'd been sucked into a vacuum. *There is no air.* He dropped like a brick, plummeting through thunder and lightning and dark, angry clouds.

Until he slammed into something that felt like concrete and blacked out.

When he woke up, he was drowning in an icy sea. As he struggled to not die, hope had appeared in front of him in the guise of a woman in an orange boat.

Now it seemed like hope had deserted him. For sure the woman had.

He'd be damned if he was going to just lie on this frozen beach and die.

There was Harley. And his mission.

He needed just a minute . . .

In his head, just as he was about to lose consciousness, he once again heard Ezra say of Rudy, "We got people waiting for him on the ground."

The harrowing thought he took with him into the dark was: this place, this island, was the only ground around.

CHAPTER EIGHT

"Get up." Crouching beside him, Gina grabbed his upper arm and shook it. His bicep was iron hard . . . his eyes were closed. His face had a grayish pallor that made him look dead. Icy spray broke over them both even as she shook him again. The waves were getting terrifyingly close. *"Get up!"*

His eyes opened.

"The tide's coming in. You'll drown if you stay here." Her voice was sharp. "You have to get up and walk. We have to *go.*"

The wind had taken on a high-pitched keening sound, and daggers of lightning lit up the bay. The sky over the water was black and boiling. The sea was blacker still, ruffled with gargantuan whitecaps that pounded the shore. Snow blew in thick and fast. The air grew colder by the minute, and yet the stranger stayed unmoving on the ground.

"We have to go," she repeated urgently.

He blinked. Snowflakes were caught in his

lashes, which were stubby and black. More settled in his hair and landed on his alarmingly slack face. They didn't melt, which was more alarming still.

"I can't carry you." Gina found herself shouting against the wind. She crouched over him. Her fingers dug into his arm as she shook him once more. "You have to *get up.*"

He breathed in with a harsh wheezing sound. His face tightened, hardened. With what she could tell was a tremendous effort, he pushed himself up onto his hands and knees, and from there managed to lurch to his feet.

"That's good." She rose with him, still gripping his arm. He staggered drunkenly, a symptom of progressing hypothermia, she suspected, and she wedged herself beneath his arm to steady him. It draped across her shoulders, hard and heavy and practically immovable, giving her the uncomfortable sensation that she was his prisoner. Shaking off that unpleasant feeling, she grabbed the thick, masculine wrist hanging from her shoulder to steady him and wrapped her other arm around his waist, careful to keep clear of his injury.

So much for not being stupid, she reflected bitterly. Apparently she hadn't changed as much as she'd thought.

Not that she was surprised at herself. From the beginning, in her heart of hearts, she'd known that it wasn't in her to leave him to die, whether she suspected he might be dangerous or not. The good news was, his condition had deteriorated to the point where he wasn't in any condition to harm her even if he wanted to.

She didn't think.

In any case, she was just going to see him safe, just going to get him out of the storm.

"Walk," she ordered with a fierceness that reflected her anger with herself, and walk he did. He seemed to be having difficulty controlling his legs, she discovered to her dismay. His gait was stiff and clumsy. Supporting him across the gritty, uneven sand was beyond difficult. They tacked back and forth, their forward progress owing much to the force of the wind.

"Where — to?"

She could barely hear him over the wind, but — God help her, was that a note of wariness in his voice?

"Away from the water," she snapped, with no breath to say anything more. He seemed to accept that, or at least he, too, had no more breath to waste on speech, because he didn't reply.

With him leaning heavily against her, they staggered up the beach. Clearly they weren't going to make it very far: he was too heavy, the going was too hard, and the storm was blasting in too fast. Already the rising surf lapped almost at their heels. Intermittent bursts of sleet bombarded them along with the snow. Even with her back to the wind, her nose and cheeks were growing numb. She could taste the faint tang of melting snow on her lips. Somewhere she'd lost her snow mask; otherwise she would have used it to protect her face.

Her clothing kept her from physically experiencing the full extent of how cold and wet he was, but she knew anyway. He was so close she could feel the chill emanating from him. His skin had the grayish pallor of a corpse. He staggered as if each step might be his last.

Casting desperate looks toward the open fields and necklace of hills that fell away from the beach, she spotted a rocky outcropping rising like a black wall through the gloom. Extending from the base of one of the smaller hills, it sat atop a small rise to their right, maybe half a city block away. It offered the only possibility of shelter she could see, and it had the additional advantage of being on relatively high ground. Like the boat, the tent was small and lightweight, no match for the current extreme conditions even if she was able to stake it — which, given the rocky, frozen ground, it didn't look like she could do. That being the case, they would need protection from the wind. The outcropping would, she hoped, provide that protection. Its elevation should keep them safe from any storm surge as well.

The problem lay in reaching it. She wasn't sure they were going to get that far. The pounding of the wind and snow was relentless. His steps were growing increasingly wobbly and his weight was wearing her down to the point where she thought her knees might give way. Her heart raced as if she were running a marathon. Her breathing was ragged. With every minute that passed, her fear of not being able to go any farther and getting caught out in the open by the full fury of the storm increased.

"We're heading up there by those rocks." She got the words out between pants for air, nodding toward the outcropping as they reached the snow-encrusted tundra that marked the edge of the beach. Despite the fact that she had to work to find sufficient breath to make herself heard, she shared their destination because she couldn't just drag him where she wanted him to go: he was too big and the rise was too steep.

He lifted his head, looking in the direction she indicated, and made a sound that she thought signified agreement. Neither of them said anything more as they started to climb. For her part, just keeping him upright and moving required all her strength. The now-solid ground was slippery underfoot, he weighed a ton and was unsteady on his feet besides, and the screaming wind gusting around them was strong enough to make battling it a constant, energy-sapping ordeal. Her cheek intermittently brushed his hard-muscled arm where it wrapped around her shoulders, and she found herself unsettled by its latent strength.

"How much — farther?" The words — the first he'd said in a while — were barely audible over the shrieking wind. She glanced up at him. With him looming over her as he was, the bulk of his body provided her with some protection from the worst of the elements. His face was mere inches away. The glint of his eyes in the darkness, the harsh lines of his strong, chiseled features, all spoke of hell-bent determination. It was, she thought, all that was keeping him on his feet. She could smell the sea on him, feel the cold coming off his skin like breath from an open refrigerator.

"We're almost there."

"What's — almost?"

"Right in front of you." Her mouth was mere inches below his ear. She still had to shout to be heard. "Maybe thirty more steps."

"Jesus," he said, not in reply but in response to the storm, the full force of which overtook them at that moment with a violence that stunned her. It was like having a wind tunnel drop down on them. The only thing that kept her from being knocked over by the ferocity of the wind was, ironically, the anchoring effect of his big body draped on top of her. Their surroundings were instantly obliterated by the swirling, rushing fog of snow mixed with sleet blowing around them. Lightning struck nearby with a boom and a bright flash, making her squeak and cringe and wringing a curse out of him. The wind turned absolutely arctic between one breath and the next and shrieked so loudly that it hurt her eardrums. She could no longer see the outcropping, or anything that was more than a foot in front of her poor freezing nose.

"*Walk,*" Gina ordered. Keeping her face down to try to protect it from the wind, she managed to keep the pair of them lurching

110

forward. Every step was a battle against being blown off their feet.

He managed to stay upright, but only barely, and only because she refused to let him go down. Moving forward, his feet dragged like they'd turned to lead. She somehow got him behind the solid, snow-capped mass of the nearest of the school bus–size rocks that jutted out in an overlapping progression from the ridge. Just like that, the wind no longer pounded them: the outcropping blocked it, blocked the worst of the storm, even better than she'd hoped. Glancing up, she saw that there was an overhang protecting them from above, too. Gina felt the sudden cessation of the wind and lashing snow with a bone-deep thankfulness. Pausing in the thick shadows at the base of the rocks to get her bearings, she felt him sway and automatically tightened her hold on him.

"I need to take a break." His voice was thick. She could sense the sheer force of will that it was taking for him to stay on his feet.

"It's all right," she told him. "We're here."

The abrupt slackening she felt in the muscles of his back and arm confirmed everything she'd suspected about how nearly impossible he was finding it to remain upright. His knees didn't quite buckle, but it was close. She let it happen, doing her best to support him as he collapsed so that he didn't completely crash to the ground. He ended up sitting with his long legs sprawled in front of him and his back resting against the uneven black surface of the first of the giant rocks.

Crouching beside him, she looked at him with concern. His eyes were closed. She thought he was conscious still, but barely. He looked totally spent.

Thankfully, the outcropping provided a small sanctuary where the blasting wind couldn't reach them and only small amounts of snow and sleet sifted in from the tempest howling all around. The air was freezing, though, and the lichen-covered ground beneath them was equally cold. She was shivering to the point where she had to periodically clench her teeth to keep them from chattering, and *she* was dressed for the weather. She couldn't even allow herself to think about how cold he had to be. The only positive element to the situation was that the now very obvious bloodstain on his shirt no longer seemed to be growing. She put that down to the cold, too, because it restricted blood flow.

"What — now?" His words emerged between uneven breaths as she shrugged out of her backpack and went down on her knees beside him to open it up. His head rested back against the rock as if his neck no longer had the strength to support it. He was looking at her through dark glinting eyes that were barely open. The grim set of his jaw and mouth left her in no doubt that he knew the score: without shelter, and warmth, he would shortly be beyond help.

"Here." Pulling out a white cotton turtleneck, part of a set of spare clothes that included sweatpants, underwear, and socks, she bundled it into a makeshift pad and passed it to him. "Press that against the injury on your side."

His hand was unsteady as he took the shirt from her. Moving like it required tremendous effort, he lifted his shirt to press the pad gingerly to his side.

He said, "We can't stay — in the open."

"I have a tent." She extracted the bag containing it from the backpack. The night before she'd slept in that same tent and the sleeping bag that was also rolled into its carrying case in her backpack, just as Arvid had slept in his, while caring for the oil-soaked eagle. She was profoundly grateful for the practical experience that had given her in setting this particular kit up. Under the circumstances, with him in the state he was in and the storm worsening by the second, there was no time to waste. "We'll have shelter in a few minutes."

He was breathing heavily and exhaling frosty clouds with each breath. His free hand was tucked beneath his armpit in an effort, she thought, to find some warmth for his frozen fingers. As she reached for her backpack again his head lifted and he seemed to do a slow visual sweep of the snowy maelstrom beyond their small oasis. Then his eyes closed. His head once again rested back against the rock. She could sense how weak he was growing. She was light-headed and wobbly with exhaustion herself, but her own survival as well as his depended on her taking care of their essential needs before she allowed herself to even begin to crash.

What she needed was stashed in one of the backpack's side pockets: two packets of chemical hand warmers. Crushing the packages to start the heat, she said, "This should help a little," and placed them on top of his chest, over his shirt — badly chilled skin burned easily, and so the insulation provided by his shirt was vital — and, roughly, over his heart.

Returning to that same pocket, she next

grabbed the Mylar blanket that had been packed with the hand warmers. Ripping open the tiny package, she shook the aluminized sheet out with an explosion of metallic crackling that had him opening his eyes to check it out.

"Space blanket," she explained, tucking it in behind his shoulders. His hand had already moved from his armpit to rest atop the hand warmers. He badly needed to lose the wet clothes, but that could come later. For now, this would have to do. Inches away, dark and penetrating, his eyes fastened on her face.

"You came back." His voice was gravelly and harsh. "Why?"

It took her a second, but then she understood him to be asking why, having run away from him when they'd reached land, she'd gone back for him when he'd collapsed getting out of the boat.

"Because you're a human being," she answered shortly. The shrieking, writhing snow beast that was the storm had enveloped the world around them completely now, and their shadowy hollow had turned as dark as night. Grabbing her backpack, she groped around through the various items in the main compartment for the flashlight she knew was in there.

He said, "You're out here watching birds — in November?"

She flicked a look at him. Silhouetted against the silvery curtain of the storm, his features were intensely masculine. There was something in his voice — mistrust? suspicion? — that gave her a prickle of unease. As though he thought there might be another reason why she was on Attu besides the one she'd given him. Once again she was reminded that she was saving the life of a man she knew nothing about, and her heart beat a little faster even as her eyes narrowed at him.

"Yes."

As answers went, it was terse, but at the moment she wasn't really feeling like having a lengthy conversation. The situation was too dire, and she was too tired and cold and otherwise miserable. However, given the fact that she had saddled herself with the man, and he might very well be dangerous, and he definitely seemed to be up to no good and mixed up in something she absolutely did not want to know anything about, letting him know that she was exactly who and what she said she was and not any kind of a threat to him probably would be wise.

She continued, "Look, as I told you, I'm an assistant professor at Stanford, I'm here on Attu with a group of scientists to study the effect of pollution on birds, and I happened to see your plane crash. And I fished you out of the sea and saved your life and here we are. That's it. The whole story."

Switching on her flashlight without waiting for a reply, she shone it inside the backpack, instantly spotting the water bottle that was her target.

His head came up off the rock with more speed than she would have thought him capable of. His hand shot out of the Mylar and grabbed the wrist of her hand that held the flashlight. She looked at him in surprise. His grip was far stronger than she would have expected for a man who seemed to be teetering on the brink of passing out.

"No light," he growled.

CHAPTER NINE

No radio. No light.

Gina's insides twisted with alarm as she suddenly understood: he thought someone was out there hunting him. On Attu, in the teeth of the storm. Goose bumps prickled across the back of her neck as their eyes met. His were no more than glinting slits. His hold on her wrist felt unbreakable.

Once again, the questions burned in her mind: *Who is this guy, and what on earth have I gotten myself into?*

The deadly gleam in his dark eyes immobilized Gina for a moment. She once again became aware of the unexpected strength in the hand gripping her wrist.

A cautious voice inside her head warned that assuming he was too weak to harm her might be the last wrong assumption she ever made.

Finally she remembered where they were, and that he needed her if he was going to survive. Which meant that she should be safe enough for now — from him. The storm was another matter. So was whoever he thought was chasing him, apparently.

What felt like a cold finger that had nothing to do with the weather ran down her spine.

Keep it together.

She inhaled, a deep, steadying breath.

First things first: for any of the rest to be a problem, she had to stay alive.

Which among other things meant making preparations to get through the storm. Which meant she needed to be able to see what she was doing, which meant she needed the damned light.

Her eyes narrowed and her chin came up.

"Do you really think anybody's going to be out in this?" Her voice was tart as she cast a comprehensive glance at the driving sheets of snow mixed with sleet that pelted down around them, hemming them into a space the size of a subway car. The wind howled like a wolf pack on the prowl. Where they were, sheltered at the base of the rocks, it was so dark she could only really see him when a spear of forked lightning split the black clouds tumbling overhead. "Anyway, the only people on this island besides you and me are my colleagues, my friends. You

119

should be *wishing* they'd find us. But they won't, not for the next few hours, at least. They're hunkered down, riding out the storm."

He slowly released her wrist, which she took as tacit permission to continue with what she'd been doing. Which she did, grabbing the water bottle and twisting off the lid.

"Scientists. Looking at birds." There was no missing the skepticism in his voice as he watched her.

"That's right." Taking a long drink herself, she handed him the bottle. "Here. It's water."

"Water." He said it almost reverently as he put the bottle to his lips. She could hear him guzzling it as she dug into the backpack again for her fire-starting kit, which was nothing more than a collection of items useful for that purpose rolled together in a ziplock bag.

Propping the flashlight up on a rock so that she could see what she was doing, she quickly made a pile of the cotton balls and small dry sticks that came in the kit. Ignoring the dread that snaked through her veins, she flicked the Bic lighter to set it alight. The small flame blazed brightly in the darkness.

He lowered the water and his head shot up off the rock in the same swift movement. The forceful but inarticulate sound of protest he made caused her to jump. The lighter went out.

"Yes, I know. No fire," she snapped, glaring at him. She was shivering and exhausted and scared and her patience was fraying. Normally the temperature on Attu in November never sank below thirty-two degrees, but they were well under that already, while the thermometer continued to drop. "Only, without a fire we're probably going to freeze to death. So whatever you're worried about is going to have to take a backseat to living through the night."

The look he gave her was hard with suspicion. She returned it with interest. His left leg moved restlessly, sliding up and bending at the knee as though he sought to make himself more comfortable. She wondered whether he'd hurt himself with his sudden movement. He grimaced, and his head sank back against the rock, as if holding it up any longer required too much effort. He lifted the water bottle again and drank. His eyes continued to gleam at her over it, but she took his lack of verbal response as tacit acceptance that she would build her fire, so she began constructing the relevant pieces.

"The people you're with — you know them?"

There was no mistaking the mistrust in his voice.

"They're college professors. Academics," she replied with a noticeable lack of patience. In a way, though, she was almost glad of the distraction he presented. The knot in her stomach as she flicked the Bic on again, then touched the lighter to the cotton and watched tiny fingers of orange flame spring to life and begin to grow, was exactly what she'd expected, but that didn't make it any easier to bear. Instead of getting caught up in horrific memories, it was far better that she concentrate on dealing with him.

"You know them?" he persisted.

Actually, she knew Arvid and Ray and Mary Dunleavy from UCLA and Jorge Tomasini from Princeton and Andrew Clark from Wash U. They'd attended several conferences together, and she and Arvid and Ray had collaborated on a grant proposal to fund a study of oil-eating microbes that was still pending. The others she'd met when they had arrived on Attu.

"Not all of them." Tearing handfuls of dry tundra from a patch near her knees, she quickly added that to the growing fire. "But the ones I don't know, I know of. I know who they are, their résumés."

"Résumés."

The skepticism in that made her frown.

He said it as if he thought the résumés might be bogus. As if he thought she and her fellow scientists might be bogus.

As if he suspected them of something.

"Who *are* you?" she demanded testily. "And who on earth do you think we are?"

He didn't answer, and as they exchanged measuring looks, dozens of horrifying possibilities for who he was chased one another through her mind. Could he be a drug smuggler? A spy? A terrorist? A fugitive? A —

Stop it, she ordered herself, and shot him a killing look. "Just so we're clear, whatever it is that's going on here, whatever's up with you, *I don't care.* It's nothing to do with me, and it's nothing to do with my colleagues or what we're doing here. And for the record, I'm damned tired of being menaced by a man whose life I'm doing my best to save."

"Menaced?" The rasp in his voice made her think of a rusty file scraping across metal. He'd finished with the water. The empty bottle was on the ground beside him, and his hand had disappeared back beneath

123

the Mylar. His eyes narrowed at her. "I haven't *menaced* you."

"Whatever you want to call it. The point is, I want it to stop. Right now. Or you can start saving your own ass." She gave him a level look and, when he didn't reply, got on with what needed to be done. Without any more fuel than was available within the small protected area, the fire wouldn't last long, but she hoped that it would last long enough to at least heat the rocks that she'd been scooping up as they were speaking and that were now piled around the edges of the flames. She followed that by also positioning the collapsible metal pan, in which she eventually meant to place the rocks, near the blaze. A fire in a tent was an invitation to disaster, and she personally, along with an equally abiding fear of flying, had an abiding fear of being trapped in a fire. But heated rocks were a different thing. Used properly, in an enclosed space such as a tent, they equaled a primitive furnace. And while the fire was burning, its heat could do some additional good: it made the bitter cold in its general vicinity a few degrees less bitter.

"Can you get your clothes off?" she asked as she began assembling the tent. He was still in danger from hypothermia despite the space blanket, the hand warmers, the water, and the fire, which hissed and smoked as stray flurries reached it from the eddies of snow and sleet that rose and swirled in miniature whirlwinds around the outcropping. His face was too deep in shadow to read, but his eyes slid her way. He had, she thought, been warily probing the darkness beyond their sanctuary. She didn't like to think about what — or who — he was looking for.

"As soon as the tent's up," she continued when he didn't reply, snapping another support into place, which suddenly made the crumpled pile of weatherproof gray nylon that was the tent start to take on size and shape, "we're getting in it, and you can't go inside it like you are. You'll get everything wet and we'll freeze. You need to strip."

"You want me . . . naked." Something in his harsh voice brought her gaze whipping up to meet his.

Too dark to read his eyes. Didn't matter.

Gina rocked back on her heels to point an I-mean-business index finger at him. "Take another step down that path, and I really will take my tent and find somewhere else to ride out the storm."

It wasn't her imagination: one corner of his mouth ticked upward in what might have been the slightest of smiles.

He held up a placating hand.

"Just clarifying," he said innocently.

The look she gave him was ripe with warning. "I have a pair of dry sweatpants in my backpack you can put on."

"Ah. Got it."

She watched him narrowly as his hand disappeared beneath the Mylar to start on his shirt buttons, then returned her attention to the tent. Two more fiberglass ribs locked into place, and the thing was done. Long and low, it was a two-man tent with zippered entrances at both ends and a vestibule to keep the weather out as you crawled into it. On her hands and knees, she pushed it as close up against the outcropping as she could in hopes of protecting it from the worst of the weather. As she had suspected, the rocky, frozen ground made staking it impossible. Instead she lugged a quartet of large rocks from their resting places nearby and placed them atop the stake loops. Dragging her backpack behind her, she crawled partway inside, being careful to keep her wet and dirty boots out of the main part of the tent. Quickly she spread out and inflated the vinyl pad that formed a barrier between the sleeping bag and the floor of the tent. With that done, she unrolled and positioned the sleeping bag on top of it.

Finished, she surveyed the space, which was the approximate shape of a hot dog bun, just about tall enough for her to kneel in with an inch or so of clearance above her head, and wide enough for two people to sleep side by side. One of them — that would be him, because he was the one with no clothes and incipient hypothermia — would get the sleeping bag. The other would sleep in her outdoor gear. With the addition of her improvised furnace, the arrangements should be sufficient to get them through the storm alive.

Crawling out of the tent, she was fuzzy-headed with fatigue until a wayward gust blasted her in the face. The arctic coldness of it was enough to shock her back into wakefulness. Pelting down just a few feet beyond the edge of the tent, a wall of sleet reflected orange from the fire. She knew it was mostly sleet now because of the sharp pattering sound it made as it hit. The small fire looked pitifully inadequate against the raging, shrieking blizzard surrounding them. The heat it put out was a puny defense against the encroaching cold. The smell of smoke was strong; her senses hurriedly reached past it to latch onto other smells — dampness and the sea.

Beside the fire, draped in the Mylar blanket, the man was a hulking shape slumped against the rocks. She couldn't be sure, but she thought he was looking out into the storm again. As if he was afraid someone might be out there.

Not liking the anxious feeling that thought gave her, she aimed her flashlight at him.

"Ready?" she asked as he blinked and looked her way. Teeth chattering, she moved toward him. The sweatpants and spare socks from her backpack were tucked beneath her parka, where, in theory at least, they were being warmed by her body heat. Her plan was to get him dried off fast with the hopefully not too bloodied turtleneck, get him into the sweatpants and socks and then the tent, and take care of whatever else needed doing — like, say, treating his injury — in there, where there was less chance of both of them expiring from exposure to the cold.

He didn't reply.

She reached him and saw why: he was not naked. Not even close. Even with the Mylar blanket draped over him, she could see that he was still struggling with the buttons on his shirt. As far as she could tell, not one stitch of his clothing had been removed.

"Oh, my God," she said, exasperation in every syllable. She was so tired she could barely move, aching all over, and cold to her bone marrow. The weather was growing worse by the minute and the fire that was warming the air was spitting and hissing in warning that the next influx of blowing snow that landed in it might well snuff it out. The only thing she wanted to do was curl up inside *her* sleeping bag in *her* tent and wait the storm out.

Instead she was going to be undressing this sinister stranger. Then giving him her sleeping bag and sharing her tent with him.

"My fingers don't seem to be working," he said gruffly. Without another word, she pulled off her gloves and thrust them into her pocket. Pushing the Mylar blanket aside, she plucked the hand warmers off him, shoved them into her pocket, too, and started unbuttoning his shirt for him.

His shirt was icy and stiff, almost frozen dry. She had to work to get the buttons through their buttonholes. As her increasingly chilled fingers brushed the glacial dampness of his skin beneath, she was reminded of what bad shape he was in. No surprise that he wasn't able to undress himself. The wonder was that he was conscious and talking.

She unfastened the rest of his buttons as quickly as she could, noticing in the process that a wedge of curly black hair covered his chest and tapered down to a narrow trail that disappeared beneath the waistband of his pants. She noticed, too, that his chest was wide and about as solid as a concrete wall, and beneath the cold and clammy skin he was all steely muscles and heavy bone.

The guy was seriously big, and seriously buff. Ordinarily she might have found that attractive. Okay, she did find it — him — attractive. Under the circumstances, however, alarm was the more appropriate response.

Once more she wondered who he was. She didn't even know his name. Which, now that she thought about it, was ridiculous.

She looked up from unbuttoning his cuff. "Think you could tell me your name now? Seeing as how I'm taking off your clothes?"

His eyes were dark and unreadable as they met hers. "I thought — no suggestive comments."

Gina moved on to the other cuff. "That wasn't a suggestive comment. It was an illustrative one, designed to make the point that, under the circumstances, I should probably have something to call you besides, *hey, popsicle boy.* So, name?"

"Popsicle boy?" His lips twitched. For just a moment a flare of amusement lit his eyes.

But still he seemed to hesitate. Why? God, she didn't want to know. Gina had just flicked another, frowning glance at him when he said, "Cal."

"Cal?" He didn't respond. "Cal — what?"

"Let's just stick with Cal."

That was it. No last name forthcoming. Or maybe that *was* his last name. No, more likely it was a nickname.

Not that it made any real difference. Whatever his name was, whatever he was into, he'd become her responsibility. Or, to be more precise, she'd made him her responsibility, by fishing him out of the sea and dragging him up off the shore and, in general, saving his life. And that would be because, she realized with a not particularly welcome flash of insight, when she'd seen his plane crash, when she'd spotted him alive in the water, she had immediately, instinctively identified with him. As in, they were members of the same club.

Plane Crash Survivors Anonymous, anyone?

"Nice to meet you, Cal." Her voice was dry.

"Likewise." He paused, then added deliberately, "Gina."

So he remembered her name. At the time she hadn't even been sure it had registered with him.

She could feel him watching her as she quickly unbuttoned his other cuff and reached for his belt buckle, but she didn't look up again.

Assuming that because they'd been through a similar experience they were somehow alike could prove to be an error of major proportions, she told herself. A *dangerous* error. Because she was growing more and more convinced that he was a dangerous man.

Meaning to wait to strip his shirt completely off at the same time as his pants so as not to leave any one part of him exposed to the frigid air for longer than was necessary, she moved on, unfastening his belt buckle with brisk efficiency even as she firmly ignored the muscular six-pack her fingers couldn't help but brush, then undoing the button below it and reaching for his fly.

"I got this part," he said. His hands were at his zipper, brushing hers aside.

Okay. She so did not have a problem with that. At the sound of his zipper being lowered, she sank back a little.

Without the pressure of his hand holding it in place, the pad he'd been pressing to his side — her turtleneck — slid from his body to the ground.

She saw what was beneath it.

A round, dark hole the approximate size of a dime. On his far left side an inch or so above his hipbone. Sluggishly oozing blood. Bruising and dark smears all around it.

His injury. The one that had stained his shirt. The one that had been bleeding all along.

She'd assumed it was a gash of some sort, the result of the plane crash.

She'd assumed wrong.

That's a bullet hole.

Surprise widened her eyes. Before she could stop herself from looking up, she did, and her gaze collided with his.

CHAPTER TEN

He'd been shot.

The knowledge hung there in the air between them.

She knew, and he knew she knew. Neither of them had to say a word.

Gina felt her heart start to thump. She remained motionless, staring at him like a bird hypnotized by a cobra as his eyes bored into hers. They were about as expressive as the rock he leaned against.

It had to have happened right before the plane crashed — on the plane? — because the wound was clearly fresh, still bleeding, with no evidence of significant clotting or that it had received any kind of treatment. And besides the one on Attu, the next closest airport was almost seven hundred miles away.

Remembering the rapid descent of the plane before it exploded, Gina suddenly had a radical new vision of what was happening in those last few minutes on board.

He'd said there were three others on the plane with him. That they were dead.

Now she found herself wondering whether it was the crash that had killed them.

At the one other glaring possibility that presented itself to her, the hair stood up on the back of her neck.

Is he a killer?

Her heart thumped at the prospect.

His eyes narrowed as they held hers. His mouth thinned. From that, Gina took that he was getting a pretty accurate reading as to the gist of her thoughts. That he wasn't happy about her speculation. About her knowledge.

The hardening of his face left her in no doubt whatsoever about one thing: the man was definitely dangerous.

While the storm raged she had no way to escape from him, nowhere to go. To run off into it would be suicidal.

The only thing she could do was stay put and play out the hand she'd dealt herself.

Her pulse raced. Her stomach fluttered. Her lungs ached with the need to expel the breath she'd been holding.

She let it out slowly. Carefully. Panic was her enemy.

Something her father had said to her once

when they were in one of his all-too-frequent tight spots came back to her: when your head is in the mouth of the bear, the only thing to do is say, *nice bear.*

"I have a first aid kit in my backpack," she said matter-of-factly, as if finding bullet holes in scary men she was trapped with were something that happened to her every day. "Once you're in the tent I can bandage that up for you."

As she spoke, she deliberately refocused her gaze on his chiseled abs and tugged his pants down his lean hips. It said a lot about her state of agitation that she didn't even really see a single ripped inch of him.

He pulled the Mylar blanket across his lap.

That caught her attention, made her blink.

Not a creep, then, she thought, then followed that with a sardonic, *Oh, yay. Like the fact that the threatening guy with the bullet hole in him doesn't seem to be a perv makes this all better.*

That's when it hit her: if he had a bullet hole in him, then somebody might really be hunting him.

Through the storm. On Attu.

Her stomach knotted. Her breathing quickened. She had her fingers hooked in his shorts — soggy, icy boxer briefs — as well as his pants and was pulling both off him at the same time. Her cold fingers clenched in a death grip around the freezing wet cloth as she darted a nervous glance out past their small circle of light, at the gusting, swirling fog of snow and ice. The near-whiteout conditions partially reassured her: it was inconceivable that anyone would be hunting him in this. Besides, if the three who'd been on the plane with him were dead, who was left to track him down?

Good question. With, she realized with a sharp increase in her anxiety level, nothing but bad answers. Because clearly he was convinced someone was.

"I'm not going to hurt you, you know," he said. She'd ducked her face to try to keep her thoughts hidden as she dragged his pants down long, hard-muscled legs. His words were so unexpected that she looked up, and thus inadvertently met his gaze. His eyes were bloodshot, and heavy-lidded with what she thought was a combination of exhaustion and pain and the effects of too much cold and too much sea. "You don't need to be afraid of me."

Great. Clearly her efforts to keep her thoughts hidden from him had failed, and just as clearly he was trying to reassure her. His gaze was calm and steady. But she thought she detected a stillness behind it, a predatory stillness, as though a part of him were crouched and waiting.

To see what she was going to do.

And God help her if she did the wrong thing.

Should she believe him, trust in the truth of what he was telling her? Trust that he wouldn't hurt her, that she didn't need to be afraid of him?

Only if she were dumb as a box of rocks.

"I'm not afraid of you," she lied. One thing she'd learned over the years was that showing fear to a predator was never a good idea. "I never thought you'd hurt me. Why would you? I've done nothing but help you. And without me, you're toast." With that less than subtle reminder, she pulled his pants the rest of the way off. "Can you get your shirt off?"

"Yeah." He struggled to do so while she yanked his socks off and hastily dried his feet and legs with the bloodstained turtleneck and thought frantic thoughts that she did her best to marshal into some sort of a cohesive plan.

Shoving dry socks onto his icy, blue-with-cold feet — he made a sound under his breath that she thought denoted pleasure at the sudden warmth — she tried to come up with some way to communicate with Arvid and the others but couldn't think of one. Wrestling her size-six but fortunately spandex sweatpants up his legs, she pondered the chances of making it back to camp in the storm but concluded that they were so small as to be nonexistent.

"Wait," he said as she got the pants about halfway up his thighs, which were thick with muscle and a real test of the cloth's capacity to expand. She paused, in action and thought, to look at him. He'd managed to get his shirt off and was reaching down beneath the Mylar that was still tucked around him to grab onto the waistband. She glimpsed brawny arms and one wide bare shoulder and then they were both wrestling with the pants.

"You're going to have to lift your butt," she told him, slightly breathless with effort.

He managed it, awkwardly, and together they got the sweats up. The Mylar blanket was dislodged in the process, and she was afforded an up-close-and-personal view of some pretty impressive male equipment that she really would rather have not seen. When the job was done and she sank back, almost warm now despite the occasional arctic blast that made it through the fire's small circle of heat and the driving wall of sleet and snow pounding down mere feet away, she saw that the black sweats that were roomy on her fit him like too-small tights. The waist hit him inches below his navel and the legs ended halfway up his calves. His every muscle and sinew was revealed by the snug-fitting cloth, along with an impressive package that she was already more familiar with than she wanted to be. A glance up his torso found that he was as totally built as she'd thought: narrow hips, flat belly, wide chest, broad shoulders, heavy on the muscle with not an ounce of fat that she could see.

She was human. She was female. She was alive. And he was smoking hot. She couldn't help the tingle of sexual awareness that pulsed to life inside her.

If it hadn't been for the bullet wound in his side and the whole I-just-might-kill-you-in-your-sleep vibe he gave off, she would have been wildly attracted to him.

The good news was, all the activity had calmed her jumbled thoughts enough to have enabled her to come up with a plan: she would do what she had to do to allay any suspicions he might be harboring about her while they rode out the storm together in the tent. Then when the storm had passed she would leave him in the tent, hike to camp, tell the others what had happened, alert the authorities to the plane crash, his gunshot wound, and everything else via satellite phone, and, acting under the guiding principle that there was safety in numbers, bring her fellow scientists back with her to both rescue him and keep him under guard until the authorities arrived.

In the meantime, she was going full *nice bear* on his ass.

"Here." Gina wrapped the Mylar blanket back around his shoulders and handed him the crumpled turtleneck, which she might have considered trying to work him into to replace his shirt except for the obvious-at-a-glance fact that the trim-fitting garment had no chance in hell of stretching enough to accommodate his heavy shoulders, to say nothing of his arms and chest. "Put this back on that."

Nodding, she indicated the bullet hole, which still seeped blood. While he did as directed she pulled her gloves back on her cold hands and turned toward the fire. Grabbing one heat-resistant handle, she began to pull the pan away from the flames.

"You have any —" he began.

He was interrupted by Gina's cry of dismay as a mini-avalanche of snow that almost certainly had been blown off the top of the rocks by the howling wind dropped directly on the fire.

And put it out.

"Crap." Gina stared with horror at the mound of snow that was already melting into the smoking, hissing remains of the fire, ruining nearly all the material that had gone into making it that hadn't already burned. Galvanized by the need to save at least the core of her makeshift furnace, she frantically started wielding the pan and a piece of scorched stick to scrape the rocks away from the sizzling mess. Moments later she had the rocks scooped up in the pan and was speed-crawling for the tent with them. She could feel the precious heat wafting off them as she went.

"What are you doing?" he asked.

"Getting us some heat," she told him over her shoulder as she entered the tent.

She'd left the sleeping bag unzipped for easier access. Running the pan of rocks along the inside of it as a kind of makeshift bed warmer, she then set the pan down in the back corner, where it would heat the small tent while still being safely out of the way. Even if the rocks were to somehow spill, though, the worst that would happen is that they would melt a hole through whatever they landed on. There was no possibility of anything catching on fire.

As an afterthought, she tucked the hand warmers down inside the sleeping bag to serve as an extra source of heat.

The only thing left to do was get him inside.

When she crawled back out, he was already on his hands and knees and almost at the door of the tent. Without the fire, the darkness was interrupted only by the narrow, focused beam of the flashlight in her hand. As it hit him, she could see that his face was drawn with effort and his mouth was tense. The air near the tent already felt ten degrees colder. The shriek of the wind howling past and the drumming of the sleet on the rocks underlined the extremity of their situation. Without the shelter the tent provided, they almost certainly wouldn't live through the night.

"I was coming to help you," she said in a scolding tone, to which he responded with a grunt. On all fours, he was a large, dark shadow the approximate size and shape of a grizzly. A grizzly with a rattling Mylar superman cape and her turtleneck tied around his waist, which made for an irresistible mental image that would have made her smile under better circumstances. If there were such a thing as limp-crawling, he was doing it. If she'd had to help him — well, there really was no way to support someone who was crawling. And dragging him inside the tent would have been impossible.

Turning to set the flashlight down inside so that he wouldn't have to find his way to the sleeping bag and avoid the makeshift furnace in complete darkness, she scooted out of the way as he reached the tent and pulled the flap aside for him.

"The sleeping bag's unzipped. Get in it. Be careful of the pan of rocks at the far end."

He didn't reply. She wasn't sure he had the energy to speak. He was breathing hard enough so that she could hear it even over the noise of the storm. As he crawled past her, she saw that he was carrying his discarded clothes with him.

"Wait! Stop! You can't take those in there." She caught a trailing pant leg, tugged. "They'll get everything wet."

He stopped, looking over his shoulder at her. "I'll need them. Tomorrow."

His tone told her that he was determined.

"They won't dry," she said.

"They'll dry some."

Stalemate, and it was too cold and she was too tired to argue. "Fine. Leave them right where you are and I'll hang them up in the vestibule."

He made a sound that she thought signified agreement, dropped the bundle of clothes, and proceeded on his way. The door of the tent was small, and he had to maneuver his way through carefully. He made it inside, and she heard the crackling of the space blanket, then a soft sound as, presumably, he collapsed onto the sleeping bag. Following him in, she closed up the outer flap, hung up his wet clothes as best she could in the vestibule, then took off her boots and left them in there, too.

Crawling into the main part of the tent, she sealed the doorway up behind her, first with a zipper and then with a Velcro flap. The sounds of the storm were suddenly muffled, like the rush of traffic on a distant freeway. Except for the flashlight's narrow column of light, the tent was dark. The corners, the ceiling, the sides of the tube encircling her were thick with shadows. She heard his breathing, harsh in that enclosed space, smelled the salty-sea scent of him, and felt her shoulders tighten. She'd never been one to suffer from claustrophobia, but for a moment the flimsy nylon of the walls and ceiling seemed to shrink around her. If she and the big, scary guy with the bullet wound had been in a space capsule on their way to Mars, their isolation couldn't have been more complete.

Stay calm.

On her knees, she turned, picked up the flashlight, and played it over the cramped, tunnel-like interior, over her backpack, over the smoking rocks in the makeshift furnace a few feet away, over the arched ceiling and the sealed flap at the far end of the tent. The Mylar blanket lay crumpled in the maybe eighteen inches of space between the edge of the sleeping bag and the curving wall. It glittered as the flashlight beam caught it.

"Glad you came prepared," he said. He lay on his uninjured side in the sleeping bag with his head cradled on his bent arm, still breathing heavily from his recent exertion. The bag was the same dark gray as the tent and the pad beneath it. It had a side zip and the top could be adjusted so that it closed around the head like a hood. At the moment that top part lay flat beneath his head and arm.

"What can I say? I was a Girl Scout." Maybe her tone was a little tart under the circumstances. Surprise: being sealed up in a virtual wind sock with him was making her nervous. The flashlight beam caught him in the process of stretching his long legs down inside the sleeping bag while pulling the loose corners of it close around his bare shoulders. At his height, she saw that he was barely going to fit. He was shivering again, which she took as a good sign. It had been a while since she'd seen him shiver. Hypothermia in reverse? She didn't know if that happened. But he was shivering.

His head lay right beside her thigh. As the light caught him he looked up at her, squinting against the brightness of the beam. "I thought 'Be Prepared' was the Boy Scout motto."

The implication in that was actually kind of reassuring. "What, were you a Boy Scout?"

"No. I beat up on kids who were."

For a moment she looked at him in surprise. Then something — a glint in his eyes, a twist at the corner of his mouth, clued her in: he was joking.

"Funny," she said. But it was good to know that he *could* joke. She didn't know any, so she couldn't be sure, but she liked to think that killers lacked a sense of humor.

As well as sex appeal. He definitely possessed that, too. Even in his present condition, he exuded a kind of animal magnetism. Raw masculinity in spades.

He was so close she could see the small lines around his eyes and the deeper ones bracketing his mouth; the elbow of the arm tucked beneath his head brushed her leg. Even lying down he was *big.* His ink-black hair appeared to be slightly damp again, and she remembered the snow that had melted in it. He was frowning: the straight black slashes of his brows nearly met above eyes that were bleary with fatigue. The blue tinge had left his mouth, which was still way too pale, just like he was way too pale. From the darkness of his hair and eyes, she was as sure as it was possible to be that vampire was not his natural color.

He was still sexy.

"Bag's warm inside," he said. "Or else I've got hypothermia bad."

She knew that feeling hot while you were actually freezing to death was a major end-stage hypothermia symptom.

"The bag's warm," she said. "I ran the pan inside it. And the hand warmers are down at the foot."

"Ah."

He hitched the silken cocoon higher around his shoulders. In the process his knuckles brushed her side. Her pulse skittered uneasily as she registered just how small the space really was, and that he took up way more than his fair share of it. His lids drooped as if he was on the verge of closing his eyes, but the prospect didn't make her feel any less anxious. She didn't know him, didn't trust him, and was more than a little afraid of him despite his assurance that he wasn't going to hurt her. To make matters worse, she was attracted to him. And there wasn't going to be any keeping her distance from him.

To say that she was uncomfortable was an understatement. She felt vulnerable and at risk, and she didn't like the feeling. The hollowing of her stomach, the prickliness creeping over her skin, were sensations that she could have lived without.

To combat them, she did what she could to take control of the situation.

"I'm going to finish setting the furnace up," she said, indicating the pan of rocks.

"Furnace, huh?"

"That's right."

Telling him what she was doing was unnecessary, but she was nervous, and talking to him, she hoped, would help mask that. If he had any evil intentions toward her, demonstrating how useful she could be to him might help ward those off, too. She crawled away from him as she spoke, pushing the pan of rocks down to the far end of the tent and positioning the blanket behind it so that its shiny metal surface would reflect and thus intensify the heat. Stripping off her gloves, she tucked them into her pocket and reached for her backpack. Rooting around in it, she pulled out two protein bars, the last bottle of water, and the first aid kit.

His head was tilted so that he could watch her.

"You got any kind of weapon in there?" he asked.

The question sent curls of apprehension twisting through Gina's bloodstream. It spoke volumes about what kind of man he was. It told her that he still thought someone was coming after him despite the storm.

It scared her.

CHAPTER ELEVEN

"No," she replied shortly. "I don't have a weapon. I have food. And water. A first aid kit."

Trying to calculate how far the glow from the flashlight might be visible after accounting for the shrouding effects of their protective nylon shell and the storm was useless. Worse, picturing the tent as a beacon of light in the snowy darkness made her feel like jumping out of her skin. Under the circumstances, the staccato drumbeat of the sleet pounding down outside was downright reassuring. The occasional blast of errant wind that rippled the silky walls around them was, too.

No one is out there in this.

As soon as it was over she was getting away from him, she reminded herself. Without him, she was in no danger at all. She just had to sit tight and ride out the storm.

Tearing open the wrapper with more force than the action strictly called for, Gina shoved a protein bar at him. It had been hours since her last meal. She wasn't hungry — she was beyond it, she thought — but some of the shakiness she was experiencing might be because she needed to eat. He definitely needed the calories to make up for the blood he'd lost, and to produce heat.

"A pocket knife? Eating utensils?" His tone made it clear that he was still harping on the possibility of a weapon. Taking the protein bar, he raised himself up on an elbow and bit into it hungrily. His voice was stronger now. She thought that the warmth plus the water he'd consumed had revived him a little.

"Try a spork."

He grimaced his opinion of the weapon potential of the combination spoon and fork.

"Mace? Pepper spray?" he continued between bites.

"Oh, my gosh, you're in luck: I have bug spray. No, wait, they're towelettes." She was eating by that time, too. The chewy combination of chocolate and oats tasted better than the finest filet mignon — or at least it would have, if chills of fear hadn't been chasing each other down her spine at the idea that he thought a weapon might be necessary. "Are you seriously expecting some kind of an attack? Tonight? Out here?"

He was wolfing down his bar as if he hadn't eaten in a week. "Depends."

That did not help. Definitely. Not.

"On what?" She eyed him starkly.

"If they find us."

Oh, God.

"They?" The question was out before she could stop it. She had a ridiculous urge to instantly clap both hands over her mouth in an attempt to stuff the imprudent word back inside. She was really, truly better off not knowing. She didn't *want* to know.

He didn't answer, not directly. Finishing his protein bar, he held out his hand for the water bottle, which she passed him. He took a swig and said, "You tell anybody about pulling me out of the sea? Over that radio?"

Gina could feel her heart beating way too fast. "I tried telling Arvid and Ray — two of my colleagues — about the plane crash, but I'm pretty sure they didn't hear me. There was too much static. Once I spotted you, I was too focused on *saving your life* to try getting hold of them again until the transmission you interrupted by *throwing my radio into the water.*"

He ignored the pointed parts of her answer. "With any luck they think everybody who was on that plane is dead. In that case, we might be all right."

There was that terrifying *they* again. Coupled as it was with the even more terrifying *we,* it was enough to make her blood run cold. The bite of protein bar she was swallowing suddenly felt like a clump of sand going down her throat. Coughing, she held out her hand for the water bottle and, when he passed it to her, chugged a few mouthfuls. Once more visions of taking off through the storm and leaving him behind danced through her head. Tantalizing visions. Which were immediately crushed by the rattling of the thin walls encircling them as another moaning blast of wind snaked around the rocks to shake the tent. Even if the storm lasted only a few hours, by the time it passed it would be the middle of the night. Only a fool would head out across Attu's rough, arctic terrain in the middle of the night.

Gloomily she faced the truth: she couldn't have been more trapped if she were chained to him.

"So you don't think anyone heard your transmission about the crash?" he said, as if he was thinking something through. He definitely seemed stronger now. She didn't know if that was a good or a bad thing. "Did your friends know where you were?"

"They knew I was out in the boat."

"They know where?"

"Not really, no. I tried telling them where the plane crash was over the radio, but I'm pretty sure they didn't get the message because of all the static."

"You took off from your camp alone?"

Gina shook her head. "A colleague and I left camp yesterday. We rescued a white-tailed eagle that got caught in some oil. Today my colleague walked back to camp, and I took the boat to follow the eagle and her mate back to their nest. I put in on the other side of Chirikof Point, but I could have gone in any direction, depending on which way the birds went."

"Good thing for me you came my way."

Gina made a noncommittal sound. *Not such a good thing for me.*

But then she thought of him dying all alone in that frigid water. She couldn't bring herself to wish things had turned out that way, either.

Neither of them said anything more until, after finishing her protein bar and taking a few more sips of water, she handed him the bottle along with a couple of pills from one of the two-pill packets in the first aid kit.

"Extra Strength Tylenol," she explained when he looked askance at the tablets she'd given him.

He eyed the small pills on his palm with disfavor. "That the best painkiller you have?"

"Yes."

He swallowed the pills, chased them with a gulp of water, and looked at her.

"Got any more?"

"Tylenol? One more packet. I suggest you save it for later."

"What about food? Water?"

"A couple of protein bars. No more water. If we have to, we can always gather snow and melt it." *That's it, Gina, you can throw the "we" around, too. Make it sound like the two of you are a team.* Although given how wet everything was going to be after the storm, gathering fuel for a fire might be a problem. But she could use the lighter flame by itself if necessary. She would need the pan, but she could dump the rocks out once they'd cooled.

She didn't like to think about the rocks cooling. Their heat had already appreciably warmed the tent. Since she didn't want to overheat — sweat was an enemy in cold conditions — she pushed back her hood and unzipped her parka. Beneath it she was wearing a red thermal long-sleeved tee tucked into her waterproof pants. Beneath the pants was a pair of jeans. The thermal tee was snug as befitted an inner layer. So were the jeans.

As her coat opened her hair spilled out to tumble around her face. Sometime over the last hour or so it had worked its way free of the bobby pins that had secured it. Shaking it back impatiently, gathering the mass of it in both hands, she ran a hand along the length of it to check for any remaining bobby pins and found none. Twisting it into a rope, she knotted it at her nape with the efficiency born of long practice. It wouldn't stay that way for long, but for now at least it was out of her face.

Finishing, she looked up to find that he was watching her. Intently. The tee had a crew neck, so she was still covered from the base of her neck to the tips of her toes, even if her shape — small but round and firm breasts above a lithe waist and slim hips — was now more readily apparent. And her hair was just — hair. No need to feel uneasy under his gaze.

But she did. Take the close quarters, add in his rugged good looks and all those muscles and his seminudity, and it was impossible for her not to be aware of him as a man. The look in his eyes made it clear that he was now equally aware of her as a woman.

Their eyes met. Something crackled in the air between them that hadn't been there before — a kind of current. An electric vibration. An elemental male-female thing.

The sudden spark of sexual heat that flared inside her as he looked at her was so urgent it actually hurt. Her chest contracted. Her throat closed.

And her body started up with a hot, sweet pulse.

She instantly, figuratively, turned her back on it. It was nothing she felt the slightest urge to acknowledge, much less pursue.

The plane crash — *her* plane crash — was five years in the past now. In the last year, she'd had precisely two dinner dates. Each with a different man, each leading nowhere. Before that, nothing. She hadn't been ready. She wasn't ready when she'd gone out on those dates. Along with her father, her husband, David, had died in the crash. Four months after their wedding. Their lives together had barely begun. He'd been her father's research assistant, twenty-six years old, blond and wiry and handsome. He'd been as reckless and adventuring as her father, and Gina had found herself agreeing to do things she never would have agreed to do if she hadn't fallen so hard for him. Reckless adventuring was not her nature, but she'd pretended like it was for the year they'd known each other, just like she'd pretended it was for her father. Maybe if she hadn't pretended so hard, maybe if she'd allowed herself to be her true careful, logical, look-before-you-leap self, she could have stopped what happened and the others would still be alive.

But she hadn't, and they'd died.

She'd lived, which meant she'd had no choice: slowly, painfully, she'd put her life back together. It was a different life than before, but it had gotten to a place where it was an actual life again. Quiet. Predictable. Stable. Good.

That was what she wanted. That was the only kind of life she could handle now, she saw.

This — this second plane crash, the apparent danger she was in because of it, *him* — was more than she was equipped to deal with.

It hit too close to home. It brought back too many memories, too many emotions. The trip to Attu had been a baby-steps attempt to get back out into the great outdoors, to embrace the wider world of adventure again, to heal herself. She saw now that it had been a mistake. She was still too raw inside, while reality was too harsh, too sharp. Too ugly.

"Something wrong?" he asked, which was when Gina realized that she'd been staring at him with who knew what kind of expression on her face.

"You mean besides the fact that I'm trapped in a tent in a blizzard with a complete stranger? Not a thing," she lied. She was still pushing the memories away, still locking the specter of sexual attraction out of her mind, still resisting the urge to zip her parka back up again and run screaming out into the storm, when he handed the half-full bottle of water back to her.

The prosaic action, the feel of the cool, slick bottle in her hand, steadied her as no amount of self-talk could have done.

"Save that," he said, and subsided back down into the depths of the sleeping bag, hitching it higher around his neck. "In case the storm lasts a while."

The suggestion was unsettling. But, like the water bottle in her hand, it gave her something concrete to focus on. She figuratively grabbed hold with both hands. "Storms on Attu usually blow over in a few hours."

"Thus I said, in case."

"Okay." Hating to entertain the thought but knowing he was right, she ate the last of her protein bar, took one more sip of water, screwed the cap back on, and set it aside.

"You say something about bandaging me up earlier?" He nodded at the first aid kit, which was on the floor beside the backpack.

"Yes." She was still rattled, but she did her best to shrug it off. Mentally squaring her shoulders, she picked up the first aid kit and shifted around until she was kneeling next to his midsection so she could get a closer look. "The one good thing is, being immersed in the sea probably helped to clean it out. And the cold probably kept the injury from bleeding as much as it otherwise would have done."

He lay on his back now with that one arm tucked beneath his head. His armpit was tufted with black hair. The arm itself was chiseled and strong-looking, heavy with muscle. Aggressively masculine, just like the rest of him. It also sported a large, darkening bruise just above his elbow. She fastened her gaze on that with a feeling very close to relief.

He said, "Kept the *bullet wound* from bleeding, you mean?"

The tent instantly seemed to shrink

around her. His expression was concealed by shadows. Her eyes jumped to his, to discover that they were fixed on her face.

So that he could weigh her response to his words? Her pulse speeded up and her stomach tightened at the thought, along with its corollary: *He doesn't trust me.*

She was hit by a sudden wave of apprehension that felt like a million tiny bugs skittering over her skin.

Thanks to her, he had shelter, warmth, food. Which in a perfect world should mean that he was grateful, right? Down in the real world where she lived, what it really meant was that he no longer needed her to survive.

He said he wouldn't hurt me.

Her chin came up. She met his eyes steadily. "Unless you have another injury I don't know about."

"Bruises and scrapes. At least, as far as I can tell."

"You're lucky," she said, remembering the violence of the plane's explosion.

"Yeah." There was a dryness to that that told her he didn't think so.

Convince him that he still does need you. Tend his wound, tend the furnace. Then, when the storm passes, when morning comes, run like hell.

■ ■ ■ ■

She pushed back the sleeping bag to find that fresh blood darkened the white cotton of his makeshift bandage. Gina frowned. Clearly the wound was still bleeding. At a guess, the only reason it had bled so sluggishly up until this point was because his circulation had slowed down as he'd gotten colder and colder. Now that he was warming up, the bleeding was worsening.

The sleeves of the turtleneck were knotted around his waist to keep it in place. Untying them, she pulled it off him, picked up the flashlight, and trained it on the wound, which was several inches above where the waistband of her sweatpants bisected his muscled abdomen.

The taut skin just below his waist was marred by a bruise about the size of the rim of a teacup. In the center of the bruise was some swelling, and in the center of the swelling was a puckered hole. A dark crust around the edge of the hole told her that it had begun to clot before something — probably everything he'd done since he'd fallen out of the boat onto the beach, at a guess — had broken open the developing scab. Fortunately, the bright red blood that welled up as she watched seeped rather than poured from the hole.

She didn't know much about bullet wounds. But she did know that a small entry wound, assuming this was the entry wound, was usually accompanied by a larger exit wound. As in, he should have a bigger, gorier hole in his back.

Since the turtleneck had already done its unsterile worst, she picked it up and used it to wipe away the blood that was starting to trickle down his side. Then she tackled the blood welling from the wound itself so she could get a better look.

"Ouch," he said as she dabbed at it.

"Can you roll on your side a little? I need to see your back."

His brows twitched together. "Why?"

"Because if you have a hole like this in your front, you probably have a bigger one in your back."

He shook his head. "Bullet's still in there."

He didn't sound nearly as worried by that as she thought he should.

"Are you sure?" Gina looked at him with dismay. He nodded. If the bullet was still in him — her chest tightened — it undoubtedly needed to come out.

The idea that she was going to have to dig a bullet out of him — with what, the tweezers in the first aid kit? — filled her with dread. A pregnant moment in which she imagined herself shoving the tweezers into that oozing hole and probing around inside his body in a sweaty, panicky, and probably futile attempt to hit metal while his blood gushed around her fingers made her feel a little woozy. It couldn't be done. Or at least, she couldn't do it. Not even to show him how much he still needed her.

The mere thought made her queasy.

"I'm not even going to try to dig a bullet out of you," she told him, sinking back on her heels.

Something glimmered in his eyes. Amusement? She couldn't be sure.

"I thought you said you're a doctor."

"PhD," she gritted.

He actually smiled at that, a quick there-and-gone smile, but a smile nonetheless. He was, she noticed sourly, way handsome when he smiled.

He said, "Then I guess you'll just have to slap a bandage on it and leave it."

She frowned at him. That was exactly what she meant to do, but . . . he sounded surprisingly okay with it.

"Don't look so worried. Amateur surgery by flashlight is way more likely to kill me than leaving the bullet in there. Besides, if it had hit anything vital I'd be dead already."

"Good point." Seeing as how he wasn't dead, seemed in no real danger of dying now that they had shelter and he was warming up, and they both agreed that her digging around inside him for the bullet was a bad idea, stopping the bleeding and then covering the wound seemed like the way to go. She positioned the flashlight on top of the backpack so that it would provide the maximum amount of light where she needed it. "One of our group — Keith Hertzinger from the University of Chicago — is a physician. He can look at it tomorrow."

"A physician, huh? I thought you were here to watch birds."

"*Study* birds. He also has a PhD with a specialty in environmental analytic chemistry. As isolated as Attu is, the organizers thought it would be good to include a physician in the group." Removing an alcohol wipe from the first aid kit, she tore it open and warned, "This is probably going to sting."

"Who are the organizers?"

"Of the trip? There are several. The National Audubon Society. The Nature Conservancy. The Cornell Lab of Ornithology. Why?" As she spoke she cleaned the wound and surrounding area, being careful not to dislodge the crust that had formed around the hole. The already taut muscles of his abdomen contracted still more as she swabbed them with alcohol. The wound was a little higher than his navel, which was an innie, and not much more than an inch from the edge of his body. She couldn't help but notice the narrow trail of black hair that traced down from his navel to disappear beneath the stretched-out waistband of her sweatpants. Or how firm his abdomen felt beneath her fingers. Or how faithfully the cotton-spandex hugged his package.

Annoyed at herself, she glanced away.

"Who paid?" he asked, ignoring her question, and apparently, thankfully, missing where her gaze had last rested. "For your group to come here," he added when, recovering, she gave him a questioning look.

"We're being funded by a grant from the EPA." By this time he was wincing at what she was doing to him. "I told you it might sting," she added as an aside, in response to his expression.

"Sting? It hurts like a mother."

"Probably because you're warming up. And because you've almost certainly had an adrenaline rush going and it's wearing off. Anyway, at a guess, I'd say getting shot tends to hurt." As she spoke, she liberally applied antibiotic ointment to the wound then placed a small pile of gauze pads over it and used her palm to press down firmly.

He yelped.

Lifting her palm, she said, "Sorry. I was applying direct pressure to stop the bleeding."

"No, go ahead," he said through his teeth. "Direct pressure all the way."

With a frowning look at him she lowered her palm to the wound again. His breathing escalated a little as she pressed, but the underlying rhythm of it was not nearly as harsh as it had been when she'd followed him into the tent. He was no longer shivering, and the sleek skin she was touching was borderline warm.

When she cautiously lifted her hand again to study the gauze pad beneath it — she didn't want to lift the pad to look at the wound itself in case lifting the pad caused more bleeding — she was relieved to see that only a small spot of blood had leaked through to the top layer.

"I think the bleeding's slowed," she said as she tore open an extralarge Band-Aid. "You probably need to stay as still as possible for a while. When I finish with this, you can just lie there and go to sleep."

And if he was still asleep when the sun

came up, then getting away from him and going for help just got that much easier.

"Thursday's Thanksgiving, isn't it?" His question was seemingly out of the blue. She nodded, and he continued, "Pretty big holiday, stateside. Why aren't you home celebrating with your family?"

Lots of reasons. None of which she cared to share. "Because I chose to come here instead."

"You got a husband, boyfriend, girlfriend, whatever, in the group you're with?"

She stopped smoothing the edges of the Band-Aid into his skin to sit up straight and frown at him. "Are you really asking me about my love life?"

"I'm just having a hard time wrapping my mind around the idea that you — a whole group of you — would spend a major holiday here in the frozen North looking at birds."

"Nobody's asking you to wrap your mind around it." Having finished with the Band-Aid, she opened another one and clapped it down crosswise over the first. Smoothing it out with a lot less care than before, she shot him an exasperated look. "It's a government-funded research project. We're here over Thanksgiving because we're college professors and that's when we get time off."

"I see." The skepticism in the look he gave her was unmistakable even through his pained grimace at her Band-Aid smoothing.

Tight-lipped at the seeming futility of trying to convince him that she was, in fact, precisely what she said she was, she finished with the Band-Aid, flipped the edge of the sleeping bag back over him, cleaned her hands with another of the alcohol wipes, and returned the first aid kit to the backpack.

"You're American, too," she stated, in the spirit of taking the battle to the enemy. "Why aren't you home for Thanksgiving?"

His expression lightened marginally. "Not a big fan of turkey."

A deliberate nonanswer answer that didn't tell her anything at all. He didn't even admit his nationality. Well, she was as certain he was American as it was possible to be, and, anyway, she didn't really care.

A muffled peal of thunder accompanied by the rattling of the tent reminded her of the storm raging outside and made her suddenly extremely thankful for the protection of their cozy cocoon.

Cozy, that is, except for the man in it with her.

She shot him a disgruntled look. She was tired of pussyfooting around with him, tired of being afraid of a man who owed her his life, and tired — exhausted, actually — in general. So tired she ached with it. She supposed that up until now she'd been experiencing an adrenaline rush, too, and that, like his, it was fading.

"So when did you start making arrangements for this trip?" he asked.

"We've been working on it for six months," she answered shortly. Then, despite knowing he was probably going to make something of it, she added, "Final approval for the funding came through two weeks ago."

He did. Doubt narrowed his eyes. "What you're telling me is that your entire twelve-person group was able to get it together and get here on two weeks' notice."

"Two weeks' *final* notice. I told you, we've been planning the trip since the end of last semester." Straightening her spine, she scowled at him. "What is it, exactly, that you suspect my colleagues and me of anyway? I'd like to know. It can't be of shooting you." She pointed a finger skyward. "You were up there" — her finger reversed itself to point at the ground — "and we were down here when it happened. Anyway, I doubt my colleagues even know you exist.

How could they? I'm as sure as it's possible to be that none of them were close enough to see your plane crash, because if they had been they'd be all over us by now. If somebody's after you, *it isn't any of us.*"

He didn't answer. Instead he gave her an inscrutable look and took the backpack from her. She hadn't been holding on to it, precisely, but to have him snag it and pull it toward him without so much as a hint of a "May I?" made her bristle.

"Hey," she protested. He'd picked up the flashlight and was shining it inside the backpack. As she watched he began to rummage through the contents. "What are you doing?"

No reply. Having apparently exhausted the possibilities of the main compartment — the backpack was relatively empty at that point — he started going through first the inner and then the outer pockets. She was watching him with growing indignation when the truth smacked her in the head.

"Oh, my God," she said incredulously. "Are you *searching* my backpack?"

"Thought you might be holding out on me about the water," he said. His search apparently finished, he tucked the backpack behind his head, where it served as a makeshift pillow. "Or maybe even the Tylenol."

"Bullshit."

His face hardened. "Yeah, okay, I searched your backpack. While we're stuck here I need to get some sleep and the way things are right now I don't like the idea of sacking out in the company of a woman I don't know. A woman who just happened to be on hand with a boat when I crashed into the sea. A woman who turned around and came back to help me when anybody with a lick of sense would have run for the hills. A woman who not only can operate a Zodiac like a pro but carries a tent with her and can set it up and start a fire and make a furnace out of a pan and some rocks, all in the space of about five minutes. A woman who's young enough, and pretty enough, to make me think she couldn't possibly be out to kill me, or in cahoots with anybody who's out to kill me. I don't know, maybe that's all just as coincidental as you say. Then again, maybe it's not."

Well, she'd known he didn't trust her.

"Seriously?" She understood from the expression on his face that he was, indeed, dead serious. "If I was out to kill you, or in cahoots with someone who's out to kill you, as you put it, why would I bother to pull you out of the sea in the first place? If I hadn't, you'd already be dead."

"You tell me."

"This is ridiculous. You're being ridiculous."

"Probably. Come here."

"What?" She frowned at him warily. "Why?"

"I'm going to search you."

She stiffened in outrage. "Oh, no you're not."

"You hiding something?"

"No!"

"Then what are you worried about?"

She glared at him. "To begin with, you have no damned right to even suggest searching me. I've been saving your ass ever since I first laid eyes on you. I've put my own safety at risk helping you. I'm all that's stood between you and freezing to death, bleeding to death, and drowning. And you have the balls to say you want to search me? How to put this, popsicle boy: Hell no!"

He met her furious gaze, and she read implacable determination in his dark eyes.

"Come here, Gina," he said softly.

"No!"

"Don't make me make you."

She bethought herself of their isolation, the storm, and the whole *nice bear* thing. Lips compressing, she opted for a compromise, shrugging out of her parka and handing it to him. "There. Search it. Knock yourself out."

He did, turning out the contents of her pockets — gloves, binoculars, ChapStick, her small notebook and pen, a pocket comb — and running his hands over her coat while she fumed. He felt the hem, the sleeves, the fur lining, the hood. If anything had been concealed in it, she thought, he would have found it.

Of course, nothing was, so he didn't.

"Happy?" she asked with bite when he was done.

"Coat's clean," he said, laying it across his legs. His gaze slid over her body, lingering in a way that made her once again uncomfortably aware of the snugness of her thermal shirt. Glancing down at herself, she saw to her dismay that the shape of her nipples was visible, jutting through the layers of her bra and shirt. If their prominence was anything to judge by, the temperature in the tent was clearly much colder than she'd realized while she'd been wearing her heavy coat. Her body's reaction did not, of course, have anything to do with him. "Come here."

She frowned. "What?"

"You heard me."

"Are you kidding me?" No, he was not. His intention to search more than just her coat was apparent in his expression. She folded her arms over her chest. "No!"

"You satisfied that I'm not carrying a weapon?" he asked.

Gina narrowed her eyes at him. Given that she'd pretty much seen him naked, yes, she was. Not that she meant to give him the satisfaction of telling him so.

"I can see from your expression that the answer's *yes.* I, however, am not satisfied that you're not carrying a weapon."

"Too damned bad. You are not searching me."

He sighed. Levering himself up onto one elbow, he wedged the flashlight into a strap on the backpack so that it provided more or less general illumination. Then he looked at her. "We can do this one of two ways: you can take off your clothes and pass them to me piece by piece and let me check each one out and then look your naked body over with the flashlight, or you can scoot on over here and let me pat you down."

She quivered with indignation. "How about *hell no* to both?"

The look he gave her was his answer: she had no choice. He might be in a weakened state, but even so he was far stronger than she was. Just as he had threatened, he *could* make her. If it came to a physical fight, he would win, no doubt about it. And flight was out. She couldn't even scramble out of his reach. All he had to do was sit up, and with the furnace blocking the far end of the tent he'd be able to grab her without even crawling after her.

Apparently reading in her face the conclusion she'd reached, he crooked a finger, beckoning. Her lips tightened rebelliously. He beckoned again, then pointed to a spot on the floor that would put her within easy reach of his hands.

"Next time I'll let you drown," she said bitterly as, capitulating, she edged forward to the spot he indicated.

"If there ever is a next time, I'll deserve it." He sat up with a grimace and a hand to his side and was immediately way too close. Close enough so that she could smell the salty, musky scent of him, close enough so that her hand that was lifting to push a wayward lock behind her ear brushed the nest of hair darkening the center of his wide chest instead before she jerked it back, close enough so that she was eyeballing the stubble on his strong jaw at what was essentially point-blank range. Her body, stupid thing, was suddenly hypernaturally aware of him. She could feel a prickle of heat moving over her skin just because he was looking at her. Jerking her eyes upward, she encountered the stern set of his mouth, the ruthless glint in his eyes, and experienced an inner shiver that had nothing to do with fear. She was reminded of his height as his head brushed the nylon arch of the ceiling before he ducked, which made it worse because she then felt like he was looming over her. Even with his sitting and her kneeling with her legs folded beneath her, he was inches taller than she was, and a whole lot broader. Being confronted by so much nearly naked masculinity was unsettling. And, as much as she hated to admit it, arousing. He was a stranger, she was leery of his intentions toward her, and there wasn't anything she could do to stop what was going to happen: he was going to put his hands all over her and she was going to let him because she had no choice. Resisting would only make the situation more combustible.

And to make matters just that much worse, he was turning her on.

Nice bear, she thought grimly, and steeled herself. The width of his shoulders and the muscularity of his bare arms and chest would have been intimidating if she hadn't been seething with temper — and if she hadn't absolutely refused to let herself be intimidated. She thought of the bleeding she'd just stopped, wondered whether he'd made it start again by sitting up, and decided she hoped so.

He said, "Lift up your arms."

Rigid with outrage, she did as she was told, then stared fixedly at him as he patted her down. Face expressionless, he ran both hands down her arms and over her armpits, her breasts, her back, her waist, her stomach and butt. Then he had her stretch out her legs so that he could feel her wool socks–clad feet and slide his hands up her legs and over her crotch. It was done quickly and with a professionalism that told her that he'd performed such searches before. His touch was light and impersonal even in the most personal places. No groping, no hint of trying to cop a feel.

Didn't matter. The feel of his hands moving over her breasts and butt and sliding between her legs made her body react in a way that reminded her, infuriatingly, that he was a man and she was a woman. Her breasts tightened under his hands; her nipples tingled. When he ran his palms over her butt, she was all too acutely aware. As his hands slid up the insides of her thighs to pass lightly between her legs, she wasn't even surprised by the way her body quivered and clenched deep inside. Despite her body's (unanticipated and unwelcome) response, the manner in which he touched her was way too invasive and intimate for it to be anything but offensive. By the time he finished, angry steam was practically coming out of her ears. Her fists were clenched, and she knew her face had to be flaming red.

"You're clean," he said as his hands withdrew from where they'd just met at her nape after thoroughly combing through her hair.

"Tell me something I don't know."

"You look mad."

"Mad? Me?" As she shook her now straggling-all-over-the-place hair back from her face, her voice was silky sweet. She was, however, all but shooting poison darts at him from her eyes. She could still feel the imprint of his hands *everywhere* — and she didn't like it. "You ever think that I might be a ninja assassin planning to kill you with my bare hands while you sleep?"

Infuriatingly, that made him smile. A full-on crooked and charming smile that smacked her in the face with how really good-looking he was. That smile hit her the wrong way. It made her want to —

Before she could finish the thought, he

slid a hand along her jaw, bent his head, and kissed her.

CHAPTER TWELVE

For a moment shock kept her frozen in place. The warm pressure of his mouth on hers was the last thing she had been expecting. His lips were firm and experienced and absolutely, unmistakably male. They moved persuasively against hers. Blisteringly hot, his tongue touched the crease between her lips. She felt a jolt of heat, a wave of longing. His tongue slid into her mouth, and she was suddenly on fire, burning up inside, *kissing him back.* Wanting more. In what amounted to a lightning bolt of sensation she felt a thousand things at once, most of which she was afraid to even try to put a name to. But she recognized the hot flare of desire an instant before it was swamped by fury, and fear.

No, her mind screamed in rejection even as, on a whole different, more conscious level, warning sirens went off inside her head: *He can do anything he wants to me.*

Here in this tent, in this storm, I'm at his mercy.

Then her spine kicked in. *Not.*

Tearing her mouth free, she slammed her fist toward the center of his chest in a hard punch guaranteed to make him think twice before he touched her like that again. He caught her fist before it could connect. Easily, his palm trapped her clenched fingers and stopped the blow in midair.

It dismayed her to realize that, besides being the approximate size of a gorilla, the man had lightning-quick reflexes.

She made an enraged sound.

"That was meant as a thank-you," he said before she could summon the words with which to annihilate him. "For saving my life. I owe you."

She jerked her hand out of his grasp. He didn't try to keep it.

"You don't kiss me," she said through her teeth. She could still feel the imprint of his lips. It was all she could do not to scrub the back of her hand over her mouth to try to wipe it away. "You don't come on to me. Are we clear?"

He held up both hands in surrender. "As glass. Gina. It was a thank-you, not a come-on. That's all."

"Next time, I suggest you use your words." Her voice was icy. It didn't escape her notice that he had used her name, but it didn't make her feel any more kindly disposed toward him. Snatching up her coat, she backed away from him on her knees, then pulled her coat on and zipped it up to the neck. Finally she gathered up her hair and knotted it at her nape again.

Fixing him with a hostile stare all the while.

"I didn't mean to scare you," he said.

"You didn't scare me. You crossed a line. I'm angry."

"I'm sorry." She couldn't quite put a name to the look in his eyes, but abject apology wasn't it.

He settled back down with his head on the backpack, pulling the sleeping bag up around his shoulders in a way that left most of his arms bare. Bulging biceps, powerful forearms dusted with dark hair, large, long-fingered, square-palmed hands — finding herself eyeballing so much brawny masculinity did nothing to lessen her antagonism. With his fingers laced together on his chest he even looked almost comfortable. Gina eyed him with annoyance coupled with mistrust. He added, "If it makes you feel any better, I now believe your story. You really are a college professor up here looking at birds."

"Wow, you're making my day." She turned away to adjust the Mylar blanket around the pan of rocks. It was a way of putting an end to their conversation — she really didn't want to talk to him anymore — and, also, it was important that the heat be husbanded so that it lasted as long as possible. Even though the sounds were muffled now, the howling of the wind and the drumming of the sleet on the rocks were a constant reminder of just how terrible conditions were outside.

He watched her in silence for a moment. Then he said, "This would probably be a bad time for me to tell you to come on over here and climb inside this sleeping bag with me so we can get some sleep."

Looking around, she bared her teeth at him in a savage non-smile. "Never gonna happen."

"So, what, you're planning to sit there thinking evil thoughts about me all night?"

"What I'm planning to do is none of your business."

"I'm not going to attack you, if that's what you're worried about. We can sleep back to back. Head to foot. However you want to do it. The key word is, *sleep.*"

She scooched around to face him. "Like I said, never gonna happen."

"You're not going to share this sleeping bag with me?"

"My, you *are* quick on the uptake."

They exchanged measuring looks.

"Right." He flung back the top of the sleeping bag and sat up again. Under the circumstances, seeing so much honed and chiseled male flesh coming at her made her nerves twitch with alarm. It was all she could do to stand — well, sit — her ground. In that she was aided by the fact that there wasn't anyplace for her to go.

Her voice bristled with suspicion. "What are you doing?"

"You take it." He rested a hand lightly over his wound as he pulled his legs out of the depths of the bag. She saw no blood on the bandage, but it was obvious the wound was hurting him. "The thing's all yours."

He was referring to the sleeping bag, she knew.

"I don't want it." Her sweatpants rendered him minimally decent, not adequately dressed. She watched his bare calves and big feet crammed into her socks swing toward her and was reminded of how nearly naked he was — and also of the ordeal he'd so recently gone through. He really needed to stay wrapped up and keep still — wait, stop, she didn't care if he hurt himself, remember? Crossly she added, "Get back in there. It's going to get cold in here later, when the heat from the rocks dies out. I'm dressed for it. You're not." When he made no move to obey, she snapped, "Get back in the damned bag."

He shook his head. "That would be un-gentlemanly."

She made a scoffing sound. "Why mess up your track record?"

That made him smile again. Which in turn made him way more handsome than she cared to think about. In response, the scowl she was directing at him turned ferocious. He was sitting up now with his knees bent and his arms resting on his knees. Strapping bare shoulders, arms, chest, abdomen, calves — his position equaled way too much raw masculinity on display for her comfort.

He said, "Look, I'm going to unzip the sleeping bag and open it up, and we can both use it as a blanket. You stay on your side of the tent, I'll stay on mine. How about that?"

Gina considered. The pad beneath them would be enough to keep the ground's cold from penetrating. Used as a blanket, the sleeping bag wouldn't provide as much warmth, but it should provide enough.

She would be relatively toasty. He would

probably avoid freezing to death.

Both were consequences she could live with.

"Fine," she said ungraciously. As he twisted around to start unzipping the bag, she winced before she could stop herself at the flexing going on with his abdominal muscles and the Band-Aids, gave up on the whole wishing-him-dead thing, and added, "Stop moving around. You'll start bleeding again. I'll do it." Eyes narrowed, lips tight, she crawled toward him. "Stay out of my way," she warned.

He stopped, slanting an unreadable look at her. "Whatever you say."

CHAPTER THIRTEEN

In just a few minutes Gina had the bag unzipped and spread out over the floor. Taking care to avoid the pan of rocks, she slipped beneath the sleeping bag and stretched out on her side with her back to him. Lying down felt surprisingly wonderful, even on so unforgiving a surface. She was so tired she was practically boneless. Every muscle in her body was sore.

On the other side of the tent, she could feel him stretching out, too.

"Here," he said.

Gina rolled onto her other side and looked at him with mistrust. Even with both of them hugging opposite sides of the tent, there wasn't more than a foot of space separating them. He lay on his side, facing her. The flashlight was on the ground now. Its beam cut through the space between them like a lightsaber. Above it, his face was deep in shadow. She could just make out the muscular shape of his bare shoulder and arm.

He was in the act of shoving the backpack toward her. "Pillow," he said.

Having him lying so close was unsettling. Gina regarded him with open suspicion as she accepted the backpack.

"Good night," he said before she could say anything, and switched off the flashlight.

The tent instantly went as dark as the inside of a sewer pipe. Gina turned her back to him again, tucked the backpack — most uncomfortable pillow ever, she could see why he'd given it up — beneath her head, wrapped her arms around herself, and closed her eyes. The memory of the way he had kissed her surged to the forefront of her mind, making her tense. Right on the heels of that came the memory of how his hands on her body had felt. Deep inside, she felt a curl of desire. Instantly, every cell in her body seized up in instinctive rejection.

What kind of person gets a thrill from a guy she doesn't know and doesn't trust?

"How does your group communicate with each other? Does everybody have a radio?"

That deep, rasping voice so close at hand, coming abruptly out of the blackness, made her start guiltily, as if there were any way he

190

could possibly be aware of what she had just thrust from her mind. Taking a quiet, steadying breath, she opened her eyes. The darkness was so complete that she might as well have kept them closed. The nylon wall flapped inches away as a gust of wind shook the tent, but she could only hear, not see it.

"Yes," she replied, totally composed, totally over what had just been going on with her.

"Now that your friends can't reach you on the radio, they're going to come looking for you, aren't they?"

"Yes." *But not before the storm clears, and not before daylight.* She didn't say that, though. It was probably a good thing for him to think that it was possible that her fellow scientists could stumble upon them at any moment. It made her feel a little safer, at any rate.

He said, "But they won't come looking for you until morning at the earliest."

Okay, so he wasn't worried about her colleagues finding them right away. Well, she'd told him herself that nobody would be out in the storm. Big mouth.

More slowly, he added, "It's better if you don't tell them about this."

Gina frowned at the noisily fluttering tent wall she couldn't see. "What?"

He repeated his words, adding, "You need to get away from me."

She blinked in surprise. "At last we agree on something."

He ignored that. "The people who are after me — you don't want them after you, too. You don't want to get on their radar."

Gina was wide awake now. "You're right, I don't."

"No one has to know that you saw my plane crash. No one has to know that you saw me."

"That's true," she replied slowly.

"If the people who are after me find out that you saw me, talked to me, it's a good bet they'll kill you."

Gina shivered. Goose bumps racing over her skin, she rolled over to stare fruitlessly in his direction, unable to see anything except a wide expanse of blank darkness.

"Wonderful."

"So you don't let them find out," he replied while an army of cold little feet duckwalked down her spine. "You don't tell your colleagues about me. You don't tell anybody about me. For all intents and purposes, you got caught in the storm and spent the night out here in your tent, alone."

She thought that over. "I can say that."

"In the morning you need to head back to

your camp bright and early, before any of your friends have a chance to track you down."

"Okay." That had been her plan anyway, although he didn't know it. Only she'd meant to tell her colleagues the whole story, alert the authorities, and come back here with them so that they could all keep collective watch over him until help arrived.

She liked his plan better. Because what he said made terrifying sense. If bad guys with guns were after him, she definitely did not want them after her and her group, too.

He said, "Once you get back, I need you to do something for me."

Her reply was cautious. "What?"

"How does your group communicate with the outside world? E-mail? Phone?"

"Not e-mail. There's no connection. We have a satellite phone."

"Ah." It was a sound of satisfaction. "Do you have access to it?"

"Yes."

"Can you make a call without anyone knowing?"

This time her answer was more uncertain. "I suppose I could."

"I need you to make a call for me. As soon as possible after you get back to camp. No one else can know."

"Who would I be calling and what would I say?"

"I'll give you the number before you leave. All you have to do is dial it and key in another set of numbers I'll give you. That will bring somebody here to pick me up and give me a ride home."

Her silence must have conveyed some of the doubt she was feeling, because he added persuasively, "One call, and I'll be gone within a matter of hours. Out of your life forever. You can pretend like you never laid eyes on me."

That sounded promising, but —

"The other people on the plane — their deaths have to be reported to the authorities," she said. "So does the crash."

"Will you trust me to take care of that?"

He must have taken her silence to mean precisely what it did — she *didn't* trust him — because he added, "Believe me, you don't want this to come back on you. I'll make sure all the right people are notified. And you and your friends stay safe."

It was the "stay safe" part that did it. "All right."

"So you'll make the call." From his tone, she could tell it wasn't really a question.

Still she hesitated. "Will I be aiding in the commission of a crime? Or committing treason or something equally hideous?"

"No." From the sound of his voice, it seemed that made him smile.

"Would you tell me if I was?" Suspicion dripped from every word.

"Probably not." He *was* smiling. She could tell.

"Then I don't think —"

"The alternative is, I can go to your camp tomorrow and commandeer your phone and place my own call, but then I'd be putting every single one of you in danger." He no longer sounded like he was smiling.

Persuasive argument. She made a face into the dark. "Fine, I'll do it."

"Thank you."

Gina snorted by way of a *you're welcome.*

He didn't say anything after that, and she didn't, either. After a few minutes, she turned over and tried to fall asleep.

She couldn't. Of course she couldn't. She didn't know why she was even surprised. The backpack felt like a stone beneath her head. Even through the pad, the ground felt almost as hard and bumpy. She was so tired she felt boneless, but her mind raced.

It was the mind-racing part that kept her awake.

It would be tricky to place the call without anyone taking notice. And she still had no real proof she wouldn't be abetting a crime by doing so. But all things considered, taking the chance to get away from him and then doing what she could to get him off the island as quickly and quietly as possible seemed like the lesser of a number of evils. Just as pretending that she'd never seen him or his plane seemed like the smartest thing she could do.

Having made the decision, she tried to empty her mind, tried to go to sleep.

He was asleep.

She could tell from the way he was breathing.

Slow and deep. Rhythmic.

Close.

Too close.

The wind screamed. The tent rattled and shook. Some combination of sleet and snow clattered relentlessly down on the ground outside. In the distance she could hear the boom of the surf, the roll of thunder, the occasional crack of what she thought must be lightning.

But what bothered her was his breathing. The more she listened to it, the more it made her tense up. Made her own breathing quicken. Made her heart beat faster.

Finally she figured out why.

It wasn't just that he was so near. It wasn't

just that she didn't trust him, or that she was, in fact, slightly afraid of him.

It was that his breathing sounded so very — male.

She hadn't slept this close to a man since David's death.

The last night of his life they'd cuddled together on a single cot in a tent in the Yucatán. They'd made love. Afterward, he'd fallen asleep and she'd lain there in the dark listening to him breathe. She'd thought, *I'm happy.*

David's breathing had sounded slow and deep. Rhythmic. Unmistakably male.

Her insides quivered at the memory.

The next morning the two of them, plus her father and sister, had gotten on that plane.

And taken off into the teeth of a threatening storm.

She could still hear the patter of rain on the fuselage —

No. Gina sat up abruptly, desperate to banish the memory. It was too late. She was trembling. Her chest felt tight. Bile rose in her throat.

"Mmm?" the scary stranger sharing her tent murmured in sleepy inquiry.

She didn't answer. Instead she stayed very still. After a moment his deep, rhythmic breathing began again.

Oh, God.

Listening, she felt her every nerve ending being scraped raw.

He was, she thought, sound asleep once more.

While she felt like she might never sleep again.

Drawing her legs up close to her body, she wrapped her arms around them. Then she dropped her head so that her forehead rested on her knees.

She didn't cry. What was the point? She'd already shed multiple oceans' worth of tears, and not one single thing had changed.

It's just breathing. She forced herself to listen to it, hoping that she would soon grow desensitized to the sound.

Her mind was on board, but her body, her senses, her emotions seemed to be having trouble adjusting.

Gradually they did. Or else she just grew so tired that she couldn't feel anything anymore.

After the shakes went away, after the knot in her chest loosened, after the bile receded, exhaustion finally claimed her. She lay down, huddled in a little ball facing away from him. Deliberately she thought about birds: the rare ones she'd spotted on the island, the eagle she'd helped save, the tests she hoped to perform to better assess the health of various species before leaving. She loved working with the island's horned puffins, the funny-faced, black-and-white clowns of the seabird world. To test their diets for pollutants, she'd placed screens in front of their burrows while they were out fishing. When they returned with their beaks full of fish, they had to spit out their catch to remove the screens, which they could do easily once their beaks were empty. While the birds dealt with the screens, she nabbed a sample of their diets. They didn't seem disturbed by her presence, and just recalling their head-bobbing, foot-shuffling dance as they approached their burrows made her smile. From there her thoughts segued to the plovers, the terns, the northern fulmars, the pigeon guillemots, all of which she'd seen in her brief time on the island. Seven hundred different kinds of birds had been identified as living on Attu. Deliberately she began ticking them off one by one, and smiled a little as she recognized that what she was doing was an ornithologist's version of counting sheep. But it focused her mind, and eventually sleep claimed her.

CHAPTER FOURTEEN

Gina was heavy eyed and cross-looking as she struggled into a sitting position inside the cramped and gloomy confines of the tent. She thrust the tangled fall of her hair out of her face, then, with a grimace, rolled her neck from side to side. The storm was history, but overnight it had gotten cold enough in the tent to turn the tip of her nose red. Watching her, Cal found himself thinking it looked cute, that *she* looked cute, actually way more than cute, and immediately dismissed the thought. He'd felt her up and kissed her and made both of them hot, but that was the end of it. His life, and maybe her life, too, and countless other lives as well, were on the line here. He didn't have time to waste on anything but managing the situation so that they all stayed alive.

"Stiff neck?" he inquired.

She gave a nod as she scrunched her

shoulders up toward her ears in an apparent attempt to ease the tension in them. "I should have let you keep the backpack."

"What can I say? Being nice has its rewards." Cal sat up, too, wincing as what felt like a white-hot poker pierced his abdomen. His hand automatically went to the wound, but other than that he ignored the pain. This bullet wasn't going to kill him, or even slow him down much. He'd been shot before, on the ground in Afghanistan, much more seriously, and had seen a fair number of others shot, too. He knew bullet wounds, and this one didn't amount to much. He was lucky there'd been a metal door between him and the gun as the shot was fired, which meant that by the time the bullet drilled into his flesh it was all but spent.

Still, the sucker hurt. When he got home, which was a beach house in Cape Charles, Virginia, that he shared with Harley and that, because of work, he left vacant for way too many days of the year, that bullet was coming out.

Chalk up one more scar to add to his collection.

"How's your wound?" she asked. Having followed his hand as it went to his side, she glanced up and met his gaze. Now that she was fully awake, he could see that she felt equal parts awkward and wary around him. He was sorry about that, some, but it couldn't be helped.

"Better," he said.

"Good." She glanced away from him, toward the front of the tent, then started to crawl toward it.

"Where are you going?" he asked.

"Out." Her tone was short. He got the distinct impression that she didn't want him following her. Probably she had personal business to attend to.

Fair enough.

It required conscious effort on his part to keep from looking at her ass as she crawled away from him. Then he slipped up, did a quick Check Six, and was rewarded by not being able to see anything of her ass at all. Between her coat and snow pants, she was well covered. Although when he'd searched her he'd been able to feel —

Don't go there.

Instead, as she un-Velcroed and unzipped and otherwise worked her way out of the tent, he turned his attention to the cold, dead remains of what had been their furnace. The technique she'd used to build it was both simple and effective. He'd seen it used before, by commandos in the field. Her knowing how to do it was interesting, but he didn't think it was especially significant.

Too many things — she was unarmed, she was clearly half-afraid of him, she went out of her way not to ask him any questions, she was too, well, young and pretty — argued against her being an operative.

The kiss had clinched it. It had gotten her hot, he knew. But after the first few seconds in which she'd kissed him back like she meant it, she'd gone cold as ice.

If she was an operative, he couldn't see where that got her.

A night spent huddled on opposite sides of the tent, a parting at dawn. Not one bit of information gleaned. She hadn't even tried.

No, she wasn't an operative. He was almost 100 percent sure.

That conclusion made him truly sorry that she'd gotten caught up in this mess. Except, of course, for the fact that she'd saved his life.

"Stay close," he told her right before she disappeared through the opening, his mind instantly going to who else might be around. There was almost certainly no one in the immediate vicinity, because if someone had known he had survived and where he was, and that someone was within range, he and Gina would already have found themselves under fire. He was taking it as a given that there was at least one enemy operative on the ground, because someone had to have fired the missile that brought down his plane. He wasn't quite sure which of many possible groups that operative was affiliated with, or which group was at that moment closing in on Attu, but he was as sure as he was that he needed air to breathe that at least one of them was. Maybe more than one. He was fairly confident, though, that there was no way anyone could know that he'd survived the crash. They had to be thinking everyone who'd been on board his plane was dead.

For the time being, he'd like to keep it that way.

But as sure as God made pretty women, whatever group had given the order to shoot down his plane would be sending backup to the island to check that the danger Rudy and his information posed had been dealt with. They would have been there already if it hadn't been for the storm.

By way of a reply to his warning to stay close, Gina sent him a narrow-eyed glance over her shoulder. He smiled at her; she frowned at him. Then she crawled on outside, and he found himself watching her disappointingly well-covered ass again until she disappeared from his view.

If she wasn't what she said she was, if she was a plant, then whoever had sent her was a genius. And she was an actress worthy of an Academy Award.

He didn't think he could possibly be that wrong about her. But then, he'd been that wrong about people before.

Ezra being a case in point.

The thought would have hurt if he'd let it. So he dismissed it. He focused on his unlikely rescuer instead.

She was, as he'd realized in the tent last night as she'd wriggled out of her parka under the unforgiving glare of the flashlight, a beautiful woman. Big blue eyes, full pink lips, slender nose, high cheekbones, delicate jaw and chin. Fair skin, long, straight hair the color of honey. Slim, but with plenty in the T & A department. At least, plenty to suit his tastes.

Add in the way she'd kissed him, and it was a shame he didn't have time to get to know her better.

But he had bigger fish to fry. Survival-level fish. National security–level fish.

He had to find a way to get the information he possessed to the people who could do something about it. To do that, he had to stay alive. And he meant to keep her alive, too.

Whatever it took.

With that resolution firmly fixed in his mind, he made what preparations he could to face the weather, then crawled out of the tent to find Gina.

CHAPTER FIFTEEN

The Zodiac was gone, of course. One of the first things Gina did upon leaving the tent was step out from behind the protection of the outcropping and look toward the bay, trying to spot it. Because the camp was much farther away by land than by water, she'd been hoping that the boat might have washed up somewhere nearby, without really expecting that it would have done so. It was nowhere in sight.

She felt a pang of disappointment, but no real surprise.

Finding her way back to camp on foot wasn't going to be a problem: directly behind the former LORAN station stood Weston Mountain. If she followed the ridge that the outcropping was part of through the pass that she could see from where she stood, she should have no trouble locating the top of the mountain, which was one of the highest on the island. To make it even harder to miss, a World War II–era lookout tower (for enemy planes) had been erected at its summit. In partial ruins now, it still stood out as a landmark against the skyline for anyone who knew where to look.

The problem she had with walking back to camp was the length of time it would take. Her colleagues hadn't been able to reach her by radio since before the storm hit, and she'd been missing overnight while the storm raged. They already would be sick with worry, she knew. By the time she walked back into camp, they would have launched a search party and done God knew what else.

At least the storm seemed to have passed. On this wintry gray morning, the waves rolled in with a murmur rather than a roar. The sea was up, covering the beach completely and extending fingers of water into low-lying areas around the rocks so that the area where she stood had been turned into a peninsula. The sky was heavily overcast. A thin layer of snow frosted the ground. Something — the force of the wind, the combination of snow and sleet, who knew? — had prevented much in the way of accumulation. While there were drifts against the rocks, the ground was covered with maybe an inch, no more.

The snow was crusted with ice that glittered even in the absence of any direct sunlight and crackled underfoot with every step.

Taking a deep breath of the moisture-laden air, Gina exhaled a soft, barely visible cloud: it was cold, but not freezing-to-death cold. Typical Attu early-morning midthirties cold. The air smelled of damp, and the sea. She looked out beyond the breakwater, where flirty whitecaps now broke in layers of ruffles against the rocks, to the sea itself. Nothing of the crashed plane could be seen from where she stood. She couldn't even tell whether the tail was still there. What was visible of the sea undulated serenely, whispering rather than roaring, with no sign of having been disturbed. Last night's violence had been replaced by a muted calm. Fog covered land and water alike, stretching as far as she could see, blocking out much of the horizon and most of her surroundings. Feathery tendrils of mist drifted across the iron-gray surface of the water, over the snowy tundra and around and over the black, rocky ridges that rose in increasingly majestic layers to peak in tall mountains in the center of the island. Sandpipers darted in and out of the foaming surf line, hunting breakfast. Kittiwakes and gulls swooped over the bay. There were no other signs of life. Gina found herself wondering about the eagles: had they made it safely back to their nests? Or, like her, had they been forced to shelter in place to survive the storm?

"How long will it take you to reach your camp, do you think?" Cal came up behind her, tall and solid in the pale dawn light. A quick, comprehensive glance over her shoulder took him in: he had the sleeping bag wrapped around him like a blanket. The waterproof bags that the tent and sleeping bag had been stored in had been drafted for use as temporary shoes. He'd bound them in place with surgical tape from the first aid kit. His eyes were bloodshot and tired looking, a day's worth of black stubble darkened his cheeks and chin, and a bruise purpled on his left cheekbone.

He should have looked ridiculous. He didn't. He looked big and tough and formidable.

He looks like a thug.

For all she knew, he *was* a thug.

A thug she did not want to know. A thug she would shortly never see again. Gina realized that she was resisting even thinking of him by his name, because he — nameless *he* — would shortly disappear from her life.

For her, he would for all intents and purposes cease to exist.

It was a good thing. She welcomed it.

"Two, two and a half hours," she replied. Abandoning her fruitless search of the sea, she stepped around him and headed back toward the tent. He made her uncomfortable. She didn't know whether it was his size or what she knew about him or what she didn't know about him or the fact that he had kissed her and put his hands on her body and made her feel things she hadn't felt in a long time or some combination of the above. She was anxious to get away from him. Anxious to put this whole traumatic episode behind her and get on with her safe and orderly life.

"Don't forget to destroy that number as soon as you use it," he cautioned, following her.

"I won't forget."

"You can just wad it up and throw it in the trash. Which I assume is burned daily."

"I will," she agreed. When he'd first emerged from the tent, he'd caught her hand, pushed up the sleeve of her coat and shirt, then smoothed a Band-Aid onto her wrist as if to cover a cut or other injury. The use of the Band-Aid was just in case, he'd told her. When she'd warily asked, "Just in case what?" he'd replied, "In case someone searches you. They're not going to look on the inside of a Band-Aid on your arm."

What was inside that Band-Aid was the phone number for her to call, plus the code he wanted her to type in after the number. Using the pen from the backpack, he'd written it on the Band-Aid's inner sterile white pad.

At the prospect of encountering the "someone" he was referring to, Gina's stomach dropped like a stone.

He'd instructed her — multiple times — to punch the numbers in once only, then get rid of the Band-Aid and forget she'd ever done such a thing or seen him or the plane. When she'd pointed out that she thought the phone would very likely keep a register of every number dialed, he'd told her not to worry about it: a computer program on the machine that the number reached would erase its number from the phone she used.

She so did not want to know who would have an answering machine that could do something like that.

"If you should run across anybody —" he began for what must have been the twelfth time. They were facing each other in front of the tent now. She was leaving it, as well as the sleeping bag and backpack and binoculars and what remained of the supplies, for his use. She would tell the others that everything had been too wet and bedraggled from the storm to carry back with her.

"I've got it," she interrupted, knowing that he meant anybody who might be looking for him, and repeated the instructions he'd given her. "Stay away from them. Hide if I can. If I can't, I know nothing about a plane crash, or you." He already had her thoroughly spooked by the idea that nameless bad guys might be scouring Attu for him. At the thought that she might have a close encounter with them, her insides quaked.

"Don't look so worried," he said. "I'm not positive they're here, and if they are you'll almost certainly never see them, especially since you're not going to be with me. They'll know the plane went down, and the logical assumption they'll make is that everybody on board is dead. They'll check out the wreckage, maybe take a quick look around to try to make sure nobody survived, but they'll probably stay as far away from you people and your camp as possible." He paused, then added, "Civilian casualties are always a bitch."

Does that mean you're not a civilian? She

213

didn't say it out loud and immediately did her best to push the speculation out of her head. Once more, she did not want to know.

Her eyes swept the area around them: a tall drift of snow had accumulated between the tent and the path that anyone who wasn't coming by sea would have to take to get to it. She guessed that most of the snow in it had been blown from the tops of the rocks. However it had happened, it formed a useful barrier if someone wanted to hide, which Cal definitely did. She knew the outcropping concealed the tent from anyone on a boat, even someone who came close to shore, and she was almost certain that the tent couldn't be seen from the path, either. Not that she expected someone to be coming along the path. This remote area high above the bay wouldn't be the first place her colleagues would think to look for her. It wouldn't be the second or third place, either.

It was just one of many rocky ridges fronting miles of irregular coastline, and since the last anyone had heard of her she'd been in the Zodiac, their first thought would almost certainly be to take the other boat and scoot around the island, scouring the shore. Of course, if whoever was looking for Cal knew the precise location where his

214

plane went down, they might be able to pinpoint his current location a little more accurately.

"Did your plane have a transponder?" she asked.

His eyes narrowed at her. "It was disabled."

Since she didn't really want to know why, she didn't ask. Instead she took full measure of the expression on his face and responded tartly. "You're wondering how I know about transponders, aren't you?"

He shook his head. "I'm assuming you read newspapers and watch TV."

"That's right, I do. So why all of a sudden look at me like you trust me about as far as you can throw me?"

A flicker of amusement came and went in his eyes. A corner of his mouth turned up in a hint of a smile. For a moment he looked seriously, scruffily handsome. She had an instant, unwelcome flashback to their sizzling kiss and her pulse quickened in response. "Maybe that's my default mode."

"It's unattractive," she informed him. "So it's possible that whoever's looking for you doesn't know where your plane went down? Or even that it went down?"

"Anything's possible."

"You don't sound convinced."

"It's nothing I'd want to bet my life on. Or yours."

For a moment their eyes held. His expression had turned grim, and reminded her that the danger he was in, and that he'd put her and her colleagues in, was very real.

It was also something she wanted no part of.

"I should go," she said. He nodded, but when she went to turn away he reached out and caught her gloved hand.

"In case you should start having second thoughts about making that call, remember that you want me off this island. The sooner I'm gone, the sooner you and your friends will be safe." His eyes bored into hers. The hard gleam in them was clearly a warning. "And if I'm not picked up within the next twelve hours I'll head into your camp and make the call myself."

She could feel the steely strength in the fingers wrapped around hers. The top of her head reached a little higher than his shoulders, and she didn't like the fact that she had to tilt her head back so far to meet his eyes. It made her feel . . . vulnerable. Like he was *letting* her go but could change his mind about that at any time.

"I said I'd make the call and I will," she told him, pulling her hand free. "Believe me, I want you gone as much as you want to be gone."

That flicker of a smile appeared in his eyes again. This time she refused to be impressed. "Good to know."

"Good-bye," she said.

She started to turn away.

He caught her arm, pulled her around, and kissed her. Just like that, his hands gripping her shoulders, his mouth coming down on hers hard.

And she kissed him back. Instantly, instinctively, without any thought at all.

Her mouth opened to his. His tongue filled her mouth, scalding hot, demanding her response. And she gave it, answering his lips and tongue with a hungry intensity that seemed to spring up out of nowhere. Her body burned for his. She went all soft and shivery inside.

As quick as he'd kissed her he was lifting his head and pushing her away.

"Good-bye," he said. He didn't smile.

Gina didn't smile, either. Her heart was thumping, her body was throbbing, and good-bye was both the last thing on earth she wanted to say — and the smartest thing she could say.

"Good-bye," she said for the second time.

Then she turned and started picking her

way across the slippery ground without waiting for him to answer. Their relationship, if it could even be called a relationship, was over, just like yesterday's hair-raising episode was over, and in the cold, clear light of dawn all she wanted to do was put it behind her and forget about it and him. She would walk across the narrow peninsula of land that formed the neck of Chirikof Point, then follow the shoreline around to Massacre Bay, where her group was staying in the buildings that had once made up LORAN Station Attu.

Would she be sorry to see the last of him? Maybe some small part of her would be.

But there was no other choice. And even if there had been, she still would have walked away.

She would make his call for him, and then she would settle back into the stable routine of the life she had made for herself. Danger and excitement were not, and never again would be, her thing.

"Gina," he called after her.

Lips compressing, she glanced back. Fingers of fog curled around the outcropping, making the landscape look like something out of Kafka. Shrouded in the deep gray of the sleeping bag, he looked as massive as one of the towering rocks behind him.

"Thank you," he said. "Again. For saving my life."

"You're welcome," she replied, and meant it.

She walked away without looking back a second time.

It took her almost five hours to travel the eight-plus miles back to camp. Although the storm had passed on during the wee hours of the morning, the storm surge she had feared had, in fact, occurred all over this eastern part of the island, cutting off many of the routes she might have taken. Most of the low-lying areas near the coast had flooded, with water in some places lying in depths of one to two feet. The deceptive film of ice that covered everything made it tricky to judge what was water and what was dry land. In addition, there were drifts of snow in unlikely places, so Gina abandoned the easier route that hugged the coastline in favor of keeping to higher, rockier ground. Footing was treacherous so she had to go slowly. By the time she got close enough to actually see her destination, from about halfway up Frazier Mountain to the east of the camp, she was cold and hungry and thirsty and so tired she had to work to keep putting one foot in front of the other.

So cold and hungry and tired, in fact, that her fear of running into one of the "strangers" he'd warned her about had receded into the category of things-to-worry-about-after-I-don't-fall-and-break-a-leg-or-collapse-from-exhaustion.

After hours of walking she hadn't seen a single, solitary soul, which reinforced her conviction that Arvid and Ray or whoever had volunteered for the search party must be out looking for her in the boat. Once she got back to camp, it would be an easy matter to contact them via the radio and tell them to come back in. Merely thinking about how much worry she was causing them, to say nothing of the time spent searching for her that was being taken away from their projects, made her feel guilty. Visiting Attu required reams of paperwork and countless official permissions. It was expensive and difficult to arrange. They all had research to carry out, both on their own and to fulfill the terms of the grant, and only a limited amount of time on the island. The likelihood was that none of them would be back.

The quicker she got down there and let

everyone know she was safe, the quicker everyone could get back to work and life could proceed as usual.

Trudging along the steep, rocky path, Gina thought longingly of food, warmth, and a shower, all of which were, she estimated, less than fifteen minutes away. All she had to do was make it the rest of the way down the mountain. With an elevation of twenty-three hundred feet, Frazier Mountain was one of maybe half a dozen low mountains that formed a semicircle around the former Coast Guard station. There were no trees to speak of on Attu, and the mountains curved behind the flat meadow just off the cove where the LORAN station lay. On a clear day she would have been able to see it below her, but there weren't many clear days on Attu and today was no exception. Fog lay over everything in a thick, gauzy blanket. But she knew where the buildings were, and she looked toward them. Solid concrete painted white, with thick walls and reinforced, black-framed windows, they were grouped closely together. The main building was two stories tall, and she could just see its rusting metal roof through the fog. The island's only runway, which was, in fact, its only paved surface, ran alongside the buildings. It ended some distance from them at a corrugated metal hangar with a red and white sign bearing the tongue-in-cheek message WELCOME TO ATTU INTERNATIONAL AIRPORT.

Peering down through the fog, Gina was able to see that lights were on in the main building, which told her that somebody was home: electricity was precious, the product of a single large generator that had to be sparingly fed fuel from the cylindrical, aboveground storage tanks that were topped off maybe once a year by a visiting freighter. Energy conservation was taken seriously on Attu, and lights were turned off when not in use. She looked toward the bay and the dock where the Zodiacs were kept tied up, but was able to see nothing through the fog.

The satellite phone was kept in the main building, which also housed the dormitory-style rooms where they all slept, women in one and men in the other. The kitchen was in there, too, along with a large common area where they ate and hung out. Just thinking about the kitchen made her stomach growl. She hadn't eaten that morning: knowing that there would be food waiting for her at camp, and not anticipating such an arduous trek, she'd left the remaining two protein bars for Cal. She'd already made up her mind about the best, most unobtrusive way to make his telephone call: if anyone was around when she picked up the phone, she would simply tell them she had a private call to make and then go outside and key in the numbers he'd given her. Then she would call her mother as cover.

Hiding in plain sight, as it were.

The more she thought about it, the more not reporting the deaths or the plane crash bothered her. She hadn't entirely made up her mind yet, but she was considering doing so once she was safely back in California. Cal would be off the island by then, too, and if he had kept his word he would have already reported the crash and the deaths, so she would be doing the right thing without endangering anybody.

Unbidden, the thought of how he'd kissed her, and how she'd kissed him back, made her cheeks heat. And her body heat. He had made her want him, and it had been a long time since she'd felt anything like that. The knowledge was disturbing, and, cross at herself, she pushed it out of her head.

The fog was heavy enough so that once she reached ground level she could only locate the main building, and that was because of its glowing windows. As she approached, light spilling through the glass panes made weird yellowish patches in the gray fog. Her boots crunched through the ice, the sound almost covered by the rush of the waves rolling into the bay behind her. The rumble of the generator grew louder as she neared the side door that opened into the mud–cum–laundry room, where they generally left their outdoor clothes.

Ordinarily she would have yelled out some version of "Hey, honey, I'm home" upon letting herself into the building. Ordinarily she would have stripped down to her socks and jeans and thermal shirt and parked her coat and boots with the others in the cubbies, then scooped up some clean clothes from her clean laundry basket — they each had two baskets, one for dirty and one for clean — in anticipation of a coming shower before proceeding farther into the building. But because she meant to grab the phone and head back outside, and really wanted to attract as little notice as possible until that was done, she didn't do any of those things.

Instead she took off her gloves and stuck them in her pocket, pushed back her hood, and carefully wiped her feet on the mat. Then she walked very quietly through to the kitchen, reveling in the warmth. The industrial-size stove and refrigerator were relatively new — as in, fewer than twenty years old — but the dark wood cabinets lining the walls probably dated from World War II. A lighter wood island that stood in the center of the room had the look of having been handmade, probably by bored Coast Guarders some considerable time before the station had been abandoned. There were no remaining signs of breakfast, not even the lingering scents of coffee or bacon. She snagged an apple from the bowl on the island on the way through because she was starving. Biting into it, enjoying the spicy scent and crisp sweetness way more than she normally would have done, she headed on into the common room.

It was large, paneled in dark wood, with a long inner wall that alternated built-in shelves with storage closets and an equally long outer wall with a pair of windows. It smelled a little of dust, a little of — was it mold? Something slightly dank and unpleasant. Three worn leather couches, plus battered coffee and end tables complete with lamps, were arranged around a striped rug at the far end of the room. They faced an outdated boxlike TV kept solely for playing DVDs, a surprisingly eclectic selection of which took up a fair amount of space on the shelves. Six mismatched armchairs complete with reading lights formed two semicircles facing each other in the middle. The section of the room nearest her and nearest the kitchen was for eating. It contained a long table covered with a red-and-white gingham plastic tablecloth with eight folding chairs arranged around it, and two smaller four-tops, one of which held a partly completed jigsaw puzzle of a beach scene that people worked on as the mood struck them. Gina personally had contributed a corner piece of blue sky.

The phone was nestled in its case on one of the shelves. With a quick glance around to make sure she was alone, hungrily munching the apple as she went, Gina headed toward the phone. Three of the lamps were on, two of the closet doors were ajar, and she could hear footsteps overhead on the second floor. Heavy footsteps: undoubtedly one of the men. But no one was anywhere they could see her.

Carpe diem.

Taking another huge bite of apple, she hurried for the phone. She would grab it, head outside —

Walking between the long table and the one with the jigsaw puzzle on it, she almost stepped on a cheery red Santa sweater. Pausing with her foot still in the air only

226

inches above it, she looked down at it stupidly. Mary Dunleavy's sweater — Gina would have recognized it anywhere. A big Santa face in the center accented by dozens of tiny dancing Santas on the sleeves and around the neck and hem. What she was seeing was a small section, but . . .

Staring down at it, Gina swallowed the bite of apple as she took one more cautious step that carried her past the tables. Her eyes widened. Her heart lurched. Mary was *wearing* her sweater. Her outflung arm lay limply on the worn linoleum floor.

Mary lay limply on the worn linoleum floor.

Gina froze in her tracks, staring down at the other woman in stupefaction.

Mary was sprawled on her back just beyond the big table. A small, trim woman in her late thirties with short platinum-blond hair, she wore jeans with her sweater and red and purple socks on her feet. Her pale hand with its bright red manicure stretched out beseechingly. Her round, cheerful face was slack and gray. Her lips were parted. Her black glasses were askew.

Her eyes were open. Usually a vivid blue, they were almost colorless now. They were also glazed over. The pupils were wide and fixed.

Mary was dead.

Gina's throat seized up. Her stomach turned inside out.

She was just registering that Santa's beard in the middle of Mary's sweater was a shiny, wet red instead of its usual fuzzy white when out of the corner of her eye she caught a glimpse of a large shape on the floor in the shadows near the wall.

She looked toward it. Jorge Tomasini lay curled in a fetal position. There was no mistaking the fact that he was dead: half his face was gone, leaving red gore where his left eye and cheek and jaw should have been. His head lay in a puddle of blood. It looked like a spill of bright scarlet paint that was slowly spreading over the scuffed linoleum.

The apple fell from her suddenly nerveless fingers. It hit the floor with a thud and rolled a few inches away.

A scream bubbled into her throat. Something — a sixth sense? — made her choke it back. What had happened to them? What *could* have happened to them?

Oh, God. Oh, God.

Whatever it was, it must have just happened. The blood — on Mary, on Jorge — was still fresh, still spreading.

Shock, grief, and fear hit her like a baseball

bat. Her chest was suddenly so constricted that it felt as if a giant hand were wrapped around it, squeezing. She tried for a deep breath and ended up with something that was shallow and painful.

Footsteps thumped on the stairs.

Her head snapped up, whipping around toward the long back hall where a staircase led to the second floor. Someone was coming down the stairs with a heavy tread.

Gina's heart leaped into her throat.

She didn't know who it was, but —

Her every instinct screamed, *Get out now.*

Pivoting, she ran back the way she had come, being as quiet as possible but hideously conscious of the soft thud of her footfalls, the slithering rasp her arms made brushing against the body of her coat, the barely stifled sobs of her breathing.

Danger was as tangible in the air as the moldy, unpleasant scent that she suddenly realized was probably blood.

She was just about to fly through the doorway into the kitchen when she heard someone open the back door and walk into the mudroom.

Two someones, she realized as she stopped dead, practically teetering on her toes inches short of the threshold. Men. She could hear them talking.

One said, *"Ty iskat vezde?"*

To the sound of the back door closing, the other replied, *"Da."*

She was no linguist, but she recognized Russian when she heard it.

Behind her a man called out in English, "Ivanov? Anything?"

Having reached the bottom of the steps, the man with the heavy footfalls from the stairs was coming along the hall toward the common room.

None of the voices belonged to her colleagues.

Stark fear turned her blood to ice.

Two of her friends had been brutally murdered — and she was trapped between the men who probably did it.

CHAPTER SIXTEEN

"Nothing," a man who was presumably Ivanov called back in heavily accented English.

From the sound of his voice she could tell he was coming through the kitchen, presumably heading for the common room. Panic sent Gina's pulse rate soaring. She could hear it drumming in her ears.

Hide.

It was the only thing to do, the only chance she had. Wildly she looked around.

Under the table . . . behind the couch . . . in the closet . . .

The closet was the only possible place to go. Everywhere else she would be spotted the moment someone walked through the room.

Juiced by a spurt of adrenaline, Gina fled toward the nearest closet with a door — a wooden double slider — that was partly open. Unless someone actually looked in it, she wouldn't be seen. Pushing the door open a little wider, she dove inside. It was maybe three-by-six feet, moldy-smelling, dark. There was a jumble of gear on the floor, snowshoes, fishing rods, a net on a long pole. Rolled-up sleeping bags piled in a corner. Clothing hanging from the overhead bar. She tripped over something — the hose of a bicycle pump — and barely managed to catch the upright metal canister part before it hit the floor. Bent almost double, with the cool metal column of the pump in one hand, she froze in place with her heart in her throat as she heard Heavy Tread walk into the room.

Stomach twisting, she realized that she'd missed her chance to slide the door shut behind her.

Maybe that's a good thing. Maybe he would have noticed that it was open and now it's shut.

"You sure it was one of these folks?" That was Heavy Tread. He was American, she could tell from his voice. It had a noticeable accent — Texas?

"Only people on island," Ivanov replied. He was in the common room, too. She caught herself on the verge of gulping in air and immediately clamped down, forcing herself to breathe in careful, quiet sips instead.

Her heart pounded so hard she could practically feel it knocking against her breastbone.

"Eto byla zhenshchina," the third man said. He was in the room, too.

Trying not to make any sound at all, carefully lowering the bicycle pump so that it rested on the ground, Gina recognized that last word, meaning "woman."

"It was a woman," Ivanov said, in a way that made her confident that he was translating. He walked into her line of vision as he spoke. Seen from the back, he was of average height and stocky build. A black knit cap hid his hair. He wore a forest-green puffy coat and black ski pants with boots. Stopping beside the long table, he glanced down.

Gina's stomach turned over as she realized that what he was looking at was Mary's body, which had to be lying almost at his feet.

"Not this one," he added, indicating Mary. "I do not think."

"Why not?" Heavy Tread asked.

"This one talked funny." Ivanov's black-gloved hand came up to rest on the table. With a surge of nausea, Gina saw that he was holding a gun.

Mary was — oh, God, *had been* — originally from New York. She'd had a heavy Brooklyn accent. If Ivanov knew about her accent, then Mary had talked to Ivanov before he'd killed her. Had he questioned her? Tortured her?

Gina felt faint.

She was still staring at Ivanov's gun when it hit her that if she could see him, he could almost certainly see her. All he had to do was turn around and look toward the closet.

Gina's vision swam briefly as she experienced a jolt of pure terror. Her heart rate hit warp speed. Her lungs begged for air. It took every ounce of self-control she possessed not to suck in big, hungry gasps.

Quiet. Breathe in, breathe out.

"Sure it was a woman?" Heavy Tread asked.

Afraid of moving for fear of knocking into something else or in some other way making a noise, Gina knew she had no choice. She had to get out of sight, which meant going deeper into the closet. Easing back step by careful step, she sidled into the corner behind the knee-high pyramid of sleeping bags. Keeping a precautionary hand on them so that nothing toppled, wary of straightening for fear of disturbing the clothes above her head, she sank down onto her knees instead. Pulling her hood up over her head, she ducked so that her face would not be a telltale splotch of pale in the gloom. She was deep in shadow, and the piled sleeping bags were between her and the opening. She should have felt safer.

But she was trembling with fear.

Careful to keep her face lowered, she couldn't resist peeking up through her lashes to observe whatever she could. All she could see of Ivanov now were his fingers curled around the gun on the table, a sliver of his leg, and the heel of his big black boot. Her mouth went dry as she looked at him. She swallowed hard. Could he see her? Only if he came over to the closet and looked inside, she decided.

With every fiber of her being, she prayed that he would not.

Ivanov said, "I am sure. We have a recording of her talking about the crash."

Gina stiffened as the possible meaning of that registered. Could it be — were they talking about *her*?

They had to be. There was no other logical interpretation.

Yesterday, when she'd seen the plane going down and called for help over the radio — they'd been *listening*? Her blood ran cold.

I know who they are. Who they have to be.

They were hunting possible survivors of

the plane crash.

Cal.

Panic assailed her.

Her hands knotted into fists so tight that she could feel her nails digging into her palms. Fighting for calm, she closed her eyes for the briefest of moments. When she opened them again, she looked out through the opening in the door and almost gasped. She actually had to press her hand hard over her mouth to contain the sound.

She didn't know how she had missed it up until now. She could only suppose that she hadn't been focusing on the floor.

Now she was, and her eyes widened with horror. Lying on the scuffed linoleum inches from the heel of Ivanov's boot was her half-eaten apple. Red and round, with juicy yellow flesh showing where bites had been taken out of it. Obviously freshly eaten and dropped.

Looking at it, every tiny hair on her body shot upright.

If they see that apple, they'll know somebody came in, saw the bodies. They'll search the room.

The taste of fear was suddenly sour in her mouth.

There was no way Ivanov was going to not see it. He *couldn't* not see it: it was right by his foot. It was just a matter of when.

"Don't matter now," Heavy Tread said. "If she was one of them, she's dead."

"Bylo tri," the third man said in his grating Russian.

"He said there were three," Ivanov translated. "Women."

"How do you know?" Heavy Tread asked.

Gina frowned as she heard what sounded like paper flapping. Judging from the direction the sound came from — behind Ivanov, rather than in front of him where Heavy Tread was — the unseen Russian was doing something to cause it.

Ivanov replied, "Paper he is waving is list. From refrigerator. It says, three women, twelve people total on island. We have found here, nine."

List? From the refrigerator? It had to be the schedule. Of cooking, of chores, of who would be using the boats when. It had been fastened to the refrigerator with a magnet. All their names were on it. Gina felt her blood drain toward her toes.

"We only found two women." Heavy Tread sounded as if he was frowning. "Where's the other one?"

"Perhaps still out on the island. At same time as transmissions from her, we picked up voices of men warning that the storm was coming. It is possible that she did not make it in."

Heavy Tread said, "We got people searching the island to make sure nobody slips through the cracks. If she's out there, they'll find her."

Ivanov said, "I hope you are right. We cannot afford any — what do you call them — screwups."

He turned, and his foot struck the apple. It rolled, traveling in a clumsy, lopsided semicircle because half of it was eaten away.

Gina's eyes riveted on it. Her breath caught. Her stomach turned over.

He's going to see it now.

He was on the move. His boot came down right beside the apple, barely missing stepping on it. Gina caught her breath. Her heart thumped so hard it felt as if it would pound its way out of her chest.

"Search the buildings again," Heavy Tread ordered. "Like you said, we don't want any screwups."

Ivanov was, impossibly as it seemed, walking away without having spotted the apple. He disappeared from view —

Gina's heart nearly stopped as he said, from right outside the closet, "What do we do about these?"

He meant the bodies, Gina could tell from

his tone. Oh, God, his gloved fingers curled around the edge of the closet door. Spotting them, her eyes popped wide for an instant. She ducked, burrowing her face into the top of the nearest sleeping bag while making herself as small as possible in the corner. Her lower spine pressed up against the wall. Her toes curled in her boots. The dusty smell of long-unused gear enfolded her.

Please God please God please . . .

The sound of the closet door being pushed farther open made Gina's heart turn over. It pounded furiously as she caught her breath, then pressed her face so hard into the rolled sleeping bag that she couldn't have breathed if she'd wanted to. She could feel the texture of the tightly woven cloth imprinting itself on her skin. She prayed that some combination of her steel-blue coat, the gray sleeping bag that she had her face buried in, the clutter in the closet, the hanging thicket of clothes, and the darkness in the corner where she crouched would render her invisible.

She could see nothing: black on black. Every other sense she possessed, though, was hyperaware.

He's right there. Only a few feet away. He's got a gun.

Her terror was so strong that she could practically feel it pulsing in the air around her. Unable to see, unable to breathe, she was claustrophobic, suffocating, wired. So frightened all she wanted to do was scream and run.

The sound of his breathing told her that he was still there. A warning prickle running down her spine made her virtually certain that he was looking inside the closet, glancing around. With panic curdling her insides and sending what felt like ice water shooting through her veins, she did her best to remain perfectly still. She visualized herself as a statue, carved from stone, lifeless and immovable.

Oh, God. Be quiet. Don't breathe.

Her heart jackhammered and the muscles in her shoulders and back knotted with tension as she waited — and prayed.

"We burn everything, them included." From the sound of Heavy Tread's voice, he was on his way out of the room. "Big mistake, keeping them fuel tanks so close to the compound. Accidents will . . ."

His words became indistinguishable as his voice faded.

Gina was afraid to twitch so much as a

finger, but her lungs ached from lack of air.

Close at hand, there was a soft scraping sound — cloth on wood? What was it? She didn't know, couldn't tell.

Do not move. Oh, God, I have to breathe.

She heard — she was almost sure she heard — footsteps walking away from the closet.

He's gone, she thought, and a shiver of relief slid over her. But — she might be wrong. Or maybe what she'd heard was the third man, the one who spoke only Russian, walking away.

Her lungs burned now. She was getting light-headed, woozy. She *had* to breathe.

As slowly and silently as possible she let out the breath she'd been holding and in-haled.

Nothing happened. No bullet slammed into the back of her head. Nobody grabbed her. There was no shouting.

Still she stayed as she was, face pressed to the sleeping bag, unmoving, quietly, care-fully breathing, until the silence, the lack of physical sensation that she thought would indicate that she was being watched, had gone on long enough that she couldn't stand it any longer. Daring to chance it, tilt-ing her head the slightest, smallest degree, she looked up.

Her worst fear was that Ivanov would be standing over her, waiting for her to make a move.

He wasn't. There was no one in the closet with her. The door was open farther than before, but the doorway was clear. Through it, she could see a good section of the common room. No one was there, at least not within her view. The overwhelming feeling she got was that the common room was empty.

There was no way she could be sure.

Sitting up, Gina took a deep but nearly silent breath.

Her discarded apple still lay unnoticed on the floor.

As she looked at it a deep shudder racked her. Her heart galloped out of control. Her stomach roiled to the point where she felt like she needed to vomit.

I could have died. I still can *die.*

Mary and Jorge lay just out of her view. Mary and Jorge's *bodies* lay just out of her view. The horror of their deaths — their *murders* — was almost impossible for her to wrap her mind around. She felt this weird sense of disconnect, as if none of what was happening could be real.

It is *real. Mary and Jorge are dead.*

For a moment everything around her went

all blurry. Blinking ferociously, Gina willed the tears back.

The others, what of them? Ivanov had said they had found nine out of the twelve.

She would make number ten. That meant two of her colleagues were presumably out on the island somewhere.

Arvid and Ray, maybe? Had they gone looking for her?

There was no way to know.

But what she had taken from Ivanov's words was that nine of her colleagues were dead.

Murdered.

By the men who were at that moment searching the compound for *her.*

If they found her, she had not the slightest doubt that they would kill her, too.

Goose bumps raced over her skin at the thought. She felt dizzy all over again.

This is no time to fall apart. Focus.

As she saw it, she had two choices: stay where she was, or try to make a run for it.

Ivanov had looked in the closet, she was sure. It was unlikely that he would look in it again.

But he might. Or someone else might.

On the other hand, if she left the closet she could run right into them. She had no idea where they were. Ivanov, Heavy Tread, third guy — they could be anywhere. In this building. Just outside. Somewhere they could see her if she emerged from her hiding place.

For all she knew, there might be more than just the three of them.

To make a run for it, she would have to go back the way she had come: through the common room, the kitchen, the mudroom, across the meadow, up the mountain. Any other route would take her through the complex, and that was too dangerous even to contemplate.

She could take the phone, call for help. Call whom? The Coast Guard? The sponsors? 911?

A question to be answered later, she decided. The point was, she could call somebody and know that help was on the way.

Heavy Tread had spoken of the fuel tanks being too close to the buildings in the context of burning the bodies — what if he meant to cause an explosion, or in some other way set the buildings on fire *now*?

The mere thought that she could be trapped in a fire made Gina go woozy. Gritting her teeth, clenching her fists, she fought to banish the disturbing images.

You can't lose it now.

The men could come back into the common room at any time.

Her chance to run would be lost.

So — go?

Go.

Moving as silently as she could, Gina picked her way to the closet door. For a moment she crouched there, listening, surveying as much of the room as she could see.

The room was empty.

Darting out of the closet, she snatched up the telltale apple and turned to grab the phone.

It was gone.

A lightning survey of the shelves confirmed it: the phone was missing. They'd taken it.

No time to waste worrying about it.

Go, go, go.

With every sense she possessed on red alert, being as quiet as she could possibly be, she dashed for the kitchen, then paused on the threshold to listen for any sound that might indicate someone was in there. Nothing.

Didn't mean somebody wasn't standing there silently.

Heart pounding so hard she could hardly hear over it, she peeked in, saw no one, and flew across the room, thrusting the apple down on top of the trash in the trash can on the way, not wanting to just drop it in case it made a telltale sound. At the entrance to the mudroom she paused again.

She listened, heard nothing. Looked, saw nothing.

Bolted for the door.

The mudroom was relatively small. Two big washing machines against the short wall at the kitchen end, two industrial-size dryers against the short wall at the opposite end with the outside door opening between them. Shelves with laundry supplies and the table with the laundry baskets taking up one long wall. The cubbies along the other. The door to the outside was solid. No window, no way to see through it.

Anybody could be out there, Gina thought as she reached it. Heart pounding, she hesitated, trying to listen, to hear anything that might be on the other side of it even as her hand wrapped around the knob. Nothing, not even the generator, not even the wind or sea. The walls and door were apparently thick enough to block external sounds. The rest of her senses were acutely attuned to the building behind her. For all she knew, someone might still be inside.

A slight creak from what she thought was

the kitchen electrified her. *Was* someone there?

She was so frightened that she could feel her knees shaking.

The sound wasn't repeated. But — maybe whoever was in there was being very quiet as they listened, too? Listened to *her.*

There was no help for it: she would have to pull the door open, scan the yard, and then run like a rabbit across the flat meadow until she reached the hills.

Thank God for the fog: it would provide concealment.

She hoped there was still fog.

Praying no one was outside, she was just tightening her grip on the knob when it turned under her hand and the door was thrust forcefully inward.

With a cry Gina went stumbling backward. Off balance, trying to keep herself from falling, she stared in wide-eyed horror at the opening door.

Her heart almost stopped as Ivanov stepped into the room.

Chapter Seventeen

Gina heard a distant roar through the rush of cold air that burst into the room with Ivanov. Someone had started up the tractor, she realized, identifying the sound using the part of her mind that wasn't transfixed by fear. The tractor was what the team had termed the big trucklike vehicle with the tank treads that was used for heavy hauling or other chores around camp.

Ivanov stopped abruptly just inside the doorway as he spotted her.

"*Hel*-lo," he said with a note of recognition as she barely saved herself from falling by grabbing on to the edge of a washing machine. There was satisfaction in his tone and in his face as his eyes ran over her. Gina barely noticed. Her attention was entirely focused on his gun.

Closing the door behind him, Ivanov raised the compact black pistol, aiming it at her almost casually.

Gina's throat closed up. She couldn't have said a word if she'd wanted to. Hideous visions of what bullets had done to Mary and Jorge sent icy spicules of fear racing through her bloodstream.

"You were hiding, yes?" he asked in a conversational tone.

Her heart and her pulse and her adrenal system all blasted into full freak-out mode at the same time.

Gina turned and ran.

"Stop!" He leaped into pursuit. Flying across the kitchen like her life depended on it, which it did, Gina heard him yell something in Russian, heard the pounding of his boots on the linoleum and the harsh pant of his breathing as he came after her.

Swallowing the scream that ripped into her throat — the last thing she wanted to do was summon more killers — she threw a terrified glance over her shoulder to find him no more than a couple of strides behind. If he lunged, could he reach her? Yes. *Run. Run.* She knew she wasn't going to make it, wasn't going to be able to escape him. There was nowhere to go.

"Stop or I will kill you," he barked. Out of the corner of her eye she saw the gun coming up —

Her heart leaped. Her shoulder blades

tightened in instinctive defense: *He's going to shoot me in the back.*

Her hood was down. Its fur-lined thickness must have made it extend a few inches behind her back, because with his free hand he was able to grab it. He yanked brutally, jerking her back toward him, sending her feet flying out from under her.

The jarring pain that shot through her as she crashed down on her back on the floor was nothing compared to the consuming horror of looking up through the haze of jumbled images brought on by the shock of the fall to find that one particular image — Ivanov — stood threateningly over her.

Even as he came into complete and total focus, panic galvanized her. Her heart beat so frantically that it felt as if it were going to burst.

There was absolutely nothing she could do.

She knew she was facing death, and every cell in her body went freezing cold even as her mind rebelled.

Getting an elbow beneath her, Gina forced her head and shoulders up off the floor. She met his gaze: his eyes were blue, and merciless. The eyes of a killer.

"It was you," he said, looking her over with

interest. He seemed in no hurry. She re-membered that he'd apparently talked to Mary before killing her. Clearly he wanted information from Gina: otherwise, she would already be dead.

He continued, "Who saw the plane —"

Gina jumped as a dark shape exploded from behind the island, behind Ivanov. Roaring something in Russian, Ivanov whipped around to face the threat. A big man in a black coat — that was Gina's initial, blurred impression of the attacker — leaped on him before he could even com-plete the turn. For a moment the two grappled — she heard a couple of solid thuds and grunts as if blows were being landed — and then Ivanov froze.

By that time he was facing her. Over the other man's shoulder, Gina watched Iva-nov's eyes widen, watched his face contort. His gun clattered to the floor, skidded toward her.

Get the gun.

It was the only thought in her mind.

Diving for the gun as the men continued to tussle, she grabbed it and came up into a crouch, clutching it. She hated guns, but she knew how to use one.

And she wouldn't hesitate to demonstrate that knowledge, if the situation called for it.

Ivanov was staggering back, away from the gun that Gina now pointed in his direction, away from the other man. He was gasping, blinking rapidly, looking down at himself. Both of his hands came up to wrap around the handle of a large knife that protruded from his chest. His puffy green coat started to darken around the knife as Gina watched in horror. She knew it was from blood. More blood started to trickle from the corner of his mouth.

Gina shuddered.

Ivanov's attacker glanced back at her, his eyes narrowing as he got a load of her straightening to her full height with the gun gripped in both hands. She was aiming squarely at Ivanov, but — the second man was within her target range, too, and as his face registered in her brain, she let out an involuntary gasp.

Cal. It was Cal. Their eyes locked for the briefest of moments, and the instant connection between them sent a jolt of awareness through her.

"Thank God," she said on a shaky exhaled breath, and realized that somewhere deep inside she'd recognized him from almost the beginning. It was the coat that had thrown her off.

"Give me the gun." Cal stretched his hand

out behind him for it as if he absolutely expected her to comply, and refocused his attention on Ivanov, who stumbled back over the threshold to the mudroom and collapsed.

Gina barely hesitated: she put the gun in his hand, which said volumes about the level of trust she apparently had in him. Until that moment, she hadn't even realized that she trusted him at all. Where he'd come from, how he'd known she was in trouble, and why he hadn't stuck with their plan were all questions that chased one another through her brain. Bottom line: she didn't care. He could answer them later. For now, he was here, and that was enough.

Handling the gun like a man who knew what to do with it, Cal followed Ivanov to the mudroom and stooped over the man's supine body. Trailing him, surprised she could even walk given how rubbery her legs felt, Gina leaned against the doorway and watched as he pressed two fingers below Ivanov's left ear to feel for his pulse.

"Is he dead?" Her voice had a definite squeak to it. She was still breathing hard, still in fight-or-flight mode. The knife in Ivanov's chest — it was one of the butcher knives from the kitchen. She'd used the set herself when it was her turn on the rotation to cook dinner for the group. She didn't know how to make much, but her pot roast was incomparable, and the knives sliced through the tough root vegetables like butter . . . She felt herself starting to hyperventilate and deliberately slowed her breathing down. Ivanov's eyes were still open, but they were glazing over as she watched. His lips were parted and blood and saliva continued to spill from a corner of his mouth. His skin had taken on a distinctly gray tinge.

"Yep." Cal said it matter-of-factly. Gina realized that she'd just watched him kill a man. Not that she objected, under the circumstances. Ivanov would have killed either or both of them without turning a hair. "You okay?" He straightened, glancing back at her and then casting a quick, probing look around the small room.

"Yes." Forget how glad she was to see Cal. Forget the pounding of her heart and the lingering aches and pains from her fall and her shaky insides from her hideous encounter with Ivanov. The horror of what lay in the common room crowded into her mind to the exclusion of all else. Her next words came out in a jumbled rush. "In the next room, Mary and Jorge — two of my friends — are dead. I think nine of them are dead. Ivanov — this one's name is Ivanov — and

254

the others shot them. Murdered them. There are two others — two more men with Ivanov. That I know of."

"I saw them." As Cal spoke, he pocketed the gun and bent over Ivanov again. "There are a lot more than that. They're all over the island. We're going to be dead ourselves if we don't get a move on. Open the dryer door, will you?"

More? A lot *more?* The thought sent Gina's heart rate soaring again. But this wasn't the moment for questions, and she brushed past him to open the door of the dryer. It was large, an industrial-size front loader. A few items of clothing lay in the bottom of it. Ignoring them, she looked back at him. He had Ivanov in his arms and was carrying him toward her. His intention was clear: he meant to stuff the dead man in the dryer.

"It'll buy us some time," he said, presumably in response to the look on her face. "Once they find the body, they'll know somebody was here and they'll be coming after us with everything they've got."

Gina's blood ran cold at the thought. Closing her mind to the horror of Ivanov's lolling head and dangling limbs, to say nothing of his sightless, still-open eyes and the blood sliding across his cheek, her question was purely practical. "Will he fit?"

"I'll make him fit." Cal grunted as he shoved Ivanov's head and shoulders inside the dryer.

"The others could come back at any minute." Fresh panic knotted her stomach at the thought. Remembering the gun made her feel slightly better, but only slightly. A shootout with an unknown number of armed murderers probably wasn't going to end well. Quick as it occurred to her to do so, she ran over and locked the door, trying to be as quiet about it as possible. The click was barely audible, but even that small sound made her wince. It was an ancient deadbolt, clearly not often used, since Attu was usually deserted. Probably the lock wouldn't keep anybody out for long, but at least it would prevent someone from taking them by surprise. She was still unnerved by Ivanov's unexpected entrance.

"See if you can find me some boots that'll fit. Size thirteen." Cal was stuffing the rest of Ivanov's body inside the dryer as he spoke. Ivanov's knees were wedged against his nose in a way that wouldn't have been possible in life.

Gina jerked her gaze away. Right now, the best thing she could do was concentrate on the things that were doable, like getting him clothes. A glance at Cal's feet confirmed that he was still wearing his improvised shoes from that morning, along with what looked like his now-dry but salt-bloomed and unsuitable-for-the-weather suit pants and the big black parka that had confused her at first glance.

Cal said, "This guy the only one who saw you?"

"Yes." Running her eyes along the cubbies, Gina saw that three were missing their outdoor gear: hers, Arvid's, and Keith Hertzinger's. Did that mean that the others — Ray? A quiver of grief ran through her as his tanned, genial face rose in her mind's eye — were all dead? Shoving the thought from her mind, she rushed to Bob Gordon's cubby. Bob was the biggest guy in the group, at maybe six-one and two-hundred-some-odd pounds. Hopefully he had big feet.

"So what do we do now?" She grabbed the boots, then snatched Bob's insulated snow pants and gloves from the hooks.

"Get the hell out of here." He was trying to jam Ivanov's arm inside the dryer with the rest of him as she ran back toward him.

"Here." Gina plopped the boots and other things down beside the dryer.

Ivanov's arm now safely inside, Cal covered the corpse with a blue towel.

"Did you make that call for me?" He was doing his best to force the dryer door closed.

"I didn't get a chance."

He shot a look at her over his shoulder. "The satellite phone somewhere you can grab it?"

"It's gone. They took it." Gina snatched two of the survival backpacks from the cubbies.

He swore. "You sure?"

"Yes." She pulled the redundant items — the tent and the ground cover — out of one of the backpacks.

Kneeing the dryer door viciously, he finally got it to latch. Looking through the dryer's round glass window, Gina would have sworn that it held nothing more sinister than a load of laundry.

"That should keep them from finding him for a while," Cal said with satisfaction. Hopping from foot to foot, he pulled off his makeshift shoes and grabbed the snow pants. Gina stuck the things she'd pulled from the backpack in the other dryer along with his discarded "shoes" and ran back to the kitchen. Behind her, he was slamming his feet into the boots.

Seconds later he followed her into the kitchen. He was wearing the boots and snow pants now, she saw. They appeared to fit him well enough.

"You say there are two dead in here? Where?"

Busy throwing food and water into the backpack she'd half emptied, Gina nodded and pointed.

"In there." Her chest tightening, she did her best not to think about Mary and Jorge. "There may be more dead. Elsewhere in the building."

He strode across the kitchen to disappear into the common room.

He came back almost at once.

"You saw . . . ?" She couldn't help but ask when he didn't say anything. Having finished filling the backpack, she zipped it shut while keeping her gaze on what she was doing. She didn't want to witness whatever effect seeing the bodies might have had on him in his face. With some difficulty, since it was now considerably heavier than before, she hoisted the backpack to her shoulder, still without looking at him.

"Yeah. I got this. Let's go." His voice sounded tight as he took the backpack from her, slung it over a broad shoulder. Refusing to think about anything other than the need to get out of there, she hurried after him as he strode through the kitchen into the mudroom.

The fact that the gun was in his hand now told her that he thought more trouble could break out at any moment. It jacked her fear level up to the roof. It also made her feel slightly — only slightly — safer.

"I locked the door," she said to his back.

"I saw."

As they neared the back door, she snagged the second backpack and lugged it along by its top strap, prepared to shrug into it as soon as she got the chance. Getting out of this alive was the goal, and if they were stuck outside for any length of time Attu's weather would kill them as surely as a bullet. Grabbing the backpacks and the extra food was her contribution to making sure they didn't die.

Cal was already at the door, hesitating in front of the solid panel exactly as she had done earlier.

The door and the windowless mudroom walls took "see no evil, hear no evil" to a whole new place.

There was no way of knowing if someone was right outside, or where Heavy Tread or anyone else was.

Opening that door required nothing short of a leap of faith.

Glancing at her over his shoulder, Cal

said, "I'm going to take a look outside. When I give you the all clear, run as fast as you can toward that mountain you came down off of earlier. I'll be right behind you. Don't stop for anything."

Gina nodded, suddenly breathless. Her stomach clenched, and it felt as if her heart, which was already racing, had just received a jolt of speed. She hauled the backpack up and slid an arm through the strap.

"Give me that," he said. Hooking a hand in the other strap, he took the backpack from her and slung it over his shoulder along with the first one. "Did I mention you need to run really fast?"

She didn't argue. Even if she'd wanted to — she didn't — there wasn't time.

He unlocked the door — she tensed at the soft click — and eased it open.

The sudden blast of cold, damp-smelling air reminded Gina horribly of Ivanov bursting through the door. The roar of the tractor, the rumble of the generator, the knowledge that armed murderers were out there, the thought of her dead friends, all came together in a nearly paralyzing rush.

"Move your ass," Cal growled.

Gina realized that she must have missed his signal. Taking a tentative step forward so that she could peek out the door, casting a single hunted glance around outside — because of the fog she could see maybe ten feet in all directions — she bolted across the stoop. Plunging into the fog, welcoming the billows of gray mist that swallowed her up and hopefully hid her from anyone who might happen to look her way, she flew back the way she had come, toward the mountain she had walked off earlier. Down in the depths of the fog she couldn't see it or the path, but she knew where they were, knew the way.

Head down, heart pumping like a piston, she ran across the crackly ice as fast as she could. With every step she took she was conscious of the treacherous surface beneath her feet and thankful for the slip-resistant, rubber-soled boots that several times arrested an incipient slide and saved her from falling. She ran so fast she got a stitch in her side, but, pressing a hand to the place that hurt, she kept going without slowing down. The crunch of her feet in the ice-crusted snow terrified her. The sound of her own breathing terrified her.

She was mortally afraid of being spotted, and shot. What was it they said about the bullet that killed you? You never even saw it coming?

Jacked on terror, she ran like she'd never

run before in her life.

Cal stayed right behind her. She could hear his footsteps crunching through the snow, too, could see the dark bulk of him looming between her and the buildings whenever she glanced back. If shooting started from that direction, he would almost certainly take the first bullet. She wondered whether he was staying behind her for just that reason.

Reaching the path that was really no more than a rut carved into the bare, rocky face of the mountain, she leaped up it like a mountain goat and kept going along the twisty trail with no thought of slowing down. Gina was so intent on putting distance between herself and the killers that she jumped with surprise and cast a startled look over her shoulder at Cal when his hand clamped around her arm and he pulled her to a stop.

CHAPTER EIGHTEEN

"Hold up," Cal said. "Let's take a break."

He was breathing hard, and Gina realized that she was, too. Gasping for air, actually, and still troubled by the stitch in her side. She grimaced and bent over, rubbing the place where it hurt.

"You all right?" he asked.

She nodded, too winded and in too much pain from the cramp to speak. They were in an area that she'd passed through on the way down, when her biggest concern had been making his phone call and she'd had no idea of the horrors awaiting her. This part of the mountain had apparently experienced a landslide at some point, because large boulders lay all around, partially blocking the path and also, she saw now, blocking them from the view of anyone who might be looking their way from above or below. Of the same near-black, volcanic composition as the mountains themselves, they were dusted with snow.

Good choice of location if they had to stop, Gina thought, then sat down abruptly on a boulder that was the approximate size and shape of a low bench. She had no choice: now that she'd stopped, her legs had turned to jelly and were refusing to support her.

You are not going to lose it.

It was an easy thing to tell herself. She was light-headed, though, and wobbly, and the boulder and the path and the steep, snowy slope behind her suddenly seemed as insubstantial as the drifting feathers of mist. Some eiders were nesting in the rocks nearby. She couldn't see them, but she could hear and identify them from the soft *rrr, rrr* sounds they made.

Closing her eyes, Gina hung her head, breathing in the thin blue air, waiting for the dizziness to recede, for the stitch in her side to pass.

Cal didn't say anything, simply sat down beside her. Never mind that she'd just seen him kill a man with a butcher knife, which officially made him the scariest person she'd ever met: he was big and solid and *armed,* all good things. Plus she was pretty sure they were on the same side. The warmth of his body so close against hers made her feel anchored, grounded. An instant, involuntary flashback to the way he'd kissed her heated her blood. That brief moment when their eyes had connected in the kitchen told the story — somehow in the midst of chaos and horror they had formed a bond. Despite everything — her uncertainty about how much she could trust him, the inescapable truth that if he hadn't fallen out of the sky on top of her, none of these dreadful things would be happening — she took comfort in his presence.

She opened her eyes, saw that he'd put the backpacks on the rocky ground near his feet, and was relieved to discover that the backpacks, and his feet, and the path, and the mountain, and everything except the fog, remained stationary. The wind had picked up. Cold and damp, it blew in gusts from the bay, smelling of the sea, sending clouds of fog scudding past them like sailboats in a regatta.

"What are you doing here?" Her question emerged as a gasp as she fought to catch her breath.

His reply was a sardonic "Saving your ass."

Gina frowned at him impatiently. "I'm serious." Her still-ragged breathing created a hitch in her words. "How did you wind up in the kitchen?"

"I followed you."

"What? Why?"

"To make sure you were safe."

She must have made an interrogative sound to go with the look she threw at him, because he added, "Not long after you left, a boat showed up to check out the crash site."

"A boat?" she interrupted on a hopeful note, because it was fixed in her mind that Arvid and Keith Hertzinger — if they were the two other survivors; oh, God, she still could not wrap her mind around the idea that the rest of her colleagues were dead — might be out in a boat looking for her.

"Believe me, it wasn't your friends. This was a fishing trawler. A big one. It stayed at the crash site, along with two of its dinghies. Another dinghy with four men aboard went on around the point. I'm assuming that's where your killers came from."

The thought of that made her stomach sink. "What makes you think so?"

"I saw it when I came after you. First thing I did when I got off the mountain was check out the bay to see if the dinghy was there, and sure enough it was, tied up at the dock. So I got a little worried and came looking for you. And that's how I wound up in the kitchen."

She was sure there was a lot more to the story, but they could talk specifics later, Gina decided. At the moment, she had more pressing concerns.

"They could find Ivanov — at any minute." Stark terror twisted her insides at her next thought. "Then they'll come looking for us."

"They'll come looking for whoever killed Ivanov. At this point, they don't know who that is. I don't think." While Gina tried to work out whether that was supposed to make a difference, he added, "Anyway, unless we're really unlucky it'll be a while before they find him."

The look she gave him was wry. "You know, I'm feeling pretty unlucky right now. Just sayin'."

That earned her a glimmer of a smile. As another gust of wind blew past, he reached out and tugged her hood up over her head with the clear intention of protecting her from the icy blast. Nodding her thanks at him, she secured her hood in place, then retrieved her gloves from her pocket and put them on as he unzipped a backpack and rooted around for a bottle of water. She knew what he was looking for because he found it almost immediately, pulled it out, unscrewed the cap, and passed it to her.

Until that moment she hadn't realized how parched her throat was. She drank thirstily and passed the bottle back. He took a drink, then screwed the cap on and stuck the bottle in the backpack. Then he produced a protein bar, which they shared.

By the time they'd finished that off she was breathing more or less normally and the pain from the stitch in her side had gone away. The base of her spine and her left elbow hurt from hitting the kitchen floor, horror at the fate of her friends lurked in the back of her mind like a malevolent shadow, and she was cold and queasy and afraid of dying, either at the hands of the killers or from exposure: they had nowhere to go and the clouds that were rolling in on the wind were low and the color of lead, which she was afraid meant more snow.

On a positive note, she was still alive.

"Better?" he asked, and she nodded. She happened to be looking down at the camp just as the wind disturbed the fog enough so that she could see the buildings, as well as headlights moving away from them in a jerky, stop-and-go fashion. The headlights could only belong to the tractor, and as she watched, the vehicle chugged into a relatively clear patch of air so she could actually see it. A cross between a Caterpillar and

a farm tractor complete with a small, enclosed cab and nine wheels in sets of three
on each side that had been wrapped in tank
treads, the thing was the canary yellow of a
school bus and about as long. Right now it
had its snowplow attachment down. Hard
at work, it moved busily back and forth,
scraping snow and ice off the asphalt.

Gina frowned. "They're clearing the runway."

Cal followed her gaze.

"Shit." He stood up abruptly. Picking up
the backpacks, he slung them over his
shoulder. "Come on, let's go."

Gina stood up, too, but she was still staring down at the tractor. "Why would they
be —" She broke off as the answer sent cold
chills sliding down her spine. "They're
expecting a plane to land."

"Looks like it." His voice was grim. He
started walking and she followed. Every
instinct she possessed screamed at her to
put as much distance as possible between
herself and what was going on below.

They were maybe halfway up the mountain, high enough so that she could see but
not hear the tractor, and at this point the
trail was wide enough for them to walk side
by side, with about five feet on the other
side of it before a sheer drop-off plunged

some three hundred feet into a snowy ravine. As it curled around the mountian, she knew from experience, the trail got narrower, and steeper.

"That can't be good," she said, catching up and falling into step beside him.

"Nope."

"Unless a plane's coming to pick them up and take them away from here?" She knew it was a forlorn hope even as she said it.

"I'd say they're bringing in more people."

"Why?" Her voice was full of trepidation. She looked back down at the camp. Except for the glow of its headlights, the tractor once again had been swallowed by fog. The light spilling from the windows of the main building created yellow rectangles in the mass of gray, keeping her oriented. She and Cal were above the dense blanket of fog covering the low-lying areas now, and as they climbed higher it was like looking down on a rolling bank of storm clouds from the window of an airplane. Up where they were, the mist was lighter and finer, more lacy tendrils and a less solid block of condensation. The honks of a formation of Aleutian cackling geese as they flew past overhead were the only sounds other than the wind and the sea.

Cal said, "They'll be concerned about

possible witnesses."

Gina digested that. "They can't afford to leave anybody alive." Her voice was hollow with realization.

He said, "We've got some time. Nobody's landing anything in this fog."

At that indirect confirmation that she was right on with her deduction, the sick feeling in the pit of her stomach intensified. "Oh, goody. We just have to worry about the killers who are already here. For now."

A corner of his mouth quirked up in response. He slanted a glance at her. "How well do you know Attu?"

"I've studied a map: I know the layout and where things are generally." Glancing back down at the industriously moving headlights, she shuddered. "I've walked some of the trails, although the farthest I've gone is about half a day's walk from camp." She flicked a look at him. His head was bent slightly, to hear her better over the blowing wind, she thought. Seen in profile, his features looked as hard and unyielding as the craggy black mountain rising behind him. "I've gone around the eastern tip of the island in a Zodiac."

"Big mistake, huh?" The hint of humor in his voice caught her by surprise.

"Oh, yeah."

He smiled at the fervency with which she said that, and once again she found herself thinking what a great-looking guy he was. Good-looking, good with his hands — the memory of their kiss and his subsequent feel-up of her body sent a reminiscent pulse through her — why, if she hadn't been on the run for her life and he hadn't been a dangerous stranger that she not only knew nothing about but didn't want to know anything about and, oh, yeah, if life hadn't smashed her romantic tendencies like a glass at the end of a Jewish wedding ceremony, she just might have been interested in him.

But given the above conditions, not a chance. Even if he was an excellent kisser.

He said, "You know of anyplace where we could hide out and still keep an eye on that runway?"

Gina frowned, considering. "There's a lookout post near the top of Weston Mountain." She pointed. The peak loomed to her left, its summit wreathed in fog that hid the tiny, tumbledown cabin on sky-high stilts that was the lookout post. "Well, the remains of one. You can see the whole camp from there. When it isn't so foggy, that is. Artillery Hill" — she pointed toward the west, where fog obscured the lower-elevation knob near the bay — "has some old Quonset huts still standing. Plus there are storage sheds all over the place. And caves."

He looked interested. "Caves?"

She nodded. "There's this massive cave system throughout the mountains. Lots of natural caves, and then the Japanese apparently dug tunnels connecting them so that they could move around the island and launch guerrilla attacks on our guys during World War Two."

"Any in the right place so we can shelter in it while keeping watch on the runway?"

"The entrance to one is up there." Gina pointed to nearby Terrible Mountain, the southern face of which overlooked the camp.

"And you know this how?"

"Some of the puffins I'm studying have burrows up around it. I've seen the entrance, but I've never been inside the cave."

"How long approximately would it take us to get there?"

"Without going back through camp" — which would be the quickest and shortest route — "probably about four hours. We'd have to go through Jackson Pass."

"You know how to get there from here?"

"Yes. Theoretically."

"That's good enough. Let's check it out.

We going the right way?"

Gina nodded. They had reached the point where the trail started narrowing, and he made a gesture to her to precede him, saying, "Lead on, Macduff."

That made her shoot him an aren't-you-funny glance over her shoulder, but she kept going, climbing doggedly up the icy path, taking the left-leading fork despite the fact that it snaked around the edge of a cliff that fell away into clouds and felt as thin and perilous as a tightrope underfoot. There were a couple of questions she had to ask, and she braced herself for answers she was pretty sure she wasn't going to like.

Glancing at him over her shoulder, she said, "Why would we rather hide in a cave than, say, a Quonset hut?"

Their eyes met, and there was something in his that told her she'd been right about not liking the answer she was about to hear.

"If they haven't already, they're going to be launching a massive search for us. Not just a ground search, but a high-tech scan of the island. Thermal imaging, infrared, satellite pictures, the whole bag of tricks. If we're in a cave, there's less chance of us showing up on anything. Get deep enough inside a mountain and even thermal imaging won't be able to spot us."

Okay, she'd known she wasn't going to like it.

"Who *are* these people?" she burst out. That was another question she really didn't want to hear the answer to, but now she reluctantly concluded that she needed to know.

He was close behind her. His broad frame blocked the worst of the wind that was huffing past in great gusts now, and once again she wondered whether he was shielding her intentionally.

He said, "I'm not sure yet. I'll let you know when I am."

That sounded evasive. She glanced back at him, but his face told her absolutely nothing. She decided to mark that as a topic to be pursued later and moved on to what she considered a more urgent question. "Why do we need to watch the runway?"

"Because after it lands, we're going to steal the plane that's coming in." He said it like it was the most reasonable thing in the world.

Gina stopped dead and turned to face him. *"What?"*

"Careful." His hands shot out to steady her, catching her upper arms and curling around them. He was clearly concerned with the drop-off beside them, while she,

having traversed this trail a number of times, barely noticed it. He continued, "We need to get off this island. That's the quickest and surest way I can think of to do it." Turning her back around, he gave her a little push that started her walking again. "Keep going. You want to be out here in the open when whatever's blowing in hits?"

That last was a rhetorical question, so she didn't reply. Anyway, even as she started walking again her mind was busy boggling. Just the thought of stealing a plane and escaping in it felt impossible.

"That's crazy." She was suddenly short of breath, and not from the climb.

"You worried I can't fly us out of here? I can."

No, no, no. Gina shook her head emphatically. "I'm worried that trying to steal a plane, much less fly it out of here, is stupid." Her mouth felt dry. "They'll catch us. The smart thing to do is hide and wait. The ship that brought most of us here will be back in five days. So will the Reever — the plane that brought the rest of us."

"You got a ship *and* a plane coming for you?"

"The Reever can carry a maximum of six passengers. And the ship is a freighter with a regular run to Siberia. It has accommodations for a few passengers, and it was just easier for some of us to travel on it. Bad weather sometimes keeps the Reever from flying, but the ship will definitely be here on time."

When he didn't say anything, she glanced back again. His expression spoke for him. It was grim, and suddenly she knew why they couldn't wait for the plane or the ship.

They were never going to make it five days.

CHAPTER NINETEEN

If he'd shown up five minutes later, she'd
be dead. That was the thought that lodged
itself in Cal's mind as Gina cast a frowning
glance back at him. Bundled up from head
to toe like she was, she still made a slender
and unmistakably feminine figure against
the bleak backdrop of mountain and fog and
threatening skies. Her blue eyes were
clouded with worry, her cheeks were rosy
with cold, and long strands of honey-
colored hair had escaped from her hood to
blow around her head. Even pressed tightly
together as they were at the moment, her
lips remained enticingly full. Kissable, he
thought as his eyes dropped to them, and
he remembered the hot way she'd kissed
him before he shook the recollection off.
Sexy as hell was his instant assessment of
how she looked as she climbed the path
ahead of him with long, athletic strides.
Beautiful and *brave* were also in the mix,

the beautiful part obvious and the brave because she was still trucking, still making rational decisions after finding her friends dead and nearly being killed herself. Not that any of that made any real difference to any course of action he planned to take. She was under his protection now, and he was going to do his best by her whether she agreed with it or not. He found himself thanking God that he'd listened to his instincts earlier and followed her back to her camp.

"I think it's time you told me what's going on." Her voice was sharp.

That the runway was being cleared bothered him. There was already a ton of muscle here — who or what were they bringing in? Pondering that question, he answered her almost at random. "We're running for our lives?"

The look she gave him told him that she wasn't in the mood for even that lame attempt at humor.

"It's the *why* I'm interested in," she said.

He couldn't tell her. His contract was subject to the rules that governed the highest security clearances, and anyway, the objective of saving her life was to let her keep living it after it was saved. Around the circles he ran in, people who knew too much tended to die young. Their current situation being a case in point. The man he'd killed back there in the camp kitchen — he hadn't known him, but he knew the type. He was hired help, a paid killer whose allegiance went to the employer with the biggest bank account. The only question was whom he was working for. Whom *they* were working for. Cal still didn't know, not for sure. Somebody who could infiltrate his company, get to Hendricks, and do what Cal would have thought was impossible, which was get to Ezra.

When Ezra had fired through that door on the jet, he'd aimed low. The only conclusion Cal could draw from that was that Ezra hadn't been intending to kill him. Although how Ezra had thought that was going to work out in the long run Cal couldn't quite fathom. He refused to feel anything — grief, loss, anger at the betrayal — for his erstwhile friend. He had no time for emotion now. Emotion got you killed. He meant to live, and to keep the woman frowning at him alive, too. It was a big job, and he wasn't going to let feelings get in the way of that.

The fact that he had one gun, a Beretta 92FS semiautomatic pistol with about half a clip in it, only served to make things interesting.

He told her, "You're better off not knowing."

Her frown turned into a full-blown scowl. "You know what you can do with that. My friends were *murdered* today. I was almost murdered today. I think I have a right to know why."

She stumbled on a rock in the path. He once again automatically reached out to steady her. He let go almost instantly, as soon as it became obvious that she wasn't going to pitch face-first over a cliff, but not before he registered that the body part he'd grabbed had been her slender upper arm, which he could feel even through his gloves and her parka.

Damn. He was still all too aware of her as a woman.

Which was a complication their situation did not need.

"Well?" she demanded, sounding testy.

In the spirit of throwing her a bone to keep the peace, Cal said to her back, "You and your friends fall under the heading of collateral damage. My plane was the primary target."

"Why?"

Jesus, she was persistent. "Because of some information we had."

"What information?" she shot back.

Okay, enough. "Can't say."

She cast another dark glance over her shoulder at him. "Oh, wow, way to be transparent."

Hugging the very edge of a five-hundred-foot drop, the path took a sharp turn upward at that point. As she looked back at him she was silhouetted against nothing but gray fog and grayer sky. For a moment there it looked as if she would fall off the side of the mountain if she took one more step, and he felt a stab of alarm over her safety.

"Quit looking back at me. Watch where you're going," he said irritably.

"What, are you afraid I'm going to die?"

If she'd ever been afraid of him — and she had been at first, he knew, and was also forced to admit that her fear hadn't been without reason — she was clearly over it. Her eyes snapped at him. Her tone was caustic.

"Falling off a cliff works as well as catching a bullet for that." His response was mild.

She made a *hmmph* sound but focused her attention on the trail. Climbing behind her, Cal absentmindedly admired her ass, admired her legs — he was nothing if not a multitasker — while turning the pieces of the nightmare they were trapped in over in his mind, trying to make sense of them. Seeing the bodies in that building, seeing the firepower that had turned out, the only conclusion he could reach was that they — the nameless *they* he couldn't quite pin an identity on yet — somehow knew or suspected that someone had survived the crash. It was possible that pictures of his rescue had been picked up by satellite. Remembering the cloud cover, he thought it was far more likely that someone on the ground, most likely whoever had fired that surface-to-air missile, had spotted Gina pulling him from the water. They would have had to have been close enough to see what was happening, but too far away to do anything about it — like, say, shoot him and Gina both and be done.

"Tell me something: are you with the military?"

There she went again, frowning back over her shoulder at him. As precarious as the trail was, her inattention to it made him nervous. And annoyed.

"No."

"Some kind of government agency? CIA? FBI? Something like that?"

"No."

"You must work for somebody. Who?"

That much he could tell her. "I work for myself."

"Is that another way of saying you're a mercenary?"

He shrugged. "We're all mercenaries, one way or another."

"You know, someday I'd love to engage in that philosophical debate with you. Right now, I'd just like a straight answer."

"I'm a private contractor. Okay? End of discussion." His tone was short, and she made another of those *hmmph* noises in response. But they'd come upon a patch of ice, and she let the conversation lapse as they picked their way over it.

In the ensuing silence, he had an epiphany: if they knew someone had survived the plane crash, they probably knew it was him. He, Ezra, and Hendricks might all prompt the degree of firepower that had been summoned to deal with the threat a survivor posed — Rudy's survival would have merited the response equivalent of a flyswatter — but Ezra and Hendricks had presumably been on the other side. Unless they'd been tricked, which he considered possible. Surface-to-air missiles had a range of only fifteen thousand feet, and there was a chance that the thirty-million deal for Rudy had been offered as a way of getting the plane to descend under that ceiling so that it could be shot down.

For safety's sake, however, he had to presume that his sole survival was known, and all this was in his honor. The intensity with which they were going about ensuring his demise made him think, too, that this wasn't just about Rudy's information, or the crash of Flight 155. The way they were going full scorched-earth here, in attempting to wipe out not only him and the others on his plane but a dozen civilians as well, set off all kinds of alarm bells in his mind.

Rudy had said that there was chatter that what had befallen Flight 155 was being set to happen again to another plane. For his survival to merit this kind of response, that almost had to be true. Whoever was behind this was prepared to do whatever was necessary to protect whatever was getting ready to go down.

Cal was willing to bet all his money that another civilian airliner was getting ready to fall out of the sky.

If he was right, it wasn't just his and Gina's lives at stake. Hundreds of others could die.

Cal blew out a frustrated puff of air. "I've got to get off this damned island."

Having reached the edge of the patch of ice she'd been negotiating with such care, Gina responded to the first words Cal had said in several minutes with a skeptical "By stealing a plane."

"Yep."

"You don't think hiding out for five days would be a better option?" Her pulse was picking up the pace big-time. Fear fluttered inside her like a trapped bird. She really, truly thought attempting to steal a plane from the midst of a camp bristling with killers (probably a whole lot more once the plane landed) was a terrible idea. That opinion was only influenced a tiny bit by the bitter truth that she was mortally afraid to fly.

She had not been on a plane since the crash that she had barely survived.

"What about you? Won't anyone be coming to look for you? You said your transponder was off, but —"

He cut in before she could finish. "It's possible, but it's nothing I'd be willing to bet our lives on. The plane was off course, for one thing. There might be some confusion about where we went down. Or even *if* we went down."

That made Gina frown. But before she could follow up with more questions, they reached the pass and started across what was basically a natural rock suspension bridge between two mountains. Sheer cliffs dropped down into nothingness on both sides, and the lowering gray sky suddenly felt so close that she could have reached up and touched it if she'd wanted to. A bucking, writhing mass of dark gray clouds churned below. Looking down at them, Gina thought that the clouds appeared solid enough that you'd almost think you could jump down on them and hitch a ride.

Without the mountain to act as a barrier, wind gusts buffeted them from all directions, some strong enough to part the clouds and the underlying fog, allowing glimpses of the silvery river that, far below, ran beneath the bridge.

"Whoa. Slow down." Cal caught the back of her parka as she strode out on the bridge with the confidence of someone who'd crossed it before, which she had: a pair of gyrfalcons that she'd been documenting had a nest on the other side.

Gina glanced back at Cal in surprise. "You're not afraid of heights, are you?"

"I'm not a fan of falling off heights, that's for sure. How about you pay attention to what you're doing?"

"I'm very sure-footed," she said. She did slow down, though, partly because it was so windy and partly because he'd kept his hand fisted in her parka. The rock underfoot was frosted over and slick, and the natural buttresses on each side were only a few feet high: it would be easy to go over. She started paying more attention to where she put her feet. As they approached the middle of the bridge she could no longer see the mountains that anchored it. All she could see was a swirling mass of gray clouds above and below. It was like being suspended in midair. The wind blew strongly, smelling of the sea, and had an icy bite to it. She had the sudden fanciful notion that if she spread out her arms the wind would catch her up and she could fly away on it.

If only.

A few moments later they were off the bridge and trudging across the face of the adjoining mountain. It was another narrow, rocky path, only this time they were going down. She was in the lead, and was acutely conscious of the vast bleakness of the jagged, treeless mountains rising all around, as well as the potential treacherousness of the path beneath her feet. The thin patches of snow weren't a problem: they were easy to avoid. The ice was harder to see. Snow-frosted boulders lay everywhere, blocking the path at times so that they had to skirt around them. This mountain and the next were like conjoined twins that became separate entities about two hundred feet above sea level, and that juncture was where they were heading. As they descended they plunged into thickening fog, and every outside sound — wind, sea, more honking geese — grew increasingly muffled. In contrast, Gina could hear her and Cal's breathing and footsteps in perfect tandem. Cal stayed so close behind her that she could have stretched a hand back and touched him, and again she was glad to have him there. He made her feel far safer than she had any business feeling under the circumstances, she knew.

"So tell me what happened back there at the camp," he said, his voice a deep rumble that cut through the increasingly high-pitched whining of the wind.

Gina knew what he meant: he wanted to know what had happened when she'd reached the LORAN station.

In careful, concise sentences that were designed to keep emotion at bay, she told him what he wanted to know. But for all her calm on the surface, as she talked she discovered that she was still shaky inside and that grief and horror had solidified into what felt like a permanent knot in her chest.

As she ended her story with his unexpected appearance in the kitchen, her heart was pounding and tears pricked her eyes.

"The guy with the Texas accent — can you describe him?" he asked.

Firmly blinking the tears away, Gina shook her head. "The only one I saw was Ivanov." Frowning, she added, "When you got to the camp, how did you even know where I was?"

He shrugged. "I headed for the building with the lights. Luckily, I was still a fair distance away when three men walked out the door. I gave them enough time to get clear and went in. I made it as far as the kitchen when I heard somebody coming and ducked behind the table thing. You ran through. I stayed where I was for a minute to make sure you weren't being chased, and then I started to come after you. Only by then you'd encountered our friend Ivanov and were running back through the kitchen the other way."

"How many of them were there? At the camp?"

"I saw the three who came out of the building, plus one other. But from the footprints I came across, I think there were at least six. The dinghy holds eight."

Gina was assailed by a terrible thought. "Oh, my God, the dinghy probably just docked and nobody had a clue that there was anything wrong." Her throat constricted, making it difficult for her to get the words out. "They probably walked up to the camp and started shooting people. No, whoever saw them pull up probably went down to the dock to meet them and *invite* them up to the camp. Mary — Jorge — none of them would even have dreamed that they could be in danger. Ivanov *talked* to Mary. I know he did, because he knew about her accent — she had this heavy Brooklyn accent. She would have had no clue what was going to happen. None of them would have had a clue. They were just *slaughtered.*"

Gina's voice quavered on the last word. The thought of Mary and Jorge as they had looked lying there on the floor refused to leave her head. Fighting to banish the image, she took a deep, shuddering breath.

"Hey." The path wasn't really wide enough for two to walk abreast, but he caught up to her anyway. She could feel the weight of his gaze on her face but she didn't look up at him because that damnable prickle of tears was back. But he clearly realized that she was upset. He caught her hand, squeezed it gently. Until she looked down at his black-gloved hand holding hers, she hadn't realized that her fingers were clenched into tight fists. Having his big hand wrapped around her fist was almost ridiculously comforting. "I'm sorry this came down on you and your friends. I can't do anything about the others, but I'm going to do my best to get you out of this in one piece."

She took a deep breath.

"It's not your fault," she said. "You didn't deliberately crash your plane."

"No," he agreed. "I didn't." He was still holding her hand, and she realized that her fingers were relaxing in his, instinctively responding to the solace he offered. She freed her hand before her fingers could do something stupid, like, say, clutch at his. Or entwine with them.

"None of that explains where you got the coat." Her voice was deliberately crisp. Succumbing to sorrow was the last thing she meant to do. Right now what she needed most of all was to keep a clear head.

"Coat?" His genuine confusion earned him an exasperated up-flick of a look. Exasperation, she decided, was a far preferable emotion to everything else she'd been experiencing.

"This one. The one you're wearing." She gave his sleeve a tug.

"Oh," he said. "A second dinghy dropped

two men off near the rocks where I was hiding. One of the men headed down the coastline, like he was going to walk around the point. The other went right on past me and took the same trail you did. I followed him, and when I got the chance I took him out. His gun went over a cliff in the struggle, but I got his coat before I pitched him after the gun. I would have taken his boots, too, but they were too small. Then I got to thinking that you might run into somebody like him, so I followed you."

Gina looked at him. He must have found a knit cap somewhere, probably in a coat pocket, because he'd pulled on a black one that hugged his head and almost touched his eyebrows in front. Below it, his eyes were as dark as the mountain behind them. His square, unshaven jaw was set and hard. His mouth was unsmiling. He looked tough. Capable. Dangerous, just as she'd suspected from the first.

And so handsome her heart beat a little faster just from looking at him.

He'd spoken of "taking out" the man he'd been following so nonchalantly, as if killing was something he was accustomed to doing. She thought of Ivanov and the butcher knife: killing obviously *was* something he was accustomed to doing.

A shiver ran down her spine.

Nice bear.

Both of those men had been killed on her behalf, she reminded herself, but that still didn't make her feel less wary where he was concerned. It was, Gina reflected, sort of like finding herself under the protection of what was so far the biggest, baddest predator in the jungle.

It was all good unless he turned on her.

"Thank you," she said. "For coming after me."

His eyes met hers. She could read absolutely nothing in them. "Like I said, I mean to get you out of this alive."

"I'm going to hold you to that," she told him.

A sudden updraft sent the fog swirling. As her eyes dropped away from his — she was afraid the sudden guardedness in hers would be all too easy to read — she got another look at the glinting silver ribbon that was the river, which, having passed beneath the natural bridge, curled around the base of the mountains before meandering off into the interior of the island.

There was an orange boat in the river: a Zodiac. In the Zodiac was a splotch of bright neon yellow. The splotch was moving, and it had a dark head, arms and legs attached. By this time she and Cal had descended until they had almost reached two hundred feet and were very near to the place where the mountains fused. From Gina's perspective the boat and its contents were rendered small by distance, but she was as sure as it was possible to be about what she was looking at.

The boat conceivably could have been any orange Zodiac, but the splotch of neon yellow in it was unmistakable: that was Arvid's parka. She would recognize it anywhere. They'd all been teasing him about its Day-Glo color since they'd first gotten a look at it.

Gina's eyes widened in surprised recognition. She stopped, grabbed Cal's arm, pointed, and said excitedly, "Arvid! There's Ar—"

From somewhere above them a shot rang out, as clear and sharp and unexpected as a thunderclap on a clear summer's day.

The neon yellow splotch that was Arvid jerked, spun, and toppled from the Zodiac into the river.

CHAPTER TWENTY

He's been shot.

Realization was almost instantaneous. Gina screamed.

Or at least, Gina would have screamed. A scream tore into her throat. Whether she would have stopped herself before letting loose with it was something she was never destined to know: Cal's hand clamped tight over her mouth, smothering any sound before it could emerge. At the same time his arm shot around her waist and he yanked her against him.

"Shh," he hissed. Her back to his front, his hand still clamped over her mouth, he lifted her clean up off her feet with his arm around her waist and bounded a few yards up the steep, uneven rise behind them. She was tangentially impressed with his strength and agility even as her head swam with denial and her heart burst with pain. His fingers dug into the soft skin of her face.

His arm around her was so tight that it was difficult for her to breathe. She must have made some slight sound, because he whispered "Shh" again, fiercely, before pushing her down behind a formation of boulders and dropping to his knees beside her. A heartbeat later they were lying chest to chest on the rocky slope. Her back was pressed against a boulder, her face was buried in his coat and held in place by his hand on the back of her head, and his hard body covered hers. There was snow beneath them, a shallow drift that had gotten caught by the boulders. With her head pillowed on his arm, Gina was only aware of it because of its cushioning properties and the cold scrunch of it beneath her as they settled in.

Shock and horror held her immobile. The image of Arvid tumbling into the river replayed itself over and over in her mind's eye. Inside she was screaming. Cal's hand was no longer clamped over her mouth and she pressed her lips together to keep from making a sound. Her hands fisted in the front of his coat.

"Don't move." It was the merest breath of sound. The arm that he had wrapped around her tightened in silent warning an instant before she heard voices coming toward them and understood that someone

298

was hurrying down the path they'd just vacated. She felt something hard in the small of her back: the gun. Cal was holding the gun. *Aiming* the gun, presumably up toward where any attacker coming from the path would first appear. She could tell by the way the grip dug into her.

Fear shot through her, colder than the snow in which they lay.

"Penyal yego!" It was a man's voice, full of exuberant exclamation, speaking Russian that she was too rattled to even try to translate. Nearby, footsteps crackled on the icy crust that covered the path. Full recognition of the danger she and Cal were in hit, and Gina froze, lying as still as a corpse in his arms. Her heart raced wildly as another man, sounding like he was practically on top of them, replied in a congratulatory tone, *"Khorosho s'yemki."*

All of a sudden the gist of the Russian words came to her. They'd said something on the order of:

"I got him!"

"Good shooting."

Her stomach cramped with sudden nausea. Her pulse pounded so hard it made her dizzy.

The thud of footsteps, the sense of people passing nearby, the sound of more voices coming from farther away, farther down the slope, sent a fresh wave of fear through her. She could feel goose bumps rippling over her skin.

Cal lay heavily against her, his body as unyielding as a brick wall, the steady expansion and contraction of his chest as he breathed the only movement he made. He was big enough to both shield her completely if more bullets should start to fly, and hide her completely from view. She could feel the steel bands of his arms around her, the pressure of his muscular thighs against hers, the hard length of his shins, the slickness of the tops of his boots where her toes rested against them. His coat was rough against her cheek. The raucous honking of more geese overhead made Gina start, and his arm tightened around her once more in warning.

Gina didn't move again, barely breathed.

From the sound of it there were four men, all heading down toward the river.

Toward Arvid. Oh, God, he'd been murdered right before her eyes.

She couldn't help it: she started to shake.

Cal must have felt it, because his hold on her changed. His broad shoulders curved more closely around her. The hand pressing her face into his coat gentled. She thought she felt his cheek rest against the top of her head.

She held on to him like he was the only safe harbor left in the world.

She didn't know how much time passed before she felt him move. It felt like hours, but from the unchanged quality of light filtering through the fog when he shifted and she opened her eyes she guessed that it had been more like fifteen minutes. Much longer than that and it would have been growing dark. Darkness fell early on Attu.

He was pulling away from her as her eyes rose to meet his. His were narrowed, with a deadly glint in them. Hers, she felt sure, were dazed and traumatized.

Feeling dizzy, she sucked in air.

"Shh." He pressed a gloved finger to her lips and shook his head at her. She nodded in acknowledgment and almost reluctantly opened her fingers to release his coat from what had been her death grip on it.

In one fluid movement he sat up and rolled into a crouch. The gun ready in his hand, he looked over the rocks that had sheltered them.

Toward the river. Toward Arvid.

Gina felt the shakes coming back.

You are not that big a wuss. But then again, maybe she was.

Curling her legs beneath her, Gina cautiously sat up, brushed snow from her coat, breathed. White tendrils of mist slid past her, as cold on her face as ghostly hands. Gritting her teeth against the image of Arvid being shot that kept threatening to undermine her fragile calm, she did her best to banish the shakes, without entirely succeeding. The fine tremors that remained made her fingers slightly unsteady and her knees feel weak.

Crawling forward until she was kneeling next to Cal, she looked down toward the river, too.

She couldn't see it. Couldn't see much of anything. Couldn't hear much of anything. The distant murmur of voices, maybe? Or was that the wind, or the river? Impossible to tell: there was too much muffling, veiling fog.

Not being able to see the river, the boat, Arvid — oh, God, Arvid! — was probably a blessing. She caught herself praying that he wasn't dead.

He almost certainly was. She knew that. But that niggle of doubt made the urge to go rushing down to the river, to try to find him, to help him, almost impossible to resist.

But going down there was the best way

302

she could think of to make sure that she also ended up dead. She *knew* that.

Cal glanced at her. His face was all harsh planes and angles. With the black watch cap pulled low on his forehead and stubble darkening his square jaw, he looked fierce, lethal, and totally badass.

She was desperately thankful he was on her side. *Her* bear.

"We need to go." His voice was scarcely louder than a breath.

She nodded and murmured the only sensible answer she could give: "Yes."

Standing up, he held a hand down to her. Taking it, she let him lift her to her feet. The fog wrapped around them, hiding them, protecting them: it had become their friend. Sliding an arm around her to pull her close against his body, pushing her hood just far enough back to uncover an ear, he spoke almost directly into it. She could feel the warmth of his breath against the delicate whorls.

"I'm almost certain they're down there by the river." His voice was so quiet that if his mouth hadn't been right by her ear she wouldn't have been able to hear him. She leaned against him, letting him take most of her weight as her knees recovered their ability to keep her upright. Her hands lay flat against the front of his coat. She didn't grip him, didn't hold on. She refused to give in to the waves of anguish that assailed her, to the urge to blindly turn responsibility for her survival over to him. *I have to stay strong.* He continued, "We need to steer clear. Can we get to that cave you were talking about without going that way?"

She had to force her mind to function, force herself to think, but she did it with a fierce determination. She nodded. "The path forks up ahead. The way we need to take doesn't go to the river."

"Good. Go. Be as quiet and quick as you can. I'll be right behind you."

Gina turned and started walking. The first few steps required a major effort of will, but as she headed steadily away from the river, leaving got easier. As he had promised, Cal stayed right behind her. Again, she thought his intent was to block her from any bullet that might come their way. Nerves jumping, hideously conscious of every rattling pebble and crackling piece of ice underfoot, Gina went as quickly as she could, blessing the whoosh of the wind, the honking geese, even the distant murmur of the river that she couldn't see, because it masked the sounds of their passing from any unseen ears that might hear.

After what had happened to Arvid, she was all too horribly aware that death could explode out of nowhere at any time.

She couldn't let herself think about that, or about Arvid, or anything else. Not now, not while she needed all her concentration just to keep putting one foot ahead of the other.

Except for the occasional, nerve-racking moment when an unusually strong gust of wind swept through and lifted whole sections of it, the fog swirled around them, gray and thick. She knew that they probably owed their lives to it. It hid them, hid the marks their boots had to be leaving on the shell of ice and snow that covered the trail. They slipped through it as silently as possible. Listening intently, she continually searched the drifting banks of mist with frightened eyes, but nothing was there. She could see the trail for no more than a few feet in front of her; she was able to follow it only because she knew where it was and how it ran.

Snow began to fall, big, fat flakes that drifted down lazily at first, then came faster and faster. She welcomed it, knowing sufficient quantities would mask the marks of their passing. The temperature dropped until her face felt like it was freezing and each breath became a frigid assault on her lungs. Her feet got cold in her insulated boots. The wind picked up, whistling through the high passes, rushing down the slopes, blowing the fog and snow into wintry dust devils that rose like dervishes around them.

They reached Terrible Mountain as dusk fell, and began to climb. The rusted-out skeleton of a World War II–era vehicle — "A Weasel!" Cal murmured reverently upon spotting it — was overturned near where the almost invisible path to their destination branched off from the main trail. It was the landmark Gina knew to look for to find the way. The new path went almost straight uphill, and grew so steep and so slippery that Gina needed handholds in places to get to the next section. Thickening darkness made it hard to see by the time they reached the last little bit, and if she hadn't had the familiar growling rumble to guide her she might have missed the final turnoff. What she had once considered an inconvenience she now knew was a blessing: the cave was not on any trail. It would, she thought, be almost impossible for anyone who was unfamiliar with it to find.

"Wait." Cal stopped her with a hand on her arm when she would have scrambled up

through the rocks toward it. Looming close behind her, he was a tall, broad-shouldered, reassuringly solid shape in a gloomy world that had been rendered almost phantasmal by the mix of heavily falling snow and shifting fog. The purple twilight made his eyes look black as coal. His hard, handsome face was grim.

Holding her in place, his grip hard enough so that she could feel the imprint of his gloved fingers through her coat, he leaned down so that his mouth was at the approximate level of her ear.

"What the hell *is* that?" His voice was just loud enough so that she could hear him. She looked up at him with a frown.

"What?"

"That sound."

"Oh." She supposed that to anyone who hadn't heard it before, the continuous low, grinding *errm* coming from somewhere up ahead of them would sound ominous. To her, the sound was comforting: it reminded her of a giant cat purring. Lots of giant cats purring.

"Puffins," she said. "They have burrows all along here, among the rocks. That's how I found the cave."

"Birds? You've got to be kidding me." He released his hold on her.

Gina would have smiled in spite of herself, but her facial muscles were too frozen. "We're here," she told him, and started to climb.

Careful not to put her hands or feet into a burrow, catching glimpses of dozens of funny little red-beaked clown faces that were the puffins peering out at her anxiously as she passed, she ascended the black, snow-dusted, nearly vertical cliff until she reached the entrance to the cave. Impossible to see from the path, it had an unimpeded view of the valley where the LORAN station was located, and beyond it to the bay and sea. The entrance was tall and narrow, a slit in the rock no more than five feet wide that was all but hidden by a jutting stone formation beside it.

It was dark inside the cave, she saw as she hoisted herself through the opening, but not so dark that she couldn't see, at least for the first few yards. After that the cave was black as pitch.

It smelled faintly of earth and various other not unpleasant things she couldn't identify. There at the entrance it was still cold, but it was many degrees warmer than it was outside and she was out of the wind and snow and relatively safe and that was all she cared about for the moment. As Gina looked out, though, she discovered that there was a problem, or at least there would be from Cal's point of view: she could see nothing but a nearly impenetrable wall of blowing snow and heavy fog turned deep purplish-gray by the coming night. She couldn't even see the lights of the buildings at the camp, which she knew had to be on and shining through the windows.

Unless there was no one left in camp to keep the generator running, of course. Unless the bad guys had gone, and all that was left behind were corpses.

She shivered and did her best to push away the horrifying images that accompanied the thought.

Having crawled well out of the reach of the wind and snow, she sat, knees bent, resting against the wall with her head tilted back against the worn-smooth stone, and watched as Cal levered himself inside, then stood up to tower in the entrance.

"I can't see anything," Cal complained. He was looking out toward the camp, so she knew he was worried about their ability to watch for the plane that was presumably going to arrive at some point. Or maybe it already had arrived. She felt sure that they would have heard any plane flying low enough to land, but maybe she was wrong about that. Maybe they'd missed it, she thought hopefully. He added, "Not that there's a chance in hell a plane landed in this."

Another hope dashed. Since she didn't feel like arguing about his plan right then, she made a noncommittal sound.

He turned away from his unproductive contemplation of the deepening darkness to walk over to where she sat. She didn't glance up as he stood there looking down at her.

"You okay?" he asked.

"Yes."

He shrugged out of the backpacks. There was the slightest of twin thumps as he dropped them on the ground beside her, then hunkered down to unzip one. Her mouth was dry, and she thought about searching through one for water, but she was too tired and dispirited to move. They'd each eaten a second protein bar on the long march to Terrible Mountain, but the effects of that had worn off and she was hungry.

"You haven't been up inside here before?" He was looking at her. She could feel rather than see his gaze on her.

"No."

"All right." Twisting the cap off a bottle of water, he handed it to her and stood up.

Just because he'd assumed she wanted water didn't mean he could read her mind, she told herself. It simply meant that he could add two and two, as in, long walk coupled with arduous climb equals thirst. "I'm going to go check it out."

"I'll be right here."

He was holding a flashlight, she saw when he switched it on. Only the smallest sliver of light escaped, and she realized that he was taking care to mask it with his fingers, not that, given the weather, there was any real chance that so insignificant a light could be seen beyond the cave. The gun was in his other hand. Seeing it, she shivered.

"I won't be long," he said.

Gina didn't reply. Instead she took careful sips of her water and watched the receding narrow stripe of light as he headed down what seemed to be a long passage before hanging a left and disappearing from view. As she sat there listening to the wind and snow and puffins, she suddenly regretted not going with him. Alone in the dark, it was much harder to keep the ghosts at bay.

She thought of sunny California, her cheerful, comfortable condo, her mother, who lived with her second husband just a few miles from her. Her calm, sensible, unadventurous mother had been her father's

311

second wife (he'd been on his fourth at the time of his death) and, while Gina had had an older half sister from her father's first marriage — Becca, another natural-born adventurer who'd died in the plane crash — Gina was her mother's only child. She knew that if she didn't make it back, her mother would grieve forever.

The thought of her mother grieving made her chest tighten.

Just don't think.

Keeping her mind blank was a useful way to avoid being overwhelmed with emotion, she had learned.

An image of Arvid in his Day-Glo coat floating facedown in the river slid past her defenses.

Her stomach twisted. Had she left him behind to die?

Save yourself.

Her father's last words to her echoed through her head.

Once more, that's exactly what she had done: saved herself.

Gina's throat closed up. She scrunched her eyes shut, but it didn't help.

Hot tears slid down her cheeks.

Stop it, she ordered herself fiercely.

When the tears kept coming, she pushed her hood back and unzipped her coat and dried her cheeks on the edge of her thermal shirt. She took off her gloves and poured some of the water from the bottle into her cupped hand and splashed her face with it. Several times. It was cold, bracingly so.

That seemed to do the trick. The tears stopped. She dried her face on her shirt again, sniffed mightily, and dug in her pocket for her ChapStick, which she applied to her lips. It tasted of cherry, which was nice. Next she pulled her comb out and started methodically working the tangles out of her hair.

Concentrate on mundane tasks: another lesson learned in how to carry on after a tragedy.

She saw the stripe of light that was Cal coming back and pocketed her comb.

"This is a hell of a cave," he said when he reached her. The stripe of light hit her face, causing her to flinch. The light lingered, and she got the impression that he was staring hard at her.

She threw up a hand in protest.

"Would you turn that off?" Her voice was sharp.

He did. It was suddenly so dark that she could barely see him. He made a movement that she thought was him pocketing the gun. Easing down to sit beside her, he said, "You crying?"

Oh, God, she couldn't believe that he'd noticed what must be the telltale signs.

"No." Her voice was sharper than before.

"Thank God. Crying women scare the hell out of me."

That made her smile. A little. Reluctantly. "In that case, maybe I am."

She could feel him looking at her. Taking another drink of water, she concentrated on the wall opposite them instead of looking back. The wall she absolutely couldn't see because it was too dark.

He took the bottle from her, drank. He'd taken off his gloves, she saw. The better to handle a weapon? She didn't want to think about it.

"Want to talk about it?" he asked.

"No."

"Pretty upsetting, seeing your friend killed like that. Several of your friends."

"Who are you, Dr. Phil?"

"If you need me to be."

She shot him a look. Not that he saw it, she thought, or that she saw him as anything other than a solid patch of darkness looming beside her. He was being *nice,* and right now nice was something she couldn't take. Especially from him. He'd come out of the same mold as the bad guys chasing them, she was pretty sure. The only difference was that right now he happened to be on her side.

She said, "I don't need you to be anything. Except quiet."

He didn't reply, just meditatively sipped *her* water. Gina's eyes narrowed as it occurred to her that he was *waiting.* For her to break down and pour her heart out to him. Which wasn't going to happen.

"That's annoying," she said.

"What's annoying?"

"You. Sitting there like that."

"You mean, being quiet?" Was there a hint of humor in his voice? "I thought that's what you wanted me to do."

If he'd been able to see it, the look she turned on him then would have fried his eyeballs.

"Why don't you go explore more of the cave?"

"I don't like leaving you here alone in the dark."

"So give me a flashlight."

"It's the leaving you alone part I don't like."

For a moment, neither of them said anything more. He sipped more water. She tried to keep her mind blank. But his words sent a fresh niggle of fear slithering through the mental barriers she was busy erecting.

"You think somebody could be in here?" She cast a nervous glance toward the impenetrable darkness he'd just walked out of.

He shrugged. "Possible. Not likely. I didn't see signs that anybody's been here in years, and as far as I can work out, unless somebody already knew this cave was here, they haven't had time to find it. And they'd have no reason to be looking for it. We just got here ourselves, and they can't know that this is where we'd head."

That made her feel a little better.

"You think they'll find it?"

She could feel his shrug. "If they look long enough."

"It's pretty well hidden."

"Yeah."

From the tone of that, Gina gathered that he thought that wasn't an insurmountable barrier. He sipped more water. She tried, unsuccessfully, not to think.

"Do you think Arvid was dead?" She couldn't help it: the words pushed themselves out before she even knew she was going to say them, a result no doubt of the thought continually preying on her mind. "I mean, obviously he *is* dead. I know those men will have made sure of it. But do you think he was dead when we left him there

316

in the river?"

"Yep. Believe me, he was dead before he hit the water."

She slanted a look up at him. "How could you possibly know that?"

"I know, okay? Trust me, I know."

Funnily enough, she did trust that he knew, although what that said about him, and about her for not being horrified that she was sitting here so companionably with him, she didn't care to think about.

Still, she couldn't just leave it. She needed more. "How do you know? The tough-guy version of female intuition?"

"There wasn't a follow-up shot. If he'd still been alive when they reached him, there would have been."

To be fair, she'd asked the question. It was her own fault if the answer made her dizzy. Anyway, as horrible as that was to think about, it relieved her worst fear: that she'd run away and left her friend behind to die without even trying to help him. She let out the breath that she hadn't realized she'd been holding in what she hoped was a nearly soundless exhalation. To her chagrin, her lips trembled in the aftermath.

"Nothing you could have done," Cal added. She guessed that either he'd heard the sigh, or that with her face silhouetted against the marginally lighter entrance to the cave he could see her profile and had seen her lips tremble.

"I know that." She sounded defensive, she realized, and pressed her lips together to keep them from trembling *again*.

"He the reason you're crying? Arvid?"

"I'm not —" Gina began, her voice tight. But he knew better, and she knew he knew better, and suddenly she didn't feel like pretending anymore. "I hate that he died like that, okay? I hate the idea that I just ran away and *left* him to die like that."

To her horror, she felt tears welling up again and closed her eyes tightly to keep them from spilling over. When that didn't work, when tears slid down her cheeks despite everything she could do and she felt him looking at her, she scrambled to her feet and started blindly walking away, back the way he had come, into the darkness that was the interior of the cave.

CHAPTER TWENTY-ONE

"Gina," Cal called after her. "Hold up."

It was, literally, so dark that she couldn't see her hand in front of her face. Gina was having to feel her way along with her hand on the cold stone wall, but she didn't even slow down. Not that she was going very fast to begin with, but still.

The sliver of light caught up with her before she made it much farther along the narrow passage. He was right behind it, his arm brushing hers as he fell in beside her. Fortunately, she'd had just enough time to swipe her eyes with her shirt, and to get the damned tears under control.

With his fingers covering it, the flashlight provided no more than a minimal amount of illumination. Even with him walking right beside her she didn't think he could actually see her face. That being the case, she was glad of his presence. Or, more precisely, glad of the flashlight that was moving over the rough stone floor in front of them to illuminate the way, even if it only brightened up the darkness slightly. Otherwise she'd be worried about breaking her neck.

"I've got the flashlight. And the gun. You want to wait for me," he said.

She made a noncommittal sound. At least, she'd meant it to be a noncommittal sound. What actually came out, to her horror, was more like a sniffle.

She could feel Cal looking at her. Then he said, "You're right. You shouldn't have left him. You should have done what you threatened to do to me: gone all ninja assassin on those four heavily armed military types and saved your boyfriend. Except, wait, he'd been hit by a bullet from a sniper rifle and was already dead before anybody had time to do anything."

When he put it that way, the welling guilt she felt seemed absurd. But still she felt it, and sorrow and anger and fear as well, even as she struggled to push such useless emotions aside. Right now, she needed every bit of focus she could summon just to keep going.

Her reply had an edge to it. "Arvid isn't — wasn't — my boyfriend. He was a friend, and a colleague, that's all. Doesn't mean I can't grieve for him. And Mary and Jorge and all the others, too."

"You absolutely should grieve for them. But you shouldn't feel guilty about something that wasn't your fault and that you couldn't have prevented no matter what you did."

Having him nail her on the guilty part bothered her. She didn't like that he had such an accurate read on what she was feeling. They didn't know each other in any substantive, real-life way, and that was how she wanted to keep it. A man like him — well, he wasn't for confiding her deepest, most personal secrets in.

A sudden petrifying thought made her stop dead and pivot to face him. "We have to find Keith Hertzinger — I think it's Keith who's still alive; his gear was missing from his cubby — and warn him. Oh, my God, I can't believe I didn't think about that sooner. Arvid might still be alive if I'd thought to try to warn him." She fixed unblinking eyes on Cal as it hit her that Keith could at any time be shot by assassins he didn't even know were stalking him, or blindly walk in on the murderous situation at the camp just as she had done, or — the possibilities were endless. She grabbed Cal's arm. "He should have his radio with him. We have to find a radio." She shook her head at her own missing of the obvious. "I should've thought to look for a radio before we ran out of the building earlier. I'm sure there was one in there. I could have warned Arvid and —"

"We'd be dead," Cal interrupted before she finished. "If you'd managed to do that, you would have led them right to us. The radio frequencies are being monitored, remember?"

The reminder was so appalling that Gina could only stare up at him. With the flashlight beam pointed at the ground and casting long upward shadows, he looked almost impossibly tall and intimidating. Menacing, even. Only, she discovered, she wasn't the least bit afraid of him anymore.

For better or worse, she discovered with a degree of dismay, he was just Cal to her now.

"I have to warn Keith." Her voice was tight with determination.

"No, you don't." As Gina opened her mouth to argue he added, "There's no way we can. We don't have a radio, and anyway radios are out. We could try flashing Morse code signals at him out the door of the cave with the flashlight, but they're a hell of a lot more likely to be seen by the people looking for us than by your friend. Or did you mean to just start screaming his name from the mountaintop and hope he shows up?"

"We could go looking for him." Ignoring his sarcasm, Gina did her best to recall the details of Keith's research project. "I think I know where he might be."

"We're not going anywhere." Cal's voice was grim.

Gina's brows snapped together. "You don't get to tell me what I'm going to do."

Dropping his arm, she turned away to head back toward the entrance. She wasn't going to leave the cave. Upset as she was, she wasn't totally stupid, and given that it was now fully night and freezing cold and there was a snowstorm and killers on the loose, she recognized that she was confined to the cave until at least daylight. But she wanted to get her bearings, to see whether she could look out into the darkness and remember where Keith had been working that day. To see whether she could think of some way to get a message to him.

If he was even still alive. Her stomach knotted and her fists clenched as she faced up to that. Probably he wasn't. Probably she was the only one left —

When Cal's arm snaked around her waist and he yanked her back against him, that was the thought that made her whirl in the hard circle of his arm and shove her palms furiously into his chest and snarl, "Damn you, let me go."

"Not a chance," he said through his teeth. Shoving the flashlight in his pocket so that only the smallest, dimmest circle of illumination surrounded them, he grabbed her wrists and backed her up against the wall and pinned her hands to it on either side of her head and leaned into her, holding her in place with the solid weight of his body. "Let's get something straight right now: I told you I was going to get you out of this alive and I mean to do it. So yeah, until then, I do get to tell you what you're going to do. Every step of the way."

"Get off me." Gina struggled to free herself. It took only a moment for her to figure out that she was wasting her time: she wasn't getting away until he chose to let her go. But in the process she became all too keenly aware of how truly big and muscular he was, of how firm and unyielding his body felt against hers, of how warm and strong the hands imprisoning hers were — and of how vulnerable she apparently was to his particular brand of way-too-aggressive masculinity.

She was furious at him. Spitting mad.

But the feel of him against her was turning her on. The weight of his body holding her more or less helplessly against the wall was making her feel things she hadn't felt in years. The crush of his chest against her breasts made them tighten and tingle with pleasure. The hardness of his thighs against hers gave her an electric thrill. The unmistakable bulge between them was large and urgent enough to be felt through the combined layers of their clothes, and it excited her more than she ever would have believed was possible.

He held her fast, his big body pressing her back against the wall, and she felt a shaft of desire so intense that she shivered.

Everywhere his body touched hers she burned.

She only realized that she'd quit struggling and was standing perfectly still, staring up at him with God knew what expression, when his face, which had been taut with anger, changed. His eyes narrowed and the tension that had thinned his mouth into a straight line eased and —

He bent his head and kissed her.

Taken by surprise, she had no time to formulate a defense. Her lips fluttered beneath the first soft brush of his, and then they parted to let him in. It wasn't a gentle kiss. What started out as a testing, a tasting, a question on his part, changed the moment she answered, the moment he felt her response. That was when his mouth turned hard and hungry and demanding, and he started kissing her like he could never get enough of her mouth. The blast of heat he ignited inside her blew her away. Her heart pounded. Her pulse raced.

She closed her eyes and kissed him back as if she'd been dying to have him kiss her like that. Her lips molded themselves to his and her tongue answered his as he learned everything there was to know about her mouth. He kissed her with a carnality that was like nothing she had ever experienced, and fireworks went off against the screen of her closed lids. Bones melting, senses reeling, she kissed him back the same way. When he let go of her wrists to wrap his arms around her and pull her even closer against him, she slid her hands up over his broad shoulders and curled them around his neck, and clung to him like her life depended on it.

Which, she thought with some irony, it actually did.

He took her mouth again and again, in a series of long, slow, drugging kisses that stripped away every last ounce of her reserve, that made her head spin, that made her body pulse and burn, that had her kissing him back just as fervently. He kissed her like he was starving for the taste of her, like he never meant to stop.

She didn't want him to stop. Arching up against him, she told him so in every way she possibly could that didn't involve words.

Words were beyond her. Thoughts were beyond her. All she could do was feel. She was on fire for him. Wild for him. Molding herself to the sturdy contours of his body, she moved her hips suggestively against the granite-like hardness of him. He made a low, guttural sound under his breath and pushed her back against the wall, rocking into her, letting her feel the unmistakable proof of how aroused he was, making her gasp for breath, turning the hot, sweet throbbing that was building inside her into a raging conflagration.

Her coat was open: his hand found and covered her breast through the thin layers of her shirt and bra. Her nipple hardened instantly against his palm. Lightning bolts of desire shot through her, and her kisses turned feverish with need. He caressed her breasts, ran his thumb over her nipples, back and forth, slow and sure. Her knees threatened to buckle and she moaned into his mouth.

Until then she'd never thought that she

was capable of something as primitive as pure, unadulterated lust. Now she knew that she was.

When his hand slipped beneath her shirt to slide up over her rib cage, she went all soft and gooey inside with anticipation. His hand was big and warm and faintly abrasive and unmistakably male, and the feel of it moving against her soft skin made her quake. It slid over the silkiness of her bra to cover her breast and she quivered and pressed closer, loving the size of it, the hardness of it, the heat.

He pushed her bra up out of his way.

When he fondled her bare breast, his touch set off a firestorm inside her. When his hand flattened on her softness and her nipple jutted into the hot plane of his palm, her body clenched and her heart raced and her blood turned to steam.

"I want you." He growled it into her ear.

Oh, God, she wanted him, too. So badly that she was ready to tear off her clothes and lie down right there on the floor of the cave and —

The cave.

Oh, no. Oh, wait.

She'd forgotten where they were. *Who* they were.

His mouth crawled down the smooth

column of her neck. The warm, firm pressure of his lips and the wet slide of his tongue felt incredible. He caressed her breasts like he owned them, like they were his to do with as he pleased. The heat and hardness of his hand made her arch up against him, made her clutch his shoulders and breathe like she'd been running for miles, made her go all light-headed and melty inside.

She knew where he was headed: he'd shoved her shirt and bra up so that her breasts were bared to him. His hand shifted to cup her breast, to hold it ready for his mouth. Her nipple was tight and eager as it waited to feel his lips, his tongue. The mere thought of it turned her insides to jelly.

He would kiss her breasts and then he would —

No. No. No.

"Cal. Cal, no. Stop." She could barely force the words out.

His open mouth burned against the base of her throat where it curved into her shoulder, right above the modest crew neckline of her shirt. It stayed where it was, all moist heat and urgent demand, while his hand tightened on her breast. His thumb swept with slow deliberation across her nipple.

A jolt of longing made her shiver. She made a tiny, helpless sound of pleasure. Her hands were on his shoulders, her fingers digging into the smooth shell of his coat, but she couldn't summon the strength to even try to push him away. She ached and burned for him.

With every cell in her body, she wanted him to —

"Cal. I can't." Her protest was breathless. Unconvincing. Weak.

His hand stilled on her breast. With an audible indrawing of breath he lifted his head to look down at her.

His eyes were black with passion. His face was hard and flushed with it. His mouth — she couldn't look at his mouth. She wanted it on her body too badly.

"I can't," she said again, meeting his gaze, knowing that her eyes had to look drugged with desire and that her lips were ripe and swollen from his kisses: a face that said yes even as she told him no.

His eyes blazed down at her. His breath hissed out through his teeth.

The steeliness of his arm around her held her fast against him. There would be no easy escape if he didn't choose to release her. His body was as unyielding as the stone wall at her back. She could feel the urgency in him, the depth of his need. The air around them was electric with arousal. It crackled with the promise of sex.

His eyes flickered down, and she realized that he was looking at her breasts. Pale in the dim light, they were round as tennis balls and taut with anticipation. Her nipples were dark, puckered, and obviously eager. Curled around her breast, his hand looked deeply tan and very masculine. His big thumb rested right beside her nipple.

The sight was so erotic that she caught her breath. With every cell in her body, she wanted to change her mind, to pull his head down and —

She watched as his hand dropped, and felt a sharp stab of regret.

Their eyes met. She had no idea what he saw in hers, but his were heavy-lidded and burning hot. That steely arm tightened around her for the briefest of moments. Then he let her go and walked away, just a few long strides but far enough, before stopping with his back to her.

Gina was left leaning against the wall, breathing hard, her body still smoldering inside as she looked at his tall, broad-shouldered form with fierce longing. Pulling her clothes down, adjusting them, she fought to banish the physical yearning that pulsed through her in an urgent, relentless rhythm. She wanted him. Badly. Nothing about that had changed.

With every rational brain cell she possessed she knew, as well as she'd ever known anything, that she was doing the right thing in calling a halt. Her incendiary response to his lovemaking had made it abundantly clear to her that she was hungry for sex. Nothing so surprising about that: it was, in fact, a good thing, a sign that she was fully emerging into life again. But however hot Cal might make her, he was absolutely not the right man for her to jump back in the sexual waters with. She wanted sex in the context of a relationship, and what she wanted in a relationship was a man who was kind and gentle and affectionate and, above all, *there.* A man who did ordinary things, who went to work at an ordinary job, with whom she could build an ordinary life.

Not a hard-eyed, hard-muscled mercenary who'd just killed a man and who'd gotten her friends killed and was probably going to get her killed before he died himself. At best, he could be counted on to provide her with a bout or two or three of steamy sex before disappearing from her life.

She knew herself: if she had sex with Cal she'd get attached to him, and if she got attached to him she'd wind up trying to put the pieces of her broken heart back together all over again.

How totally stupid would she have to be, to open herself up to something like that?

Probably, if she survived this and made it back home, she ought to try dating again, she decided.

In the meantime, she needed to get her act together and deal with the man in front of her.

Cal hadn't moved. The rigidity of his back made her stomach muscles tighten. His hands were curled into fists at his sides. It occurred to her that she actually knew very little about him — such as how he took rejection. Was he angry or —

Her hands were unsteady as — in instinctive, unthinking reaction to what had just happened between them rather than because of the temperature, which this far into the cave was relatively mild — she zipped her coat back up. The metallic sound it made was jarring to her senses. He heard it, too: she saw his head lift.

"Cal." Her voice was husky. It didn't help that her bra now felt about two sizes too small, or that her mouth still tingled from his kisses, or that the hungry throbbing deep inside her hadn't abated.

He turned to look at her. Since the flashlight was tucked in his pocket still, the small circle of illumination surrounded him. She was able to see his face, while hopefully she was deeper in shadow and he couldn't see hers well enough to read anything in it. His eyes were still black and hot. His mouth was iron with control. His body radiated tension.

His eyes slid over her, registering, she could tell, her zipped-up coat. He said, "Hmm?" without any intonation at all.

She took a breath. "Can we talk?"

"About what?" There was a harshness to his voice that confirmed, as if any confirmation was necessary, that he was still at least as turned on as she was.

Her lips compressed. "About what just happened. About the fact that we — kissed. About why I can't let it go any farther."

He took a breath. It was deep and ragged enough that she both saw and heard it. When he spoke, his voice was slightly less harsh than before. "You have a perfect right to call a halt anytime you want. I'm fine with it, okay? So is there anything else you want to talk about?"

She searched his face. Those ruggedly handsome features could have been carved from stone for all the emotion they revealed.

Yet she could see the enormous amount of self-control he was exercising in everything from the curl of his fingers to the tension in his stance.

She said, "I'd really like to know what you're feeling."

He made a sound that was the grim equivalent of a derisive hoot. "So who's playing at being Dr. Phil now?"

"I'm not playing at anything."

His eyes were black and unfathomable as they held hers. "You want to know what I'm *feeling*? Fine, I'll tell you. How about — horny?"

At the sudden blast of heat that flamed at her from his eyes, the world seemed to tilt on its axis. She couldn't tear her gaze from his. The truth, the horrible, incontrovertible truth, was that she felt the exact same way, although she would never have put it so crudely. Plus her state was specific to him, while she guessed that for him being sexually aroused was probably something way more frequent and generic, as in, any young and reasonably attractive woman in his vicinity would do. But to her dismay she discovered that giving a name to what she was feeling only seemed to make the condition worse. If he came toward her now, if he took her in his arms and kissed her again, she wasn't sure she'd have the strength to call a halt a second time.

"You don't have to look so worried." His voice was dry. She abandoned the hope that he could not see and read her expression. Obviously he could. "I'm not going to jump you. What just happened was an accident."

Gina frowned. "You make it sound like we had a car wreck."

"That pretty much sums it up, doesn't it?" Pulling the flashlight out of his pocket, he masked its brightness with his hand and gestured down the passage with it. "Come on, let's go."

Gina didn't move. She was having to work to keep her breathing even. Her body was still all soft and shivery with arousal and, despite how ready he seemed to be to dismiss what had just happened, electricity still arced palpably between them. None of which was good for achieving the kind of working partnership that she felt their situation called for. Striving for honesty, she also wanted to do what she could to clear the air. Their survival — *her* survival — might depend on it.

"Cal, listen: I loved what we just did. It was good. Great, actually. That was some truly impressive making out." Watching his face tighten, she hesitated. When she continued her tone was earnest. "It's just — I can't go any farther. I can't get involved with you."

His eyes narrowed. After a moment he said, "Honey, there's a big difference between getting it on and getting involved. And that thing we just did? It falls smack dab into the category of getting it on."

That whole speech, from the generic "honey" to the getting-it-on shot, made the hackles rise on the back of Gina's neck. Clearly he hadn't liked what she'd just said. Well, she didn't like his reply right back.

"All right," she said, her tone several degrees cooler. "I can't *get it on* with you."

"Probably a good call under the circumstances. How about we forget it ever happened?"

Gina nodded, nettled but trying not to show it. "Consider it forgotten."

Her knees still felt wobbly, but she managed to step away from the wall. Not for anything was she going to let him know how shell-shocked she still felt from the intensity of the desire he had roused in her. There was no future in wanting him: she not only could not, she *would not* let this thing — the blazing sexual attraction, the tentative friendship, the building trust, whatever it was that the sum of those parts added up to

— simmering between them grow into anything more.

The truth was, there was no way he would be in her life beyond Attu.

Provided they even survived Attu.

That thought was the wake-up call, the reality check she needed as she walked toward him. Forget sex; think survival, she told herself grimly. It was enough to at least cool her blood a little, and to take the hot, shivery feelings that she still couldn't seem to rid herself of down to a manageable level.

Without waiting for her to reach him, he turned and started walking away, heading down the passage with the sliver of light skipping ahead of him.

"I still want to warn Keith," she said to his retreating back. It was absolutely true, but it was also in the nature of underscoring the fact that she hadn't given in: she might be walking after him now rather than walking away as she'd been doing before he'd grabbed her and they'd kissed, but that did not mean he was the one calling the shots. Necessarily. Only if she agreed with what he suggested. She'd spent most of a lifetime giving in to people who thought they knew best, against her better judgment, and she wasn't about to make that mistake again.

"We've had this conversation." He flung that over his shoulder at her.

"Yes, we have." Her tone was sugar sweet. "And nothing's changed."

That stopped him. He turned to wait for her. "I meant what I said."

She smiled at him. "And I meant what I said: you don't get to tell me what to do."

"Honey, I'm bigger than you, and badder than you, and way more experienced with living through the kind of situation we're dealing with here than you. So I think that makes me the one in charge."

"I am absolutely prepared to listen to everything you have to say. And make my own decisions on the basis of your recommendations."

He snorted. "Be careful I don't let you live with that."

"Is that a threat? Because I'm not impressed." With a glinting look thrown his way, she walked on past him into the dark. "And don't call me honey," she added over her shoulder. The flashlight beam danced ahead of her, pointing the way down what seemed to be a long, narrow passage.

He caught up with her. She flicked a glance up at him to find that his eyes glinted and his jaw was hard.

"You don't like 'honey'?" There was steel

in his voice. "As long as you're doing what I tell you, I'll call you anything you want: baby, sugar, darling, sweetheart —"

"Gina," she snapped. "If you can't manage that, Dr. Sullivan works. And I'll do what you tell me just as long as I agree that it's the best thing to do."

Their eyes met and clashed. The air was suddenly charged with hostility. Or, to be more exact, hostility infused with sex. Because the sparks were definitely still there.

"*Gina,*" he said with elaborate emphasis. "Do you honestly believe that you have a snowball's chance in hell of getting yourself off this island alive without me?"

The passage crooked to the left again and sloped downward. Gina rested a hand on the smooth stone of the wall as she negotiated the turn. "I think waiting for rescue might be our best option."

He made an impatient sound. "If you 'wait for rescue,' you'll wind up dead."

"Sooner or later someone is going to come looking for us," she argued stubbornly. "I think we should hide until then."

"Yeah. No." His tone said *Discussion over.* "You saved my life. I'm going to do my level best to save yours. Which means we're getting the hell off this island just as quick as we can."

340

"What about escaping by boat?"

He shook his head. "We have a thousand miles of ocean to cross. We'd be caught before we got anywhere near land."

"There are other islands around. Attu is part of a chain. And the Commander Islands are only a few hundred miles away."

"The Commander Islands are Russian territory, and the rest of the Aleutians are deserted. If we even made it to any of them, which I doubt we would because they'll be coming after us with everything they have, we'd be in the same position there as we are here. Running and hiding until they find and kill us." He gave her an assessing look. "I can fly us out of here. Trust me."

The sad thing about it was, she did. Trust him. About wanting to save her life, at least. Not that it made any difference as to how she felt. Stealing a plane and trying to fly away in it to safety sounded . . . undoable. Her heart sank at the prospect.

I could tell him, she thought, but outside of the accident investigators who'd come to her in the hospital and the therapist who'd helped her at least put the memories in a box, she had never talked about the plane crash in detail to anyone. Not even to her mother, who she knew didn't really want to know, and whom she didn't want to burden.

Even now, all these years later, the memories had the power to make her feel sick and weak and dizzy, and she'd learned that the only way to cope was to avoid them at all costs. Anyway, strictly apart from her phobia, she thought that his escape plan was a really, really bad idea. That thousand miles of ocean he'd said they had to cross by boat? The distance didn't change just because they were in a plane.

"You do whatever you want. I'm going to hide. *And* try to warn Keith."

There was a moment of charged silence as her words hung in the air. The air in the cave had changed subtly, Gina noted as, ignoring the darkening face of the man who was now a step behind her, she followed the flashlight beam around a pile of fallen rocks. Deep into the mountain as they now had to be, it was drier, and warmer, and outside sounds were nonexistent. When she reached out to touch the wall the stone felt cool rather than cold, and bone dry.

"This is you being pissed at me because I kissed you and got you hot, isn't it?" Cal's voice grated as he caught up to her. She refused to look at him, so she couldn't be sure, but she thought he was scowling at her: a man on the brink of losing his temper. "What's the big deal about that anyway?

Are you married or something?"

The question hit her like a blow to the stomach. She winced before she could stop herself.

"No." Her voice was sharp.

"Oh, yeah? Then what's with the face you just made? And why did you say you *can't* get it on with me? Sounds like married-woman guilt to me."

She glared at him. "I'm a widow, okay?"

"A widow." His eyes flickered, slid over her. "How old are you?"

"Twenty-eight."

"How long has your husband been dead?"

Gina focused her gaze straight ahead. Except for the small circle of stone floor revealed by the flashlight beam, there was nothing to see but pitch darkness. "I don't want to talk about it."

"But, see, I do." She could feel his eyes on her. "You want to tell me how long, or do you want me to start guessing?" He paused, seemed to wait, then continued: "A year? Two?"

"Five years," she snapped.

"You've been a widow for five years."

"I just said that, didn't I?"

"How'd he die?"

"I *really* don't want to talk about it."

"How'd he die, Gina?"

She shot him a furious glance. "My God, can't you just let it alone?"

"No. He must have been young. In his twenties? So probably an accident. Did he die in an accident?"

She felt the floor start to tilt beneath her. To keep from stumbling, she had to stop walking and put a hand on the wall to steady herself.

Cal stopped, too. He loomed up beside her, frowning down at her. She refused to look at him.

"What kind of accident?" he persisted.

"It was a plane crash," she said, and closed her eyes as the darkness started to shimmy around her.

"Ah," Cal said, adding something that she couldn't quite hear, because the blood pounding in her ears drowned everything else out. Her heart raced and her stomach churned. Leaning against the wall, she took a deep, even breath as she fought to get herself under control again. Then she gritted her teeth, opened her eyes, and shoved away from the wall. Chin up, ignoring his frowning gaze, she took a few tentative steps. Her knees felt so weak that she had to stop and lean against the wall again.

"It's all right, I've got you," she heard him say over the drumming in her ears. He

344

wrapped an arm around her shoulders, slid the other one beneath her knees, and scooped her up in his arms. Then he started walking with her.

CHAPTER TWENTY-TWO

I'm fine, put me down, is what Gina wanted to say, but she didn't, because she couldn't.

Her throat was too tight to allow her to say anything at all.

She didn't struggle, either.

Instead she looked at his hard, masculine features and realized to her dismay that in his arms was exactly where she wanted to be. She felt safe there. That wasn't good, and she knew it, but at the moment she was too upset to even try to police what she was feeling. Giving up, she hooked her arms around his neck and rested her head on his wide shoulder and closed her eyes, working on getting her equilibrium back even as she surrendered to the novel experience of having a man take care of her. He smelled of snow and the outdoors, and he carried her as if she weighed nothing at all. After a few moments in which she resisted acknowledging it, she broke down and silently admitted that she found his display of easy strength mind-blowingly sexy. It appealed to some primitive part of her that she'd never even suspected existed.

She had to face it: *he* appealed to some primitive part of her that she'd never even suspected existed.

He's not for you, she warned herself even as she relaxed in his hold.

But she tightened her arms around his neck anyway. The hard muscularity of his arms, the wide expanse of his chest, the solid breadth of his shoulders cradled her, and for just that little span of time she was prepared to let them.

A few minutes later he stopped walking. She opened her eyes to discover that the flashlight that he still held lit up a wooden door set into the stone. The door was ajar, and Gina was still blinking at it in surprise as, stepping carefully over what was apparently a threshold, he carried her through it.

Her head came up off his shoulder as she looked around, wide-eyed.

Surprise gave her her voice back as Cal played the flashlight over their surroundings: a large natural cavern with a soaring domed roof and — furniture?

He'd said it was a hell of a cave.

"What is this place?"

But even as she asked the question, she knew what it had to be, or at least what its purpose once was: she'd studied up on Attu before arriving. The Japanese had used the extensive cave system that riddled the mountains to hide from, and launch sneak attacks on, the numerically superior American forces. The Americans had been forced into fighting a guerrilla war in which they'd ended up claiming most of the caves for themselves.

"Looks to me like it was used as a military barracks at one time," Cal replied. He seemed to be striding toward a particular target — an old metal table surrounded by four folding metal chairs, still set up as if whoever had last used them had merely stepped away for a short period. The dust covering them was the only indication that they'd waited like that for a long, long time, Gina saw as the flashlight beam hit them. A moment later Cal nudged a chair out from under the table with his boot, lowered her feet to the ground so that he could pick it up and shake the dust off it, then settled her into it.

"Don't move," he told her. Dropping the backpacks on the ground beside her, he walked away.

Left alone in what was — except for the

bobbing flashlight beam that was moving steadily away from her — pitch darkness, she instantly missed his arms around her, instantly felt cold and bereft. Folding her arms over her chest, she tracked his movements by watching the flashlight. But then the flashlight went stationary, as if he'd put it down on something, while she could still hear him moving around.

"Cal."

"I'm right here." His words were accompanied by a series of scratching sounds. The faint scent of sulfur had just reached her nose when a match flared to life. A moment later the tiny flame found its way into a storm lantern, and the area around it was lit by a spreading glow. The flashlight beam vanished.

The lantern, metal-framed and glass-sided with a single fat candle inside, came toward her. Cal was carrying it, and he set it down in the middle of the table.

"What happened to the flashlight?" Gina asked. She was glad to focus on the here and now, and practical things. If she could do it, she would stuff everything that had happened from the time she'd pulled him out of the sea until this moment into a mental box and never think of it again.

Except, maybe, for his kisses. And the way

his kisses made her feel.

"It's in my pocket. I turned it off to save the batteries."

"Good idea." She was looking around.

"I thought so," he replied. She could feel him studying her. He was standing right beside her: with her peripheral vision, she could see his long, muscular legs, his over-size black boots, mere inches from her own. She was not, she discovered, quite ready to look up and meet his gaze. Uneasy as it made her to recognize it, the dynamic between them had changed. The sexual charge was unmistakable, but with it was a new sense of emotional intimacy that she actually found more disturbing.

The last thing in the world she meant to let herself do was develop feelings for this man.

"Feeling better?" he asked, and the gravelly rasp of his voice slid over her like a lover's touch.

She actually shivered. From nothing more than the sound of his voice.

This is ridiculous, she told herself sternly, and lifted her eyes to meet his even as she responded with a cool "Yes, thanks."

His eyes were impossible to read in the flickering, uncertain light. His face likewise revealed nothing. His mouth was unsmiling.

Grave, even.

Sexy.

Gina found that she couldn't look at it, because looking at it made her pulse quicken and her body start to tighten deep inside. She had an instant, involuntary flashback to those blistering kisses. Heat flashed through her.

Rattled, she glanced away.

"You really did mean a barracks," she said, with equal parts surprise and satisfaction at finding a neutral topic of conversation, as her gaze lit on what looked like stacks of broken-down metal bed frames piled against one wall.

"Looks like it." He moved away from her, and her breath escaped in a soundless sigh of relief.

The farthest reaches of the cavern were deep in shadow, but she could see that more chairs like the one she was sitting on were piled against another wall, along with a number of folded tables, a stack of wooden pallets, and a row of metal garbage cans with the lids on. Open metal shelving held a hodgepodge of objects. Everything was covered with the fine silt that was the cave version of dust. But the room was dry and surprisingly warm and there was light.

Cal closed the door — he had to lift it by

the handle to get it to move, and the hinges squeaked in protest — and returned to stand by the table just a few feet away. Knowing that avoiding doing so would reveal more than she wanted to, she met his gaze in what was meant to be a casual glance. From the thoughtful expression on his face as he returned her look, she figured he was on the brink of initiating a serious conversation. She tensed, wary about what the topic might be.

She did not want to talk about David. Or the plane crash that had killed her family. Or anything hard or painful. She was tired to the point of exhaustion, aching in every muscle, scared to death, shaken, grieving — and so aware of Cal that she could feel her body tightening just because he was near.

"We should be okay here until daylight," he said. She got the feeling that it wasn't what he'd intended to say, and wondered what he'd read in her face.

"That's good," she replied, grabbing on to the neutral topic gratefully.

He'd removed the watch cap and was running a hand over his hair. It looked seal black in the uncertain light. His eyes looked black, too, as they moved over her in an assessing way that worried her as she tried to work out what he was thinking. The chiseled planes and angles of his face were harsh with shadows. He looked tired and wired and big as a tractor trailer and tough as nails — and so handsome that her heart beat a little faster just from looking at him.

This is bad. You cannot *fall for him.*

She found herself watching as he pressed a hand against his coat just below his waist, and immediately had the distraction she needed.

"Are you bleeding?" She frowned as she nodded toward his wound, which was what he was pressing his hand against through the layers of his coat and other clothes, she knew. "You probably tore the wound open carrying me."

And how was that for being matter-of-fact about something that still had her pulse tripping?

He lifted his brows at her. "Honey — oh, sorry, *Gina* — you're not that heavy. And if you think that's the most strenuous thing I've done all day, you obviously missed something." As she acknowledged the truth of that with a little grimace, he unzipped his coat and pulled up yesterday's crumpled and dried-stiff shirt to peer down and probe at the Band-Aids still adhering to his honed abdomen. As she blinked in bemused admiration at the strip of tanned, hard-muscled flesh thus exposed, he added, "It's not bleeding, I don't think. It hurts some, is all. Not enough to worry about."

"Let me look at it," she said, resigned to getting as up close and personal as tending his wound required despite the fact that, right at this moment, the idea of touching his bare skin set off all kinds of warning bells in her head.

To her surprise, and relief, he shook his head. Dropping his shirt, he looked at her semihumorously. "Weren't you the one who said something along the lines of 'getting shot is supposed to hurt'?"

She was, but she now discovered that she didn't like the idea of him hurting. Worse, she didn't like the idea that she didn't like the idea of him hurting. What that told her was that she really was starting to get in too deep with him, and her poor damaged heart recoiled at the thought. Under different circumstances she would have *insisted* on looking more closely at his wound, but, worried by the turn their association was taking, she glanced down at the backpacks instead and said in a neutral tone, "You should probably take some Tylenol. There should be some in the first aid kits."

"I will," he said. Even though she was no longer looking at him, she could feel him watching her like a cat at a mouse hole, and it made her uncomfortable. To forestall the conversation she knew in her bones was coming, she hurried into speech again.

"We need to eat." She tried to remember what she'd shoved into the backpack during her fraught foray through the kitchen cabinets. "Something besides protein bars."

"You're right." He crouched beside the backpacks, unzipped one, and started rummaging around inside it. That brought him close enough so that she could have laid her hand against his bristly cheek — and the unnerving part was, she wanted to. He pulled out a first aid kit and handed it to her. "You fish out the Tylenol, and I'll find us some food."

"Okay." As she accepted the plastic box their fingers brushed, and instantly electricity shot through her. Her fingers withdrew noticeably too fast, their eyes collided, and something in the depths of his woke butterflies in her stomach. The desire in them was unmistakable, but there was more than that, and it was the *more* that scared her. Neither of them said a word, but contained in that exchange of looks was a silent acknowledgment that things had changed between them: they had forged a connection, a bond, that hadn't existed before.

Unnerved, Gina hastily broke eye contact, opening up the first aid kit and delving inside it for a packet of Tylenol. When she came up with one he was no longer looking at her, but instead was pulling more items from the backpack.

"Tylenol," she announced, waving the packet.

"Thanks." Taking it from her, he ripped the little package open, popped the pills in his mouth, and swallowed.

"You don't need water?" Gina asked, scandalized.

"Nah." He went back to searching through the backpack and she set the first aid kit on the table.

"I forgot a can opener." Chagrined, Gina followed his movements as he pulled out cans of tuna, soup, and beef stew, followed by a rolled bundle of clothing. From what she could see of it, the clothes were the generic white tee and black sweatpants that came in the backpacks, which was good because that meant she couldn't identify whose backpack it was from the clothing in it. Which didn't prevent her from suffering a fresh pang of horror and grief over the fate of her friends. The thought of which she immediately did her best to banish: right now her emotions were too close to the surface for her to do anything but keep resolutely moving forward. There would be time later to mourn — if she survived.

Cal reclaimed her attention by tossing the bundle of clothes in her lap.

"I'll see about the food," he said, and nodded in the direction of an arched opening in the stone wall opposite the door. "If you want to wash up, there's hot water in there. I think they used that area as a bathroom. Here, take the flashlight."

"Hot water?" Instantly dazzled, Gina reached for the flashlight even as she glanced wide-eyed in the direction he'd indicated.

Cal nodded. "Why do you think this room is so warm?"

"How is that even possible?" Gina was already on her feet, clothes tucked under her arm, flashlight beam leading the way as she headed off to check it out.

"Looked like a natural spring to me," he called after her.

Turned out it was indeed a natural spring, a hot spring, bubbling up through the rock into a time-worn depression about the size of a kitchen sink that nature had carved into the floor. As the flashlight illuminated it, Gina eyed it with delight. At some point in the past, someone had put up pipes connected to an overhead can contraption that appeared to be designed to work as a shower, but the pipes were rusted and she had a healthy mistrust of what might lurk in the can, so she decided not to test it. There was also a crude toilet in a corner, the workings of which she refused to think about even as she used it. Afterward, kneeling on the smooth stone beside the hot spring, she cautiously checked the water: hot but not dangerously so, fresh, with only the slightest tang of minerals.

At that point, a spa tub at the Ritz-Carlton couldn't have looked better to her.

When she unrolled the bundle of clothes, a ziplock bag with a hotel-size bar of soap, a folded washcloth, a mini toothpaste, and a new travel toothbrush fell out.

Her cup runneth over.

"You stay out of here," she called to Cal, whose answering grunt at least told her that he'd heard.

That was all she needed: she stripped, and bathed, and rinsed out her undies and hung them up to dry on a pipe, which, given that both her bra and underpants were flimsy nylon, she expected they would do in a few hours. She hadn't realized how grungy she'd been feeling until she was clean and dressed again in the tee, which was of the Hanes underwear variety, and sweats. Both were a man's medium, which meant they were too big for her, but even though the elastic waistband hung loosely from her hip bones, it was enough to keep them up. Underneath she went commando, because the included boxers were impossibly large.

Combing out her hair, she twisted it into a loose knot at her nape, shrugged into her coat, which she left unzipped, pulled her boots on over fresh white half socks, and, carrying her discarded clothes, headed back toward the main room.

Cal was down on one knee in a corner and gave her only a cursory glance as she entered. Tucking her bundled clothes and the flashlight into the emptier of the two backpacks, she headed toward him. He'd kindled a fire in a small iron camp stove that clearly he'd found somewhere in the room. She eyed the stove with some misgivings as she approached, but an upward glance following the wisp of smoke it put out told her that there was ventilation: the smoke drifted off through a crack in the ceiling and she suspected that he had chosen the location for exactly that purpose. And one of the great things about a room carved out of stone was that it was not conducive to a spreading fire.

The tantalizing aroma of cooking food made her stomach growl. She was *starving.*

"How was it?" he greeted her as she stopped beside him to look down past his black head and broad shoulders to what was heating on the cooktop: two opened, individual-size cans of beef stew. She had no idea how he'd managed to get them open without a can opener, but she wasn't surprised that he *had* managed. The man, as she had already learned, was efficient.

"Heavenly," she replied, and he smiled. It was a crooked, charming smile that warmed his eyes and caused her heart to unexpectedly skip a beat, but before she could react in any other way he stood up, which brought him so close to her that she nearly took a step back. Tilting her head back to look up at him, she — barely — managed to stand her ground. It wasn't fear of him that made it feel dangerous for her to stand so close; it was that the sexual charge between them was too strong.

"Keep an eye on this. I won't be long."

That prosaic remark was about the food. Repressing her misgivings — the fire was small and encased in an iron stove, for heaven's sake; what could go wrong? — she nodded and watched as he headed for their primitive bathroom, then glanced around.

He'd dusted off the table: as she looked at it, her eyes widened. Besides the lantern, maybe a half dozen rifles now rested on it, presumably found in the same search that had turned up the stove. From the look of them, they were leftovers from World War II.

While the thought of having more fire-power was appealing, the sight of them gave Gina the willies: it looked like he was preparing to take on an army. Besides, she was skeptical that after all this time they would even still work.

Looking past them with effort, she discovered that he'd spread out their sleeping bag bed on two pallets that he'd dragged flush against the wall just behind the door. Two things struck her about that: first, her automatic assumption that it was *their* bed, which meant that they would be sharing it, and second, that behind the door was an interesting choice of placement for it. Anyone coming through the door would be blocked from seeing the bed and the people in it until the intruders were all the way inside the room. Did that mean that he was expecting somebody to come through the door? Or was it simply a precaution?

Either way, even considering the possibility was enough to send a cold chill snaking down her spine.

Once again, she was reminded that the name of the game here was survival.

As he'd promised, Cal was only gone briefly, and when he came back the stew was bubbling. The smell alone was making Gina salivate, but the sight of Cal all washed and clean and dressed in a snug white tee along with his own suit pants was enough to get her mind off her stomach and take her thoughts in a whole different and entirely unwelcome direction.

"Rifles, huh? Where'd you find them?" she asked as he dropped his coat and snow pants on top of the backpacks and then stopped by the table to gather the rifles up, partly because she wanted to know the answer and partly to redirect her thoughts *again.*

"Trash cans," he said, nodding toward the row of them as he leaned the rifles carefully against the wall. "Ammo, too, and other things, all carefully stored. Everything looks mint."

"Think we'll need them?"

"Can't have too many weapons."

With that surprisingly cheerful-sounding observation, he joined her by the stove.

The fire in the stove was already burning itself out, but she noticed with approval that he took the time to smother it completely before carrying the cans over to the table, using his gloves as pot holders. He'd found a collection of measuring spoons and a single knife, which she'd carefully washed, and they each dug into the stew with a spoon while sharing the knife to cut the bigger pieces of meat. She'd gotten so warm as she stirred the stew and stayed by the stove waiting for his return that she'd shed her coat: it hung over the back of one of the chairs.

Except for the flickering circle of light cast by the lantern, the cavern was dark and full of shadows. The short-sleeved tee she wore was way big on her, and her braless breasts were on the small size and firm, so she didn't feel self-conscious about revealing too much as she sat down across the table from him.

She was, she discovered as they ate, soon self-conscious about something else entirely. She had trouble keeping her eyes off him. Sitting there eating by lantern light, he looked disturbingly handsome and vaguely piratical with more than a day's growth of stubble darkening his chin. His teeth were even and white and his brows were straight black slashes above dark brown eyes that had acquired gold glints from the reflected light. The same type of ordinary white tee that she was wearing took on an entirely different appearance on him: in it his shoulders looked about a mile wide and the truly impressive muscles of his chest and arms visibly rippled and flexed against the clingy cotton whenever he moved. She found her pulse quickening just from watching him eat, from admiring the play of the lamplight on the bronzed bulge of his biceps and the hair-darkened length of his powerful forearm every time he lifted the spoon to his mouth, from observing the deft movements of his square-palmed, long-fingered hands. She caught herself wondering what it would feel like to be crushed against that muscular chest without the inches-thick layers of their winter clothes between them — and then she realized to her embarrassment that she was staring at him, and he'd noticed.

To that point, they'd been busy eating and hadn't been talking, or at least nothing more substantive than "This is good" and "Shame we don't have bread," that sort of thing. But at the look in his eyes as she accidentally encountered them, after she'd watched with close attention for what was probably the two dozenth time as he raised his arm to take another bite of stew, she felt a rush of flustered consternation and hurried to think of something to say that would send his thoughts in another direction.

"You know, if we could locate Keith, that would give us one more person on our side," she said. "If those rifles work, he would even be armed. There would be three of us. Can't have too many people shooting those weapons."

Having turned his words back around on him, she watched his eyes narrow at her: distraction completed.

"Another civilian would be a liability, not a help." His gaze slid over her face. When he continued, it was in a tone of careful patience. "Gina, look: trying to warn your friend is out. If we start running all over the island like chickens with our heads cut off, we're way more likely to run into the guys who want to kill us than we are into him. You *know* that."

She did know it. She just hated to face it — and what it meant for Keith. "If we don't warn him, he'll be killed." The thought made her feel sick. She put down her spoon abruptly, wishing she'd waited to bring the subject up. She'd never meant to let the matter go, but if she hadn't been so intent on refocusing his attention on something other than the way she had been looking at him, she would have held off until morning.

"*We'll* be killed if we try. For all you know, somebody else in your group managed to warn him. Got a call out to him over the radio or something. Before —"

He broke off, but she knew what he meant: before the person doing the warning, Mary or Jorge, say, or one of the others, was killed.

"You don't believe that."

"I don't know one way or the other. And you don't, either." Something in her face made his mouth twist. "Once we get off this damned island, we can send help back, okay? Anyway —"

He broke off again. Gina frowned at him. His expression had suddenly become closed off, unreadable.

"Anyway what?" she demanded.

He shook his head. Clearly he didn't mean to elaborate.

"Either we're in this together, or we're not," she said, looking at him hard. "It's not going to be just you running the show. It's you and me, partners, or else it's nothing." He'd put down his spoon, too, which would have been a more impressive indication of the effect of her speech on him if he hadn't eaten all his stew by that time. Observing that, her eyes narrowed at him. "So you want to finish what you started to say? Anyway . . . ?"

His eyes were dark and intent as they met hers. His mouth was suddenly grim. "If you're so eager to share everything, why don't you start by telling me about the plane crash that killed your husband?"

Pain twisted through her. She'd *known* he was going to want to talk about that. And she couldn't. Just could not.

So she strong-armed past the pain, gave him a level look, and said, "I asked you first. *Anyway* what?"

His eyes slid over her face. His jaw tightened. "Okay, *partner,* here it is: my plane didn't just crash. It was shot out of the sky by a surface-to-air missile. Given our altitude and location when we were hit, someone here on Attu or in the waters right around it had to have done it. It's possible that one of this group who's coming after us now was already on the island at that point, but I don't think so, because storm or no storm, if they had been on the island, it wouldn't have taken them until the next morning to show up. I think they got called in after my plane was shot down. As far as I know, your people were the only ones on the island at the time, and if that's the case, then one of you had to have fired that missile."

It took a moment for what he was saying to click into place.

"You think *Keith* shot your plane down?"

"I don't know. If you and he are the only ones left — and we don't know that; without eyeballing the bodies there's no way to be sure — then I'd say he's at the top of the suspect list."

Staring at him, Gina mentally reviewed all she knew about Keith. He was a scientist, and a physician, and —

"He was the last person added to the team," she said slowly. "That was about a week before we left. I thought at the time that he was going to have to scramble to get everything he needed together in order to do the project he meant to do here."

"Tell me about him. Everything you know."

Gina did. It wasn't a lot.

"So you'd never met him before he joined your group on Attu?" Cal asked, and Gina shook her head no. "Did any of the others know him?"

Gina thought back. "I'm pretty sure Arvid didn't." The thought of Arvid made her wince, but she determinedly kept her focus on where it needed to be: the present, in which she was remembering everything she could about Keith. "I don't know about anyone else. He didn't seem to have any particular friends among the group." She frowned at Cal. "It's difficult to get permission to conduct research on Attu, you know. We all had to go through this unbelievable application and screening process. If there was anything wrong with Keith's credentials — with any of our credentials — the screening process almost certainly would have caught it."

Cal sat back in his chair. "Ah, but what you've got to ask yourself is, who conducted the screening process?"

"We had to go through a ton of government agencies . . ." Her words faltered at the look on his face. "Are you saying *our government* is involved?"

"I'm not saying anything at all. I'm still trying to work out who's involved."

She refused to let him off the hook that easily. "Ivanov and the men who shot Arvid were speaking Russian. How could they be from *our* government?"

"The international situation tends to get complicated sometimes." His tone told her that as far as he was concerned the conversation was over, even before he cast a meaningful look at the stew remaining in her can. She had only eaten about half. It was good, and it was still warm, but she couldn't take another bite. He said, "You should eat the rest of that."

Shaking her head, she shoved the can across the table toward him. "I can't. You eat it. You're way bigger than me, and you need more food. And while you're eating it you can tell me —"

She broke off as his fingers encircled her wrist, trapping her with her arm stretched out across the table.

"What?" She looked at him in bewilderment, only to find that he was staring down at her arm.

Following his gaze, she saw to her dismay that the lamplight had caught the fine tracery of scars that covered her forearm like a spiderweb and turned them silver.

They were why the extra set of clothes in her backpack had included a white turtleneck instead of a tee and why she almost never wore short-sleeved or sleeveless shirts anymore.

With the help of skin grafts, the scars had shrunk and faded until they were no longer disfiguring, until they were no more than pale, hair-thin lines crisscrossing her right arm, but they were there: a permanent reminder.

Like she needed one. Like she would ever, could ever, forget.

"Those are burns," Cal said, and ran a gentle forefinger over her scars. Her eyes flew to his. She would have been sucking in air except that what felt like the weight of the whole world had just dropped on her chest, making it impossible for her to breathe at all. "How'd you get them, honey?"

CHAPTER TWENTY-THREE

There it was again, that generic "honey" that she didn't like, only now it didn't sound generic at all. It sounded almost impossibly tender and like he meant it just for her.

Gina couldn't say a word, couldn't move. She felt as if she'd been paralyzed. Steeling herself against the memories of how she'd gotten the scars, she found herself unable to pull her gaze from his. The gold flecks in his eyes seemed to glitter as he looked at her. His lashes were short and thick and as black as his hair, she noted abstractedly. The fine grid of lines around his eyes caught her attention: they were deeper than she'd ever seen them. From concern for her, she thought.

"The plane crash that killed your husband." Cal's voice seemed to come to her from across a great distance. "Were you in it, too?"

Pain slammed her. If she wasn't careful,

she thought, she would slide right off the chair into a little puddle on the stone floor.

I'm stronger than that.

Gritting her teeth, she jerked her arm free and at last managed to breathe.

"Why would you think that?" Her tone was wintry, hostile — but her voice was hoarse.

He made a sound that could have been a laugh, only there was no amusement in it.

"For one thing, I've seen scars like those before. You were showered with burning airplane fuel, weren't you?"

The words couldn't have hurt more if they'd been blows. The memories pounded in harder. Pushing her chair away from the table, Gina started to stand up, meaning to walk away, to put distance between them, to go as far from the source of the pain as she could — only she was suddenly too dizzy, and too sick to her stomach, to stand up.

Before she could get herself together enough to escape, he came around the table and crouched in front of her.

He looked as big and immovable as a mountain, she thought resentfully. The sheer mass of him hunkered down in front of her was enough to keep her from standing up and walking away even if she had been able to move, which at the moment she could not. Their eyes were nearly on a level. His were dark and grave. When he reached out to take her hand — she only realized that it had gone ice cold when she felt the warmth of his long fingers curling around hers — she gave him a look of total antipathy as she tried unsuccessfully to tug it free.

" 'Either we're in this together, or we're not,' " he quoted her words back at her. "Tell me what happened."

She glared at him. Stupid to be angry at him, she knew, but she suddenly was, because he was dredging up what it had cost her a lot to bury and hurting her in the process. Under the circumstances, though, she knew his question wasn't out of line. She should tell him. She knew she should. Her answer affected both of them. He needed to understand about planes — about how she felt about planes, about flying. He'd seen her scars now. He'd guessed the cause. All she needed to give him was the barest outline and he would know why stealing a plane and flying it out of there was not going to work for her.

But the memories were sharp as knives, shredding her composure.

She only realized that she was gripping his hand so hard that her nails were digging into his palm when his thumb stroked soothingly over the back of her hand. The gentle caress caused her fingers to relax a little.

"Gina," he prompted. His eyes held hers. "Tell me."

The steadiness of his gaze steadied her in turn. *Bare bones,* she thought, *I can do.* Wetting her lips, taking a breath, she kept her eyes fastened to his as if they were a lifeline.

"I was the only one who survived." She did her best to speak normally, but still the words emerged as scarcely more than a croak. "My husband. My father. My sister. All died."

His face tightened. "Ah, Jesus," he said. "I'm sorry."

She nodded, unable to say anything more because her throat had closed up. Pain welled inside her as the memories ripped free of their moorings and she saw it again, all of it, in a terrifying flash that lasted no longer than a split second. She held on to his hand like she never meant to let go as the fear and grief and horror washed over her in a giant wave and then receded, leaving her cold and shaking in its wake.

He glanced down at their joined hands, then raised them to his mouth and pressed his lips to the back of her hand. His lips on her skin felt warm. Possessive. As if they belonged there.

Heat surged through her as his mouth shifted to kiss each one of her fingers in turn. Glorious, life-giving heat.

He's a gorgeous guy, she thought with a surprising degree of detachment as she watched his black head bent over her hand while he pressed his lips to each of her fingers. The feel of his mouth on her skin made her body tighten with awareness. Hard-eyed, hard-bodied, handsome, aggressively male: what woman wouldn't want a man like that?

More than that, he was someone she'd learned she could count on. Someone who'd become surprisingly important to her.

"It's okay," he said, lowering their hands to look at her. "That's all I needed to know. You don't have to tell me any more."

She nodded and exhaled. He didn't let go of her hand. She didn't try to pull away. Instead, she entwined her fingers with his and held on.

"I can't really — talk about it." Her voice was ragged. "But I'm glad you know."

"Yeah, me too."

She smiled at him a little unsteadily. Her

heartbeat accelerated as she met his eyes. They flamed at her. Other than that, his face was impossible to read.

But she could see the tension in the set of his broad shoulders and the hardness of his jaw. She could read it, just like she could read what was in his eyes.

He wanted her. She had no doubt about that whatsoever. But she'd told him no before, and it was clear that he wouldn't cross that line.

In her book, whatever else he'd done, that made him a good guy.

The chemistry between them was off the charts. She could feel it sizzling in the air. It was there in the heat of their linked hands, in the intensity of their locked gazes. The blistering kisses they'd shared were permanently branded in her memory. Her body was aware of his like a flower is aware of the sun.

Here, she realized with a blinding flash of insight, was the key to the prison she'd been locked in. She might die tomorrow. Was she really going to let the poor maimed thing her life had become be the last chapter of her existence? He wanted her. Well, she wanted him, too — badly. There was no logical reason why she shouldn't take what she wanted. She didn't have to worry about getting pregnant: she had long-term protection from that. And if they weren't together permanently, so what? There was nothing wrong with being together for right now. She could have a relationship with a man with forever potential later. Forget getting involved with him: that didn't have to happen. To put it in his terms, they could simply get it on. This thing with Cal would be her very own red-hot love affair, an icebreaker to catapult her back into the sexual arena. When this nightmare was over, if they survived and parted, maybe she'd be on her way to being free to live her life again.

The prospect intrigued her.

The thought of sleeping with Cal dazzled her. It made her heart start to pound.

Tightening her grip on his hand, she leaned forward and pressed her mouth to his. She kissed him softly, provocatively, sliding a hand behind his head, her lips molding to the warm firmness of his as if she would memorize the shape and taste of them. Her pulse began to race. Her body began to quicken. She touched her tongue to the crease between his lips, slid it that first little bit into his mouth, found the tip of his tongue. His mouth was scalding hot. The wave of heat that swept over her made her stomach quiver.

He made a slight, harsh sound against her lips. Then his tongue was in her mouth and he was kissing her fiercely, taking control, his mouth slanting across hers, his lips hard and demanding. She closed her eyes and kissed him back, wanting him so much that she was on fire with it. Her pulse hammered and her body burned and her toes curled in her boots.

His arm came around her waist and he stood up, pulling her up with him, pulling her tight against his body. When they were both on their feet he stopped kissing her and lifted his head. Dizzy with wanting him, she opened her eyes and looked up at him. She was plastered against him, her arms around his neck, her head thrown back so that she had a perfect view of his hard, handsome face. His arms were locked around her waist and he looked down at her with passion blazing from his eyes, but she thought she detected a hint of wariness in the set of his mouth.

"You want to tell me what this is?" There was a hint of wariness, too, in his husky question.

"Make love to me." Her voice was throaty, breathless. She felt hot all over, as if flames were licking at her skin. Maybe from the heat of his body pressed so closely against hers; more likely from the intensity of her own desire. He'd been able to read her from the first. Now his eyes darkened as they absorbed the sultry promise in hers.

For a moment they simply stared at each other while the air around them turned to steam. His jaw clenched as his eyes slid over her face. When they met hers again, what she read in them sent an electric charge through her body.

The raw carnality smoldering back at her from his eyes took her breath away.

Her heart lurched. Her body went up in flames.

Without a word he started to kiss her again, deep, hot kisses that made her dizzy, that made her tighten her arms around his neck and go up on tiptoe and kiss him back with increasing abandon. She pressed her body against his, reveling in the feel of him against her, in the hardness of his muscles, in the sheer size of him, in his strength. She felt the rigidity of his erection between them and her body clenched fiercely in response. His big hand slid down to cup her bottom and press her closer yet, and the rock-hardness of him against her sent long tremors of arousal coursing through her.

He kissed her cheek, her ear, slid his mouth down the side of her neck while she shivered and quaked and clung and pressed hot little kisses along his bristly jawline. Dying to touch him, she stroked both hands down his wide chest to circle his waist and delve beneath his shirt, sliding up over his bare back. She was entranced by the hot sleekness of his skin and the steely muscles beneath it.

His head lifted at the feel of her hands on his back, and he made a sound under his breath that was almost a growl.

Gina opened her eyes to find that he was looking down at her, his eyes black as coal and glittering with passion.

"You sure you want to do this?" His voice was hoarse.

She loved that he cared enough about her to check with her one more time. She loved how tall he was, and how strong, and how totally male. She loved the iron bands of his arms around her, the solid muscles of his chest against her breasts, the powerful length of his legs against the slenderness of hers. She loved the way his back felt under her hands. He was hard with wanting her, and huge with wanting her, and she loved that, too. She could feel the size and shape and urgency of his erection pressing against her, and knowing how turned on he was turned her on even more. She was breathing way too fast, her heart was pounding way too hard, and she was all soft and shivery inside.

And she loved every bit of it. She loved the way she felt. She loved the way her body throbbed and burned. She was, as she had suspected, hungry for sex. But not just sex, she discovered: what she was really hungry for was sex with him.

"I'm sure," she answered in a voice she didn't even recognize, and reached up to kiss him again.

His jaw went hard and his eyes leaped at her just before her lips found his. Kissing her back like he could never get enough of her mouth, he picked her up, carried her over to their makeshift bed, and put her down on it.

He was still kissing her as he came down beside her, but then his mouth pulled free of hers. She made a wordless sound of protest and opened her eyes. Her breathing was fast, irregular. The flickering lamplight lent his face a fierce masculine beauty, and the hot blaze of passion in his eyes set her on fire. Her hands were deep under his shirt by that time, stroking over the flexing muscles of his back, pressing into the flat planes of his shoulder blades, following the smooth indentation of his spine. As he moved they slid down to his waist, where they lingered on the honed muscles there, and her mouth slid down to kiss the sturdy column of his neck. His skin was hot and sandpapery with whiskers and tasted faintly of salt, and she loved the feel of it beneath her lips and the taste of it on her tongue. He sat up to pull his shirt over his head and she found herself completely dislodged. Breathing unevenly, awash in the most delicious sensations imaginable, Gina leaned back on her elbows to look at him.

He was so very big, with hard, solid muscle everywhere she looked. His broad linebacker's shoulders and wide chest tapered down to a flat stomach and lean hips. The wedge of black hair on his chest was blatantly male. He was mouthwateringly gorgeous, and just the sight of him made her so hot that she felt as if she were melting inside.

"You must work out a lot," she said as their eyes met, and knew she sounded idiotic even as the words left her mouth. But the thing was, she was so intoxicated by the thought of what they were getting ready to do that she wasn't quite thinking straight.

The slightest of smiles curved his mouth. "Some." His voice was gravelly and low. "Did I mention I want you like hell?" What she read in his eyes made her shiver.

Before she could reply, he leaned toward her and kissed her, his hand sliding along her cheek to bury itself in her hair. The touch of his mouth was a total aphrodisiac for her now. She kissed him back like she would die if she didn't and felt a hot, intense throbbing pulse to life between her legs. Reveling in the fact that she could touch him at will, she pushed her fingers through the crispness of his chest hair, stroked his wide pecs, slid her hands up over the bulging muscles of his upper arms and along the firmness of his broad shoulders. She felt her bones dissolve at the feel of his chiseled body beneath her hands — and at the intensity of his response to her touch. His breath seemed to rattle in his throat. His body grew harder, hotter. His kisses scalded her mouth. Everywhere they touched she burned.

She let him ease her back down onto the silky gray expanse of the sleeping bag as the delicious feelings surging through her turned into a tidal wave of need.

"Gina." Leaning over her as she lay flat on her back looking up at him, he smoothed her hair away from her face in a gesture that was surprisingly tender. Then he took her mouth in a hot, lush kiss and slipped a hand beneath her shirt to find her breast. She could feel the whole hard-muscled length of him stretched out on his side next to her, and the weight of the leg he'd thrown over her thighs. She could feel the body heat he radiated, the brush of his bare skin. She could feel the slide of his hand up her rib cage. His touch was electric, searing her skin.

"Cal," she whispered against his lips as his hand covered her breast, and she gave a little gasp as her nipple tightened and her breast surged into the hardness of his palm. Her body pulsed with need as he fondled her, caressing her breasts like a man who knew what he was doing. He was shoving her shirt up out of his way and kissing a blazing-hot trail down the side of her neck when a not particularly welcome thought occurred to her, penetrating the steam fogging her brain. On a ragged little laugh she said, "Oh, God, I don't even know if Cal's your real name."

"It is." Her breasts were bared to him now. He'd lifted his head to look at them, and as he shifted his gaze to meet her eyes her world went slightly out of focus at the intensity of the arousal she saw in them.

"Is there more? Like, say, a last name?" She was determined to get an answer even as her mind threatened to shut down to everything except the way he was making her feel.

"James MacArthur Callahan. I go by Cal." The thickness of his voice, the way he was looking at her, threatened to undo her completely. His eyes gleamed with sexual intent. His face was tight with it. His mouth was hard with it. So was his body.

She was shaky with excitement, breathing way too fast, and so hot for him she suddenly understood how spontaneous combustion might work. Long-fingered and dark against her pale skin, his hand curved around her breast. She knew what he was doing: the same thing he had done before. He was holding her breast ready for his mouth. Only this time she was going to let it happen. Her nipples were puckered and tingling. She wanted his mouth on her so much that she trembled.

"Cal." There was something else she needed to know first.

Leaning down, he just grazed her nipple with his lips: a tease, a promise. The jolt of sensation that went through her at that featherlight touch was unreal. Her nipples instantly hardened into tight little points. She barely managed to hold back a moan. As he lifted his head, her back arched in a futile attempt to keep her breasts in contact with his mouth. She went all hot and liquidy inside.

"Um?" He looked down at her with hungry, heavy-lidded eyes. He was breathing hard. Twin flags of color rode high on his cheekbones.

She took a steadying breath. Oh, God, he'd almost made her forget what she'd been about to ask. Looming above her, he shifted his gaze to watch the rise and fall of her breasts with concentrated interest. His body was taut and primed for sex. She could feel the leashed power in him, the latent strength. She could feel the carnal vibes he was giving off. Heat raced through her like a flash fire. Deep inside, she felt her body clench. It was all she could do not to squirm with excitement beneath the heavy leg that was pinning her down.

"You're not married, are you?" Her voice was faintly unsteady.

"Nope. No significant other. No sexually transmitted diseases. No condom, though. Is that a problem?"

She shook her head and sucked in more air. Shirtless, with the lamplight flickering over his body, he was the embodiment of practically every sexy dream she'd ever had, and her heart beat faster just from looking at him.

"Anything else you feel the need to ask me about right now?" The words were polite. His voice was a dangerous-sounding growl.

Gina shook her head. Her heart thundered so loudly that it was like a drumbeat in her ears. Her body was tight, pulsing, eager.

He bent his head and took her nipple in his mouth. For real this time. The scalding heat of it made her senses reel. Ripples of pleasure shot along her nerve endings. She gasped and buried her hands in the short, thick strands of his hair.

He kissed and sucked and licked until she was mindless, until she was arching up against him and moaning, and then he pulled her shirt up over her head and threw it to one side and started kissing her mouth again. Shivery with arousal, she kissed him back, loving the weight of his chest against her sensitized breasts, loving the roughness of his kiss, loving the possessive way he fondled her breasts before his hand slid down inside the sweatpants and between her legs, touching her where she most wanted to be touched.

She cried out, moving against his hand, burning, melting, absolutely on fire. Wanting more, needing more, she reached for his belt buckle, fumbled at it with fingers made clumsy by urgency, ran unsteady fingers over the rigid bulge in the front of his pants. He muttered something short and profane against her mouth and lifted himself away from her and sat up. Her eyes popped open and her fingers sank into the softness of the sleeping bag, but before she could ask him where the hell he thought he was going or what was up or anything like that, he hooked his fingers in her waistband and yanked her pants down her legs, pausing only long enough to pull off her boots before stripping her nude.

She lay propped up on her elbows on the silky gray sleeping bag, awash in golden lamplight, her tawny hair streaming down her back, her knees bent, her legs slightly raised. She felt just a little shy under his hard gaze but also incredibly turned on. He looked at her with open lust, and she found that the idea that he was seeing her naked brought its own fiery thrill. He took in every inch of her, and it was almost like she could see herself through his eyes: tousled hair, flushed face, lips swollen by his kisses; creamy round breasts with darkened, erect nipples; slim waist, flat stomach, gently curved hips; long, toned, tanned legs with a strip of fair pubic hair between.

"You're beautiful." His voice was hoarse. His eyes glittered at her like black diamonds.

Too turned on to answer, she murmured something wordless by way of a reply and watched him unashamedly. He'd shucked his boots and unfastened his belt buckle while he was looking at her, and the tiny sound his zipper made as he lowered it made her quake.

Then he was shedding his pants, and she saw that he was, indeed, as huge and hard as he'd felt.

Her heart pounded as if she'd been running for miles.

"Oh, my," she breathed, and as he saw what she was looking at, a corner of his mouth ticked up in the briefest of smiles.

He leaned toward her, kissed her with a naked hunger that made her go up in flames, and bore her back down into their makeshift bed, his hands all over her, his big body pressing her down. When he had her wild for him, when she was moving beneath him and moaning and so hot, so ready, that she thought if he didn't come into her right that very minute she would lose her mind, his mouth left hers and his body shifted. Opening her eyes, she murmured, *"Cal,"* and clutched at him in protest.

That's when he kissed his way down her body to the cleft between her legs, and pressed his mouth to her and licked her and did other thrilling, secret things.

Until her body clenched hard. And she came, and came, and came.

She was still shaking, still shuddering, still gasping for breath, when he levered his big body on top of her and pushed himself inside her so fiercely that she cried out. He was hard and hot and filled her to capacity and then some. He took her with a single-minded ferocity that had her quaking and burning and wanting *again,* and she did the only thing she could do: wrapped her arms around his neck and her legs around his waist and held on. It was the most erotic experience of her life, and the end, when it came, was so hot and intense that she thought she would die right there and then from the sheer explosive pleasure of it.

She bucked, and clung, and cried out his name. "Cal! Cal, Cal, *Cal!*"

He drove into her one final time, groaning as he found his own release. Then he held himself shuddering inside her.

CHAPTER TWENTY-FOUR

She'd made him tremble. He was a grown-ass man, a highly trained veteran of battle campaigns, firefights, clandestine forays, and any number of life-and-death situations, to say nothing of countless rolls in the sack, and the last time he remembered trembling was when he'd lost his virginity at fifteen.

Dr. Gina Sullivan, ornithologist, college professor, uptight, angst-ridden twenty-eight-year-old widow, was by no means his type, which tended toward busty platinum blondes who liked to have a raucous good time in bed and out. She was beautiful, all right, but not in the eye-popping, head-turning way of his usual. Hers was a quieter, more refined type of beauty that Cal saw now had been sneaking up on him until finally it hit him over the head, which had happened with all the force of a baseball bat swinging for a line drive the moment he saw her naked. Then he'd realized: hers was a face and body to die for.

He'd wanted to fuck her senseless.

Instead he'd taken his time, reined himself in, been mindful of her hang-ups and history and almost certain relative lack of sexual experience, and set himself to making it good for her, first and foremost.

She'd been so hot for him, so hungry and eager, that it had been all he could do to keep himself under control. By the time she was coming hard against his mouth, his body had been screaming with the need to take her. As he'd lifted himself over her, more than ready to get down to it, his arms had trembled.

That was when, finally, he'd given up on the whole self-control thing and let his animal instincts rule.

The memory was making him hard all over again.

Right now she was sprawled on top of him, silent and sated and limp as a glove, because after he'd finished rocking her world he'd rolled with her, not wanting to crush her with his weight. The heavy mass of her hair lay across his shoulder like a blanket. He could feel the flutter of her breath just over his heart. He could feel other things, too: the swell of her tits against his chest; the small, hard points of her nipples. The brush of her sweet little bush on top of his abs. The heat between her long, sexy legs, which were open and sprawled on either side of his.

That heat was doing a number on his thought processes, to say nothing of his cock, which was assuming the approximate size and consistency of a log again. That heat was drawing his hand down from where it had been idly resting on the warm, silky skin of her back to stroke over the curve of her gorgeous ass on its way to investigating it. That heat was fogging his brain to the point where, when she stirred and braced a forearm against his chest and lifted her head to unexpectedly pin him with her big blue eyes, all he could think to say was, "Hey."

She smiled at him. A warm, intimate, you-just-got-me-off smile that did a number on his heart rate. With her honey-colored hair spilling like a waterfall over one of her pale shoulders and her eyes all dreamy-looking from sex and her knockout body all slim naked curves painted gold by the lamplight, she looked hot enough to fuck into next week. Again.

"That was amazing," she said. Her voice was husky and low.

"Yeah?" So he wasn't up to making brilliant conversation. His cock was currently doing all his thinking. It was a wonder he was even able to talk.

"Yeah."

"Glad you think so." His hand was on her ass, palming the smooth, warm curve, and he tightened his grip and shifted her just a little so that she was lying right on top of his erection. Jesus, that felt good.

Her eyes widened as she felt him stirring under her. Her lips parted to give him a glimpse of her pretty white teeth. Then she gave a little wriggle, pressed her hips deliberately down, and —

Holy Mary Mother of God, if he got any hotter he'd catch fire.

His hand slid on down to check out that enticing heat of hers.

"Oh," she said as his hand moved between her legs, parting her folds, stroking, exploring. He pushed two fingers inside her and was blown away by how tight she was, how hot and wet. She said "Oh" again, on a squeaky little note of surprised delight that instantly made him so big and hard that the marble monolith of the Washington Monument had nothing on him.

She closed her eyes with one of her sexy little moans that made every muscle in his body tighten, every time she did it. Then, with his fingers moving purposefully in and out, with her body undulating on top of his like she was deliberately trying to drive him out of his mind, with her panting and flushed on top of him and her nipples practically branding his chest and enough heat rising off the pair of them to steam up the air, she opened her eyes, gave him a dead-sexy look, and said in a throaty growl, "I knew there was a reason I pulled you out of the sea."

That surprised a laugh out of him. First time he could remember laughing while he was in the middle of some serious foreplay, with his cock begging for action and his balls aching like they were getting ready to explode.

"Lucky me," he said, meaning it, and rolled so that she was beneath him again.

Their gazes met as her arms came around his neck and he bent his head to kiss her. Her eyes were hot for him, just like her body was hot for him, but there was something else in those big baby blues of hers, too, something that he couldn't quite —

"Lucky *me*," she said softly, and lifted her mouth to meet his.

The instant before their lips touched, he had it. He knew what was looking out at him from behind the blaze of torrid passion in her eyes: vulnerability. And trust.

What do you do with a woman who looks at you like that?

He fucked her until she screamed.

Afterward, she passed out, while he managed to stay awake long enough to get up and retrieve the flashlight and his weapon, which he wanted to keep within easy reach.

Ordinarily the phenomenal sex would have been enough to occupy his thoughts, but as he rolled their coats into substitute pillows and then blew out the lantern, Cal found himself once again turning over in his mind the unwelcome scenario that had first occurred to him when Gina had described the Texas accent of the gunman she called Heavy Tread. Cal's CIA handler, Lon Whitman, who'd hired him for this job, was from San Antonio, and his twang was as Texas as they came.

Was it possible that Whitman had sold him and the operation out?

That would mean that Whitman had gone rogue, a possibility that Cal ordinarily would have rejected as impossible. He'd known Whitman for a number of years, and the guy was a straight-arrow, by-the-book operative whose integrity he'd never had any reason to doubt.

But someone had gotten to Hendricks and Ezra. Hendricks he could, very dimly, envision being corrupted by any number of unsavory interests. Ezra? Cal once would have said, never could happen. It had happened, though, and the only way Cal could envision that going down was if Ezra was approached by someone like, say, Whitman, their trusted CIA handler. With some plausible reason why Rudy should be prevented from returning to the United States and why Cal should be kept in the dark about this, along with a promise, coupled with the power to follow through, to make the less-than-positive repercussions from their losing Rudy after obtaining him from the Kazakhs go away. Plus the money. Thirty million was a lot of money. Having that much on the table certainly would have inclined Ezra to listen when Whitman talked.

When Ezra had shot Cal, he hadn't been shooting to kill. In what possible scenario could Ezra have thought that was going to work out? Not killing Cal after turning traitor on him and shooting him was like leaving a live grenade in your own house, and Ezra would have known that.

Unless Ezra had been assured that everything would be smoothed over and explained once the alternate disposal of Rudy was accomplished. Just about the only person Ezra might have trusted to be able to smooth over what he would have known Cal would see as a base betrayal was their CIA employer, Whitman.

Ezra had said Cal would get his share of the money. He would have been counting on ten million dollars going a long way toward mollifying Cal, too.

The scorched-earth magnitude of the response to his survival would have been exactly what he would have expected if the CIA — that is, Whitman — was directing it.

If he was right in what he was thinking, and Cal profoundly hoped he wasn't, he and Gina were in exponentially more danger than he had thought. Cal knew his own skills and abilities, and had every confidence in them. But if Whitman, with his CIA resources, was behind this, the technology and manpower they might be facing would be overwhelming. With Cal alive, Whitman would have everything to lose. He would stop at nothing to make sure no one who could tell the tale lived to do so.

There were other possibilities, of course. So many bad players on the world stage made for a large pool of suspects. But Cal kept coming back to that Texas twang. What were the chances that there were two drawling Texans involved in this?

Very small, Cal judged. In fact, almost infinitesimal.

Shit.

Nothing to do about it at the moment, he told himself grimly. Tomorrow would be time enough to deal. For now, he needed to sleep.

Gina was still sleeping soundly when he stretched out beside her, but she must have felt him slide the pillow beneath her head and then subconsciously registered the warmth of his body next to hers, because she turned over to snuggle against him. He managed to get her tucked up against his side and pull half the sleeping bag over them both without waking her. They had these few precious hours in which he judged they were relatively safe, and he had no idea when they'd get an opportunity to sleep again. If he had any chance in hell of getting them out of this alive, he would need a clear head and a body that was as functional as possible. On that thought he closed his eyes, concentrated, and was gone, falling fathoms deep asleep in an instant as his military training had taught him to do.

Cal woke abruptly, shaken out of a sound

sleep by — he didn't know what. It was pitch dark. His body was comfortably covered, but the air around him was cool and smelled like musty earth. He couldn't see a thing — but there was a woman in his arms, warm and slim and silky soft. Naked, just like he was naked. Then realization clicked, and he was fully alert, fully aware of where he was and of the identity of the woman sleeping with him and the deadly situation they were in.

In the total absence of light the cavern felt vast. Tiny sounds echoed, making it difficult to zero in on their source. His muscles tensed as his body went into automatic defensive mode. He turned every sense he possessed to rapidly scanning the surrounding area for a threat.

Gina didn't move. Except for her breathing, which seemed abnormally fast. Was she awake? He couldn't tell, and he didn't dare to even so much as whisper her name in case someone was near. She lay with her back to his front. His arm was draped around her waist and her delectable ass pressed against his crotch, which was already sporting significant morning wood, although he was as sure as it was possible to be that they'd only been asleep for a few hours and it was still the middle of the night. Strands of her hair tickled his face, she smelled of soap and woman, and his hand was full of a soft, warm tit. She felt slender and supple and sexy as hell against him. So much so that he felt a stab of regret that at the moment he had more urgent things to think about than how horny she was making him.

Carefully he removed his hand from her breast and reached up for his weapon, which he'd tucked beneath the coat his head was pillowed on, and brought it down to rest on the part of the sleeping bag that covered her hip.

Asleep under battlefield conditions, which he considered these to be, he almost never woke up for no reason. Something had jolted him back to awareness. But if there was anything that shouldn't be there in that cavern with them, he wasn't picking up on —

She gave a little mewling cry, startling him, and began thrashing around in what seemed to be a desperate attempt to escape the shrouding sleeping bag. Careful to keep his gun hand out of the fray, he grabbed her to keep her from throwing herself out onto the stone floor, caught a heel in the kneecap and an elbow in the ribs for his pains, and had his answer: *she'd* woken him up.

From the small distressed sounds she was making, he was pretty sure that she was having a nightmare.

"Gina." Placing his gun carefully back beneath the pillow, he wrapped both arms around her, imprisoning her flailing arms. He threw a leg over hers to keep from getting kicked again and nuzzled her ear. "Gina, wake up."

She did, with a gasp and a shudder, then went stiff as a board in his hold as, he thought, she struggled to get her bearings. She was still facing away from him, and he could hear her agitation in the raggedness of her breathing.

"It's okay, I've got you." He freed her trapped arms and legs while still keeping a precautionary arm around her waist, and at the same time reached for the flashlight, hoping that feeling less physically restricted and being able to see something besides utter blackness might help her get oriented. Switching on the flashlight, he was treated to a glimpse of a fall of tawny hair and a slim shoulder and a beautiful bare breast emerging from the confines of the sleeping bag as she turned her head to cast an alarmed glance back at him.

Her big blue eyes, awash in tears, glistened as the light caught them.

"Cal." She breathed his name with obvious relief, then said, "Turn the light off, please," in a constricted voice that confirmed it for him: she was crying.

The knowledge unexpectedly made his gut clench.

He switched off the light, returning the flashlight to its place beside the gun. She wriggled around to face him, and he gathered her up, turning onto his back with her, cradling her in his arms. She snuggled close, naked skin to naked skin, her head and a hand resting on his chest, a slender, sexy leg sliding over his thighs. He could feel her heat, her curves, the satin of her skin, pressing full length against him, but what got to him most, what garnered his attention and made his stomach twist, was the hot dampness leaking onto his chest.

Tears, he knew.

Her crying disturbed him on a visceral level, and why that should be he had neither the time nor the energy to try to sort out at the moment. What he knew for sure was that it wasn't a positive development, details to be worked out later. Grimacing at the niggling unease his reaction to her tears caused him, he set himself to calming her.

He smoothed a hand over her hair: silk against his palm.

"Bad dream, honey?"

She replied with a sniffle and a shudder as she pressed even closer against him. Which might have worked fine for getting him to think about something else — like, say, sex — if it hadn't been for the tears that were spilling like rain onto his chest. Or if the knowledge that she was crying didn't make him feel like someone was working him over with a club.

"Gina. Talk to me."

"It was just a stupid nightmare. I get them occasionally, okay? I'll be all right in a minute. I'm sorry I'm crying all over you."

Accompanied by a gasping breath, a tremor that shook her from head to toe, and more dripping tears, that truculent response made him tighten his hold on her and press his lips to the top of her head. He had a shrewd idea about the subject of her nightmare: the plane crash that had killed her family members. The difficulty she'd had talking about it earlier, along with her emotional response to the little she did say, told the tale.

"You can cry on me all you want. What I said earlier about crying women scaring me — that was just a dumb joke. Nightmares are the pits. I used to get one that made me cry every time I had it."

He could feel her settling herself more comfortably against him. Silky skin, tits, legs, a beautiful naked woman in his arms who was his for the taking — and all he could think about was stopping her crying. She was shivering, and he tugged the sleeping bag more tightly around her shoulders. The softness of her breasts pressing against his chest, the slide of her smooth, taut thigh over his, the nudge of her bush against his hip, pointed him toward a hell of an enjoyable way to give her thoughts another direction fast. But her tears stopped him. Knowing that she was hurting stopped him. If he was right about the cause of her nightmare, and he was 99.9 percent sure he was, the pain she was suffering went deep. He knew, because he'd been there. What she needed most was to talk it out.

Forget the urgings of his cock: he was there to listen.

"Really?" She sounded deeply suspicious, but her tears seemed to be slowing.

"Yes, really. After my mom was killed in a car accident, I would dream that I saw her walking through my bedroom door. She would smile at me and disappear. I would wake up every time bawling my eyes out." It was the truth, and although it had been at least twenty years since he'd last had that dream, he could still remember the wrenching agony of it — and how lost and alone he'd felt waking up crying in his bed and knowing that if he didn't muffle his tears, if his father heard him, he'd come in and berate or beat some manliness into him.

He could feel her attention focusing on him like radar. "*Was* your mother killed in a car accident?"

"Yep."

"How old were you?"

He told her.

"Oh, my God. Poor little boy." Her hand moved up his chest in a sensuous slide that he was acutely aware of. Her arm curled around his neck and she pressed closer in silent comfort. He could feel the imprint of her naked body against his with every cell he possessed — right along with her sympathy, her sorrow for the little boy he'd once been. She said, "I'm so sorry," and he dropped a kiss on the top of her head.

"It was a long time ago. But I understand nightmares."

She took a deep breath. He realized that he no longer felt tears falling on his chest. *Good.*

"After your mother died, who took care of you?" Her voice was steadier. There was a note in it that told him how eager she was

407

to focus on him rather than herself for the moment. He was fine with that if it helped her.

"It was just me and my dad until I left home after high school."

She snuggled herself against him some more. "Then what did you do?"

Cal hesitated. The need for secrecy and anonymity had been ingrained in him over the last few years, but his background wasn't confidential and, somewhat to his surprise, he found himself wanting her to know.

"I attended the Air Force Academy. Became a pilot. Then, Air Force Special Ops."

"I knew you were military." There was a wealth of satisfaction in her voice. She was no longer sounding so small and scared, and she'd quit shivering. He congratulated himself for that.

"Not anymore. Like I said, I'm a private contractor."

"Doing what, exactly?"

"Right now, trying to stay alive." His voice was dry. Ignoring the growing erection that her wriggling around against him wasn't helping, he settled himself in to chat.

"You're not going to tell me, are you?"

"Nope."

She made a sound that combined annoyance with disgust, then said, "What about your father? Is he still alive?"

"Yes."

"The two of you must be close."

"We manage to exist on the same planet and that's about it."

"Is he very different from you? Like, an accountant or an insurance agent or something?"

"He's a retired Air Force officer. When I was growing up, he was a hard-ass and I was rebellious. My mother was the buffer. When she died, our relationship went to hell on a slide."

"That's sad."

Cal shrugged. He didn't find it particularly sad. He and his father had no problems now that he was grown. They'd achieved a kind of détente, the key to which was never seeing each other. "It is what it is."

She took a deep breath, then confessed what he'd been almost certain of all along. "That's what my nightmares are about, too. My family — the plane crash that killed them." She sounded like she was having a hard time getting the words out, but at least she was talking about it. That was the result he'd been aiming for with his own confessional: kind of an I'll-show-you-mine-if-you-show-me-yours deal. A high school guidance counselor had once done the same thing for him, and not long after that the nightmares had stopped.

"There were only the four of you on board?" he asked carefully, not wanting to push her too far too fast.

He felt her jerky nod. Then she said, "Yes," as if she was just remembering that he couldn't see her, and added, "We were in Campeche, in the Yucatán, at the site of a newly discovered Mayan city. My father was Dr. Gavin Sullivan. He was an archaeologist and a professor emeritus at Stanford. He was pretty famous, at least in academic circles." She stirred against him, and Cal got the impression that she was looking up at him through the darkness. "I don't suppose you've ever heard of him?"

"No. But then, I don't spend a whole hell of a lot of time in academic circles."

"No, I don't suppose you do."

He detected what he thought was a flicker of a smile in her voice, and some of the tension in his gut eased. She was emerging from the miasma of the nightmare, and that was good. What he wanted to do was keep her talking until she got it all out. Tomorrow they were catching a plane out of there if he could find any possible way to manage it, and it would be better for both of them if she'd aired her fears before then. At the very least, he'd know exactly what he was dealing with.

He said, "So you flew out of Yucatán. Who was at the controls?"

"My father. He owned a Piper Cherokee that he flew to archaeological sites all the time. He was an experienced pilot. He —" There was a sudden catch in her voice and she broke off, then started again. "He was good at everything like that, everything he did, really. Sometimes — sometimes, though, he tended to overestimate his abilities. Or underestimate the risks."

A shudder racked her. Cal guessed that she was thinking of the plane crash. He tightened his hold on her.

"Who was acting as copilot?"

She took another deep breath. "David. He had his private pilot's license — my father helped him get it for just that reason — but he hadn't had it very long and he didn't have a lot of experience. He was proficient enough, though, and getting better all the time. But he was another one to sometimes overestimate his abilities and underestimate risks. Probably it had rubbed off on him from my father."

"The two of them worked together?"

"Yes. By the time of — the crash, David

411

had been working for Dad for a couple of years as his graduate assistant while trying to earn his PhD. The two of them were tight. Almost father-son tight. Becca — she was my half sister from my father's first marriage; she was the same age as David, twenty-six — worked for my father, too. He wanted a documentary made of his work and he hired her to be his videographer."

"What about you? What were you doing there?"

"I was working for him, too. From the time I was a little girl I'd spent part of my summers and a lot of school breaks traveling with Dad to archaeological sites, usually really remote ones, which is why I know things like how to set up a tent, and make a furnace for a tent." Her tone had turned slightly pointed, and Cal remembered expressing suspicion of her abilities in that regard. He rubbed an apologetic hand up and down her arm. She continued, "Dad offered me a job right out of college, to complete the team, he said. I was in charge of making all the necessary logistical arrangements, like where we would sleep and what food was available and finding us cars, porters, specialized equipment, that kind of thing. My father called me his ground control officer." Again Cal got the impression that she gave a faint smile. "It was supposed to be a temporary position because I had plans to go on to grad school, but then there was David, and I stayed."

"You fell in love." Cal kept his voice carefully neutral. He discovered that he actually didn't much like the idea of that, even if it was younger, more naive and idealistic Gina falling in love with her father's almost equally young assistant. Even if the relationship was long over. Even if the guy was dead.

"We fell in love," Gina confirmed, her voice soft with reminiscence. "David was handsome and smart and funny and kind of brash, and I was absolutely thrilled that he chose me. Becca had a thing for him, too, you see. Becca was beautiful, and she was like our dad, outspoken and ready to take on anything, anytime. I take after my mother: I'm quieter and more careful. My father used to call my mother 'domestically inclined' because she got tired of traveling around with him all over the world. She wanted a stable home life. She's very organized, very down-to-earth. Also very loving and kind."

"I like the sound of your mother."

"She's been my rock all my life. Dad was more like a shooting star blazing across the heavens. Dazzling, but —" She broke off.

"Not as reliable?" Cal guessed.

"He liked excitement. He was always on the go, always chasing the next big find, always testing himself and everyone around him. My mother used to say that one of these days he was going to get himself killed. Turns out she was right." Her voice went a little unsteady as she said that last.

"Can you tell me what happened? With the plane?" His voice was carefully gentle. She'd told him a lot, but she was still circling the tragedy that haunted her like a wary animal fearing a trap.

She was silent for so long that he wasn't sure she was going to answer. He did what he could: held her and waited.

Finally she made a restless little movement, and her arm tightened around his neck.

"There was a tropical storm coming in when we took off," she said. "It hadn't hit yet, but it was on the way. I wanted to either wait a few days until the storm system passed, or take a commercial flight out of Cancún, which was only a few hours away, but Dad and David and Becca voted me down. The three of them were all adventurers, natural-born risk takers, and an approaching storm that at that point wasn't anything more than some wind and overcast

414

skies was nothing to them. I was the official wuss." She took a breath. "They were always calling me that, teasing me about being so cautious and careful. I *hated* having them think I was a wuss. If I hadn't hated it so much, I might have stuck to my guns and *insisted* we take a commercial flight if we had to leave that day, or else wait until the weather cleared. But my father wanted to get back and wouldn't hear of waiting, and as they all pointed out to me we could be almost all the way home by the time we drove to Cancún and got through the airport onto the flight I'd found, and anyway it wasn't even raining yet. So I caved. I *caved.*"

Her voice caught, and she shivered. He hugged her closer.

"So you took off under the threat of an incoming storm," he prompted. "How long were you in the air before it hit? Presuming it did hit."

"It hit." Her words were flat. Cal could feel her pressing closer, and he slid a comforting hand down the smooth curve of her back. "We'd been in the air about forty-five minutes when it started to rain. Only a little at first and then a deluge. Sheets of water pouring down, sluicing over the windows, drumming against the fuselage.

Big peals of thunder along with flashes of lightning. We were over the jungle, there was no place to land, so that option was out. Dad tried getting above the storm, but he couldn't. It was too big. We were flying in clouds so thick and black that it was like the darkest of nights. He had to switch to flying by instruments. The wind was the worst. We were bouncing all over the place, hitting wind shears without warning, going up and down like we were in an elevator. Dad was calm. David and Becca were calm. I was scared to death, but I tried not to let it show." She paused, and Cal felt her fingers digging into the back of his shoulder. "Then a huge wind shear took us down in what felt like a free fall and somehow the tail broke off. The plane went into a dive and crashed in the jungle. I was thrown clear."

She stopped. He could feel the tension in her body, hear her too-fast breathing, sense her rising agitation.

"The others?" he asked gently.

"They were still with the plane."

He smoothed the hair back from her face and pressed another kiss to the top of her head. He knew how hard this was for her. His stomach went tight with reaction to her distress.

"Can you tell me the rest of it, honey?"

She clung to him like a barnacle to a boat, like he was her anchor, and the knowledge that this beautiful, brave, resourceful woman was depending on him to get her safely through her emotional storm messed with his own emotions. He felt her getting in under his guard, sinking in hooks where he took good care hooks should not be sunk, but there was nothing he could do to prevent it. He was deep in the maelstrom with her, and he sure as hell wasn't letting her go.

When she spoke, her voice was so low he had to strain to hear. "I was knocked unconscious for a few minutes, and when I came to the plane was on fire. Just a little bit, just a few flames licking up around where the tail had been. The fuselage was all crumpled up like an accordion and was wedged in this grove of trees. I ran over to the plane. The cockpit was ripped open and I was able to see inside. My father was slumped over the controls. David —" Her voice quavered, but she swallowed and went on. "David was lying there on the nose of the plane, covered with blood. He'd gone through the windshield. I could see at a glance that he was dead. Becca — she was all twisted up in the wreckage. I thought she was dead, too. The only one I could reach was my father. I grabbed his arm and shook him. The fire was spreading, and I was screaming and trying to pull him out, but I couldn't. He woke up and kind of shook himself and tried getting himself out and he couldn't do it, either. His legs were trapped. The fire was racing toward us. I could feel its heat on my back but I wouldn't look around because I was afraid of what I would see. We were both desperately trying to pull his legs free when he looked past me and said, 'Get back, you have to save yourself,' and pushed me away. Then the plane blew up. Just went *boom* and was engulfed in flames. I got thrown backward, and that's when my shirt caught fire. You were right: it was burning fuel. It rained down all over me."

Her voice shook. He held her close and thought of the lacy tracery of scars on her arm, wincing as he imagined the pain she must have suffered getting them. The worst thing was, that pain was nothing compared to the psychological pain she still suffered, was suffering now.

He said, "It's in the past, it's over. I've got you now."

She whispered, "I keep — seeing them die. *Hearing* them die. Becca was alive, too. I know, because she started screaming as

418

the plane burned. My father screamed, too. They were alive. They screamed. And I — you know what I did? — I couldn't stand watching, or listening, so I turned and ran away and left them to die."

She started to cry, deep, harsh sobs that shook her from head to toe and stripped him raw inside. He held her and rocked her and kissed her and murmured whatever inane words of comfort came to him and felt his gut twist and his heart break for her.

That's when he knew, for sure, that he had a problem.

Forget getting it on, he was getting involved.

Hell, face the truth: he *was* involved.

In the end, when she was all cried out in his arms, he loved her back to sleep.

Then, unable to sleep himself for the first time in as long as he could remember, he got up, got dressed, and started making preparations for the coming day.

As a last act before waking her, he headed out to the mouth of the cave to check the weather and see what he could see.

The fog had cleared. It was still snowing, but only moderately. No blizzard involved. There was a stiff wind, and it was still bitterly cold. Cal thanked God they'd had the protection of the cave during the night. The sun was just coming up, adding streaks of pink and orange to the leaden gray of the sky. The birds on the slope directly below him were stirring, emerging from their burrows and hopping around, making a surprising amount of noise. He ignored them, first squinting at the camp and then looking at it through binoculars to make sure.

Yes. He gave a mental fist pump as he spotted the de Havilland Beaver on the runway. There was no snow accumulation yet on the wings, which told him that it hadn't been on the ground long. This particular one looked a little battered, but the Beaver was a small, hardy Alaskan bush plane and would do the job he needed it to do.

Already turning back into the cave, busy making plans, Cal was startled when the puffins below him took off in a squawking, wing-beating mass, rising into the dawn sky in a noisy black cloud.

His gaze followed them automatically. As it did, it alighted on a sight so ominous that his blood froze. Whipping back around, he jerked the binoculars up to his eyes again to make sure.

Moving along the path he and Gina had taken the day before, with all the deadly silence of a squadron of stealth bombers, was a group of about twenty armed men. They had almost reached the fork in the trail that would take them up to the cave, and they were being led by a pair of what looked like native Aleuts with their tracking dogs.

CHAPTER TWENTY-FIVE

"We're going to do *what*?" Gina squeaked. Cal gripped her hand tightly, pulling her after him as, flashlight illuminating the way, they raced up the last, steep section of the pitch-black stone tunnel that at its end would open out into nothingness at the top of Terrible Mountain.

"Jump."

If his reply was terse, it was because the situation was desperate. Anyway, her question was largely rhetorical. She'd heard him perfectly well the first time he'd said it: he was proposing that they jump out of a cave entrance some three thousand feet up, on a different side of Terrible Mountain from the cave where they'd entered the mountain last night. With a parachute. A World War II–era parachute. That had been stored since the war ended in one of the garbage cans in the cave along with a couple dozen other parachutes and all kinds of other military odds and ends.

The horrible thing about it was, she couldn't think of a better alternative.

"There has to be another way," she said. Alarm spiraled through her system at the very idea. At his urging, her feet flew over the uneven stone floor. She'd stumbled several times already. His iron grip on her hand was all that had kept her upright.

He glanced back at her. "Look, I know what I'm doing. I've jumped under worse conditions than these. I'll get you down alive."

"Are we even high enough for a parachute to work?"

"Yes."

The brusqueness of his reply told her that he'd made up his mind. But she hadn't yet made up hers. She'd already had an object lesson in the inadvisability of letting domineering personalities make life-or-death decisions that affected her. She had to decide for herself what the best thing to do was — and she wasn't feeling that parachuting off a mountaintop was going to be it.

Moments before, Cal had urgently wakened her. She'd dressed at light speed while he'd gathered the supplies he deemed they needed and explained the situation. Then they'd headed upward through the tunnel as quickly as they could go. Apparently during the night he'd found a map of the tunnel system, and both the cave they'd slept in and this other one, which was right below the summit on the western face of the mountain, were clearly marked. Gina had seen the higher entrance before as well, in a notation on a birder's map, because a colony of ptarmigans nested near it. That it existed wasn't in question.

The need to jump out of it was what had every brain cell she possessed screaming at her to put on the brakes.

Only, on the way up they'd paused at the first entrance for just long enough so that she could look out. What she saw had frightened her into turning tail and running with him, and kept her from digging in her heels and shouting *Hell no* now.

Armed men were swarming up the side of the mountain. The scarily silent tracking dogs that were leading them had been right below the now empty puffin burrows when she'd looked out. Gina had had a brief flashback to Arvid's death, to Mary's and Jorge's bodies on the common-room floor, and had known without a shadow of a doubt that if she and Cal were caught, they would be killed.

At Cal's insistence the two of them were

now dashing for the fissure near the top of the mountain instead of fleeing through the interconnecting tunnels that would take them into the adjoining mountain, and from there into other adjoining mountains, because, as he'd pointed out, the dogs could track them through the tunnels as easily as they could along the trails outside. And she had just minutes in which to make up her mind about whether she was going to go along with him and jump.

Gina was still shuddering at the thought when, as they pelted around a bend in the tunnel, she saw gray fingers of light stretching down from what had to be the cave opening. A waft of fresh air reached her. The temperature dropped by at least ten degrees.

Her stomach dropped straight to her toes.

Oh, God, she thought as Cal pulled her after him toward the light, *we're here. This is it.*

The area right inside the opening was the size of a small room with a flat, relatively even floor. After racing through it, Cal stopped at the edge of this fissure in the mountain's face to look out. Hauled up to stand beside him, Gina stood on the black lip of the precipice and got her first glimpse of the dizzying vista he was expecting her to leap into. Jagged mountain peaks turned a misty lavender by the frosty light of the newly risen sun surrounded them, the tallest of them piercing a fast-moving field of dark clouds. A frigid wind gusted from the east, its force slanting the heavily falling snow sideways. Below them, Terrible Mountain fell away in a sheer straight drop for at least several hundred feet before shooting up a secondary peak and ridges and a whole solid mountainside. That they could crash into. If they tried parachuting down.

It was a long, long way to the ground. Almost three thousand feet, to be exact. The river skirting through the mountains appeared so tiny from Gina's vantage point that it was no more than a glinting silver thread in the vast white fields of snow. Just looking down gave her vertigo.

If she didn't jump, she wondered frantically, what were the chances that she'd be caught and shot?

"Come here." Grabbing her before she could reach any solid conclusion, Cal pulled her away from the edge. She was wearing her snow gear, as was he, and he zipped her coat the rest of the way up to her chin. "Make sure your hood is on tight. It's going to be cold."

She secured her hood, watching with

dismay as he shrugged into the army-green, backpacklike parachute housing and secured the straps around his chest and waist.

"How about we try *climbing* down the mountain?" Still faintly breathless from their flat-out run, she looked up at him despairingly, already as sure as it was possible to be that she knew what he was going to say.

"You saw the dogs. If they're here, they're able to track us. They'll have found Ivanov by now, and they probably put the dogs onto our scent from there." He bundled her into one of their regular backpacks as he spoke. Its contents had been pared down to the bare essentials they needed to survive, and it was light. "If they're not in the cave yet, they will be at any minute. They'll follow us up here. As long as your feet are touching ground, you can't hide from dogs. We could stand and fight, but I don't like our chances: there are too many of them. If we try climbing down from here, there's no way we'll be out of rifle range before they spot us, because the dogs are going to bring them *here.* Even if we did somehow manage that, they'd still be right on our tail. If we jump, we lose the dogs and buy ourselves some time. If we don't, we're essentially dead."

"If we jump off a mountain and the decades-old parachute doesn't work, or something else goes wrong, we're just as dead." As she spoke he was wrapping rope he'd found in the cavern around her waist and between her legs.

"I checked the rigging and the canopy: it's all good. Anyway, I thought you weren't afraid of heights." He knotted the rope at her waist. She remembered their exchange at the natural bridge and grimaced.

"I'm not a fan of jumping off heights, that's for sure." She threw his words, slightly modified, back at him.

Apparently he also remembered, because a corner of his mouth ticked up in a quick flash of a smile.

"It'll be fine. You'll see."

"Shouldn't I at least have my own parachute?" Her voice was getting higher pitched again as she realized that the ropes he was knotting around her formed a makeshift harness.

He shook his head and tied a final knot at her waist before stepping back. "We'd get separated. Anyway, if you tried jumping by yourself, you'd die."

"Oh, that makes me feel all better."

"I guess what it boils down to is, do you trust me?" He pulled the straps of two of the rifles over his head so that he was wearing them like a woman might wear a crossbody purse, and stuck the pistol in the pocket of his coat. He looked big and tough and competent, Special Forces to the max — and also, just incidentally, so handsome he stole her breath.

"I trust you." Her tone was grim because she could scarcely believe that she was saying it. She was so nervous that she was jiggling from foot to foot. Her heart was beating a mile a minute and her stomach was in a knot and she had a really bad feeling about what they were getting ready to do — but she'd spoken the truth: for better or worse, she did trust him. That's when she knew her decision was made: she was going to jump off a damned mountain with him. God help her.

"That's my girl." Cupping her face in his hands, he bent his head and kissed her. It was a quick, hard kiss, but her lips opened under his and she kissed him back in helpless surrender to the way even that brief caress made her feel. Her body softened and her blood heated and her head spun. They hadn't had a chance to discuss anything — not the earthshaking sex, not the soulbaring confidences he'd coaxed from her or his own revelations — but the night had changed everything, at least for her. As juvenile and anachronistic as it sounded, she now felt like *his girl.*

Breaking the kiss, he pulled her hard against him. Unfortunately, the action felt anything but romantic. Gina tensed. Her breathing quickened. Inside her gloves, her palms began to sweat. It was *on,* she knew.

"Put your arms around my neck." His tone was all business, and as she complied he wrapped the trailing end of the rope that he'd tied around her around his own waist and hers several times before knotting it. "From time to time I'm going to need both hands free to operate the 'chute, but we're tied together now. I need you to hold on tight, but even if you let go, you can't fall." Sliding an arm beneath her bottom, he lifted her off her feet. "Wrap your legs around my waist."

Struggling against panic, Gina complied. In the distance, she thought she heard muffled sounds. Hushed voices. The thud of footsteps. The scrabble of claws on stone.

Alarmed, she glanced back down the passage. "Cal —"

"I hear it." His voice was perfectly calm. "Hang on." His arm clamped around her waist. He started to run, carrying her with

430

him as if her weight was no hindrance at all.

Gina's eyes widened. Her heart lurched. Her pulse pounded. She twined herself around him and clung like the proverbial monkey in a hurricane, bracing herself for — a horrifying drop into oblivion? A quick, hopefully painless death? A —

"Whatever you do, don't scream," he said in her ear.

Then he leaped out into nothingness like an Olympic long-jumper going for gold, like Superman launching himself into the stratosphere — only they fell like a stone.

It felt like getting hit by a train. Air slammed into her back with all the force of a ten-ton locomotive, forcing the breath from her lungs. Her heart rate skyrocketed. Every muscle she possessed went rigid with fright. If she'd wanted to scream — and she did — the g-forces would have made it impossible. It was almost impossible to breathe. Staring wildly up into the tumbling gray clouds, watching in helpless terror as the overcast ceiling receded above her head at an incredible rate, Gina felt the wind rushing past and practically saw her life passing before her eyes. Fast-forwarding through every prayer she'd ever heard in her life, she hurtled toward earth flat on her back, her arms and legs locked desperately around Cal's hard body, which was no help at all because he was falling through the sky, too. Terrible Mountain's black, snow-dusted face seemed to shoot upward, too horrifyingly close as she fell down it. The sheer drop that she'd looked out on from the cave entrance flashed past, and she arched upward in terrified anticipation, sure that at any second she would smash into the peak below, be broken, and die on solid rock —

The chute deployed, bursting into the air above them like a silken rocket, the narrow column of flimsy rope and gathered white cloth streaking toward the massing storm clouds.

It billowed, opened —

Just like that they were jerked upright and sent shooting skyward like a rubber ball on an elastic tether. The jolt was so unexpected that Gina almost became dislodged. It didn't help that Cal's arm, which had been clamped around her waist during their free fall, was no longer there. Instead, she saw in a terrified glance, he was holding on to two triangular handles that seemed to be attached to the parachute. In that same glance she caught a glimpse of his face. His jaw was hard, his mouth was tight, his eyes were narrowed, and he seemed to be looking down. He appeared intensely focused, but — thank God! — perfectly calm.

He must have felt her glance, because he yelled in her ear, "Doing okay?"

She didn't yet have enough breath back to yell an answer. Instead, quaking with reaction, she nodded and tightened her death grip on him and watched Terrible Mountain falling away below them. They were soaring up and away, being borne along on the wind through the blowing snow, flying higher than the highest of the peaks, ascending into the clouds —

That realization scared her enough to shriek a question at him. "Shouldn't we be going down?"

"Updraft," he shouted back, not sounding at all alarmed but, rather, like a man in his element. He was holding on to the handles, using them to keep the parachute steady in the face of the buffeting wind that sent them skittering this way and that, and also, as she discovered as she risked a look down, to steer. He sent them around the backside of Terrible Mountain, then did his best to keep the parachute following the valley between the peaks. They were so high now that she could see a V-shaped formation of cackling geese flying below them. "We're good now.

Relax and enjoy the view."

Gina almost choked. Her heart pounded and her pulse raced and her stomach felt as if it were lodged in her throat. Dangling from the floating mushroom above them, she and Cal rocked from side to side. The sensation of being suspended in mid-air, with nothing but a rope and her death grip on him standing between her and a fall of thousands of feet, was nightmarishly surreal.

"Enjoy the *view*?" she screamed at him disbelievingly, tipping her head back just enough to allow her to get a good look at his face.

He grinned, got a load of her expression, and said, "Or not."

Then he kissed her. Another of those brief, hard kisses that thrilled her clear down to her toes. And, freaked out or not, she kissed him back.

The snow-covered landscape below *was* bleakly beautiful, she had to admit, once he quit kissing her to concentrate on getting them safely back to solid ground, and she recovered enough equanimity to actually look down and check it out. Soaring above it, she might even have appreciated the scenic side of their death-defying stunt if she hadn't been busy keeping a wary eye out for bad guys with guns, and if her right leg hadn't been developing a cramp, and if she hadn't been totally scared to death because they were sailing along thousands of feet above the ground.

The descent was gradual. They dropped into the shadow of the mountains, went down past a nesting colony of rare red-legged kittiwakes (the location of which, under better conditions, she would have been itching to record), and skimmed rocks and snowdrifts before touching down in a narrow, horseshoe-shaped valley surrounded by mountains as softly as one of the snow-flakes falling around them. She'd thought that she would see the ground rushing up at her, that they would hit hard and maybe roll or something, but his feet touched and he took a few running steps while apparently doing something that freed the canopy part of the parachute. As the white silk went billowing away without them, he slowed and stopped.

"Thank God," Gina said devoutly, mentally kissing the ground, which, since they'd landed in Henderson Marsh, was spongy tundra beneath about six inches of snow. Unwrapping her poor, cramped legs from their death grip on his waist, she let them drop with a sigh of relief, only to find as her feet touched the ground that they were full of pins and needles. Her arms slid down from around his neck until her hands clutched the front of his coat for stability, and she rested against him thankfully as her legs regained their feeling.

"You did great." He rubbed her back in apparent congratulations, then cut her free of the rope that had harnessed them to-gether. She hadn't seen the folding knife, which he pulled from his boot and which he'd apparently found in the cave before.

"You enjoyed that," she accused, resting her cheek against his wide chest.

"I haven't jumped for a long time." His faintly nostalgic tone made it an admission that she was right. After freeing her of the rope, he lifted the backpack off her back, then set it down in the snow. Not quite hav-ing recovered the full use of her legs yet, she sank down cross-legged in the snow beside it while he unstrapped himself from the parachute case and buried it by kicking snow over it.

"Do you think they saw where we went?" Pulling the backpack onto her lap, Gina dug inside it for essentials: water and a protein bar. They hadn't yet had a chance to eat anything that morning, and the way she was feeling, she needed to if she was ever going to move again. Unscrewing the top of the water bottle, she drank.

"Not unless we're really unlucky. We dropped so fast that they couldn't have seen us go, and I steered us around the far side of the mountain once we had lift, so I don't think the men with the trackers could have spotted us. And if anyone had seen us land — well, we'd know about it." He hunkered down in front of her, a big, dark figure against the background of towering mountains and endless snow.

"They'd have shot us by now, you mean." Glumly Gina passed him the water bottle and broke off half the protein bar and handed that over, too, before biting into her half. With the knit cap pulled down low over his eyes and the black scruff on his jaw and chin growing in thick, he looked so disreputable that if she were to see him coming when she was walking alone down a street, she would cross to the other side.

"You don't have to worry. I told you I'd get you out of this alive, and I will."

Under his steady regard, Gina, to her own astonishment, found herself feeling suddenly shy. She had an instant, way-too-vivid flashback to the things they'd done together in bed, to how uncharacteristically wild he'd made her, to how passionate he'd been, and as her heartbeat sped up and her body heated she took refuge in flippancy.

"You sweet-talker, you," she said, and treated him to an exaggerated batting of her eyelashes.

He grinned, said, "Eat up, we need to go," and demolished his own protein bar in four bites.

Then he pulled the binoculars from the backpack, stood up, and started scanning the surrounding slopes with them. By the time she finished eating and he reached down to help her to her feet, this reminder of the danger they were in had her insides twisting with anxiety.

"Nothing," he said in response to the look she gave him. "And there's almost no cover, so I'm pretty sure I would have spotted anyone who was up there."

That was good, and she felt a tingle of relief.

"Now what?" she asked as he tucked the binoculars back into the backpack and shrugged into it.

He started walking, his boots crunching in the snow, and she fell in beside him.

"Now we go steal a plane."

She'd known he was going to say that. Her stomach turned inside out at the thought, but she didn't say anything, just kept trudging along at his side through the falling snow. But something of what she was feeling must have shown on her face, because after a glance at her he said, "You trust me, remember."

She sighed, faced the truth of that, and said, "I do."

"I just need you to trust me this one more time. Just till we get home."

Home. That was the word that did it. Because she knew that his idea of home and her idea of home were two entirely different things. The knowledge that at home, in the real world, they had no place in each other's lives stabbed sharp as a knife through her heart. Which, because of its implications for the future state of that heart, scared her to death.

She stopped dead. As he turned to frown questioningly at her, she folded her arms over her chest, lifted her chin at him, and said, "Just so we're clear, I haven't flown in a plane since the last one I was in crashed and burned. I haven't had sex with anyone but you since my husband died. I live a quiet, peaceful, stable life as a college professor, and I like it. I don't do death-defying stunts, and I don't do one-night stands with dangerous men who flit through my life like a puff of smoke and then disappear. I'm not brave, or adventurous, or sexually uninhibited. That isn't me. It won't ever be me."

"Gina." His eyes slid over her, then rose to meet hers as he reached out to catch her by the arms. She couldn't quite read what was in them, but his mouth curved in the slightest of wry smiles, which made her think she was amusing him, which had her frowning direly at him. "You parachuted off a mountain with me: in my book, that makes you pretty brave. You came here to Attu, which makes you plenty adventurous. As for sexually uninhibited" — his eyes glinted at her in a way that served as a graphic reminder of everything he'd done to her and she'd done to him, and, not coincidentally, set her heart to knocking — "you'll do. You have my personal guarantee."

Shaking her head no, she burst out with, "But that was a one-time thing. That isn't *me.*"

"Maybe," he said, "that's you with me."

That rendered her speechless. She searched his eyes, and at what she saw blazing at her from the coffee-brown depths, butterflies fluttered to life in her stomach. Maybe the crazy-hot attraction she felt for him, maybe the way her body quaked and burned at his slightest touch, maybe the explosion of passion she'd experienced with him that was like nothing she'd ever felt before had an explanation just that simple. This was a different, fresh relationship. This was how she and Cal were together. This was *them. You with me.*

Her mind boggled. Her heart skipped a beat.

He continued, "As far as I'm concerned, last night wasn't a one-night stand, and I'm not planning on vanishing from your life like a puff of smoke unless you want me to. I think what we have going on here, this thing between us, might be the start of something special. We could try it out. I could bring you flowers, take you to dinner, that kind of thing. See where it goes."

Something — hope, happiness, a promise of fresh, new love — burst to life inside her heart like the first delicate spring crocus shooting up through a long winter's worth of snow.

She smiled at him, a beautiful sunburst of a smile, which immediately turned into a suspicious frown as a thought hit her.

"You're not just saying that to get me on that damned airplane, are you?"

He laughed, pulled her into his arms, and kissed her. Hot and sweet at first, the kiss soon turned hot and urgent, and by the time

he let her go the snow was practically melting around them and Gina was blissfully
convinced that he'd meant every word he'd
said.

CHAPTER TWENTY-SIX

During the hours-long trek to camp, the weather deteriorated. More heavy gray clouds rolled in to hang low in the sky and turn what had been a pale but relatively clear morning as gloomy and dark as if dusk had fallen. The temperature dropped and the wind picked up until it bit at their cheeks and whistled around their ears. Fog blew in, not in a heavy blanket but in thick wisps that formed islands of mist floating just above the ground. The snowfall grew heavier, wetter. Every indicator was there: another major storm was on the way. The only questions were, when would it hit and would they be caught out in it.

Gina devoutly hoped they wouldn't be. She was freezing cold, dead tired, aching in every muscle, and scared to death. Under such conditions, it was difficult to maintain a warm little glow of happiness. But she was managing it.

Cal seemed pretty cheerful, too, for a man armed with two rifles, a pistol, and a knife in his boot, who was keeping a wary eye out for anyone wanting to kill them so he could kill that person first. At her urging, he told her about his beach house in Cape Charles, Virginia, and his company, and his dog, Harley, whose very existence Gina found completely charming. Without revealing too much, he also filled in more details about the circumstances surrounding the plane crash that had dumped him in her lap. In turn, she talked about her life, telling him about the time she'd spent in the hospital and how she'd passed the long, slow days of her recovery watching the birds they kept in giant cages there and developing a fascination with them, which had spurred her, when she was released at last, to go on and get her master's and PhD in ornithology. She told him about her life as a college professor, and her condo, and beautiful, sunny Northern California.

At length they found an old army road, which Cal instantly mistrusted even though Gina assured him that, to her knowledge, there were no operational land vehicles on Attu other than the tractor. He felt that the road made too obvious a target for a search party, and also that there was no way to

444

know whether the bad guys had brought something like, say, ATVs with them. But since they were sure to hear anything like that coming, and walking was so much easier with the firm surface of the hard-packed dirt road beneath the snow than with the squishy tundra, and time was of the essence, they were trudging along it anyway.

Cal said, "With the weather looking like it is, the trackers and any other search parties will most likely be heading back to the Coast Guard station. We want to beat them there if we can. It'll be a lot easier to steal a plane out from under the noses of a few men than twenty or more."

As much faith as she had in Cal, the thought of attempting an escape via plane still made Gina queasy.

She said, "Don't you think somebody's going to notice when the plane starts to move? I mean, the only way it can go is down the runway right past the buildings."

"Once we're moving, it's too late."

"Aren't you the person whose plane just got shot out of the sky by a surface-to-air missile? What's preventing whoever shot your first plane out of the sky from shooting you out of the sky *again*?" If there was a note of exasperation in her voice, it was because they were getting worrisomely close to camp and close to the whole steal-a-plane scenario, which she wouldn't even have dreamed of agreeing to if it had been presented to her by anyone other than Cal.

"First, I wasn't flying the plane when it got shot down. Second, as far as I'm aware nobody had any reason to suspect we might get shot down. Now that I'm flying, believe me, us getting shot down just ain't gonna happen."

That cocky flyboy answer earned him a jaundiced look. But, whether it was idiotic of her or not, it also made her feel better. It both unsettled and alarmed her to discover that her trust in him apparently knew no bounds.

"Which brings me to something I've been meaning to do," he said, and stopped walking to pull the pistol out of his pocket. She stopped, too, looking silently down at the gun in his gloved hand before glancing up at him. Even through the veil of thickly falling snow, he seemed suddenly bigger and more formidable. His jaw was set, his mouth was unsmiling, and Gina realized that he'd gone into warrior mode: she was face-to-face with the hard-eyed, scary man she'd first encountered. For a second she was taken aback. Then she got a grip and reminded herself that he was now *her* bear.

"In case of — anything," he said, his tone as grim as his face — the slight hesitation told her that the "anything" he was referring to was something bad — "I want you to be able to protect yourself. I'm going to give you this, along with a quick lesson in how to use it."

Okay, now she got it: the "anything" referred to his death or incapacitation. *Nice.* Gina looked at the gun, looked at him, and held out her hand.

"Can I hold it?" she asked sweetly.

A slightly wary look flickered over his face. He passed the gun to her, grip first. It was big, black, and heavy.

"Basically, all you have to do is point and shoot," he instructed, leaning close. "But first you have to release the safety, right here —"

Before he could finish, she released then reengaged the safety lever on the back of the slide, ejected the magazine and the chambered round, snapped the magazine back into place, and pulled the slide back to rechamber a round, all in a series of crisp, practiced movements that, when she finished and looked at him, had him rocking back on his heels with his eyes wide.

Pocketing the gun, she raised her eyebrows

447

at him. "What is it they say about assumptions? I traveled to some very unstable regions of the world with my father. I learned to use a gun."

Recovering from his surprise, he practically crowed with delight, then wrapped his arms around her, rocking her from side to side as he hugged her against him.

"So, okay, I'm an ass," he said, clearly getting her "assume makes an ass out of you and me" reference. "That was awesome. *You* are awesome. Gorgeous, sexy, smart, can handle a gun. Honey, you're my wildest dream come true."

He was grinning as he said it, but then as he looked down at her and met her eyes his grin faded. A serious, intent expression took its place. Gina was instantly dazzled by the look in his eyes. He kissed her, a slow, lush kiss that made her all melty and dizzy and had her kissing him back as if the world would stop spinning unless they generated sufficient heat. The thought that beat like a pulse through her brain as she twined her arms around his neck and returned the hungry insistence of his mouth was, maybe, just maybe, *he* was *her* wildest dream come true.

Sleet broke them apart. Not just a sprinkling of sleet. A deluge, as if the angry-looking clouds overhead had gotten tired of politely seeding the island with snow and had decided to disgorge their contents in a massive, freezing moisture dump.

"Holy shit," Cal said as he flipped the waterproof hood of his coat up over his cap. One arm was still around her and his mouth was close to her ear as he raised his voice to be heard over the loud rushing sound of the falling sleet. "We got to move. If we don't get in the air soon, the wings will ice over and we won't be able to take off."

Grabbing her hand, he took off at a brisk walk — anything faster was dangerous to impossible given the worsening conditions underfoot — and pulled her along with him. Bending her head against the pounding sleet, Gina didn't know whether to be glad or sorry that the camp was only about half a mile away. The thought of trying to steal a plane and fly away in it made her stomach knot. The thought of trying to steal a plane with possibly iced-over wings and fly away in it into a sleet storm caused her stomach to twist into a pretzel.

By the time they were close enough to see the buildings, Gina was so cold and so physically miserable that she would have been pulling out the tent and taking shelter in it until the weather improved, and never mind what Cal thought about that, except for the fact that they'd left the tent behind in the cave to lighten the backpack's load. She was shivering uncontrollably, her face stung, and she could no longer feel her hands and feet. They skirted the camp's perimeter, skulking low like animals on the prowl for fear that their dark shapes against the white snow might be visible even through the gloom and the driving curtain of silvery sleet. It was early afternoon, although the weather made it seem much later. The main building appeared to have only a few occupants: Gina saw a couple of indistinct shapes moving past the windows. She could only suppose that anyone not at camp when the sleet storm hit had taken shelter in place, as she would have liked to have done. While Cal searched the shadows for sentries — there didn't appear to be any — she listened to the rattle of the generator, looked at the light pouring out of the windows, and felt envy mix with her fear. What she wouldn't give to be inside where it was warm and dry! The only thing she wanted more than to thaw out was to be safe.

"The plane's gone." Gina saw with relief that the runway was empty. Until that moment, she hadn't realized just how tense she was, how tight with anxiety her stomach was, how dry her mouth was at the prospect of getting on a plane.

"Somebody had the good sense to move it inside the hangar," Cal replied. They crouched behind the fuel tanks for cover, and he had his hand up, shielding his eyes from the driving sleet, while she had her hood pulled low over her eyes for the same purpose. Looking farther down the runway, Gina saw that he was right. The door to the hangar was open, the first time she'd ever seen it that way. The shadow inside had to be the plane.

Her breathing quickened as she realized what that almost certainly meant: his plan was still on. She could feel the sudden thumping of her heart.

She said, "The runway's solid ice." That was easy to see: sleet had formed a visible layer over the pavement that gleamed even in the muted light.

"We'll have to risk it."

Cal was so close that their bodies brushed. Looking at him, she saw that he was assessing the runway, his eyes intent. Determination was visible in every hard line of his face. She could feel him gathering himself, preparing for whatever the next step was. Her gaze flitted desperately around, looking for danger, for some reason to call a halt to what she now, more than ever, really, truly did not want to do. What she saw made her pulse skitter with horror. She grabbed Cal's leg.

"They're here," she whispered to him, leaning in close and gesturing urgently at the large party of armed men who appeared like wraiths out of the sleet. The men were at the eastern edge of the compound, jogging at double time toward the buildings. Alarm made her stiffen and reach toward the gun in her pocket, only to abort the maneuver. The falling sleet would coat it with ice in seconds, just like she and Cal were coated with ice. She wanted to keep it dry and operational for as long as she could. Anyway, Cal had one of the rifles, both of which he'd tucked inside his coat when it became obvious the sleet wasn't going to let up, in his hands. "Oh, my God, did they track us here?"

She didn't dare raise her voice to the level they'd previously been using, which had been fairly loud to be heard over the combined noise of the sleet and the generator. Cal heard her anyway. He shook his head.

"They're not coming toward us. Look."

He was right: they were heading straight for the buildings. From the pair of dogs with them, she deduced that these were the men who had tracked them to Terrible Mountain. She shut her mouth and shrank against the nearest ice-coated tank: the search party was passing terrifyingly close. At that moment only the twelve or so car-size capsules of fuel stood between her and Cal, and them.

Her heart started to slam against her breastbone.

Thankfully the men seemed to be more interested in getting out of the storm than they were in looking around. It was obvious that they had no inkling that she and Cal were anywhere in the vicinity, and she prayed that nothing happened to clue them in. Nothing did. Minutes after Gina first spotted them, the last of them filed inside the building.

She drew a deep, shaking breath of relief.

"We're going now. Run as fast as you can to the hangar. Stay low. I'll be right behind you."

Cal's words sent her gaze slewing around to him. Her stomach seized up, and a hard knot formed in her chest.

"But we can't — they'll see us. They'll see the plane. Did you see how many of them there are?"

"If we don't go now, we won't get another chance. As soon as the sleet stops, this yard is going to be crawling with gunmen. And in the meantime, all it's going to take is for one of those dogs to have to take a leak and in the process pick up our scent, and we're done."

Their faces were inches apart as they leaned closer to make themselves heard. Their eyes met and held. Gina realized that this was it, the fork in the road, the moment of choice. All she had to do was say, *you know, I think I'll give this a miss.* He wouldn't leave without her, she knew.

Wordlessly she got up on the balls of her feet, then took off at a sprint across the icy open field toward the hangar. She stayed low, her back bent against the lashings of sleet, her boots slamming through the layer of ice that covered the stabilizing snow. The pounding of her pulse in her ears was louder even than the drumming of the sleet hitting the hangar's corrugated metal roof.

Bursting through the open garage-style door into the shadowy darkness beyond, Gina processed the instant absence of pelting sleet with a rush of gratitude. Then she looked at the small plane with its large single propeller in front of her and felt her stomach sink straight to her toes. The thing was yellow and white, about the size of a mosquito, and looked like it was held together with duct tape.

She had zero confidence that it could make it into the sky, much less carry them across an ocean.

Cal was right behind her. His eyes touched on her, seemed to register that she was in one piece, moved around the interior of the hangar as though checking for any potential threat — it was empty — and fastened on the plane.

"Come on." He headed toward it.

No. No, no, no. Every instinct she possessed screamed in protest. Gina followed him anyway. The ice that had accumulated on his clothing fell off in thin sheets as he did a quick walk around the plane, checking it out. She supposed that ice was sliding off her in a similar fashion as well. She was too agitated to look.

Hoping for a locked door was hoping for too much, Gina knew even before Cal pulled the door open. The plane's dark interior yawned before her, as terrifying as anything she'd ever seen: the mouth of the beast.

She thought, *I can't do this.*

"Put your foot there and climb in." He patted a wing strut even as he turned to look at her. She didn't know what he saw in her face, but she knew that her heart had pushed way beyond pounding to go into panicked palpitations.

"Hey." He turned to her, cupping her face in his hands. Her cheeks were frozen. His gloves felt frozen. Neither was as cold as the blood pumping through her veins. "You trust me, remember?"

"Oh, God." She gripped his wrists, nodded jerkily.

He kissed her, a quick brush of his lips against hers. His lips were cold — and firm and possessive. It was a measure of her terror that she didn't even respond.

"I've got you. I've got this," he said as his hands dropped away from her face and he patted the strut again. The look he gave her was compelling. "Gina. Climb in."

Mute with fear, she looked from his face to the big gloved hand resting on the fragile-looking strut to the darkness waiting for her beyond the open door.

Then she steeled herself and climbed in.

The interior smelled old and musty. The narrow cylinder was cramped enough that she had to bend her head as she made her way toward the nose. If there had once been passenger seats, they'd been removed in favor of making cargo space: only the pilot and copilot seats remained. There were dog crates and other items in the back: it seemed

456

pretty certain that the tracking dogs and their handlers had arrived on this plane. She didn't really look at anything else, because she didn't care.

She was too busy keeping it together, keeping a lid on the panic that washed over her in waves. It was bad. Her nerves felt as if they were jumping beneath her skin, her stomach had turned inside out, and her chest was so tight that it required effort to breathe.

Cal was behind her. She concentrated on him and tried not to think about the fact that she was inside a plane. That she would soon be *flying* in said plane.

The cockpit was so small that she had no other option but to sit down in the copilot's seat to make room for Cal to enter. Memories crowded into her mind. She forced them back, mentally slamming the door in their face. Instead of looking at the windshield curving so close in front of her, she pulled off her gloves, pushed back her hood, and looked at Cal. He had the rifles under his arm and was carrying the flashlight, she saw as he tucked the rifles away on the floor behind the pilot's seat. He switched the flashlight on, shielding the beam with his fingers as he played it over the instrument panel: old wood, a dozen or more round, glass-fronted dials, twin yokes. Her gaze steadfastly followed the light's path.

"Don't you need a key?" she asked faintly as the light zeroed in on the ignition.

"No. Hold this steady for me, would you?" He passed her the flashlight.

She took it, restricted the beam with her fingers so that it focused only on the ignition, and refused to let her hands shake. Instead she watched Cal work. He'd stripped off his gloves and his long fingers moved dexterously, despite how cold she knew they had to be, as he inserted what looked like a straightened paper clip into the ignition, following it with the blade of his knife.

"You know how to hot-wire a plane?" she asked.

He was manipulating the blade and the wire simultaneously. "A basic skill learned in Air Commando 101."

"Seriously?"

"Sometimes stealing a plane is the best way to move across hostile territory anonymously. They can't track you if they don't know it's you."

Without warning the engine roared to life.

The sound was so unexpected that Gina jumped. The flashlight wavered, but Cal didn't need its light anymore: he'd already withdrawn his improvised tools from the ignition.

"Won't they hear?" she asked in alarm as he took the flashlight from her and switched it off before folding himself into the pilot's seat. He had, she saw, pushed back his own hood and pulled off his cap. His black hair was ruffled. His hard, handsome face was taut with concentration as he checked the dials. Her seat vibrated with the force of the engine's gyrations. Beyond the windshield, she tried not to see the propeller coming to life, rotating with increasing speed until it was no more than a blur.

Clenching her teeth against the emotional meltdown she could feel hovering, she focused on remaining very, very calm.

"They might. I'm hoping that it's noisy enough out there to block the sound." He frowned, tapped on a dial with a forefinger, then glanced at her before reaching past her to undo the latch on the small, triangular window beside her. "Get the gun out."

His businesslike tone was calming. So was having something physical to do. She looked a question at him as she complied. "Why?"

"I'm going to be busy flying this thing. If we run into trouble, you may have to provide cover fire."

Fear twisted around Gina's heart.

"If they start shooting at us, you mean." Her voice sounded hollow. Big surprise, she felt hollow. Like there was a huge empty space where her stomach used to be. But at least she wasn't quite so worried about being rendered catatonic by memories. A jolt of stark terror, she discovered, was a potent antidote to losing it.

"I'm hoping they won't. I'm hoping we can just roll on out of here and sail off into the sky." Reaching across her, he grabbed her seat belt and fastened it for her. Then he kissed the corner of her mouth. Firm, cool lips, the scratch of beard. "You're doing great. We're going to get out of here in one piece, I promise."

He pulled on his own seat belt.

Goose bumps prickled over her skin. She swallowed in an effort to combat her suddenly dry mouth. Her heart thumped like it was going to beat its way out of her chest. Her mind screamed, *No!* even as she braced herself.

He reached for the throttle, eased it back, and they were moving, taxiing through the open doorway out into the relentless sleet. It beat a staccato tattoo on the plane's metal skin, rattled down on the windshield. As they picked up speed, the interior of the plane vibrated forebodingly. One hand clenched into a fist, the other tight around the gun, Gina sat rigid in her seat, her gaze focused straight ahead.

"Shit." Cal was fighting the yoke and working the throttle at the same time. The plane fishtailed down the runway, its tires clearly unable to find a purchase on the ice. But what had prompted his exclamation wasn't anything to do with the plane: it was the men spilling from the buildings, charging toward the runway, opening fire.

A series of bullets smacked into the fuselage, the sounds as sharp as slaps.

"Gina." Cal looked her way, and she knew what she had to do. Shaking off the near paralysis that had been holding her in thrall, she girded her loins, shoved the little window open, stuck the pistol's barrel out a few inches, and fired back at the closest of the dark shapes darting toward them through the sleet. Whether she hit anybody, she had no idea. She was suddenly as icy cold inside as the wind rushing in through the window. More bullets smacked the fuselage as the plane picked up speed, slip-sliding toward the end of the runway like a drunken speed skater.

Her worst fear — oh, God, she couldn't even stand to entertain the thought — was that a bullet would find the gas tank and the plane would —

Do. Not. Go. There.

Out of the corner of her eye Gina saw something moving, something big, looked at it fully, and realized with a spurt of mortal fear that the tractor was lumbering toward the runway at full tilt.

"*Gina.* You don't have enough bullets. Shoot one of the fuel tanks. Did you hear me? *Shoot one of the tanks.*" Cal was yelling at her, had apparently been yelling at her all along. Between the roar of the wind and the roaring in her ears she hadn't heard a word, until this fresh burst of horror had juiced her with adrenaline and cleared her head.

She instantly saw what Cal meant: the men were bunching in front of the fuel tanks, using them for cover, firing at the plane from there, and the tractor was just about to barrel past the white metal capsules on its way to blocking the runway.

The fuel tanks were only a few yards beyond the end of the runway. The plane was racing toward them, too.

"Shoot the tanks," Cal bellowed.

Sick with dread, screwing up every last bit of courage she possessed, praying that she was not making a fatal mistake, she put her faith in God and Cal and snapped off some bullets at the damned tanks.

They exploded in a tremendous fireball, sending the tractor flipping end over end and bodies flying and a wall of flames shooting a hundred feet into the air.

The plane achieved liftoff and soared over the blaze with what, to Gina, felt like inches to spare.

The smell of fire was strong, freezing Gina in place. Sparks peppered the sky, glowing red like a million burning eyes. They flew through them as all around, everywhere, the sleet and the clouds and the sky turned a shimmering orange. The concussion from the explosion hit with jarring force, shoving the tail up and the nose down. The plane hurtled toward the ground, tipping left, threatening to roll as it plummeted toward what, below them, looked like an ocean of fire.

Fear grabbed Gina by the throat, strangling all utterance. Dropping the gun, she clutched the edges of her seat with both hands and hung on. Her heart pounded and her stomach dropped with the plane. Too terrified to close her eyes or even pray, she stared wide-eyed through the windshield and waited to crash and die.

The plane steadied. The wings evened out. A moment later they were bumping up through the sleet into the clouds, and the only orange she could see was a slight reflection on the shiny surfaces in front of her. Then the clouds swallowed them up, and the fire was left behind.

"You okay?" Cal reached past her to close the small triangular window that, until that moment, she hadn't realized was still open. The freezing cold, the rushing roar, immediately lessened.

"Yes." It was all she could do to reply. She felt limp, wrung out, exhausted from acute terror. Her chest still felt like it was caught in a vice.

"You did fantastic back there."

"Thanks." She was still having trouble talking. The plane rattled and bumped as it barreled through the clouds, and as she faced the fact that there were hours of this yet to go, her insides twisted with fright.

"The worst is over. I'm going to get you home safe." Cal's voice was soothing. Gina managed to turn her head enough to look at him. He did not look frightened, or even worried. He looked like he had when she'd jumped off the mountain with him: coolly competent, a man in his element.

Gina's death grip on her seat lessened. She even managed a deep breath. This was not a man who overestimated his abilities or underestimated the risks. This was a man who had proved to her that he could do exactly what he said he'd do.

"I know," she said.

CHAPTER TWENTY-SEVEN

Some five hours later, Cal set the Beaver down on the northwest runway at Eielson Air Force Base near Fairbanks, Alaska. The sixty-three-thousand-acre home of the 354th Fighter Wing would not have been his first choice of refuges, but the mission was too urgent and the margin for error was too small to let any type of personal consideration weigh with him. The flight had been a little rough, as he'd had to stay low to avoid detection by radar and thus evade any pursuit that the opposing side might have been able to launch. The end had gotten slightly hairy as fuel, even with the extra juice from the auxiliary tanks, had run critically low. It had been full dark by the time the bright lights of the base had appeared on the horizon. He'd been operating under visual flight rules since taking off from Attu, and since the instruments were a little wonky he'd had to basically guess how much farther they had to go. Without a word to Gina — he didn't want to alarm her — he'd been nursing the fuel to make it last, and the sight of the base, which was basically a small, self-contained city, was a considerable relief. Grim triumph was his strongest emotion as the Beaver rolled in past the control tower and on down the runway: they'd made it.

As he had expected, as soon as the plane taxied to a stop it was surrounded by a full contingent of MP vehicles; being in a civilian aircraft of unverified provenance, he would necessarily have been accorded a look-see. What he had not expected, at least not so soon, was the large black limousine.

He was tired. He was hungry. He was worried about the woman beside him, who'd gotten paler and quieter as she'd white-knuckled it through the buffeting they'd received five thousand feet above the waves. But one look at the limousine and he could already feel his hackles beginning to rise.

"We rate a limo? And a police escort? Or are we about to be arrested?" Gina was looking out at the surrounding cars with surprise. She'd shed her snow gear during the ride and was sitting there beside him looking stressed but beautiful in her snug red thermal shirt and tight jeans, her hair finger-combed and confined in a loose braid that hung over one shoulder. Faint blue shadows beneath her eyes gave them a slightly bruised look that did something to his gut. He wanted to wrap her up in his arms and sweep her off somewhere to rest and recuperate. But he couldn't: not right now.

Cal sighed. Having unfastened his seat belt, he reached over and unfastened hers.

Then he got up, leaned over, and kissed her.

She kissed him back, her lips softly clinging, her mouth hot and sweet and luscious. He felt himself getting hard in response, recognized that now was not the time, and pulled back.

Those big blue eyes of hers were almost his undoing. If it hadn't been for his certain knowledge of who was waiting for him in that limousine, he would have taken his time and kissed her breathless. As it was, he dropped one more quick, hard kiss on her lips and lifted his head.

Her slim, cool hand was still lingering on his cheek when he looked back out at the tarmac and saw that the rear door of the limo was being held open by an airman at full attention. The combination of the cars' headlights and the runway lighting meant that the tarmac was as bright as a football stadium on a Friday night in October.

Straightening as best he could given the low ceiling, Cal said, "I realize it's probably a little early in this relationship for us to start meeting the parents, but brace yourself: you're about to meet my father."

Gina's face tipped up toward him. "What?"

Cal nodded toward the tall, silver-haired man who was just stretching to his full height as he got out of the limo.

Gina looked. Then she looked back at Cal. "But — that's a general."

Cal nodded. "Yep."

Grabbing her hand, he snagged both their coats and headed out of the cockpit. "Let's go."

"Your father's a general," she said from behind him. Her fingers were wrapped around his. He tightened his hold on them.

"Yes, he is."

"I thought you said your father was a retired Air Force officer."

"He is an Air Force officer, and he is retired. He's here at Eielson acting as a consultant to the 354th Fighter Wing." Having reached the door by that time, Cal opened it and jumped down. Then he reached up to lift Gina down. As he set her on her feet she was looking at him wide-eyed, but she didn't say anything, probably because she was as aware as he was of their audience. He helped her on with her coat, shrugged into his, and was just turning around to head to the limo and get the confrontation over with when a deep, gravelly, and way too familiar voice spoke in an abrupt tone behind him.

"I got a message saying you were landing here."

That message had no doubt come via the control tower, when Cal had had to identify himself before being given permission to land. Well, his plan had been to get in contact as soon as he was on the ground anyway. Suspicious as he was of Whitman's, and possibly the CIA's, involvement in what had gone down, he'd made the decision not to head for the small private airfield where he was supposed to return with Rudy for a rendezvous with Whitman, but to come to Eielson instead. The flash drive in his belt, and the information he possessed, were vital to national security. At this point, there were two institutions the integrity of which he felt he could trust absolutely, and that were also equipped to deal swiftly and effectively with whatever was on that flash drive: the Air Force, and his father.

"Hello, General." Cal turned to face his father. Neither offered to shake hands. The devil of it was, they looked alike. The old man was heavier, jowlier, more squinty-eyed. Plus the silver hair. And the full uniform. But the resemblance was unmistakable.

"You in trouble?"

"I was going to call you when I landed. We need to talk privately." Cal put a hand on Gina's arm, drew her forward. His father had already raked her with a look, and, knowing his father, Cal knew what the old man was thinking: this was one of Cal's quickie chickies, as he called them. Only Gina wasn't, as Cal meant to make clear. "This is Dr. Gina Sullivan. She's a professor at Stanford. Gina, meet my father. Major General John Callahan."

"How do you do, General," Gina said with perfect, exquisite composure, offering her hand.

With a quick, glinting look at Cal, who knew that he was thinking something along the lines of *DOCTOR Sullivan? You're coming up in the world,* his father shook hands. "Pleasure to meet you, Dr. Sullivan." His attention returned to Cal. "What can I do for you?"

It was cold, and windy, and Cal wasn't

about to leave Gina standing around on the tarmac while he answered that question. On the other hand, his business was urgent — and private.

"We can talk here, but I'd like Gina to wait in your car," he said. For security purposes, to thwart any possibility of being bugged or spied on, having an unscheduled conversation in the great outdoors was probably as good as it got.

His father looked at him, nodded, then said to Gina, "Dr. Sullivan, if you'd care to —" and made a gesture toward the limo.

"I'll just be a few minutes," Cal told her. She nodded and headed for the limo. He waited until she was ensconced in the rear seat — the airman who still stood at attention by the rear flank of the car opened it for her — and then drew his father away until they were standing alone on the tarmac.

Then he told him everything.

"We've got Detachment 632 here on the base. They can check that flash drive of yours out," his father said. Detachment 632, Air Force Office of Special Investigations, specialized in counterintelligence investigations, among other things, and their capabilities and reach were absolutely on par with the CIA's or any other government agency's.

Cal had known that D632 was based at Eielson, which was another reason he'd chosen the base. Along with his father's clout, which would get the wheels rolling instantly.

"I don't want to hand the flash drive over to you out here. It's probably best if as few people as possible are aware of its existence."

His father was looking thoughtful. "We'll drop Dr. Sullivan at the hotel here on base — I presume you don't want to stay in my house" — which was an absolutely correct assumption, especially since Cal was planning to share a room with Gina — "and take that thing over to D632. They've got hella good IT specialists."

Cal wasn't sure how much his father knew about IT specialists, but as that had been more or less his plan for the flash drive, too, he agreed, with one proviso.

"Gina stays with me." When the general gave him a look that Cal knew was a prelude to some kind of lecture along the lines of *This is not the time, keep it in your pants,* he added, "She's a witness. She heard the man who I think might be Whitman talking, and she can identify his voice. If anyone knew, if Whitman knew, he'd pull out all the stops to eliminate her."

His father frowned and jerked his head in the direction of the motorcade surrounding his limo. "You don't trust those boys to protect her?"

"I don't trust anybody to protect her. Not until she listens to Whitman's voice and identifies it, or not."

"You think this Whitman will come if you tell him to? Won't he suspect you're setting him up?"

Cal shook his head. "I'm going to let him think I'm wounded — which I am, by the way; I took a bullet in the side a couple of days ago, no big deal — and that's why I came running here to Eielson and my dear old dad. He wants that flash drive, and he'll come get it. And he doesn't know Gina heard his voice."

His father frowned thoughtfully, then nodded. "All right, then. Get in the car and let's go."

They were both striding back toward the car when Cal said, "Oh, and a crew ought to be dispatched to Attu. There's at least ten dead and a hell of a mess out there."

His father snorted. "Sounds like the story of your life. I'll pass the word on."

Then the airman was opening the door for them and Cal slid in beside Gina.

Twenty minutes later, the flash drive was

in the hands of IT specialists at D632. And under the supervision of a cadre of fully briefed D632 agents, Cal was dispatching a message to Whitman. Using code and the secure phone connection that he'd told Gina about on Attu, he relayed the information that he was wounded, at Eielson, and had a flash drive given to him by Rudy: the "proof" Whitman had been seeking. Only Whitman was going to have to come and get it, because Cal wasn't going anywhere anytime soon.

After that, he and Gina sat down with his father at the cafeteria in the building and had a quick meal. He was starved, and he and his father weren't exactly chatty at the best of times, so once Cal made a courtesy inquiry about the well-being of his step-mother — his father had been married to his second wife, a very nice former flight attendant named Sharon, for ten years — and learned that she was fine and, at that moment, visiting her mother in Chicago, most of the conversation took place between Gina and his father. By the end of the meal, the old man was calling her Gina (nobody ever called the general anything but "sir" or "General") and making her smile as he caustically recounted some of Cal's teenage exploits.

"He always could find trouble," the general concluded, and gave Cal a censorious look. "Here we are a decade and a half later, and as you can see, he hasn't changed a bit."

"He saved my life," Gina said over her last sip of coffee. "I think he's pretty great."

Cal smiled at her, met his father's gaze — the old man's look said as plainly as if he'd shouted it, *This one's too good for you* — and stood up. The agents at the adjacent table, who were tasked with providing security for Gina until she was able to confirm, or not, that Whitman's was the voice she'd heard, stood up, too.

Having thus ended the meal before his father's reminiscences could turn acrimonious, as they tended to do, Cal borrowed a couple hundred dollars from him — all he and Gina had were the clothes they were wearing, and he thought he might need some cash — and exchanged surprisingly civil good nights with the old man. Then Cal and Gina were driven to the base hotel, The Gold Rush Inn. As spare and utilitarian as was just about everything Air Force, the inn was a foursquare and solid three-story beige brick building with a small lobby and adequate but far from luxurious rooms. Agents escorted them to their room, waited while a bag of clothing and other necessities from the base shopping center were brought up to them, then stationed themselves in a room across the hall where they would remain to provide security through the night.

When they were alone, Cal looked at Gina, who was glancing around the spartan accommodations with a slight frown as she took off her coat and hung it in the closet just inside the door.

He was familiar with Air Force lodging, but he tried to see it through her eyes. A queen-size bed with the bag from the shopping center on it. A small table beside it with a lamp. A chest across from the bed that held a TV. A couple of narrow windows set high up in the wall. A couple of cheap, framed prints. Brown carpet, brown curtains, brown bedspread, beige walls. Basic, white-tiled bathroom, attached.

She'd had a hell of a trying day, and he could tell how tired she was by the strain around her eyes and mouth and the slight droop to her slender shoulders.

"You doing okay?" he asked.

"Mm-hmm." She moved over to the bed, rummaged through the shopping bag, and extracted a few items from it. "I think I like your father."

Cal managed to repress a snort. "He

seemed to like you, too."

Clutching what seemed to be a jumble of toiletries and a nightgown close against her body, she gave him a level look and said, "Are you going to tell me why we have intelligence agents escorting us everywhere we go and spending the night across the hall?"

Cal couldn't tell her the truth, and he wasn't going to lie to her. She knew nothing about the danger she was still potentially in, because neither he nor anyone else had told her that the man she called Heavy Tread might very well be Agent Lon Whitman, CIA. Or that her identification of Whitman's voice, if identify it she did, would be what brought him down.

All she knew was that Cal was wrapping up the job he'd been carrying out when his plane had gone down, and that she was needed because she was a witness to what had happened on Attu. The agents felt, and he and his father agreed, that telling her anything more might conceivably compromise her ability to be impartial when she heard Whitman's voice.

Cal said, "No."

Gina's lips compressed. "That's what I thought." Turning toward the bathroom, she said over her shoulder, "I'm going to take a shower."

He nodded, and she went into the bathroom and closed the door. He thought about joining her — as tired as he was, the idea of taking a shower with Gina was enough to make him realize that he wasn't *that* tired — but knowing how tired she had to be dissuaded him. When she emerged, looking sweet and slightly ridiculous and amazingly sexy all at the same time in a long-sleeved, ankle-grazing pink flannel granny gown that he was as sure as it was possible to be was like nothing she ever wore, he allowed himself one look before managing a gruff, "Go to sleep," and retreating to take his own shower.

When he finished and came back out into the bedroom, he was wearing a towel around his waist, a fresh Band-Aid over his wound — the bullet was coming out in the morning — and nothing else, because the plaid flannel pajamas that had been folded into that shopping bag for him weren't going to happen.

To his surprise, she was still awake, propped up in bed in a room that was dark except for the blue glow of the TV, flipping through channels.

He stopped beside the bed to look down at her. Her tawny hair was loose and fell in a silken slide over one shoulder. Her fine-boned face was a pale oval in the gloom. The covers were tucked up under her armpits, so basically all he could see of the rest of her was the pink ruffle at the neckline of her gown and the long, full sleeves that ended in more ruffles at her wrists.

He was a sick man, he decided. Pink flannel granny gowns obviously did it for him. One look and he was instantly hard.

"I thought you'd be asleep," he said.

She shook her head, flicked him a look. "I waited for you."

"Oh?" He dropped the towel and slid into bed beside her. Taking the remote from her unresisting hand, he turned the TV off, dropped the remote on the table, and leaned over her. "I hear you think I'm pretty great."

There was just enough light from the halogens in the parking lot filtering in around the edges of the curtains to enable him to see that she was looking at him, to see her slight smile.

"I do." She put her hand on his shoulder. Her fingers felt delicate and cool.

"I think you're pretty great, too." His voice was husky. Coming from her, the faint, clean scent of the same soap he'd showered with that hadn't done a thing for him at the time now teased his nostrils like the headiest of perfumes. "And beautiful. And sexy as hell."

"You do?" She snuggled close, and he got treated to some full body contact with a whole lot of Downy-soft flannel. Suddenly he was so consumed with lust that he ached. Jesus God, maybe he had a granny night-gown fetish. Who'd known? His hand closed on a firm round breast with an eager little nipple that he could feel nudging his palm through the cloth.

"Mm-hmm." He kissed the breast his hand had captured, opening his mouth and teasing her nipple with his teeth and tongue until the flannel was wet and she was gasp-ing and clutching at his shoulders and straining up against him.

Then he kissed her mouth.

By the time the nightgown finally came off — half a dozen confoundingly tiny but-tons at the neck made removing the damned thing more of a challenge than he had foreseen — her legs were wrapped tight around his waist and he was thrusting hard inside her. His mouth was on her bare breasts and her hands were buried in his hair and she was moving beneath him and moaning. He couldn't have been hotter if he'd been set on fire.

His last semilucid thought before he succumbed to the flames was, *I ain't letting this woman go.*

CHAPTER TWENTY-EIGHT

Whitman showed up on schedule, as Cal had been sure he would. The moment Whitman realized that Cal had escaped from Attu, it would have been his top priority to hotfoot it back to his office in Seattle, because as far as he knew, Cal had no inkling that Whitman had been involved, and he would take the greatest precautions to make sure Cal never found out. In fact, if it hadn't been for Gina and her description of Heavy Tread's voice, Cal might never have suspected. Also, if it hadn't been for Gina, he probably wouldn't have been alive to worry about it.

So he owed her a lot. And as he'd told her that morning when he pulled her into the shower with him, he always paid his debts. In full. With interest.

Whitman arrived at Eielson that afternoon.

They were ready and waiting for him.

Cal in a blue hospital gown, stretched out in a semireclining position in a hospital bed, white blanket tucked around him up to the waist, an IV taped to his arm, in a white-walled hospital room complete with beeping monitors, should have looked a lot more helpless and vulnerable than he did, Gina thought.

Watching through a two-way mirror from the room next door, she decided that the man looked about as helpless and vulnerable as a rottweiler.

"Boy doesn't look sick a bit," Cal's father observed with disgust. He was beside her, sitting in a cushioned office chair just as she was. With them were two D632 agents, also seated. All of them were focused on the room next door. When she'd been driven to the hospital some hours after Cal had left early that morning, Gina had thought that she was being taken to visit him in his sickbed. It had been obvious to her from the moment she'd been ushered into this adjoining room and discovered that she could both see Cal and most of his room through the two-way mirror — what kind of hospital room had a two-way mirror? — and hear everything that was going on in said room, that something else was up.

Just what it was she wasn't quite sure, but she was tense with anticipation.

"He had surgery this morning," Gina pointed out mildly. "To remove a bullet."

"Outpatient surgery. Could have popped that thing out with his fingers." The general shook his head. "Doctor told me that it was right there under the skin. Not much worse than a splinter. Damn it, he's supposed to look like he's on his last legs. He never could pretend worth a flip."

Pretend? Gina cast him a sharp look, but was distracted by the opening of the door in Cal's room.

A man walked in, closing the door behind him. He looked to be around forty, with short, well-groomed, tobacco-brown hair and an open, pleasant face. He was over six feet tall, slightly stocky in build, well dressed in a camel overcoat over a dark suit. Gina supposed he could have been described as possessing all-American good looks, although the broad smile with which he advanced on Cal struck a wrong note in her somewhere.

"Whitman," Cal greeted him, and held out his hand.

"Was I ever glad to hear from you." Whitman shook Cal's hand. "The intelligence I got — it said you were all lost along with the plane. I —"

Whitman kept talking, but Gina stopped listening. His words, uttered in a slow Texas drawl, seemed to buzz around her head like bees. Then she realized that the buzzing was in her ears, and that her ears were buzzing because she was light-headed, and she was light-headed because —

"Gina. Is something wrong?" The general leaned toward her, gripping her hand as it rested limply on the arm of her chair. His hand felt surprisingly like Cal's, big and long-fingered and strong. The realization gave her something to focus on, an anchor to help pull her back from the dizziness that threatened to swamp her, and she gripped his fingers in turn.

"I know that voice," she said. "That man was on Attu. He was involved in the murders of my friends."

"Dr. Sullivan." The two agents were on their feet. One of them, Captain Brady — thirtyish, bald, medium height, wiry — leaned closer. "Are you sure?"

Gina took a breath, tightened her hold on the general's fingers. "Yes."

The agents exchanged glances and left the room. Even as she looked back through the mirror at Cal, at the man talking to him, she realized why she was there: to identify the voice of Heavy Tread.

Just as she had that epiphany, the agents entered Cal's room and walked briskly toward his bed.

Their guns were drawn.

Whitman turned, frowned at them.

"Lon Whitman, get your hands in the air!" Brady barked. "You're under arrest."

As soon as Whitman knew the jig was up, and the death penalty was on the table unless he talked, he confessed all.

Sitting in on the interrogation, which was conducted in a secure room in D632 headquarters by their agents, Cal felt his anger build as he listened.

The short version of what was an hourslong confession punctuated by many questions and asides was this: Flight 155 was, indeed, brought down to eliminate Jorgensen, aka Steven Carbone. Putin and his allies had nothing to do with it, however, just as they had nothing to do with the murder of Putin's rival Volkov. A few corrupt CIA officers, combined with a cabal of Russian dissidents and an international criminal cartel that wanted Putin out of office and replaced with someone who answered to them, had arranged Volkov's murder to incriminate Putin. Jorgensen, who was in on Volkov's murder, was planning to testify to that effect. Therefore, Jorgensen had to be eliminated. Unfortunately, Jorgensen was a trained operative who was hard to kill. The commercial plane crash made killing him both doable and deniable. The other passengers on board were written off with a shrug as collateral damage.

Keith Hertzinger was, indeed, a CIA operative. It was he who had shot down Cal's plane on Whitman's orders. Whitman claimed not to know whether he was alive or dead, but Cal was as certain as it was possible to be that Hertzinger was dead. Along with Gina, Hertzinger would have been one of the two survivors of the horror that had befallen the research party on Attu, and as such he would have been subjected to some pretty severe questioning as soon as the authorities had shown up to investigate. Whitman couldn't have risked that, because Hertzinger knew too much about Whitman's involvement in what had gone down. The simple solution: kill Hertzinger. Which, if Hertzinger was still alive at the time of Cal and Gina's escape, Cal was certain Whitman had done before leaving Attu.

Ezra had been induced to fall in with

Whitman's plan when Whitman had convinced him that the US government had made a deal to sell Rudy and his knowledge to a valued ally. Whitman had told Ezra that Cal wasn't in the loop on the new deal because he supposedly had some issues with that ally, a Middle Eastern government that Ezra knew Cal did, indeed, mistrust, and that, therefore, Cal couldn't be counted on to cooperate.

"We done here?" Cal asked Agents Brady and Rincon, who'd taken the lead on the interrogation, when Whitman quit talking at last.

Brady nodded. "Yeah, we're done."

Rincon and another agent were already pulling Whitman to his feet, getting ready to handcuff him and cart him off to wherever it was they kept traitors until he could be picked up by higher authorities and taken away.

Cal stepped up to Whitman, looked him in the eye, and slammed his fist into Whitman's face. He felt the crunch of bone with a rush of savage satisfaction. Blood spurted from Whitman's nose. Reeling back with a cry, Whitman fell to the ground.

"That was for Ezra," Cal told him, then shook off the agents who'd leaped to grab him and walked away.

Word came down from D632 early the next morning: the hole in the software that allowed the outside takeover of Flight 155 and other commercial airliners had been plugged. It was a simple fix, and the best part was, the patch included a worm that, if anyone tried to do such a thing again, would allow investigators to trace the attempt back to its source.

The perpetrators would be identified, and neutralized.

And so the day was saved.

Chapter Twenty-Nine

A little more than two weeks later, Gina's doorbell rang.

She was in her condo in sunny California, it was seven o'clock on a Saturday night, and she had a date.

With Cal.

It was their first. Kind of.

The chic little black dress she wore with diamond studs and killer heels was slim-fitting, short, and extremely becoming. It had been chosen expressly to wow the man on the other side of the door.

Whom she hadn't seen since she'd left Alaska, when he'd put her on a commercial flight to California. He'd then flown off to DC, where he'd been "requested" to appear by the CIA to give his account of Whitman's perfidy.

In the meantime, they'd talked on the phone. A lot. He'd flown in this afternoon, and tonight he was taking her to dinner.

Her pulse fluttered as she pulled open the door.

He stood there in her hallway, smiling at her. Tall, dark, and dangerous.

He was all of those, and also so handsome that her heart beat faster just from looking at him.

He wore an expensive-looking dark gray suit and was holding a big bunch of red roses.

"Hi," he said, and stepped into her apartment as he handed them over.

She smiled at him as she took them and closed the door. "Thank you."

"Hey, I promised you flowers and dinner. I always keep my promises."

"Just like you always pay your debts?"

He grinned at her, clearly remembering, as she was, exactly how he'd "paid his debt" to her. "Just like that, yeah."

Then he bent his head and kissed her.

And the heat of it, the instant sizzle, the I'm-melting-into-a-little-puddle-on-my-floor-and-I-wouldn't-have-it-any-other-way impact of it, totally blew her away.

As she went up on tiptoe and twined one arm around his neck — the other was curved around his roses — she felt as if a whole garden of flowers were springing to life in her heart.

She was *happy.*

She kissed him back like he was the best thing that had ever happened to her, like he was exactly what she had always wanted.

This, she thought, dizzy with the promise of it, is me with you.

ACKNOWLEDGMENTS

To make a book requires more than just a writer: it requires a team. I want to thank Lauren McKenna, editor extraordinaire; Elana Cohen, her fearless assistant; Louise Burke, our leader; and the whole incredible group at Gallery Books.

ABOUT THE AUTHOR

Karen Robards is the author of more than forty novels and one novella and is a regular on the *New York Times*, *USA TODAY*, and *Publishers Weekly* bestseller lists, among others. She is the mother of three boys and lives in Louisville, Kentucky.

The employees of Thorndike Press hope you have enjoyed this Large Print book. All our Thorndike, Wheeler, and Kennebec Large Print titles are designed for easy reading, and all our books are made to last. Other Thorndike Press Large Print books are available at your library, through selected bookstores, or directly from us.

For information about titles, please call:
  (800) 223-1244

or visit our Web site at:
  http://gale.cengage.com/thorndike

To share your comments, please write:
  Publisher
  Thorndike Press
  10 Water St., Suite 310
  Waterville, ME 04901